Dexter

❧Book Three❧

Mistress & Master
of
Restraint

Dexter

Copyright ©2012 Erica Chilson

Wicked Reads
PO Box 29
Nelson, PA 16940

www.ericachilson.com/wicked-reads

Printed in the United States of America

First Printing, 2015

ISBN-13: **978-0692544693**
ISBN-10: **0692544690**

Dedication

To my very patient fans

Titles by Erica Chilson

Mistress and Master of Restraint
-series order-

Restraint
Unleashed
Dexter
Dalton
Queen Omnibus*
Jaded*
Queened*
Checkmate*
King
Faithless
The Hunter
Integrated

-Coming Soon-
Hero/Empowered (tentative title)

BLENDED
-Series order-

Good Girl
Wildly Wedded Wife (Blended #1.5)
Widow
Wanton (Blended #2.5)

-COMING SOON-
Warped

RUSTY KNOB
Rusty Knob
Tarnished
Stainless (coming soon)

Master of Restraint and sadist, Dexter Hayes has always used the following adage as a form of self-preservation: *never ask questions when you aren't prepared to hear the answers.*

Dexter turned a blind eye on Maître du Jeu's activities, only doing as he was told without question. His sole focus for the past few years had been on his girlfriend, Monica James, and their housemate, Tobias Kline.

When the riots began at Restraint, the two halves of Dexter's world collided, putting everyone at risk. Adelaide Whittenhower published the Mistress & Master of Restraint, exposing the secrets of Dominion's underground. The book drew the public to Restraint, and it has been spiraling out of control.

Dexter tried to maintain his stance of never knowing too much, but he was swept into the fray. He had lost control of Monica, allowing her insecurities to ruin her from the inside out. Tobias flexed his newfound independence by no longer following Dexter's instruction. The members of Restraint were running rampant, forgetting their training and doing whatever they wished.

Dexter felt he knew the people in his life, but as the questions he never asked were being answered, he learned they were always complete strangers.

As the battle lines were drawn, Dexter learned a valuable lesson–pleading ignorance may have been his greatest downfall yet.

Chapter One

"Where's our girl?" Kat walks into my parlor, and then makes herself at home in one of my chairs. We have an open-door policy with a very small handful of people– Kat being one of them. She wears a playful smirk as she gets comfortable on the antique chair. She's never voiced it, but it's always sitting on the tip of her tongue.

"Dexter, why are you obsessed with Victorian furnishings?"

I answer Kat's spoken question, but never her unspoken one. "At the gym." I sigh heavily, hating how that trait of my grandfather's manifested in Marcus and me, with Ezra adopting it as his own. "Again."

"Jesus," Kat hisses, getting the gravity of the situation. "What's that make? Five times this week? Twice today? I've asked Ezra to counsel Monica."

I reach forward to grab my smoke out of the cigar box resting on my coffee table. "Excuse me if I'm not too confident in Ezra's psychiatric abilities," I drawl, but Kat doesn't get offended.

Laughing at the lunacy of a psychiatrist with a mental illness, Kat grabs the bowl out of my hand before I can stop her. "Tobias?"

"At the gym–" with the rasp of the lighter, Kat's taking a toke before I can finish my sentence since my resident recovering drug addict isn't home. "With Monica. Bad day?"

Kat holds up one finger, unable to talk while the pot fills her lungs. Smoke billows out her nose, and a second later she comes back to life. "Bad life," she rasps in a husky voice, dry from the smoke. She gives my bowl back, sharing my weed with me as if it was hers. "Seriously, we need to do something about Monica. I think she's left anorexic and has entered bulimic territory. Because I practically have to force-feed her two snacks and lunch every day at work, and she's getting skeletal."

Instead of taking a hit, I contemplate Katya's curvy body. I love Monica with every cell in my body, and I want her to be happy and healthy. It took me several years to come to terms with the fact that it wasn't me who was manifesting Monica's illness. We've had many fights with me shouting how I find curvy girls sexy so she doesn't need to starve herself– look at Heidi. I never mentioned Katya, fearing a rift would form between the friends. While Kat has tried to get Monica to eat, she herself has packed on a nice padded layer of flesh that makes me hornier than hell.

Katya may be my friend, but I'm still a man. Relaxed, eyelids shuttering the green of her eyes, I enjoy the view of the stoned woman sitting across from me. Light skin flushed pink, her mouth parted, she's sucking on my bowl like it's a fat and juicy, tasty cock.

Shifting on the sofa, I try to ignore the effect the woman has on me. It's not totally lust; I like our easy rapport. Effortless friendship is hard to come by. It's even more important when you and your partner find someone you both equally respect and appreciate. Erection be damned, I'll behave for that reason alone.

"I force breakfast and dinner on Monica. Tobias stalks her with smoothies in his hands, trying to make sure she gets enough vitamins. The harder we work at it, the less she eats. It doesn't matter how thin she gets, she's not happy with the results. I don't care how much Monica weighs, as long as she's healthy. I wake up in the middle of the night with the cold sweats, expecting her organs to fail while she sleeps."

Wincing, Kat lights up again to erase the words I had spoken. Katya loves Monica as much as I do. Finishing another hit, she passes the bowl back to me. Our fingertips touch during the handoff, which I find as a comfort.

When I don't immediately light up, Katya coaxes me. "Smoke up! You need it." Sighing, finally able to relax, she rests her head on the back of my grandmother's velvet-covered chair. "Monica is a strong woman who needs a stronger man. She is testing you, setting you up for failure until it proves she's as worthless as she feels on the inside."

"Tell me something I don't already know," I mutter to myself as I stare down at my fingers holding the swirled glass.

"According to Ezra, anorexia is a mental disorder, and it has nothing to do with weight, appearance, or sexiness. It's an addiction of sorts. It's how Monica feels in control. She's out of control right now. She's floundering, and it's going to kill her."

When I don't take a hit, Kat's eyelashes flutter open, revealing emerald fire. She tips her chin in my direction, so I do as she bids— I fill my lungs with the marijuana smoke, exhale, and repeat until Katya is satisfied that I'm relaxed enough for whatever painful advice she's about to administer. She understands Monica better than I do, so I listen because I haven't been helping matters.

"Ezra explained how our pushing food onto Monica will only make her rebel, making the problem worse." Noticing my narrowed stare, "Ezra may be fucking nuts, but that's why he knows how his fellow lunatics operate," she defends her criminally insane husband. "Do you love Monica?"

"This is killing me, Kat! Of course I love her!"

"Then you need to take charge. Our girl isn't capable anymore. If you love her, you will take her in hand as you did with Tobias. Anorexia is no different than a drug addiction."

"Goddamnit, KAT!" I charge to my feet, the pot not doing a damn thing to calm my nerves. I pace around my living room, having a care not to harm its priceless contents. Even in a fit of rage, I'd never put an angry fingertip on my grandmother's belongings.

"I want to marry Monica. I don't want to have to lord over my own wife. What if we have kids? I don't want that responsibility, having to raise my kids while raising my wife. I don't want that sort of life."

"Tobias is a good, young man. He's intelligent. He's graduating from college. He's ready to join you at the office. Toby's starting to disobey you, which means he's finding his sense of self. I'm not telling you to take away Monica's freewill. I'm saying you *must* until she gets her head on straight. Then slowly give Monica her independence back."

"I don't know if I can do it." I tug at my hair out of frustration–a nasty familial habit I picked up from Toby. "Obviously I have no issue telling submissives what to do if that's what they need. But outside of teaching dominant beings, I get no pleasure out of controlling them. Toby needed me, so I helped him."

"Monica is a strong woman. Sometimes a woman needs the man to be the man, even if she loves wearing the pants in the family. An alpha woman either needs a man strong enough to be her equal, or one even stronger."

"You're saying she doesn't respect me because I'm allowing her to behave this way?" I'm trying to listen to the words Kat is *not* using.

Tiny red eyebrow hitching high, "Yes, Dex. That's *exactly* what I'm saying," Katya drawls like she thinks I've lost my dominant traits. "Boundaries. Monica came to me three years ago needing just that, and that's why I gave her to you. But outside of playing in the dungeon, you're not giving Monica what she needs, and she's going off the deep end. If you love her, you'll control her."

Calming, I retake my seat on the settee. "I need some time to formulate a plan and fortify my nerves. I can't start the minute she comes in from the gym."

"I understand. It's not life or death. *Yet*," Kat stresses, scaring the piss out of me because she's right. "Here," she tosses me a good-sized baggie. "Alex sends his regards. You're going to need it if you plan on taking Monica in hand."

Rubbing the cellophane between my fingertips, I contemplate what she's advising. "That's a lot of fucking weed, Kat."

"Monica's not an easy woman, Dex," she says in the same inflection. "I love her. She's the first best friend I've ever had in my life, and I don't plan on getting a second one. If you won't fix her–I will."

The hair on the back of my neck bristles up, my need to possess Monica finally revealing itself. The only thing keeping me from challenging Kat is the fact that she has tears staining her cheeks and a calculating glint in her eyes, like she knows encroaching on my territory will force my hand.

"Well played," I mutter begrudgingly as I toss the baggie into the cigar box. "Is it our girl who has you toking up, or do you need a friend tonight, too?"

"I need a friend, and Monica isn't capable of being one right now." Kat's lips curl into a devious smirk. "Congrats! You're my last resort."

"Only having one friend must suck." I shake my head back and forth, marveling at how blind Kat is. Everyone is drawn to her. Her unflinching dominance, combined with the way she looks down on us like we're her underlings, has us all wanting her approval. "You are so peculiar. Your husband is a psychiatrist who is also mentally ill, and you buy your weed from a drug and alcohol counselor."

"Well, I'm also '*married*' to an author who doesn't write, and the mother of three children that I father because that author won't let me mother them. Which is why I need a friend."

"Troubles in paradise?" The main reason I enjoy Kat's company is because her life is a bigger train wreck than my own.

Eyes glassy with her pupils blown, cheeks rosy, Kat looks higher than a kite. Beautifully unkempt, and completely open to me because she trusts me. The intimacy is more intoxicating than any drug. "You know when you have a litter of puppies or kittens, or a nest of chicks?" …And not making a goddamned lick of sense.

Not having an inkling of what Katya's getting at, I wonder how burnt she could possibly be. "Kat, you do realize I grew up in a house exactly like this one, right?" I gesture around my parlor as we sit in a Victorian three-story house with a turret and mansard style roofline. I rebuilt my grandmother's house exactly as I remembered it– the house I grew up in, the house that burnt to the ground when I was in college. Rebuilt with the exception of the servants' quarters, the garage built specifically for my grandfather's precious Spyder– which I gave to Marc because I was terrified of harming the car – and the stables.

"I work for a living by choice. I was raised with a chef, a butler, a driver, a housekeeper, a stable of servants, three gardeners, and a tutor in every known subject. I've never touched an animal in my life. Not even a dog or cat. I don't have a fucking clue what you're getting at."

"Shit!" Kat's eyebrows knit together out of sheer frustration. "This is why I need Monica. She would have understood what I was trying to say before I even did."

Lips curling up at the sides, I humor Kat. "Try me." She rebuffs me with a throat-clearing noise– the woman positively loathes the elite, refusing to see she is one. "I live in the real world now. Try me."

"Fine…" Kat mutters begrudgingly. "Animals are always about dominance. When you have baby animals, they tend to push the rest from the nest, or keep them from the teat. Cort's driving me nuts, to the point the only way to deal with him–"

"–Is to push Cort from the nest? Yank his spoiled mouth off Ezra's dick? Erm… I mean teat." Enjoying myself tremendously, I'm so thankful those bastards brought Katya into my life.

Katya flashes me a conspiratorial smirk, like I'm being a good replacement best friend. I try not to preen underneath her appreciative gaze. "I wish," she mutters underneath her breath. "I believe Cort is trying to force Ezra to push *me* from the nest. Other than having to go through Cort to see my children, I haven't had a conversation with him in months. Sometimes Cort doesn't even come to bed, saying he's '*writing*'. He's not having any affairs, other than I fear his cocksucking has evolved into something more."

Now that is something interesting. I lean forward, intrigued. "Tell me more about this cocksucking. Who?"

The stupid sonofabitch must have a death wish. Rumor has it, Ezra's hands are stained red from ordering others to eliminate his opposition. Adelaide is locked away in Wintercrest Asylum for life. With Cort being Ezra's most prized possession, the man who Cort sucks off must either have huge balls, a low IQ, or afflicted with suicide-by-lunatic.

Kat flinches, which means I know this person.
Who?

Voice distressed, dripping with desperation, I stop wheedling Katya. "It's too twisted to explain. Ezra's stressed, and that scares the fuck out of me, because I don't know what he's capable of doing if pushed to the brink."

"I have no clue what advice Monica would give in this instance. But I can tell you that your fears are valid." I lean back against the sofa, folding my arms over my chest. "This '*game*' they are playing is nothing new, Katya. This is how it's always been. Cortez starts to want more with Ezra, which freaks him out, so he begins to act like the biggest asshole in all of creation. Then he gets off on how it upsets Ezra, who doesn't know how to handle it while staying sane. People get hurt, Cort gets his ego fed, and then they fall into bed. I had hoped they'd finally grown up since they married you and had kids."

Cheeks stained red, tears glistening in her eyes, Katya looks more frustrated than anything. "I knew this coming in. I accepted it. But sometimes you love someone so much, it kills you to see them hurting. This is hurting Ezra because he did break the cycle. I wholeheartedly believe that it's different this time. Ezra is cleaving onto me like he can feel the storm brewing, and he's doing everything he can to keep it at bay. Cort isn't trying to get attention. He resents Ezra because I'm there."

"Kat, I don't believe that." I lie. I try to think like a female, channeling what Monica would say, but that's all I can come up with. Judging by the grimace twisting Kat's face, she doesn't buy it.

"Monica is my friend because she's brutally honest," Kat reminds me, and this time I grimace. "You should see Cort with the kids– he won't share them with me. He'll even walk over and take them from my arms. But if Ezra is holding one of the twins, Cort gets moony-eyed." In a dead voice, Katya whispers, "Cort got what he wanted from me, and now he wants me to leave."

I'm honest this time. "Why would you give that spoiled asshole what he wants? I care for Cortez, but I'd rather whip him, even knowing he hates pain. You're where you should be, with your husband and children. If I know anything, it's that Ezra loves you unto death do us part."

Blinking away tears, Kat still refuses to show me her weaknesses. I often wonder if she shows them to anyone. "I know

Ezra loves me. But sometimes I think I love him more. Love him enough to give him what he needs, what is healthy, what will make him happy. What if that isn't me but Cortez? Only Cortez? What if Cortez is transitioning because he wants me to go away because he's now ready for it to be just Ezra and him?"

This time my voice drops low, seething, because Katya is scaring me. "I ask again, why would you give that asshole what he wants?"

"Because I love them," Katya breathes, "that's why."

"You want brutal honesty? Fine. Cortez isn't there yet, or he wouldn't be playing games, acting like a child, pushing Ezra's buttons, or yanking the kids from you. That is not how a man behaves. That is not how a father who loves his children acts. He would want them to be with their mother, to give them a full, loving life. Ezra recognizes this, which is why he's going full-out lunatic mode again."

"Master Ez is terrifying," Katya whispers, and I shiver for her.

"Whatever Ezra does is his own fault, and not a reflection of anything you've done. The same as Monica not eating and obsessively exercising is not because of anything you or I have done. If I were you, the day I would become frightened is the day Cortez starts behaving like an adult. Because that's the day Ezra will be forced to choose."

"I won't let Ezra choose. I promised I wouldn't."

"Then you better hope Cortez never grows up. But something tells me you love Ezra, Cortez, and your children so much, you'd sacrifice yourself for that day to come." I warn, "Don't do it. Let this run its natural course. It's painful and chaotic. But it's a cycle they've been living for thirty-three years."

I feel pity for Katya as she runs her palms over her face, trying to pretend even for a few minutes that life for her is normal. It never was, nor will it ever be. "We both have something very uncomfortable to do. I have to be mean to Monica for her own good, and it's going to kill me. You have to let Ezra and Cortez destroy their own lives, while keeping strong enough so they don't drag you and your children down with them."

I lean forward, plucking the baggie from the cigar box. "Here," I toss it in Katya's lap. "You're going to need it."

Laughing, truly laughing the most beatific sound of happiness, Katya tosses the baggie back into the cigar box. "I've got my own." She yanks another baggie from her purse, this one bigger than the last. "I knew I needed it more than you did."

"Toby alert! Toby alert!" Monica shouts as she walks into our parlor. "I sent him on a phony errand when I noticed Kat's car in the drive." She leans down to give Kat a quick hug. Whispering, "Bad day?" as she pulls away.

"Bad life," Katya repeats, earning a knowing chuckle from Monica.

The love of my life doesn't greet me. Instead, she looks sheepish, knowing I see her clearly and I don't like what I see. It's a standoff I despise. I cannot live this way anymore. It's not healthy for Monica, and it's not healthy for Tobias.

It's not healthy for me.

I'm not a selfless martyr. I won't back down like Katya is. If she wants Ezra, even if he taints her, she should fight for him. If she realizes he's toxic to her, she should leave to protect herself and her children. Kat needs to be selfish and make it about her and her children. We live in reality, not in the in-between state of imaginary land where unicorns ride rainbows and love can withstand lies, betrayals, and criminally insane behaviors.

Until death do us part does not mean you stand by while your partner slowly kills you emotionally. Katya and I have that in common as well. I deserve the real Monica, because I give her nothing short of the real me.

Tonight I will plan the first battle of the war, knowing I have to do just as I had with Tobias. While it will be uncomfortable for me, it will be painful yet healing for Monica.

I place the baggie of marijuana in the box, fish the key from my pocket, and then lock it up tight. The girls chat while I stow the cigar box in the liquor cabinet, and lock it to remove any temptation Tobias might feel. His drug of choice was heroin. But an addict doesn't care what they can get their hands on when in the throes of a craving.

Toby's issues were visible, while Monica's are not. Being an enabler, I let it fester for over two years, not understanding how she was damaging herself, our budding family, and our relationship.

I settle back on the settee, watching Monica and Katya interact. I understand how Katya feels right now. I love Monica so much my heart throbs. Sometimes I feel physically sick when I look at her. Sometimes I hate her guts with such passion I fear I might kill her to protect myself from the slow suicide she is forcing me to witness.

I hate Monica because she could stop it– she could stop our pain. She could make our lives better. Which is how Katya feels around both Cortez and Ezra.

Sometimes I hate myself because I'm no longer physically attracted to Monica. The thought of sex turns my stomach, because when I look at her, all I see is a sick person who is near to death. But then I watch her struggle, think of losing her, and I realize I couldn't love her more if I tried.

"I have the munchies," Katya announces. "You should toke up and join me for some snacks."

I rest my head in my hands, laughing silently at the ludicrousness. Katya and I started smoking weed for two reasons: neither of us could relax because our significant others were consuming us and we both wanted Monica to join us in the hopes she would get the munchies and actually eat for once.

In the end, Kat and I are marginally dependent on the drug, we've both gained a good twenty pounds, and Monica has never taken a single hit because she's smarter than the rest of us.

Chapter Two

I've always wanted to recapture what I had when I was growing up. Not the mourning and loss, but the strong sense of family. Grandfather and Grandmother Zeitler instilled in us how the simple things were important. You went to work, you followed your dreams, and at the end of the day, you spent time with the family you created.

Dexter Zeitler was an incredible, self-made man, and Rebekah was the heart and soul of our family. Yet somehow they managed to birth a son and a daughter who were power-hungry, money gatherers who bulldozed over everything in their paths– Marc's father and my mother.

After we lost our grandfather to a heart attack, tainted by their lust for green, our parents tried to break my grandmother. In the end, our parents' greed killed them, leaving our grandmother to continue teaching us her path in life.

Rebekah Zeitler immigrated to the United States from Israel. She knew real pain, loss, and hunger, and she made sure we did too. Our grandmother was our mother, our father, our teacher, our religious leader, and she was our grounding force.

Every step I take in life is guided by my grandmother, even if she is no longer on this earth. My decision to become one of the United States government's Boogiemen in the most hated profession was to police those greedy bastards like my mother and uncle.

My home is a replica of Rebekah Zeitler's in homage to her, but more so as a comfort to Marcus and myself. Our parents' evil deeds haunted us years later, when in retaliation, the same people who murdered our parents burnt our home, while those opposed to the decision removed all of our cherished belongings. My grandmother died of grief less than a week later at Whittenhower Estates, with her friends by her side. The land our home rested on is empty to symbolize the power and destruction of greed.

I have more money than anyone I know, because I refuse to spend it. My mother was a criminal, not only breaking the laws of man but the laws of nature. I work for a living. I teach anyone who is willing to learn. I ignore what is right in front of my face, because I am not my mother, my ignorant father, or my uncle and his cutthroat wife.

My life is not how I want it, and the slow burn of irritation is growing into the need for change. After working all day while being called an asshole for making people pay their due, instead of coming home to a happy wife and children, I have Tobias, who is more of a son than I ever expected, and Monica, who is committing slow suicide by making herself the waste she believes herself to be.

Worse, I spend my nights at Restraint because I'm angry. Angry at life. Angry that the good guys get fucked left and right while the bad guys always win.

By default, I'm one of the bad guys, and I loathe myself because of this.

Maître du Jeu is the same organization that killed my parents, and I want to thank them for saving me from their influence. But they are also the same ruthless assholes who burnt my house to the ground. I turn the other cheek because that's what Rebekah would do.

Instead of being at home with Monica, and any kids we would have had if she wasn't destroying her body to the point of infertility, I'm policing Restraint for Maître du Jeu.

Police raids. Riots. The patrons charging the doors to fill the building past fire code regulations. All of this is putting us on the radar of Maître du Jeu, who is threatening us to get it under control, or else they will.

I don't confide in Marcus on this front as I'm the eldest and it's my job to protect him. If I were to think like my cousin, I might venture a guess that it's Maître de Jeu themselves who orchestrated the chaos and destruction as an excuse to invade us, or it could be someone they pissed off. Hell, it could be Ezra destroying his own club for shits and giggles just because he's that fucking nuts.

But I'm not a conspiracy theorist. I just do as I'm told without asking any questions, because questions mean answers, and answers can get you killed.

All I know is that I don't want to be here, being sucked into the same life that murdered the Zeitler family, with the exception of Marcus and myself. They've always had a hard-on for our money and influence. If I could guarantee my continued existence, I'd give them every cent to my name to buy myself out of their organization. But that would leave an ignorant Marcus without any protection.

Exhausted, sick to death of the direction my life is headed, every night I walk into Restraint like it's a battle zone. Tonight's no different as I lean against the wall with my tired eyes tracking the crowd.

"Can you feel that?" Aaron puts his hand on my shoulder. "The need for violence is charging the air. Any minute now it will erupt, and we'll have to step in."

"I'm in the mood to bring the pain," I mutter underneath my breath.

"I bet you are." Aaron chuckles while he slaps my back.

"If this goes on any longer, they'll shut us down," I say in his direction, but my eyes never leave the crowd. "I don't mean the city– they love the revenue we're bringing in." I know Aaron knows all there is to know about Maître du Jeu, and I know he's not allowed to divulge their secrets. "You know who I mean."

"No clue what you're talking about, my man," Aaron gives his usual statement when I make ambiguous comments about the organization. I trust him not to try to kill me for saying anything, but apparently he doesn't trust me with an answer. Or maybe Aaron is protecting me from the truth.

The air heats, almost suffocating with the crack and sizzle of pressurized violence. The first time I felt it I didn't recognize it for what it was. There's always a five second span of time where you can breathe, and then you suffocate on the toxicity.

Right on cue… "Hey! Hands off, Asshole!" a dinky blonde woman is struggling with a war-hardened man. I'm not worried about the blonde or the asshole. It's the blonde's boyfriend that's going to be an issue– he has that glint in his eye that Ezra often wears.

"Better call it in. It's gonna escalate fast. I don't want a mob mentality to fall prey upon the club, where everyone goes batshit," I order in Aaron's direction. When he doesn't move, I turn to stare at him.

Frozen in indecision, Aaron's wearing a *'you've got to be fucking shitting me'* expression, and then he unthaws and goes into the action. He presses the Bluetooth at his ear– all of Restraint's employees are wired together. "All hands on deck. Surround 'em and pound 'em. Roarke, inform Ezra we have The Whore, the Magic Eraser, and GI Joe in house as ground zero."

I'm not going to ask Aaron what his message meant, but I got the gist. The riots are being started on purpose. Tonight is going to be the worst. I can sense the violence weaving its way through the crowd, infecting all of the patrons with its taint.

Just as I know Restraint's ten bouncers who were supposed to be on duty tonight aren't down because of an epidemic of the flu spreading like wildfire, when there is not a single case reported in Dominion. Ten isn't nearly enough. We need two outside the door, one inside the door, one to protect Kris at the bar, one at the entrance to the bathrooms, and a dozen spread out around the club. We used to have them posted inside the dungeon, but as the chaos escalated, we had to yank them out.

Five men in black security t-shirts surround the hissing blonde as she attacks the guy with the air of a soldier who had the audacity to hit on her. She's dressed like Mary Freaking Sunshine– a petite woman in her forties, who looks a lot younger than she is, with natural blonde hair and huge, wounded blue eyes, wearing a dress Monica would kill to possess. She has every right to say no, but she's not throwing a fit because GI Joe propositioned her. She didn't say no, she went postal on purpose.

With surprising rage, GI Joe snarls into the blonde's face. "You've fucked everyone I know, ya whore."

I lunge forward the instant *whore* leaves his mouth with Aaron on my heels because the other fellow with the glacial blue eyes has death on his mind. The man is frothing at the mouth like a rabid dog.

Lunging, "You better not have actually meant that, fuckface," Rabid Dog warns as if GI Joe's statement hit too close to home. He pulls GI Joe to the ground with surprising ease, and then the two of them begin pounding the ever-loving piss out of the other. Swinging meaty fists pounding flesh, the sound in time with the bass from the stereo system.

Restraint's depleted security force enters the fray, but the crowd swallows the five men as they drag Rabid Dog into the middle of the dance floor with GI Joe now beating on my men.

I unleash my dominant nature– the caveman who dwells deep inside of me, who rules my actions. I grab the blonde and bitch-slap some sense into her, furious that she did this on purpose.

I toss her ass to the nearest booth. "You move an inch and your ass is arrested for inciting a riot." I growl at her and dive into the fray.

"Aaron," I yell above the music, the screams of outrage, and the impact of bruising flesh. "Get everyone out of the dungeon! We're going to need assistance. Call the PD."

I allow myself a second to assess the situation. Eyes flicking around wildly, I note the dance floor is a writhing mass of fists, with arms raised high, elbows being thrown, and kicking feet sticking out of the wave of carnage. The innocent and the not-so innocent scatter like rats and plug up the exits, blocking everyone in the vicious stew.

"Dexter!" A sharp scream pierces above the din of the music and the thumping of flesh against flesh. Hair on the back of my neck rising as if electrified, I instantly go on alert. I ignore my heart beating in the back of my throat and the way my curled fists are sweating. I've never heard my protégée sound so frantic. Not Syn. Never Syn. She is the epitome of strength and control.

"Syn!" I shout over and over again, waiting for a reply, as I rush through the crowd with no destination in sight. "Syn!" She's exactly five feet tall, and I can't see the top of her black hair in the writhing mass. "Syn! S-Y-N!" I need her reply to give me her location. It's a sick version of Marco-Polo, instead of water it's a sea of inebriated douchebags.

"Get off her!" I hear Syn scream at someone in a terrified, tight voice. She never screams. She's never terrified.

Blood surging through my veins, I can't see my protégée but I run in the direction her voice flows. Another altercation is taking place near the bar, and my mind instantly seeks out Kris.

Two large men are on the ground tearing the dress off a tiny gal– her smooth, creamy pale skin means it's not Kristal's tan, tattooed flesh. Grabbing at assaulting hands, Syn rides the back of one, but she can't take both of them on at once.

"Oh, shit! Fate!" My stomach twists with pain when I realize who is being brutalized. Sweet, docile Fate. A pair of twenty-somethings has the submissive on the ground with her pink dress torn from seam to seam, her small breasts exposed.

Syn's punching one of assailants in the back of the head, but they're either too high or drunk or numb to react. With his cruel mouth descending on Fate's breast, Syn reaches forward to fishhook the asshole. With a sharp backhand, I watch in slow motion as Syn flies several feet to where her head hits on the corner of the bar with a thunderous crack.

Enraged, I understand with Syn out for the count it will only take seconds for Fate's scare to turn into a living nightmare. I fight my way through the crowd as they flow in the opposite direction. Shoving me, jostling me two steps back for every step I take forward. Frustration pounds in my blood, fueled by unadulterated fear and rage. As a sadist, I believe giving pain is a gift. Tonight is the first time I want to annihilate someone because I want them to hurt, not because I want them to heal.

The oblivious, riotous morons slow my rescue attempts. Selfish, they only think of themselves, hindering those trying to help instead of stopping to help themselves. With the exits blocked like Thermopylae, everyone is pushing and shoving, hurting themselves and others instead of just... "STOP! Just fucking STOP moving!"

It's like being in the epicenter of a tornado, with the loud, roaring rush of sound eclipsing all else. The force defying the nature of gravity. I reach down to yank a young lady to her feet who was sucked to the ground by the rolling wave of feet. She was seconds away from being trampled by sneakers and stilettos. I receive a sharp jab of an elbow to the face for my efforts, and then a swift kick to the back of my knee as the swarm tries to swallow me to the floor.

I fight my way against the current. I can't see anything but a mass of arms and legs and panicky eyes as several hundred people flee for the front of the club, knowing they will never get out until the clog disperses. I only know I'm on the right path because I'm pushing in the opposite direction of the herd.

I get spit out of the flow and hit the side of the bar. Rebounding from the force, it takes a split-second for the dizziness to fade. Eyes clearing, Fate is being assaulted a few feet from me, her blonde hair feathered against the dirty tile flooring.

My vision turns red as I watch two men grope and prod Queen's sweet submissive. One is yanking her legs apart, fingertips dimpling the flawless skin of her thighs. The other reaches down, tearing protective silk from the apex of her thighs. With a laugh, the man wears the panties on his head. As if, in battle, being a rapist is a badge of honor.

Crack! Crack! Crack! My fist flies over and over, all of my rage fueling my strength. I don't stop until I feel the cartilage give beneath my bruised knuckles. Squashed flesh, nearly flat to his face, his nose will never be the same. The fucker deserves nothing less. I turn to the man trying to force his way into Fate, but Regina is already on him.

The six-foot tall beast of a female is beating the man to death, with Fate lying prone and helpless beneath him. His face is a mass of red pulp, blood splattering the bar, Regina's face, and Fate beneath.

"Syn!" I yank my sadist up and give her a rough shake, trying to bring her to consciousness. "Get Fate to a room and shower with her, comfort her. I have to get our girl off of that asshole before she commits homicide."

Snapping into action, Syn is yanking Fate free from beneath the battle. Hands fluttering, she checks out the tiny woman. "Shh… It's okay. Regina always protects you." Syn picks up the ninety pound gal when she herself barely weighs more, and then carries her around the back of the bar toward the dungeon.

Syn is showing a protective, female lion instinct I never knew she possessed. Vicious, brutal, powerful, but never vulnerable and caring. If anyone would bring tears to Syn's eyes, it would be Fate.

Fate was lucky she had Syn and Regina, but not lucky enough. She was a hairsbreadth away from being full-out raped. But a lack of penetration doesn't lessen the impact this will have on Fate's life.

"Regina!" I shout into her ear, but she continues to ignore me while she rearranges the guy's internal organs. Tugging forcefully at her shoulder, I can't stop her. Helpless, all I can do is watch as Regina breaks the bones in her hands with the force of her hits.

Satisfied with her destruction, the two hundred pound woman hops off her prey and immediately mounts the one who I took out. "Fate was mine to protect," she utters in a cold, calculated voice, so unlike the warm Regina I've known since she was fourteen. "Where's Kris? It'd be just my luck that both my girls are hurt." She moans as if in pain but doesn't let up on bashing the fucker's face in.

"Shit," I hiss underneath my breath. I look for the familiarity of those I know through the crowd of strangers. I spot Whitt protecting Kris and two other submissives as he pushes them through the crowd to the dungeon.

"They're safe. Pretty boy's got Kris, Heidi, and Kayla taken care of. Stop beating on him." I coax Regina, hating how any other female would listen to my command instantaneously. Having equals sucks when they are going on a rampage. I shake her again, and she barely registers my presence.

"No," she growls at me. Then Regina punches the fallen man in the nuts– fist connecting with the floor through his flesh. He screams as if being slaughtered, causing her lips to twist up in the corners in a sadistic version of pure pleasure.

Regina is completely unhinged. She's allowed her dominant nature to take over. Protect. Eliminate the threat. Don't stop until everyone is safe. She's working with a prehistoric brain, no longer registering logic and reasoning.

Regina's submissive best friend was abused, and she could do nothing to prevent it. I can imagine the feeling of powerlessness the sensation would elicit. It flipped a switch inside of her that she doesn't want to turn off. A switch that keeps the guilt at bay.

"Regina, I can't stop you, so go ahead and kill them." I stand over her, speaking in a bored tone when I'm anything but. "Bear in mind, Master will kill you if you do." She pauses her arm momentarily when I mention Marcus, but then throws another forceful punch.

I feel so damned worthless, but she's almost a foot taller than me and fifty pounds heavier. The glint in her eye screams that she'll take me on if I try to stop her.

I look around the chaos of Restraint. When the DJ fled for safety the music stopped. The sound of fists on flesh is no more; instead moans and shouts dominate as a flood of blue waves through the door in riot gear.

"Regina, knock it the fuck off," I command. She ignores me. Queen likes to pretend she's one of the weakest of us, but she's as strong as Marcus. Mentally. Physically. Sheer force of will.

I kick her in the butt to gain her attention. "Fuck, you're going to get arrested for assault," I mutter hopelessly.

"Queen," Whitt's deep voice commands, returning from taking the submissives to the safety of the dungeon. The very young boy-next-door has a unique hold over the woman. Whitt squeezes the back of Regina's neck between two fingertips, and her hands instantly fall to her lap. Lifeless. It's like he hit her off switch.

When Daniel Whittenhower II grows up, I hope he uses his immense power for good.

"Queen wasn't here. She didn't do this and no one saw anything," Whitt says to me as he lifts the large woman into his arms.

Regina's splattered with blood, a sadistic version of war paint. Tears of frustration flow from her eyes in a wave of powerlessness. She buries her face in the crook of Whitt's neck and sobs– I will never erase the sound from my mind. I watch as Whitt walks to the security door and enters the dungeon as if none of this ever happened.

I turn back to the boys in blue. We have a lot of explaining to do... again.

Chapter Three

I'm asked no less than five times a day what Tobias is to me by those who are confused about our relationship. At work, where I take the young man on a weekly basis to show him what his life will soon be, my co-workers see Toby as my personal assistant, the boy I've turned into a man, and my surrogate son. In the dungeon, those who understand see Toby as my outlet, yet those who don't, think him my abuse sufferer. In reality, Tobias is all those things. But mostly, he's my comfort object– when I gaze at him, I see all that is right with the world as my greatest gift stares back at me with unflinching trust and patience.

"Is everybody going to be okay?" Toby grips my hand tightly as we walk through the silent club. To an outside observer, we either look like gay lovers or Toby looks like a frightened child. I'm good with either because I don't give a fuck what others think.

We just experienced unadulterated violence during the riot, watched our friends be harmed, and then we were subjected to hours of interrogation. If Toby wasn't upset, I'd think something was wrong with him. I'm upset but trying to hide it, and Toby is allowing it because he has no other choice. So his need for comfort is my way of giving and receiving comfort while saving my pride.

"Queen and Syn won't let anything ever happen to Fate. It was a close call this time, and it won't happen again."

"I was worried about them." Tobias is highly empathetic, taking on the pain of others. Which is why we will probably be visiting my basement to release the unwelcome emotions when we finally arrive home.

Squeezing his hand slightly to keep his attention, "I want you to stay home in the evenings, you and Monica. I don't mean this as an insult." I tread lightly, not wanting to harm the twenty-one-year-old's burgeoning pride. "But you're a liability to me at Restraint. It's no longer about playing in the dungeon. I'm here to work. I worry about you first and foremost, and I couldn't live with myself if someone hurt you."

"Okay," is his go-to answer. It's always said in an emotionless voice so I can't interpret the underlying emotions. Toby may obey, but I never know if he wants to or not.

"It's not that I think you're weak, Toby. It's because I care for you so much it physically hurts me to think of anyone taking advantage of you. Fate will not be back until this is taken care of. Aaron forbade Kayla and Heidi from stepping foot into Restraint. It's not just me demanding you stay home."

"Okay," Toby repeats, but this time there is emotion present. He seems happier now that I've explained myself. "I'll use the extra time to study... but–"

"I'll take care of your needs at home," I answer Toby's unspoken question.

With a sigh, he visibly relaxes, leaning into me for support. "Are they all Catholic?"

I smile my first real smile in over five hours– not the placating bullshit twists of my lips I fed the police officers. *"I have no idea what is happening, Officer."*

Laughing lightly, I tug the slightly taller man under my arm, hugging him to my side. "Yes, they are all Catholics." I laugh harder. "Syn is a Protestant of some kind, but I don't know if she's your kind." Toby shudders underneath my arm, making me laugh harder. "So I guess you won't be offering guidance, my friend."

"I would speak with Master Syn if she would allow it." Toby shows bravery when you least expect it. Raised by a warped Presbyterian pastor, he was shaped to become one himself. There is a reason I saved Tobias Kline– he is a good human being. "But it's a comfort to know she has faith in her life."

I laugh so hard I nearly stumble. "Oh, boy... you have no idea." I drop my arm from around Toby's shoulders, coming to a standstill when we exit Restraint and enter the alleyway. He flashes me a look of hurt, like I'm mocking him for his belief system. "No, Toby. You know I believe we all must have something bigger to believe in when our lives are at their lowest. I was laughing at the irony of Syn not having faith, is all. She's never without faith."

Nodding solemnly, Toby doesn't get it, which makes me chuckle some more. "Sorry, I'm being a dumbass tonight. Have you called your father lately?" In the beginning, I demanded it. But as Toby found his independence, I allowed him to make the choice.

Sheepish, Toby's refusal to look at me is answer enough. "I talked to my brother and sister last night. I called Mom the day before yesterday. I even spoke to Auggie for an update on Tina. But I will never call my father," is said in a voice waiting for me to argue.

"I didn't mean for you–"

"Oh! A kitty!" my apology is cut short by Toby lunging down the alleyway, head nearly careening with the filthy dumpster. He comes to rest on his knees in a puddle of disease.

"Get up!" I order, temper short tonight. "You're ruining your khakis."

"A kitty," Toby croons, turning to face me with a small creature cupped in his palms. He strokes a fingertip lovingly down the hairless head. "Aren't you sweet?"

"Drop it!" I command in my Master Dexter tone, heart pounding a vicious tattoo in my chest. Wild animals are unpredictable and they carry disease. "Now, Tobias! That is not a cat. Drop the rat!"

Face twisting like a defiant child, Toby scowls up at me, ignoring my order. "I grew up in the country, Dex." He holds up his cupped palms, presenting the hairless, filthy creature. "This is a kitten." He flips the *thing* over, lifting its tail. "It's a girl kitty. Probably three or four months old, and it's hungry. Can I keep it? Please?"

Tiny, helpless, blond, blue-eyed, and angelic, Tobias Kline is just like half of his fucked up family– the female half– all taking after the sinful pastor. A prominent branch off Toby's family tree are manly men– huge, red-haired domineering bastards. Toby takes after the females because one look into his eyes and you melt, wanting to give him anything he has ever asked for.

I'm just like the men in Toby's family. "No," I state simply, not drawn by his pleading when my job is to protect him. "Put the rat down. This is its natural habitat."

Pout replaced with eyes filled with daggers, Toby does as he was told. He places *it* on the ground by the dumpster. Still glaring at me, he pulls his backpack off his shoulder, and starts fiddling inside.

"The night draws long," I warn Tobias to hurry the fuck up. The filth staining his pants reminds me too much of when I first met him– terrified, malnourished, drug-addled, and emotionally destroyed. His niece, Tina, was with him that night, and I shipped her ass back to her father, keeping Tobias for myself. I'd be worried about Toby, except for the fact that the anger he's directing at me proves he's a stronger man than ever.

"I'm getting my hand sanitizer, Your Meanness." Toby makes a show of squirting the green liquid in his palm, still glaring at me in challenge. It takes everything in me not to grin like I'm the winner.

I *am* the winner. Toby's display proves I did a fantastic job raising him. Most dominants would kick him back down to where he used to be, thinking he belonged there. But Marcus and I were raised to lift those who follow us to our own level, making us stronger as a unit.

Breaking our staring contest, Toby turns around so I can't see him putting his hand sanitizer back into his backpack. The sound of the zipper fills the air, and then he's standing. "I'll make sure not to get the car dirty."

"That's all I ask," I reply quietly, relieved the rat is nowhere in sight.

Toby strides down the alleyway like a man on a mission– a grown man with his own needs, wants, and the wherewithal to recognize he can have whatever he wants as long as he reaches out and takes it.

Chapter Four

"We're going to the Brownstone." I warn the silent man sitting next to me in the car, as he protectively clutches his backpack to his chest. "I need to speak with Marcus." Toby doesn't respond, because he knows he's my passenger in my life as I wait for him to take over driving his own.

As I drive, then park in my designated spot in Jamie and Alex's garage, and then walk to the rear door with my shadow not far behind, my mind wanders.

I was raised to lead the Zeitler family fortune. The first male grandson, I wasn't doted upon like my blond counterparts in Dominion. We aren't blue bloods. We earned our money with hard work and innovation, and my grandfather made sure Marcus and I knew this. My grandfather's daughter and son were entitled pieces of shit, so his grandsons were educated to become the patriarchs.

After Grandfather's death, Marcus was thrown away– sold to Diane Holden by his own father, who pocketed the money like the scum of the earth he was. My own mother thought she could control me, but I was incorruptible. Then a tragic plane crash took their lives, saving our family from total destruction. Afterward, my grandmother took over, but it was too late for Marcus, as he was already married.

I wasn't in Dominion when our home was razed to the ground, with Marcus shouldering the burden. Somehow, I was immune to the evil spinning around us. So with my grandmother's passing, I rewarded Marcus for his commitment to our family by giving him everything to the Zeitler name, with the exception of our grandmother's belongings.

Everyone looked at me like I was an altruistic saint, when in reality I spent billions of dollars to ensure my freedom, and Marcus was easily bought.

I find the object of my thoughts lounging on a settee in the Brownstone's parlor– Marc's slice of the past he's carved out for himself within our childhood friend's home. Here sits a commanding man, with more power and money than the leader of the free world, but he's not free.

With no home of his own, because he lives in Ezra's territory, Marcus hides out in Jamie's hideaway, with the scant few pieces of Grandmother's furniture he stole from me. Lounging on the velvet sofa, Marcus looks like he owns the world, but there is a tightness in the corners of his eyes that worries me.

"Rough night?" Marcus smirks at me as the words leave his mouth, knowing exactly the direction of my thoughts. "Jamie and I were just watching the footage Alexander fetched for us." He points to the doorway, and Toby takes his cue to give us privacy.

My back tingles a pleasant warm sensation, informing me Marc's comfort object is lingering in the shadows. "Jamie, can you fetch Tobias a saucer of milk, please? He's hiding a rat in his backpack."

The silent shadow breaks from the wall to ghost into his kitchen.

Black brow arching, Marcus slides down the sofa, giving me a place to sit. "Your minion is disobeying you again, I see."

"You know how it amuses the hell out of me when Tobias takes what he wants." I chuckle at how proud Toby's acted since he snuck the hairless creature into his bag.

Shifting on the sofa to face me, Marcus tucks one leg beneath the other. "A rat?"

"Nah– a Siamese or hairless cat, or maybe a mixture of the two. Hopefully it's not diseased. I'll call a vet in the morning and set up an appointment."

Marcus sighs deeply, resting his head on the back of the sofa. He turns to the side to pin me with his whiskey stare. "I don't want to talk about Restraint."

Understanding, but not backing down, "We all know Ezra was fucking with his own club. This is fact. I understand he can't help himself when he goes off the deep end. But I'm no longer only terrified for Katya and the kids. Master Ez is a menace."

"I know." Marc's eyelids clench shut tightly, shuttering himself from the outside world for a heartbeat. "Please, not tonight."

Feeling the pain he must feel over his adoptive son, I try to lessen his burdens. "I love Ezra, Marc. I get it." I reach over for my cousin's hand, and his fingertips immediately clench against mine. "Tonight wasn't Ezra."

Eyelids snap open, and hope and fear blaze out at me. "What?"

"Whatever Ezra started has now been picked up to be used against him by whomever he pissed off." I don't mention Maître du Jeu. I may have relinquished our business holdings and our wealth, but I never passed the torch to Marcus within the game. They know I like being in the dark, and they know I'm protecting Marcus, so they allow me to stay where I am as long as I obey without question.

"They finally found an excuse to come back to Dominion," Marc utters cryptically, shuddering in revulsion.

Marcus has never spoken of his time in Las Vegas, but I know it haunts him to this day. It was his year-long taste of Maître du Jeu, and I've sheltered him since. It was their way of controlling me. I refused them, so they took the young man I saw as my brother– my only blood on Earth. They took Marcus and harmed him, irrevocably changed something vital in him. So I've toed the party line ever since.

Maître du Jeu finds your currency and exploits it.

I don't know who they are, or who is in charge. I don't know if they are just a pawn being toyed with, having their loved ones exploited for money or power. They may have had no choice in the matter; the same as I didn't in order to free Marcus from his Las Vegas prison. I only get a vague sense of who is involved by the things they say, or don't say.

When I hear an order from anyone, I just know it was handed down the ranks and it must be obeyed. Which is a very difficult thing to swallow for a man such as myself.

Marcus had been speaking as my mind took a nightmarish vacation, believing Maître du Jeu is an international BDSM group which we all belong to. "I'd hoped to never see them again. No doubt they waited for an in, where they took the advantage. The Fontaine Las Vegas sect will descend on us like a plague of locusts on Egypt."

Biblical Marcus is a petrified Marcus. "They created their own in. But no fear, cousin. I'll take care of it. While you're a master of diplomacy, I'm a master at finding someone's motivations and giving them what they want to get rid of them. You concentrate on keeping Ezra even-keeled, and I'll keep them off his ass. They will be coming to Dominion, no doubt. I'll make sure they leave."

"Thank you." Marc's eyes flick to Jamie's chair, seeking out his comfort object. As if called, Jamie glides in from the entryway. Marc finally takes a deep breath and relaxes when his eyes light on the small man.

Over a decade ago, we almost lost our childhood friend in this very room. Marcus held him during the ambulance ride, where the man died and Jamie was resurrected. Sweet, gentle, beautiful, tragic, and brooding, Jamie hated his previous life– hated being the heir to a twisted kingdom. He couldn't survive the tarnish on his soul. Unlike me who simply gave my money and power away, Jamie nearly lost his life, lost his voice, lost his family, lost his children... lost everything while gaining his freedom.

Jamie's fingers start signing a mile a minute. "Slow up, bro. I suck at this shit, no matter how hard I try." I turn to my translator, who's smirking like a sonofabitch but nowhere nearly as bright as the mute man.

When Jamie smiles the sun rises, even with the scars on his cheek pulling at his mutilated skin. The smile is his birthright. The silence and scars are a gift from Maître du Jeu, where I'm positive Jamie reigns in Hell right next to those who mutilated him.

Jamie is usually my messenger, using me to protect Marcus. It's odd to obey someone so submissive.

"It's a good thing I'm here, so you don't have to rely on texting," Marcus murmurs wryly, knowing I use texting, emails, and expressive looks and gestures to communicate with our friend because my sign language skills are a joke. "Your disobedient boy is being counseled by the house therapist while getting a handjob, and there is a dirty kitten napping in his backpack. You've lost control of your minion."

"No shit?" I ask Jamie, who releases a grisly sound from his throat. Vocal cords damaged, Jamie's laugh is scary as fuck, but a welcome sound to my ears. It brings tears to my eyes, since the man had the softest, most soothing voice– it was almost a caress. When his eldest son, a taller clone of his father, failed to sound like Jamie after he reached puberty, Marcus and I consoled each other. Last year, when Jamie's youngest son grew into a young man, we wept for another reason. The boy looks nothing like his father, but his voice is a perfect facsimile. All is not lost.

"Why don't you pick out a nice girl for your boy to play with?" Marcus chats over top of Jamie's signing, watching the conversation with one eye. "I get how Alex is a giver.... Oh!"

"Jamie, stop!" I warn, glaring at his fingertips. "If Tobias is confiding in Alex, it's not your place to spill it to Marc." I stand from the sofa. "Lest you forget what silenced you in the first place. The loss of your voice killed something vital in all of us. The loss of your words would cripple not only you." As I leave the room, I warn over my shoulder, "Careful, or your fingers will be next."

I cross the twenty feet spanning between Marc and Jamie's territory to Alex's– the Brownstone's entryway between the parlor on one side and the living room on the other. Half of the building is Alex's home and the other half is Marc's BDSM training playground, with the bedrooms upstairs. The Brownstone was purchased with Jamie's money but placed in Alexander's name– all of Jamie's money is filtered through Alex.

I can't wrap my mind around the amount of trust between them. I gave my money to my cousin, while Jamie gave his to a dying drug dealer who he'd never shared a single word. Once Alex healed from a gunshot wound to the chest, Jamie killed who he used to be.

I lean on the doorjamb to Alex's living room– a comfortable, lived-in man cave at complete odds with Marc's parlor. Both men sense my presence but don't bother to halt their conversation. The Brownstone is a safe haven. All those who cross the threshold are trusted with our secrets.

"Ask Dexter to let you have a girl." Alex picks up where Marcus left off. "A man has needs, and you don't like guys."

Tobias leans back on the sofa, softly stroking his kitty who is lying on his chest. A satisfied smirk flirts with his lips, no doubt from the handjob Alex administered. The cheeky bastard winks at me, fingertips rubbing under the kitten's chin.

I win!

No, I do because you're growing up into a fine gentleman.

"I'm allowed to fuck whoever I want." Tobias finally admits that I'm not a cruel bastard who's cock-blocking him. I refuse to pick girls out and toss them at him like they are whores. "My dad stuck his dick in anything warm. I love my dad. He's a righteous man with a sex addiction, and I refuse to carry on the family tradition."

"My girl is an addict, so I get it." Alex plucks the kitten from Toby's chest, flips it over, and tickles its belly. "But I don't see why you won't settle down with a girlfriend."

I wait with bated breath to see if Toby will talk about this. He hasn't voiced it since our initial meeting. I had whipped him until the words flowed like water. Afterward, I contacted Toby's family, informing them they were a bad influence and their boy was mine now. In the years since, I've made acquaintance with Toby's brother, Patrick Kline.

Toby retrieves his kitty. "I won't have sex with someone unless I know they've never stepped foot into Massachusetts or their mother hasn't. I wasn't born until after the shit hit the fan, but I've lived in the aftermath."

"I'm lost," Alex whispers. The counselor is used to this type of conversation, so he's patient while he waits for clarification.

"My mom was a young girl in Dad's congregation. After I was born, my grandparents delivered me to my father, and I've never met them. They moved away. My birth certificate has my father and his wife as my parents. Way before I was born, Dad didn't meet his kid until after it was too late. Like when his pregnant daughter brought home the boy who was asking our dad for her hand in marriage."

"What?" Alex's shocked reaction mirrors my own. His black hair swings around his chin as he shakes his head left and right in mystification.

"My siblings are married now, but it took almost thirty years of hell to get there. Good thing about lying birth certificates, the government can't stop you from marrying. Bad thing about the truth, it haunts you. I was raised with my niece– we're the same age. She ran away and came back a different girl, and then she told me the truth. See, I didn't know I was a throwaway kid with a brother. I thought I was a son with only an older sister, a brother-in-law, and an older nephew and niece."

"That's why you started using?"

"Mom couldn't have kids– Dad got her some kids. My sister is a drug addict because she couldn't deal with the truth. So my brother has the same profession as you to protect her from herself. But the truth infected us. Tina, my niece, got me hooked on drugs when we both learned the truth. She and I took off on a bus, not caring where we landed. We ended up in Dominion. The night I came to Restraint, I was trying to talk some sense into her, wanting to go home. Her brother owns a club, Rush, and a BDSM group called the Playroom, and she was missing home. That's what called us to Restraint. But then Dexter found me, took me in, and sent Tina back home and kept me."

I leave Tobias to confide in Alex in peace. He knew I was lurking in the doorway, but didn't mind since I already know all of the Kline family's dark and dirty secrets.

I make a detour to the kitchen to grab a couple of beers, and then weave my way down the long hallway to the front parlor, passing many doorways to small BDSM training rooms on either side of the hallway.

Marc and Jamie are engaged in a silent conversation when I return. I watch them briefly, the power of a lifetime of friendship washing over me.

It's been the three of us since we shit in our diapers. I'm older than Marc by a little over a year, with Jamie a few months younger than me. Our grandmother and Jamie's mother were the best of friends. It's a comfort to know someone so completely where they can no longer speak but you can still hear them in the silence.

"Jamie's not deaf, ya know?" I razz them both. "If I was paranoid like our Ezra, I'd swear you were discussing something I wasn't to know."

Bronze skin pinking, Marc flounders, readying to deny my accusations, but Jamie's rough cuff of a laugh is answer enough.

Handing them both a beer, I take my seat at the end of the sofa. "I'd rather not know if you don't wish me to know. You know that already." I crack my beer open, never imbibing at home because of Toby. But he understands that sometimes even his master has to unwind.

"Heads up," I warn both Marc and Jamie. "Regina is threatening to close Restraint, saying it's a liability. But Ezra was adamantly against it."

"He must be pissed at me right now," Marc mutters underneath his breath. Moving his lips silently, Jamie concurs.

"Excuse me?" I lean forward, breaking into their line of sight. If Marc can't see Jamie, they can't communicate. "Come again? What did you do to piss him off?"

Turning redder by the second, "Don't worry about why." Marc waves his hand to clear the air. "This explains why Ezra was creating riots in his own club, trying to get Maître du Jeu to leave Las Vegas."

This time Jamie and I share a loaded look. Marc's right and wrong.

"Ezra must be pissed at me and he's forcing my Boogieman to come for a visit, trying to destroy the BDSM infrastructure I've worked so hard to put into place."

Jamie signs: *That must be it.*

"I ask again. What did you do to piss Ezra off?" I lean into Marc's personal space. "Do I need to warn Kat?"

"Something that hasn't pissed him off in nearly fifteen years." Marc closes his eyes, thinking very hard, shame and guilt scroll across his features. "You know Ezra gets insulted if one of us sneezes sideways. I'll take care of Ezra. Don't worry about Katya. I'm positive she could guess what's rubbed him raw at last."

"Adelaide," I say at the same time Jamie signs the woman's name. I might feel sick to my stomach, but poor Jamie almost passes out from the thought. "She was Ezra's collateral damage that definitely effected Katya."

Adelaide Whittenhower has been rotting in Wintercrest Asylum for the past three years. Her health is poor, her face is scarred, and rumor has it she refuses to speak to anyone. The young woman was twisted in the head– twisted by someone. My guess was Maître du Jeu. At his sentencing, Raymond Hunter told Marcus he thought it was Ezra, which is why he turned himself in as the one who committed the crime.

"I'm my son's target this time." Again, Marcus waves his hand in the air, like that will cause the subject to be dropped. "Imagine enraged hornets defending their nests– The Fontaines. Let them pester the membership to keep them occupied. As long as I keep Ezra on his leash–"

"I'll take care of The Fontaines when they finally show up. Fair?" Marcus nods in assent. "Thoughts?" I turn to Jamie, who raises his hands, clearly saying, *"Leave me out of this shit!"*

"Fuck..." Marcus leans forward, his fingertips combing through his ringlets. "I've got to get back to Shadow Haven." He lunges to his feet, like he needs the courage to go home to the other half of his family. He'd never leave the Brownstone if he could get away with it.

Following after my cousin, "Ezra's not going to harm you, is he?"

Laughing without humor, Marc terrifies me. "Harm me?" Amber eyes connect with mine. "No, not physically. He'll make me pay for something he feels I've taken from him. Harm me? Cerebrally, of course."

I snap my fingers at Toby when we hit the entryway to gain his attention. He pockets the kitten into his backpack and comes to me, with Alex following at his heels.

"Cort's pulling his usual bullshit," I warn Marc. "Does this have anything to do with that?"

"Ya think?" Marc releases a strained laugh as he stalks from the house and into the night. "I know Cort's moods better than anyone. I'll call you in the morning. Night."

I turn to catch Alex and Jamie having a conversation solely in sign language. I only catch bits and pieces because I suck. Giving up, I descend the front steps, with Toby behind me.

As soon as the looming red door with the gargoyle knocker shuts behind us… "Jamie told Alex to prepare accommodations for their guests." The quiet, unassuming ones are who you should watch out for. Tobias Kline is great at ferreting out secrets. "Jamie said that he was sure Ezra had already taken care of it, seeing as how he's the asshole who put out the bat-signal."

"Well, now that that is confirmed," I mutter underneath my breath as I slide into my car.

"I caught Alex signing that we were to think it was only about Restraint ruining the image of the BDSM lifestyle. He caught my eyes bulging out and learned I know ASL."

"So much for that now, eh?" I turn to Toby, laughing that he finally got caught *eavesdropping*. "About the cat—"

"I'm keeping it," Toby demands, squeezing his bag to his chest. "Minion is my kitty. I'll take care of her."

"We'll get supplies in the morning," is all I can say in the face of Tobias becoming a man and taking what he wants.

Chapter Five

"Tobias, do you want any more eggs?" I ask over my shoulder as I scrape the last of the scrambled eggs from the cast-iron skillet. Minion is weaving her way around my ankles, chirping and meowing for a snack.

The hairless alien kitten was given a clean bill of health last week, and immediately taken to the groomers for a thorough scrubbing. Toby put her potty box in his bathroom, and his bedroom is decked out with a spoiled cat tree. Minion loves me, is so-so about Tobias, and loathes Monica.

Cats– nature's biggest assholes.

"No, thank you, Dex. I'm stuffed." The young, blond man pats his tummy while wearing a satisfied smile.

"More for me then," I mutter as I sit at the breakfast nook.

"What's on our agenda for the day?" I ask around a mouthful of food and feel rude. I hastily swallow and take a drink. "Excuse me. Sorry. It was a late night and I'm starved. We had to get more security for the club and it's not helping matters. We had another riot."

Wrapping a palm underneath Minion, he hoists the cat into his lap. Head-butting his hand, the kitty asks for a snack. "Another one?" Toby tilts his head to the side and squints. "What does that make, three riots?"

"Five," I answer in awe. "The more riots we have, the more people who show up at our door. In Restraint's case, bad publicity is definitely not better than none. We're losing control, Tobias. I don't think we can fix it."

"I have no doubt that you all will protect us," Tobias says with infallible confidence in the Masters of Restraint. "You have an audit at one o'clock and nothing before lunch. You should get caught up on the paperwork for the Joffre's case this morning." He looks down at the digital tablet that never leaves his side. Minion head-butts that next, rubbing her chin on the corner.

Cats– territorial assholes. Minion is a budding master or mistress, whichever she prefers.

"I don't know what I would do without you." I try not to tell Tobias this too often, as I fear the sentiment would be rendered meaningless if I did.

"What are your plans for the day?" I happily spear a sausage link and chew. I have to eat the meat before Monica gets into the room. She isn't a vegetarian, but she doesn't want me to eat fatty foods, even though we all work out on a weekly basis. I'm a man who believes a meal should be about pleasure and sustenance, and Monica even takes the fun out of eating.

It's difficult living in a house where I have to hide all the addictive substances, including cold and flu medications. No mouthwash. Aspirin under lock and key. That is a cost of caring for Tobias, which I gladly pay. But add on top of that, my partner in life despises food. What the fuck is left to live for?

Toby is rambling on about his day while my mind takes a vindictive vacation. He knows I'm not paying attention, so I'm positive he's repeating it until I finally hear him. "I'm sorry," I mutter, feeling exposed.

"Understood, Dexter," Toby says kindly. He nabs a bit of sausage off my plate to feed to Minion as payment for my absent-mindedness. "I have to clean the house this morning and study for a few hours. I'm taking Monica's car to the repair shop to be inspected. Oh, I made those reservations you wanted, Dexter, for seven p.m. at the Bistro. I even managed to get you the corner table that you sat at on your first date." Toby's blue eyes glow with pride for getting me exactly what I wanted.

"Thanks. I want tonight to be perfect." I smile around a big bite of sausage.

Monica entering the room cuts off our conversation, especially with a hiss emanating from Minion. I'm positive the cat's hair would be on end if she had any.

Two pussies in the same house isn't working out for Tobias and me.

Monica looks miserable, an expression she's worn for months. She's dressed as usual: her hair bound tightly, hiding its natural beauty, same as the bland clothes that hide her slim figure. No matter how much I shower Monica with attention and affection, with words of praise, she sinks further into herself. It feels like the more I do, the worse it gets.

"I'll get your breakfast," I say and hop up from my seat. I pull Monica's chair out for her and wait for her to sit.

"Dexter, you don't have to do that. I'm not even hungry." Monica issues a protest, just as she does every meal we eat at home. When was the last time she allowed herself to be hungry– to enjoy a meal? To be relaxed in my presence? She is never relaxed because of the monologue playing out inside her own mind. "Really, Dexter. I'm going to be late for work." She moves to stand, but I press her back down with a palm on her bony shoulder.

"I'm sure I can get your boss to go easy on you," I mutter teasingly, causing Toby to snort. Monica's boss is Katya, her own best friend. Ezra is the owner of Edge Publishing, a member of our family. Monica's just doing her usual by trying to avoid food at all costs.

Monica is actually earlier than usual.

I understand what Katya was saying about anorexia being an addiction. A disease. It's the lies, especially the lies to themselves, tearing relationships apart. I don't want to hate Monica for putting us all through this, but it doesn't mean I'm not feeling what I'm feeling.

"You didn't eat anything for dinner last night, and I bet you haven't eaten since yesterday morning." I grab Monica's plate from the oven I'd set to warm. I quickly spread a thin layer of cream cheese on her bagel. I hand her a plate with half a whole-wheat bagel and scrambled egg whites.

"Thanks." Monica smiles up at me sweetly. It's genuine for a change, but still a facsimile of the woman I fell in love with.

She grabs a knife and scrapes most of the cream cheese off her half bagel. I scowl at her. Last night I noticed that Monica's smaller than she was the last time we were intimate. It's been a few weeks because Toby and I have been busy with tax season, Restraint is exploding, and Monica has taken on a few more authors at Edge. I cringe in remembrance of how her bones protruded from her skin, her hips as sharp as blades, her breasts were empty bags of flesh.

"Eat all your eggs, or no dessert for you," I tease, tapping the edge of her plate with my fingertip. I wish she'd eat dessert.

Monica pushes her food around and pretends to eat. The past year she's been more insecure and that is an amazing feat since she was very insecure to begin with. I know all the tricks she pulls to hide her anorexia. What I don't understand is where this bullshit is stemming from. I can't fix it if I don't know the cause.

Feeling utterly helpless, I lose my cool. "Eat it all, Monica. I fucking mean it." I command her in my Master Dexter tone. I'm done coddling her with this shit. I'm sitting at the breakfast table with two of the most important people in my life. The people I consider my family. We have an easy life and we're comfortable. I cooked a healthy, nutritious breakfast, and she's being disrespectful by ruining the moment– something she's notorious for lately.

I quickly text a message to Tobias with my phone in my lap: *make sure she doesn't toss it back up!*

Toby nods his head at me when he gets the message. Both Tobias and I have been managing her lately. I love her so much, but I'm not sure how to help her. Helplessness and powerlessness are not emotions I want to feel.

I watch as Monica eats her eggs as quickly as possible, not even pausing to breathe or chew as she swallows.

I've been reconsidering the relationship I have with my girlfriend. We're at an impasse. I want a wife and children, not a girlfriend I have to be terrified will have a stroke, organ failure, or die in her sleep. Monica is draining me. I never wanted to treat Monica as I had treated Tobias in the beginning, but she no longer has the capacity to do it for herself.

I've treated Monica with respect as she treats herself with none.

But today is not the day to begin treating Monica as my slave. It's the three-year anniversary of Katya's initiation. The very day I took Monica as my own, but I forgot what that truly meant. All of Monica's poor decisions and destructive behaviors are on me. She needed me and I failed her.

The life as we've known it changes tomorrow night.

"Good girl," I murmur to Monica when her plate is empty. "I have to get to work. It seems I have some free time to attack that pile of shit on my desk. I can't wait until you're ready for the office, Toby. I need you there badly."

Tobias smiles at me in pride and the tension Monica brought to the table dissipates.

"We have a date tonight if memory serves me correctly. Please be ready at six. I'll meet you here at home." I cup Monica's cheek in my palm and kiss her lightly on parted lips tasting of cream cheese and salt.

Her confidence issues disappear as I kiss her passionately, tongue tasting tongue. Anyone who saw me with this woman would know I'm completely taken with her. It's too bad she's too blind to see it.

"I love you, Monica. I'll see you tonight." I quickly kiss her again. If I linger, I would pull her back to our bedroom and never see the light of day. "Have a good day, boys and girls. See you guys tonight sometime. I'll talk to you later, Tobias."

Chapter Six

Wanting to play pretend, even if it's for the evening, the illness is insistently wafting around us, impossible to ignore. "My God, this steak is fantastic. It melts in my mouth." I groan in pleasure as my taste buds explode from the buttery meat. Monica smiles at the expression of pure bliss written across my face, but it's muted somehow.

Monica must feel ill all the time. When I miss a single meal, I turn into a foraging angry bear. But missing so many meals until your body is cannibalizing itself, I can't imagine the lethargy, the agony of an empty, protesting stomach, and the nausea. Monica must be in constant misery, inside and out.

Toby and Katya confirmed my greatest fears this evening. Monica used the bathroom prior to leaving for the office this morning, and Toby heard her purging out the breakfast that I spent so much energy coaxing her to eat. Later in the day, when Kat forced lunch down Monica's throat, she slipped off to the bathroom, and Kat picked the lock to catch her in the act.

I'm furious, but it's the same type of fury you feel when someone is dying. I'm allowed to feel powerless and helpless, but I'd be an asshole to hate someone who is obviously not doing this on purpose.

"I appreciate how we're keeping up tradition," I begin, trying for polite conversation, hoping to spark Monica with a walk down memory lane. "Same restaurant as our first date, even the same entrees."

"That was what I loved most about you." Monica plays along, or she's actually being genuine. It's hard to be sure with how much she lies to the both of us lately. "You were so stable, solid, in control of yourself and everyone around you at all times. I loved how ritual mattered to you."

Monica's *I need that now* is unspoken but screaming across the table.

"You can thank my grandmother for instilling those traditions into me. I'm thankful that you weren't from a religious family.

Rebekah Zeitler would have rolled over in her grave if I'd married a Catholic like Marcus."

"Not a love match, though," Monica teases me, a wicked light glinting in her eyes. I try not to get sad as I hang onto this moment. This thread of the Monica I fell in love with used to be her 24/7, but currently doesn't make an appearance even once or twice per day.

I miss Monica. I miss her so much it physically hurts. But I believe Monica misses her true self even more than I do.

"As I said, I love the ritual of it. I may not be fully invested in the religious belief aspects of Judaism, but I appreciate the traditions and values. I do wish someday I can give to you what you've always given me. Stability. A strong sense of family and belonging. Comfort and contentment."

The sincerity in Monica's voice draws tears to my eyes, and I finally see the addict dwelling deep inside her. Addicts want to believe what they say, even knowing it will never happen. Monica doesn't want to be this way, and stopping is not about willpower.

A woman who can go without eating while hungry, while fighting dizzy spells and low blood sugar, is a woman with an insane amount of willpower. One who also has a mental illness that needs to be taken in hand.

Monica wants a life with me, a happy life like the one we both long to have, but for some reason she doesn't feel she deserves it, and it's killing her. Literally.

"How's the sea bass?" I gaze pointedly at her plate– a plate that is more than half full. Rice is scattered all over the platter and bits of fish are flaked apart, all in a quest to make it look eaten. The broccoli is the only item that disappeared from her plate, but probably into Monica's napkin.

We both play pretend tonight. "It's delicious," she says sweetly in a tight voice because she's angry I brought attention to her illness. However, she does try to make an effort to eat a bite of fish.

I want to command Monica to eat, but it's a special night and I don't want to push her. It feels disrespectful to boss someone around when you see them as an equal. It's the double-edged sword of tough love. It hurts both parties.

"How about some molten lava cake for dessert, just like the first time we were here? We could share it." I lick my lips to show how much I'd love to share the chocolatey, gooey treat with Monica. I leer at her chest and lick my bottom lip again. I earn a girlish giggle for my trouble.

Later, after paying the bill, I take Monica's hand in mine and walk her down the street. I suggest we walk off our dinner, just so we can spend a few moments together than aren't about everyday life. Monica quickly jumps on the request for exercise because she did have several spoonfuls of cake, for which I'm thankful.

I quickly grab a blanket from the backseat of our car and we head to the park. It's a beautiful night. The air feels like bathwater caressing at our skin. I spread the blanket out beneath one of the huge willow trees that dominates the center of the park, and then I pull Monica down with me.

Gazing at me with love dwelling in her brown eyes, Monica rests her palm over my heart. "Happy third anniversary, Monica. I've never been as happy as I am now with you. I love you so much it hurts." I profess and I mean every word. "It doesn't matter how big or small, we will get through anything. Together."

I pull Monica to my chest and flutter a kiss on her lips. She moans into my mouth and her small hands fist my shirt. I love it when she responds to my touch with fervor and intensity, as if she's as addicted to me as I am to her.

Pulling back slightly with kiss-swollen lips, Monica's fingertips brush the hair off my forehead. "Your best feature is your forehead," she mutters wryly. "Not the tightly coiled muscles, or that huge cock." Chuckling throatily, she leans forward to kiss my forehead. "I love your hair, but there is just something about your forehead that turns me on."

"It's the big brain beneath," I tease her back.

"It most certainly is," Monica agrees, turning serious, almost regretful. "Beauty fades, and in order to spend a lifetime at someone's side, it has to be about more than looks, more than a quick fuck." She looks away from me, the dark silence wafting around us. Then she whispers so quietly I can barely hear her over the beating of my heart in my ears. "I'm deeply flawed. In body, mind, and spirit."

"I don't believe that, Monica." I try to pull her into my arms but she won't allow it.

"Someday when you finally see me clearly, you'll regret saying that," she says as a challenge. "I'm just a plumber's daughter. I was not raised to know anything but work. I was told from a young age I had to work for whatever I needed to survive because I couldn't fall back on my looks."

Tortured brown eyes connect with mine. "My dad believed women to be his equal, and I understood why he did what he did. As children, boys are told they are strong and girls are told they are pretty. But every time someone said that to me as a child, my father would correct them. '*Monica is neither pretty nor beautiful. She is smart.*' I get that he was trying to make me feel like there was more to me than what was between my legs, but it hurt when I would dress up and would be told I wasn't pretty. On purpose."

"Monica," I sigh sadly, realizing she's finally letting me in, yet it somehow feels like a goodbye.

"I'm smart, but I'm not smart enough to be the best in my profession. Katya holds that top spot. I couldn't be pretty. I couldn't even be attractive. But I also couldn't have the job I thought I deserved. I hated Katya for having it all until I got to know her and realized she was not vapid, shallow, and making fun of me with every breath she took. I cherish our friendship, but it doesn't take the sting away when my dad tells me I'm nothing. Now I'm neither pretty nor smart."

The agony in Monica's voice takes my breath away, leaving me speechless. I do the only thing I can. Show her how much I need her in all ways. I roll Monica over onto her back and make out with her as if we're teenage lovers, not adults in our late thirties.

Monica never says she loves me back, but I know she does. I can see it in her gaze. I can feel it in her touch. And I can hear it in the tone of her voice. Right now, I can feel it in the way she clings to me like a lifeline.

Actions speak louder than words if you know how to interpret them.

I kiss Monica's neck and I feel bad that she's missing the piece of jewelry that binds us to one another. "I'm sorry that your collar isn't repaired yet. It should be finished at the jeweler's sometime tomorrow afternoon. I tried to get it for tonight. I thought it would be special to give it back to you three years after I gave it to you."

"I don't need it to know that we're connected, Dexter." She gazes adoringly at me and twines her fingers in my hair. I gaze back down at the love of my life and wish I could bottle this moment, because it's only going to get worse before it gets better.

Chapter Seven

"Finally a quiet night, eh?" Aaron says to me in passing, large white teeth glowing in the darkened club. "Maybe this will keep Queen from shutting us down."

That must rankle the man when he puts his heart and soul into Restraint, but Ezra will follow Regina's directive versus Aaron's. "Is Ezra here tonight?" I ask as I type in the security code to the Dungeon. The slight tilting of Aaron's chin has me saying, "That would be why it's quiet. Chaos follows Master Ez. If he's not here, it's calm."

Blushing high in his cheeks, Aaron fails to comment. Trailing a devious chuckle, I enter the dungeon. My eyes take in everything surrounding me. Seeing Syn work a man on the St. Andrew's cross has a coil of sadism tightening in my gut.

Between Tobias feeling stressed with his school work, Monica acting like she wants me to whip her when she's never shown a masochistic urge before, and the feeling of powerlessness over what I have to do later this evening, I almost want to break the tenets of my gift.

One does not strike out to cause pain out of anger, frustration, or a lack of power, because that means one is no longer in control.

Sadism is a gift you bestow on a masochist. One never hits someone who doesn't need release. That is an abuse of power and trust, not kindness and respect.

The sadist uses pain to heal the masochist, to extinguish a build-up of emotions that they are otherwise incapable of releasing.

The sadist finds pleasure and pride in the masochist finding relief, not in the delivery of pain itself.

Sadism is a gift and a curse. Not many have the stomach to harm someone until they are healed. The curse is in others seeing you as a sociopath who finds great pleasure in causing pain, when it couldn't be farther from the truth.

A sadist and a masochist are both highly empathetic. A masochist cannot handle being a sponge for the emotions surrounding them, unable to distinguish their own from others.

Whereas a sadist feels the pressure the masochist is under, and neither will be comfortable until the union takes place.

I appreciate Syn's work while slowly breathing in and out to unloosen the coil deep in my belly. After a few moments, the snap of the whip no longer has all parts of me aroused for action. My palm still itches because the leather handle of my whip is not resting upon it. I curl my fingertips, nails biting into my palm, to combat the need.

I about-face, turning to walk down the hallway to our private rooms, unable to stand in the dungeon proper for fear I will fall under its intoxicating spell and find me a toy for the evening.

My sadism has belonged solely to Tobias these past few years, with my body and heart belonging to Monica.

A master who is not ethical, logical, faithful, and in control at all times, is no master at all. Which is why we have Maître du Jeu breathing down our necks, as Ezra and Cortez do not exhibit the signs of a true master, and when it comes to the Ezes, neither does the master of all of us– Marcus.

Masculine moans echo down the hallway toward me as I approach my private room. I smirk to myself, glad someone is having a good night when I cannot. The moans increase in volume as I get closer, to almost porn-like quality. Fake enthusiasm. My interest piques about who could possibly be in the throes of an endless orgasm, like they're a siren calling in the hedonists from the dungeon.

Ezra is doing the work of the insane elsewhere with Katya and Cortez. Aaron is in the club. Syn is in the dungeon. Alex is at the Brownstone with our master who never sets foot into Restraint. Pretty Boy was having a drink at the bar, teasing Kris. Queen is no doubt running operations from Ezra's office.

That only leaves the asshole Dalton, and I'm beyond surprised. Other than a penchant for epic-level douchebaggery, I've never seen him have sex.

Letting it go, not faulting whomever is having a great time, I open the door to my private room and just stare. Just stare in a mix of horror, awe, and agony. I'm so shocked my mind can't catch up to the emotions of it, completely shutting my system down. The only parts on me that move are my eyeballs and my fists clenching, fingernails drawing blood in my palms.

Dalton's a lucky bastard all right– he's trespassing in my room and using *my* very skilled submissive. My girlfriend. The woman

I've spent the last three years building a life with, while considering spending the rest of my years with her.

Hours shy of her intervention, Monica betrays me, meeting the challenge she threw down last night. *Someday when you finally see me clearly, you'll regret saying that.* I breathe through the fury and pain, lest I lash out in violence.

"Ah– Dexter." Dalton grunts dramatically as he ruts on my woman. Fully clothed in several layers of clothing with his freakishly small hands gripping Monica's bony hips, he rocks as if performing. His mud-brown, muted eyes shine with triumph, and something else I can't name moves beneath the glassy surface. "God, Monica's sooo good. I just had to take her." He uses arrogance to bait me into doing what he wants. "Tight. So tight."

Dalton wants to hurt me and I have no idea why. The sadist in me scents him as a masochist, no matter how hard he may try to disguise it. Part of Dalton is lashing out to hurt me, while part is begging for me to heal him. It was no different than how Tobias behaved when we met.

Scenting Dalton's hidden masochism doesn't change anything. I would not mourn his loss should he fall dead right this moment. I would deny it later, but I would celebrate the occasion.

I might not know Dalton's twisted motivations, but I do know why Monica wants to hurt me. She wants to push me away so she has an excuse to cuddle with her sickness, to validate the insanity in her mind.

Dexter says he loves me, but I don't believe him. So I'll do whatever it takes to prove to him that he can't love someone like me.

In retrospect, I understand this. But I am still a goddamned man with testicles and a huge motherfucking cock. There is a man inside the woman I possess, and the caveman dwelling deep inside of me can't be reasoned with. The all-encompassing wash of red violence flickers in my vision, and only Monica soothes the savage beast readying itself to erupt.

Monica immediately starts to bawl when she sees me standing in the doorway. Perhaps the movement of air from the hallway alluded to my presence, because she was out of it when Dalton was speaking to me– utterly blank-faced. Large wracking sobs shudder through Monica's body, only the ropes containing her keep her from collapsing on the floor.

The hollowing sound of Monica's agony drives a knife deep within my heart. I want to rub the pain in my chest, but it would show my displeasure. As a Master of Restraint, I learned how to project myself as calm no matter the storm brewing beneath the surface.

A master's moods should not affect the submissive's emotional climate. We are here to guide and lead them, not the other way around. Any true dominant has the ability to read body language, and my master taught me early on to mask my own body language. To express outward emotions in the dungeon, or anywhere else for that matter, is a sign of a poor dominant.

"Carry on, Dalton. Don't stop for my benefit. If you wish to disrespect me, do so thoroughly. I'll watch."

Dalton's face betrays his shock. He wanted me to attack him, and I don't accept his poor attempt to control me. It is taking all of my restraint not to do so, as I'm in love with the woman he takes so brutally. I refuse to engage bullies, either negatively or positively. Even if it makes me look like I'm turning the other cheek.

With all his douchebaggery, Dalton has always thought that the way to become the top master was through antagonizing his fellow masters. There is no top master. He never understood that it is pure talent. Dominance is innate inside your soul. It cannot be learned, only crafted, honed, improved, and fostered.

Leaning back on the doorframe, I cross my arms over my chest to stop myself from rubbing the pain away. I simply watch.

Dalton stares at me for a moment, testing me. He turns back to Monica, who is strung up against the wall in ropes. She is trussed up so tightly the skin dents in from the tension of the ropes. In some spots, I see dried blood from rub burns. This is not entirely Dalton's fault, and exactly why I haven't engaged in BDSM activities with Monica in almost a year. She is too fragile, with not enough life in her to do so safely.

Monica holds my eyes and cries, tears streaming down her face in a torrent. The look on her tortured face is begging for me to make him stop. But Monica has a voice, and she has the ability to use it. If she wanted to be treated as my submissive, than she shouldn't have betrayed me.

No. All it would take is a no. A safeword. Any utterance would halt Dalton on the spot. I can even feel his reluctance in this entire affair. I have no doubt that Monica entered this scene willingly. I did not give permission for Dalton to use Monica. But in the past three years, we moved past a relationship between a master and a submissive to that of a committed couple. Dalton only needed Monica's permission because I am not her master.

Monica wanted a master, and she wanted him to be me. That is where I've failed. She wanted a solid life-mate. All I gave her was a doting, coddling boyfriend without a backbone because he fell in love with a broken woman who was desperate for his help.

It kills something vital in me to witness the lost expression on Monica's face, as if she just now came to realize I will never abandon her. But I will also never allow her to control me through her destructive behaviors.

"Aren't you going to punish us, Dexter?" The little fucker tries and fails to bait me. Smarmy fake voice. Odd brown hair that almost looks like an old man's toupee. Lifeless brown eyes. A body clad in layers upon layers of clothing hanging off his slight frame. Large shoes that don't look quite right on his feet. Dalton is just as pitiful as Monica.

"A master doesn't beat an already beaten dog. Sadists are not sociopaths. This is not a perverted romance novel, Dalton," I mutter dryly. "Maître du Jeu's Masters of Restraint will not bastardize the BDSM culture. You want me to kill you, don't you? That is not BDSM; it is assault. You both have freewill, and the consequences of said use rest solely on your shoulders. The breach of our trust, the loss of my respect, and your guilt and shame will be punishment enough."

I point between their connected bodies, giving Dalton and Monica impassive eyes. Challenging me as if a child would, Dalton begins thrusting anew– to punish us all since I won't do it.

Monica's sobs twist the knife in my heart. The exaggerated grunts flowing from Dalton's throat are all for show. I've been with countless women and one man. I know the guttural, animalistic sounds people make, and his are poorly rehearsed renditions straight from a porn video. For years, Dalton's theatrics have been talk among the busybody masters. We all want to break him of it because it's just saddening.

"One does not punish his girlfriend," I say to the adulterers as they fuck in front of me, none of us enjoying it. "That would be considered domestic violence, and would also make me weak."

Monica's skirt is hiked up to her ass, panties pushed aside. Her blouse is still buttoned. Her hair is still smooth and perfect. All of Dalton's body is covered in fabric except for his hands and face, with only a slight view of his cock sliding in and out of Monica.

The only flaw on Monica is the mascara creating black tear-tracks down her cheeks. She looks utterly beautiful in her broken state, and I've never loved her more. Just as it takes courage to destroy your body, it takes just as much to destroy the love of your life.

Using their tortured facial features to my advantage, I speak to both Monica and Dalton. "A real man has enough pride to understand how his girlfriend cheating on him is because something is wrong inside of her. She's either trying to fill a void, or destroy what is good, to prove she is unworthy. A real man will figure it out and fix it, not blame her and throw her away, even if that's what she thinks she deserves."

Monica's sobs increase in volume as she realizes her mistake, how even unspoken I do understand. Never blinking, instead of telling Dalton no like she should, she holds my stare as a grounding force. I start to doubt myself. Is Monica so far gone she is incapable of safe-wording out?

Dalton quickly looks at me from over his shoulder, appraising my expression. He thrusts awkwardly, as if he's unused to his own body. "You're not going to punish her?" He sounds disbelieving as he tests my limits.

In a flat, emotionless tone, I mutter. "No, I figure that fucking you is punishment enough."

Dalton shouts his nasal voice at the ceiling as he climaxes. Even his twisted orgasm face is a turn off. I may not enjoy the sexual company of men, but I always enjoy the sound of their release. It usually means a job well done. But this time it's different. Exaggerated moans turn to no panting or breathlessness as Dalton pulls from Monica's body, flagging cock looking to be that way from a lack of arousal, not from climax.

"FYI, Dalton. A spent cock looks a helluva lot different than a flaccid one." I can't help the edge of superiority from creeping into my tone.

Glaring at me but otherwise silent, Dalton turns from me as he tucks his cock away in his brown dress pants. I focus on how everything about him is brown, pretending that his cock didn't appear to be bigger than mine. It had to be an optical illusion since I have a thick ten-incher.

Remorse and defeat bleeding from his pores, Dalton removes Monica's binding. I hold my wince as the rope is pulled from her flesh. It sticks in the dried blood and peels fragile skin as the rope is yanked away.

I want to so badly run to Monica and offer her aftercare. But this is not my scene. I will not provide her loving aftercare when she's hurt me so deeply. My having to watch this scene and the aftermath that plays out before my eyes hurts just as badly as her betrayal, but nowhere nearly as badly as witnessing her pain causes upon me.

Monica's skin is red and splotchy around her injuries. The rest of her flesh is so pale I worry. She whimpers as she walks toward me, begging for my attention, affection, and my forgiveness.

I want to fall to my knees and hold Monica to my chest, to erase what has been done. I want to join her as she cries out her pain. But she created my pain. She created her own pain.

Monica is at the root of our problem, and it's time I take responsibility for the role I played in allowing her sickness to infect not only our relationship, but our lives and how I interact with the world.

Words forceful, commanding, I leave Dexter behind and become one with Master Dexter the sadist. "Are you through? Are you through punishing yourself by punishing me? If so, I suggest you make your way home, where I expect you to sit and think over your life choices, and how all actions have a consequence. Understood?"

"Yes, Master." Monica's voice holds a wealth of agony. But even deeper is the relief, as if she's waited three years to say those two words and she cannot believe she hears them coming from her own mouth. "Yes, Master."

Turning, I walk away, out into the hallway and beyond, leaving the love of my life groveling on the floor. I leave my heart smashed into pulp at her feet.

Chapter Eight

I rush through the crowded dungeon at a fast clip. Everyone gets out of my way, but not for the expression on my face, because there isn't one. I'm neutral, but terrified and seething beneath the surface. Everyone just knows not to fuck with me because I mean business. It's too damned bad that Dalton hasn't learned the lesson yet.

Brain taking over, I move automatically to the point I don't register who I've passed or when I've entered the club and left the dungeon behind. I know deep in my subconscious that Monica feels incomplete and that causes her to act out. However, the part of my brain that is archaic, from the time when we lived in caves, hunted prey, and dragged our women around by their hair, is yet again refusing to be reasoned with.

A dominant's mind is made from the part of human nature that evolution bred out of the population. We are few, and we don't think like the normal beings of this world. This animal part of my brain wants me to run back to my personal room and kill Dalton for having the audacity to touch my woman. It also screams for me to punish Monica within an inch of her life so that she knows never to cross me again. After that, I would fuck her senseless, marking her with my scent and filling her with my seed until it germinates. I want to scream to every male in this club that Monica is *mine*.

Instead of allowing my nature to control me, I make my way through the club entrance, discreetly flicking the tears that betray my frustration. I can't do what the caveman wants, no matter how satisfying that may be.

Monica is in great need of tough love, and I will be strong enough for the both of us to administer it. Just not this second. I need a moment to clear my head before I begin. I'll make her sit at home, contemplating her mistakes as a teaching tool.

I lean on the bar and absorb the chaos swirling around me. Kris is working her tiny tail off as the bartender, with some added security and help tonight. The strobe lights flicker with the bass pounding from the speaker system as the DJ shows us all who's the master.

It's all just a big headache for me, and I'm sick and tired of the politics of it. When we first started our BDSM chapter here in Dominion, it was about the lifestyle. With the advent of Restraint, that all changed, as did what I do with my nonexistent free time. Policing a wild crowd is not what I had in mind. I long to teach those in my lifestyle just as much as I crave practicing it. But the cost of doing so is to clean up Ezra Zeitler's temper tantrums.

While riot-free tonight, Restraint is at maximum capacity thanks to media coverage. It all started when Ezra finally caught Katya, with the release of the details of her rape and Ava's conception. Then Raymond Hunter was released, only to attack both Adelaide and Katya at Aaron and Kayla's wedding. The media storm caused Restraint to burst at the seams. Years later, Adelaide Whittenhower released a tell-all book titled the *Mistress & Master of Restraint*. Then weeks ago, the riots began, attracting customers like flies.

I hate the news hounds, the paparazzi, and the constant spotlight. Every member of Restraint has been targeted by those blood-sucking mosquitoes. When will it ever end? We promise members anonymity and fail on all accounts. Now random people flock in droves to become a part of the membership as we lose valuable members from the unwanted attention. Soon Restraint will devolve into the violent joke the paper makes it out to be.

All of it was Ezra's fault. From what I gathered from Marcus, Ezra was trying to get Maître du Jeu's attention so they would show up and be Marc's ultimate boogieman. All of this was Ezra's '*fuck you!*' for some slight that doesn't involve us but always takes us down with the sinking ship. Judging by the last riot, the riot that had Fate a nanosecond from penetrative rape, he did get Maître du Jeu's attention.

Now it's just a waiting game.

So here I am, dealing with my own life falling to shit, cleaning up Ezra's mess. I slouch against the bar, needing a drink and then hating myself for the thought. I'm a master for shit's sake. I need to own how I feel, not allow it to control me. So what? Monica got fucked by Dalton, and neither of them enjoyed it. I feel betrayed but Monica is her own person, allowed freewill to make mistakes on her own.

Monica's actions are not about me, and to think otherwise is immature and arrogant. But that doesn't mean it doesn't feel like a wrecking ball to the nutsack.

As a master and a sadist, even I think it's barbaric to treat women as lesser beings. Regina Regal is proof of that. Katya Waters is proof of that. Monica's behavior is proof of that. Her father was trying to instill this same ethical code by not making beauty the sole reason for his daughter's existence, but he went overboard and caused a neurosis.

I won't allow Monica to create a neurosis in me. I'm a problem solver. We have a problem. I will make sure Monica fixes it… after I take a breather.

Monica cheated on you.

Shut up, caveman! Shut up and let me think without emotion. Damn you!

You may not want to own a woman, but your woman wants to be owned by you.

Shut up!

No, you need to listen to me. Own Monica to heal her.

I will, caveman. Just go away.

Without a word, Kris slides a lowball glass of scotch my way. With a sad twist of her lips, she goes back to attend the rush at the bar.

My inner caveman is pissed at me, craving the urge to go fuck Monica and kill Dalton. *You're human. Drink it.*

I'm better than using a substance to numb my emotions, pollute my body, and taint my reasoning skills.

No, you're not, pothead!

You're right. The amber liquid is sliding down my throat before I even register it. Warmth radiates from my belly, spreading to my arms and legs to relax my muscles. Sighing, my mind floats away.

Restraint is ironic: the name of the club versus the clientele. No one shows any restraint as they gorge themselves on liquor, sex, and music. Even my iron-willed restraint isn't immune. The intoxication allows their dampened primitive mind to resurface, as evident by their mating dances, the violence, and the hedonistic acts being displayed all around me.

The purpose of the main club at Restraint is a hunting ground for the members and visiting masters. It gives us new conquests and restocks our membership to keep things interesting. Most patrons don't realize they are being watched constantly. We look for the markers of a submissive or dominant, with ninety-nine percent being overlooked because we find them lacking.

The fake doms prey upon the misinformed, and things get messy. They dress up in leather and pretend to command their friends, or they use it as a piss-poor excuse to abuse their significant other who isn't submissive in nature. They aren't properly educated on how to be a dominant being, and it's to everyone's detriment.

The biggest population at Restraint is the Fifty Shades wannabees. They flock to Restraint looking for their personal Christian. They're looking for some excitement in their lives– a bit of slap and tickle –where they will tell their friends, their bosses, their spouses, how they were taken by a real BDSM Master. They look at us like we're sideshow freaks, or trapped in viewing cages at a zoo.

These entitled, drunken, loose-tongued, roaming-hand women feel they have permission to proposition us, simply because they paid a cover charge to enter Restraint. They travel in hordes and treat us like meat, worse than male strippers and prostitutes who are getting paid for a service, when we're trying to provide for their safety. They laugh when we push them off, telling their friends right in front of us how we must be gay or our dicks are broken. If the tables were turned, we'd be slapped with sexual assault charges. If their husbands did the same thing at a club, they'd say he was cheating. They believe we have no right to say no because we are brooding sex machines put on this earth to be their ultimate fantasy.

By popping their fantasy bubble, yanking them back into reality, I make sure these two forces never collide: the fake doms and the Fifty Shades wannabees. With its union is the bastardization of an entire culture.

The sadist side of me sometimes lets the women who grabbed me by the crotch be preyed upon in retaliation. But the human side of me steps in to stop it before it turns into the bored, straying wife's ultimate fantasy turned nightmare.

Restraint's version of Christian suddenly turns into a jobless creep, who is grabbing tits and reaching under skirts with the same entitlement they showed me, and then the woman screams bloody murder.

The politically correct response would be to say she wasn't at fault. But the part of me that is firmly in reality wants to point out how none of it would have happened if she would have stayed home, or at least not poked the beast into action.

Don't slap me, and then play the victim when I punch you back.

BDSM is not a joke, nor is it about sex. It should be taken seriously. It's not an excuse to abuse, carry out an assault, or victimize. When no care is taken, people *will* get hurt. It's also not fair when someone comes looking for an adrenaline rush, and then calls foul when they get more than expected. Ignorance is no excuse.

You don't drive a car if you don't know how, and then act confused as to how you managed to kill three people on the freeway during an accident. You should not enter into a BDSM establishment as a rite of passage or out of curiosity, then taunt and tease the natives and expect to walk out the same way as you entered. Especially when it is a culture built upon trust and respect. You are a stranger in our house, disrespecting us, so expect to be taught a valuable lesson before you leave.

My job is twofold, as it is for the rest of the membership. We look for clientele who possess the traits that make for an excellent submissive or dominant, and we remove the irritants from the club. Members are part bouncer– part hunter –part salesman.

In the past, I was a vicious hunter. I would stalk my prey with pinpoint accuracy. Ever since Monica came into my life, I've abstained from the game. It almost feels strange to stand here and look to the crowd knowing I could pick one and fuck them into oblivion.

I won't do it, though.

I may love Monica, but that isn't the reason I abstain from the hunt. If I were to pick someone for the sake of revenge sex, then I'd be giving control to Monica and Dalton for betraying me. Not only would I be disrespecting the unsuspecting soul, I'd be disrespecting myself.

Other's actions should never alter your own.

A good hunter is always patient and never stalks in anger. Which is why I am playing observer instead of meeting Monica at home, where I may harm her mentally, emotionally, and most certainly physically in a fit of rage.

My favorite part about observing the crowd is the people. They come from every walk of life, every tax bracket, and offer endless amounts of entertainment, especially the naïve.

If I were hunting, and I tell myself I'm not. *I lie.* The hunter's mind cannot be shut off. I would cull the innocent and the desperate from the herd. My eyes immediately light on the one who doesn't belong in the club. She's all by herself. A huge no-no. Easy prey.

There are three types of women who frequent the club: those who submit, those who dominate, and those who are just here for the show and to get a cheap thrill.

Those who submit are dressed conservatively. They are not here alone, as that would lead to bloodshed. They are safe and secure with their friends, or a spouse, or a true master. They aren't dressed salaciously, as that would be looked upon as soliciting unwanted attention. Archaic as it may be, it's human nature to not only look but to reach out and take.

Those who dominate are dressed in a wide array of styles, ranging from cliché domme in full leather, to showing off their distinct personalities. They don't need to impress anyone because they are comfortable in their own skin.

The Fifty Shaders are in their slut clothes– the super tight, super short, ass hanging out the hemline with their tits overflowing the bodice. Dinky, skinny, curvy, chubby, they all shop in the same store, none of them having an individual personality. Everything has someone else's name stamped on it for approval, as if they can't make a decision without consulting everyone else on the brand. These are wives and girlfriends to either insecure men, or rich men who need brainless arm-candy to shut up and look pretty.

Their small scattering of friends are patiently humoring the horde while exuding pure confidence. It's not by how much or little flesh is on display. They have an air of self-assurance weaving around them that is attractive to anyone looking for a cerebral connection after the lust wears off.

But the majority are more insecure than Monica, needing validation by a guy getting a hard-on as proof they are better than those who stand near them. These are who a hunter culls from the herd. They are easy prey after you get them far from their confident, protective friends. They are prey who are ignorant, or desperate, or are too ashamed to report an assault once it happens.

As a predator, I recognize them with only a passing glance. As a human being, I do my damnedest to save them from themselves. These women aren't unintelligent. They are broken inside and believe any man will fix them, not realizing they need to heal themselves.

In the sea of dominant, submissive, and lost women, one woman stands out amongst the crowd. She doesn't fit any of these categories if you go by her choice of clothing. She's average height for a lady, but slightly pudgy for someone who frequents a club looking to get laid. The biggest giveaway is the tan dress pants and flower print blouse. The majority of the patrons in the club wear either fetish wear, Goth style clothing, or strips of fabric to keep them from indecent exposure.

Her eyes dart back and forth, roving over the crowd until they finally come to rest on me. She shakes her head yes, just a nod up and down once, as if I was exactly who she was looking for. She promptly makes her way toward me while weaving around drunken dancers.

Voice infused with confidence, she steps right in front of me, looking me dead to rights. "Are you a master?"

"Yes." I answer flatly, unsure of her motives but instinctively knowing she's not hitting on me.

In my world, when one doesn't belong it's because Maître du Jeu sent them. Judging a book by its cover, she is a professional woman in her early thirties. The fact that she passed curvy a few dress sizes ago is a dead giveaway. She also has soft mocha skin, which is completely at odds with the basic white girls who flood our doors.

With amused patience, I allow her to look her fill as I do the same in return.

I raise an eyebrow, silently asking her to continue. I'm here. She's here. Might as well go ahead and either order me to do something or ask me a question. This is how it always goes, but usually it's Jamie bothering me in secret.

Is this lone woman the Las Vegas retinue of Maître du Jeu?

Doubtful that she would scare Marcus to death. But you can never be too sure when it comes to those with power, influence, no ethical code, and no fear of breaking the laws of man or human kind.

My face betrays nothing as she stares at me, waiting to see which one of us breaks first. I could be singing children's songs or dirty limericks and no one would be the wiser. I enjoy this part of my control, because it's what has kept me in as normal of a life as I could ever have.

After what feels like several long minutes of a staring contest, she says matter-of-factly, "I want to train," completely taking me off my game.

"For what?" I feign confusion, still not buying her reason for being here.

"I want to train as a dominant." She nods her head *yes* again— so succinct. No bullshit with this woman, which is a dominant trait.

"Why? And what makes you think we do that here?" I sigh and act bored. I pick a hangnail on my finger as if I'm not paying her any attention. "We're just a club. Booze. Dancing. A place to pick up a fuck-buddy. Does it look like we train anyone here?"

"Master Dexter Hayes. IRS Agent. Lives in the Crestview gated community with the rest of your rich friends, at the very edge of the community in a huge Victorian house that sticks out like a sore thumb among the micro-mansions. Cousin of Marcus Zeitler, who is the adoptive father of Ezra Zeitler. Ezra Zeitler, who is the owner of Restraint, reported to being a part of the BDSM community, where he said he was a Master of Restraint. It wasn't a leap."

Oh, you are so Maître du Jeu, aren't you?

"Are you a reporter?" I glare the woman down, and her hazel eyes don't so much as even flinch. "We've had our share of those come around here looking to pester us. Is this a new tactic? Inside reporting from the dark and scary depths of Restraint's dungeon?"

"A reporter?" She snorts, and it's not the type where you're trying to cover up a lie. It's derisive yet frustrated. "I figured learning to release my dominant nature is better than self-defense training. It only gives you an outlet if you have an attacker. But here I could do that on someone who wants it."

"No." I shut her down immediately. Maître du Jeu or not. "I'm sorry, but we're not for you. BDSM is a lifestyle choice, not a whim. It would be irresponsible and abusive to use a submissive out of frustration or anger." With a backward glance, I begin to walk away from her, not that I can get far with the crush of bodies in my way.

"No!" She yelps in frustration, and then taps me on the back. "I explained myself wrong."

I slowly turn to her with a bored expression on my face. I gaze at the hand that touched me and smirk. "Now that I've told you what we aren't, you're going to change your tactic in hope of choosing what we are, correct?"

Stunned that I hit the nail on the head, she begins to stammer rapidly. "I wouldn't be angry or frustrated. I have things I want to work out with help. I need to feel in control of something. I... I'm a nice person. I wouldn't be mean."

I'm curious to see how far she will take this, whether she is a snoopy bitch, for real, or a minion sent from the higher-ups trying to keep an eye on Restraint from the inside. I raise my hand in a goodbye gesture and start to walk away again.

She immediately grabs one of my wrists to halt my escape. "Listen, I'm not some freak. I'm a strong person who has needs. Something happened to me and I don't want to be the victim any longer." Her light, feminine voice is strong and sincere yet showing signs of vulnerability.

I'm a sucker. "What's your name?" I decide to be charitable, realizing if I let her in, I can keep an eye on her, too.

"Greta," she says softly as she pulls her shoulders back in pride, and I believe her. "Greta Wilson."

"Okay, Greta. I'm going to tell you a secret. There are only two people who train in the area. One is me and the other is the master of all of us here at Restraint. He currently has a young trainee and will be unavailable for at least the next two years. After that, he has a waiting list a mile long. I haven't trained anyone in a few years, and have a waiting list pressuring me to get back to work, as well as a shit-ton of obligations. I really have to think about this. This is a real commitment that must be taken seriously."

"I understand." Greta's eyes cast down to the floor. It's the first fissure in her confidence that I've seen, and I hate it. I don't enjoy breaking the strong. My job is to elevate them, including the weak.

"Dex!" Aaron's voice calls to me as he weaves through the crowd, with Ezra, Cortez, and Katya behind him, then Marcus comes into focus. Startled, I'm momentarily frozen when my cousin's terrified amber eyes connect with mine. "Our guests have finally arrived."

Shit! I didn't think it was possible for my night to get any worse.

If I had any doubts on whether or not Greta Wilson was Maître du Jeu, they are vanquished when her gaze follows my family with a wealth of knowledge and hatred.

"It seems I have an important meeting to attend." I have no choice but to let this woman into my dungeon and into my life. These are the unspoken rules amongst the organization. It's best not to ask any questions as I fear the answers. She may be friend or foe, I'll never know.

"I have to go, but I will think it through this evening. Meet me here tomorrow night at seven p.m. and I will give you an interview. It's hard to judge someone in this light with the music blaring and the chaos swarming around us. We need to sit down and discuss this. Understood?"

"Yes!" Greta sounds relieved. "Seven o'clock tomorrow night." She turns on her heel without another word. I watch as she weaves around people blocking her path and walks right out the front door.

Who am I kidding? I know I'm going to train her, and not only because I have no choice. Because I can feel her control and self-respect. The hunter in me has found another hunter to mentor. I smile because at least one good thing came out of this evening. This will be interesting.

Chapter Nine

As we wait for the meeting to start, I sit next to my cousin, Marcus–our terrified master. Just a few minutes ago, a man who has only stepped foot into Restraint during initiations, and only from the backdoor, entered from the front and walked through the club to the dungeon and the hallway beyond to our meeting room.

As Dominion's District Attorney, he's a career politician who has to be above reproach. When Ezra came out as not only the owner of Restraint, but a member of its secret BDSM community, Marcus caught some flak for that. When Ezra admitted to marrying Katya while living in a polyamorous relationship with another man–Cortez – Marcus lost many constituents in his run for judge.

In that instance, I didn't blame Ezra for being honest and owning the life he wanted to lead, but it did Marcus no favors. But what I do blame Ezra for doing is bringing the very people who held Marcus captive for an entire year right to our doorstep.

No matter the reason, once you invite someone in, you are no longer in control of what they do while they visit or when or if they will ever leave.

I stare at the man who puts my power to shame. Even if he wasn't family, I would trust Marcus implicitly. We were raised with the same tenets, the same sense of loyalty. Younger than me by a little over a year, I'd do anything in my considerable power to keep him safe and to have him remain ignorant to keep his innocent soul intact.

My cousin and I share similar features, black ringlets that I despise and warm brown eyes. The bastard got my share of the height, but I got the muscle definition, so it's a wash. I smirk at the man and he smirks back.

Marcus sits at the power position at the head of the table because he earned this right during his trials in Las Vegas. When he returned, he created the Dominion branch of Maître du Jeu, not realizing he was simply allowing the organization into the backdoor of his life after I had shut the front door.

Calling Maître du Jeu a BDSM community is like calling a mafia kingpin the owner and operator of a carwash-laundromat combo. The BDSM community is a front for whatever nefarious, illegal acts they perform. I don't want to know so that when the authorities swoop down, I can plead ignorance while they all rot in prison.

We are seated by hierarchy, which is the first clue that this is not your normal run-of-the-mill BDSM club. We're not about meeting bi-weekly, sharing stories and a safe place we call a dungeon. No, we are a world-wide organization that doesn't allow you entrance unless you have something they want or need in return.

Everyone seated around this table is a member of Maître du Jeu the organization, whether they realize it or not. Many are in the know, as I believe Ezra reigns supreme in hell. Which means Aaron knows everything via Ezra, the same as Alex knows from Jamie. Most realize something is amiss, like Katya and myself, but would rather not be involved for sanity's sake. The rest are blissfully ignorant, like Marcus, Regina, Whitt, and Dalton. Cortez? He's too egotistical to care either way.

We're seated by when we were inducted as master, not by our strengths and weaknesses. Marcus is at the head of the table with me to his right and Ezra on his left, Cortez is on my right directly across the table from Syn. By rights she should sit next to Cort, but the pair will come to blows. It's best to keep them separated when it's bad enough with them facing one another. On Cortez's right is young Daniel Whittenhower II– aka Whitt or Pretty Boy. Across from Whitt is Queen, and next to her is Dalton, who won't meet my eyes. Alex, Katya, and Aaron are relegated the farthest from our master, like they're sitting at the little kids' table during Thanksgiving, which puts them smack-dab in enemy territory.

Marcus is sweating bullets, but only I take note because I've had nearly four decades of practice at reading his body language. At the opposite end of the table are our visitors. The Las Vegas retinue of Maître du Jeu, the creators of the BDSM organization they use as a front for their true purposes, whatever they may be.

A petite, young brunette is seated primly, delicate hands folded on the top of the table. She's silent, seemingly nonthreatening, but looks can always be deceiving. We weren't yet introduced, but she finds us all utterly fascinating. Particularly Syn and Whitt, but she can't keep her eyes off Dalton. Two men stand behind the young woman, looking more like security personnel than into the BDSM lifestyle. My guess is the girl is the eyes and ears of Maître du Jeu's master.

We were told to sit quietly, awaiting *The Master*'s right-hand-man. *She* couldn't be with us this evening, and we were to take directives from Devlin Conrick as if she were speaking to us directly. I was shocked to learn a woman was in control of the entire organization.

At the mention of Olivia Fontaine, I thought Marcus would go into convulsions, so terrified Ezra moved to comfort him. But it was Dalton's reaction that confused me even more. Already looking as if he wanted me to kill him, when the tiny brunette showed up with information on Olivia Fontaine's impending arrival and to welcome Devlin Conrick with open arms, Dalton looked as if he was already dead.

Blurting out of nowhere, "Accept my sincerest apologies," I whisper to Cort, the man I betrayed years ago. I hadn't realized the intense pain associated with the act of adultery until I saw Monica with Dalton.

"For what?" Cortez has a confused smile playing along his lips.

Ten years ago, as I was training Ezra as a dominant, I experienced my first and only sex with a man. Looking back, I realize what I thought was from the high of connection, the intense intimacy between a teacher and student, was most likely premeditated by Ezra. At the time, I hadn't known the complications between Ezra and Cort, thinking them not together romantically for years. In a fit of rage, Cort blackened my eye and swore to never touch Ezra again. Going by the fact that they took marriage vows, the threat didn't come to fruition. Even after trying to train Cortez and Syn at the same time, it was never right between us again.

I'd betrayed Cortez's trust, his friendship, and broke his loyalty. I could blame Ezra for his part in it, but as a lifetime of regret has taught me, he didn't make me have sex with him. I did it of my own volition, and I should have to pay the consequences. Just because Cortez forgave Ezra, doesn't mean he should automatically forgive me.

"I now know what it feels like to see the love of your life betray you. I'm sorry for any pain I may have caused." I say with the greatest sincerity I can muster.

Cortez looks around, trying to figure out who betrayed me, but his eyes quickly glide by the actual perpetrator. "All is forgiven, Dex. You know that. I don't blame you– I never did. I blamed myself for a long time, but I've finally let it go." He grasps my shoulder in a manly touch of affection, squeezes three times, and then drops his hand. "We're good, right? You're gonna be good too. Whatever Monica did, it wasn't about you, true? I know she's a difficult woman to handle, but if anyone can, it's you."

"I know that to be the truth, but it doesn't make it any easier," I admit loud enough for Dalton to overhear. In fact, everyone at the table is eavesdropping, including the sweet little girl who shouldn't be here. She can't be a day over twenty.

"It's still raw." Cort is Captain Obvious. "It will be raw for a long time. But eventually things will get better between the two of you, and you'll only feel it during the bad times."

Ezra chuckles sinisterly and Katya coughs, *"Bullshit!"* into the palm of her hand. I'd be pissed, but their theatrics defrosted Marcus enough to crack a genuine smile.

"Piece of advice– rewrite the memory. I asked that when you and Kat finally have your reward, for Ezra to join you. This time I would give him to you freely and it would be my decision."

Stunned, I recoil in disgust. "First of all, it's been three years. I highly doubt Kat and I will ever use our reward, and I refuse to touch Ezra in any way other than with familial affection. Secondly, no way could I stand to watch Monica and that asshole torture themselves again." My stomach rolls at the thought, bile forcing its way up my esophagus.

"Yeah, I get that. I see you as a friend so it's different. I suggest someone close in trust to you. Watch them together and overwrite the memory. It will make it a mutual decision, not a betrayal. It's what Ezra, Kat, and I finally did to erase what I felt was a betrayal when they were first together."

"Thank you. I truly appreciate the advice." I raise my eyebrows at Cortez, because he doesn't have a selfless bone in his body. "Do you really want me to fuck your husband? Your wife?"

Everyone at the table laughs in answer for Cortez, even Dalton coming to life with a bizarre giggle that doesn't sound like his own. The young lady at the end of the table becomes animated, as if she knows us personally and gets the gist of our conversation. Poor Katya's alabaster skin is a brilliant shade of red, but not nearly as badly as Ezra's albino-white flesh turned crimson.

The doors to the meeting room burst open, and in walks Devlin Conrick. Nearly seven feet of suffocating power. I fight the urge to cower in my chair by sitting up straighter.

The Master of the *BDSM Lifestyle Authority's* right-hand man is terrifying. His rolling gait is reminiscent of a stalking panther. He's as black as midnight, bald as a cue ball, gigantically tall yet formed from long, striated muscles coiled and at the ready for attack.

Not one to notice fashion, I can't help but be mesmerized by how amazing the man looks in his black suit and purple shirt. What captivates everyone in his path are the glacial blue eyes of a husky gazing at us from his dark face. It's almost as if he's glaring at us through fresh water, which is the seat of his commanding power.

Never one to give a shit, suddenly I develop a massive case of envy. This man I would allow to take my first born if it pleased him.

Devlin comes to rest next to the young brunette girl, who smiles serenely up into his enraged face. "What do you have to say for yourselves?" Low and deadly, his tone of voice would be perfect as he sang the blues while fucking your wife.

We turn as one to Marcus in confusion. We have no clue what this meeting is about. He gives us calm eyes and shrugs, eyes flicking toward Ezra for a bit of help.

"We have nothing to say for ourselves since we've done no wrong." Marcus finally replies with smug arrogance to hide the terror trying to break free and quiver in his voice. Devlin's presence is fracturing Marc's even demeanor.

Standing, refusing to sit, the man is so tall he has to lean his fisted palms on the meeting room table just to look into our eyes instead of over our heads. "Explain why I keep getting complaints as members leave your area in droves. You're the only club in our organization in New York State, providing a dungeon for its members as well as the option to train. You hold one of the largest clubs in the country. It's a position of power, and you're doing a lousy fucking job."

"You had to have walked through the dungeon on your way in here. You have to sign off on any potential members before we give the okay. You know how booked our membership is almost as well as we do. Clearly we have no issue keeping members when our membership is at an all-time high."

"Marc, don't feed me a line of bullshit, buddy." Devlin slides into a chair next to the young girl, the entire time he shakes his head left and right.

"Don't talk to me like you know me," Marcus warns, seething. "I'm not the same person I was eighteen years ago, locked in a fucking room for nearly a year. Obviously you're not the same person, either. So I suggest you treat me with some goddamned respect!"

Every eye notes how Ezra reaches over to Marc's arm and presses his fingernails in, unable to break skin through his shirt. But the message is clearer than if it had been spoken aloud.

"Fine," Devlin allows, but he's not calm. If anything, he's storing his frustration and anger, which will make it that more powerful when it erupts. "Yes, you do have a lot of members. It's the quality of the membership that disturbs me. We're an exclusive club, allowing riffraff to join our ranks is an embarrassment to the community." Conrick's fist hits the table once per word of his last sentence– boom… boom… boom… echoing throughout the room. He needs a lesson in emotional restraint.

I actually see Devlin's point. If Marcus has been allowing people to join without being vetted by the higher-ups, then we are allowing people into our organization that shouldn't be there. This is not about a BDSM club, and that is what Marcus doesn't and can't understand… I hope he never does.

"Our club provides all the amenities that a master could dream up. The influx of new customers means a greater variety of prey to choose from. I cannot turn people away who wish to apply for membership. If they meet all the requirements– which *you* put into place –then I allow them to join. That is why we have rules. I will not change the rules on a person-to-person basis. This goes against the covenant we live by."

Marcus seems to get cooler, more rational, the more Devlin Conrick loses his shit. It makes me wonder about what type of relationship they used to have. I wouldn't guess enemies by the way they speak to one another so freely. Because if Devlin were my enemy, I would hold my tongue around him.

"The publicity that your family has brought down upon our community is sickening." Devlin's eyes pass over Katya and Cortez very quickly, but light on Ezra. Narrowed gunmetal eyes have Devlin flinching back. "The more members the weaker the pool. You're watering down the system."

"We're going to have to agree to disagree on this issue. If you want a smaller pool, you will have to place a vote on more restrictive rules." Marcus hides behind the rules that Olivia Fontaine put into place.

"Fine. I agree on this concession. However, the publicity is a huge issue amongst your membership. Many members have gone underground because their anonymity has been compromised. They were contacted by the press and publicized in print and film. You may have no issue with your lifestyle being on display, but many do. Parents don't like it when their child's teacher likes to be tied up and fucked," Devlin spits. "People won't vote for a politician when they find out his adoptive son is shacking up with his own cousin."

"Dev, don't!" Marc barks sharply in warning. "My son and his family didn't wish to be in the limelight. They wanted anonymity just like the rest of us. I surely didn't want my dirty laundry aired. I'm an elected official running for Judge. My campaign advisors said it's ridiculous to run because of the recent controversy. So don't tell me about anonymity. It is an unfortunate incident and all we can do is wait it out."

"Unfortunate incident? Didn't wish to be in the limelight? We all know Ezra put this all into place himself, for whatever insane reasons he may have." Devlin glares at Ez, but so do Marc, Cort, and Kat.

"I truly don't believe I did what you're accusing me of," Ezra mutters innocently, genuinely looking confused. His facial expression twists up, like he's thinking too hard. "I probably did. Who knows?"

"Amnesia, Ez? Really? That's more Cortez's speed." Devlin proves he knows a lot more than I ever gave him credit for.

"I suggest that you don't engage me in a hostile way," Ezra mutters politely, but his eyes have shifted, a darkness lurking beneath.

Devlin isn't as afraid as he should be. "You fucking arrogant Zeitlers piss me the hell off. You think because of your clout, political standing, and financial backing that you're without consequences. Billionaires or not, losing your affiliation to the BDSM Lifestyle Authority is nothing compared to the mass of people who have left our organization. I don't give a shit if we lose your money, because at least with you gone we'd gain some privacy. This is beyond ridiculous."

Maybe Devlin Conrick actually is concerned about the BDSM Lifestyle Authority, because kicking out Maître du Jeu's henchmen wouldn't make any sense otherwise. I can sympathize with the organization that wishes to remain secret. If the shit hits the fan, we're all going down with the ship. Ignorant or not, I have done things I'm not proud of doing for the sake of keeping Marcus safe.

I'd bet most of us at this table have been called upon for favors with our families' lives held in the balance as collateral damage.

"Hate me all ya want, Dev." Marcus flashes a mouth filled with big, white teeth. A feral smile of warning. "But I do agree with you. This is ridiculous. You're complaining about a small part of your life– what you do in the dungeon. Try living our lives for five minutes. If we sneeze crosswise, it hits the national newspapers and spreads across social media like wildfire. Did you know I had a steak and au gratin potatoes last night? No? Well, everyone on the planet knew before I took my first bite."

"You can't complain about being inconvenienced due to the fact that your son is insane and put you on the national media's radar. Your political leanings also put you there. So stop playing the martyr, Marc. I thought that was Ezra's tactic."

"Fuck you!" Marc shouts across the table, words landing like physical blows. "It's not our fault Adelaide Whittenhower published a goddamn book about the BDSM Lifestyle Authority!"

Devlin relaxes in the face of Marc's outburst. "Your membership needs more extensive training. I don't just mean the masters sitting around this table. But all those who pass the threshold from the club to the dungeon. Plus those idiots of yours who cull unsuspecting innocents from the dance floor and drag them into the dungeon. That has got to stop. Anyone who got laid and regrets it could go to the press and expose us. Train them, or can them."

"I am currently training a dominant," Marcus admits.

"Oh, and what a dominant he is. He's a seventeen-year-old minor who will tie you up for the next several years. He also happens to be the nephew of the cunt who outed our organization to the media." Devlin mutters snidely, "Excuse me if that pisses off the membership."

"Young Daniel was brought to us by one of our masters. He has ties to all of us sitting at this table. He needed the guidance my strong hand can provide. Discipline. He was in great need of learning how to harness all of his power, so that he could lead his family in the near future. My training Niel has nothing to do with sex and bondage, and everything to do with having restraint."

Devlin levels a glare on Whitt, as if he is solely at fault for Adelaide Whittenhower's actions, as well as Niel being in Marc's care. "I need reassurance that your nephew is nothing like your sister, and that neither of you were involved with this shit-storm. Adelaide Whittenhower published a book detailing private situations that she had no way of knowing without inside information. My money's on you, Pretty Boy," Devlin accuses as he points at Whitt.

My money's on Ezra.

"I would never betray Marcus. He's like a father to me, more so than my own. He's doing wonderful things for my nephew– the kid is like a different person. I will apologize for my sister's actions, even though I shouldn't have to." Whitt drops his gaze.

I feel bad for the kid. Whitt is only twenty-three years old, dealing with the consequences of his older sister going off the deep end. The Whittenhower family was torn apart by Adelaide's actions. I trust Whitt. But Devlin is correct– we have a mole. Adelaide Whittenhower published a short exposé detailing Restraint from the inside. She named all the masters, most of the submissives, and more than half of our membership. Even from the inside of Wintercrest Asylum, the woman is creating havoc.

"Back to the topic at hand." Devlin changing the subject speaks volumes, as he must truly believe Whitt is innocent of any wrongdoing. "Training. You can't train one member every two years when you have ten new members a week. Just because you like to feel self-righteous with your elite Masters of Restraint amongst the populous of untrained dominants and misinformed submissives. The results have been disastrous."

"There are too many to train for Dexter and myself on a one-on-one basis." Marcus finally sees the real problem. Finally. I never wanted to open Restraint's dungeon to the public. I fought long and hard, but Marcus and Ezra always do what they want to do.

"While you were patiently waiting in here, I was watching the idiots in the dungeon. Someone is going to get hurt, and you have no monitors to stop it before it turns into a nightmare."

"No monitors?" Marcus snorts. "That's rich, considering you pulled all of us away from our duties, and then judged us for not being there. The climate in the club has caused us to yank many of the monitors away. We had to switch companies that provided us with security services. The last three were compromised. I believe we have a handle on it now," Marcus says confidently.

"Yeah, a handle on it," Devlin mutters sarcastically. "That's why an anti-riot squad was called in last week, and several times prior. If you don't believe this place is out of control, then you're living deeper in denial than Ezra. Only he has mental illness to fall back on as an excuse."

"We believe all these incidences are tied together. Our compromised security caused us to have a shortage of manpower, and the fights being incited pulled everyone from their posts. I believe someone wants us to remain in the headlines and plastered all over social media." Marcus runs his fingers through his tight curls, displaying his frustration. "During these same times, things have gone awry in the dungeon as well. It can't be a coincidence."

"Do you have proof?" Conrick inquires, probably hoping there is none, as it might point in his direction.

"Nothing concrete, but we're working on it."

"Back to the training. If you had more trained dominants who could monitor, you'd have more help. Clearly this is spiraling out of control. You have to see that." Devlin flashes his eerie, pale stare down the table and challenges Marc.

"I can train and retrain three simultaneously. Will that appease you?" Marcus puts on a helpful face, hoping Devlin will go away.

"Yes. What about him?" Devlin points at me. "Dexter hasn't trained anyone in well over two years. His delicate sensibilities prohibit it." His sneer informs me that he finds monogamy ridiculous if it prohibits you from doing your job.

I haven't trained anyone since Katya gave me Monica, fearing a sexual and emotional attachment would grow during the training process. Now that Monica shit on our monogamy, I tend to agree with Devlin that I've allowed matters of the heart to taint my duties here at Restraint.

"I have a new trainee as of this evening. We're starting tomorrow night." Everyone in the room turns their gaze of disbelief on me. I smirk. It's nice to shock the masses for once.

"I can take on one other if it's necessary. Each trainee needs different levels of individual instruction. I was also thinking of starting a course for dominants and submissives together. A lot of the untrained dominant members train their submissives incorrectly, leading to an abuse of power. I think training to become a true dominant and as well as a proficient submissive is necessary to keep the issues we've been having at bay. I also feel a lot of us sitting around this table need a refresher course in emotional restraint."

"I like you," Devlin says cheerfully. His white teeth flash bright against his dark skin. "You will stay after the meeting. The three of us will sit down and discuss a way to fix this mess."

"Understood, sir. But perhaps another master like Marcus and myself could further their training. We could use a third instructor," I offer.

"Good. Good. Meeting over– everyone get out and do your goddamned jobs for once."

The room empties before Devlin Conrick finishes the sentence. Even the young brunette and her two goons leave. Devlin is a power to be reckoned with, but he allows his emotions to get the better of him. Pounding on the table, shouting, swearing at those around the table, that is a mark of someone who is never fully in control, and I can't trust him if he can't control himself.

Just as I can't trust my own blood when it comes to rational thought pertaining to Ezra. Marcus would allow Ezra to raze our lives to the ground while standing idly by with his hands tied behind his back and a passive but loving smile etched across his face.

Hopefully I can get everyone else behaving, but it's a tough row to hoe when the least in control are the ones who lead us.

"I'm staying in the area for the foreseeable future," Devlin announces that he has no plans to leave Dominion any time soon. "The Fontaines and I are staying in your son's old apartment in The Edge Building."

Marcus jerks backward as if struck. "I see," he utters coldly. "I see very clearly."

"I want daily meetings between the three of us scheduled. I need progress reports on your training sessions. Your current trainees will need to meet with me on our next meeting. While they might have individual needs, I believe it would be easier to drop everyone in a classroom. The dominants hearing what the submissives need to do, and the submissives what the dominants want. This would remove any abuses of power. It would also ensure everyone is getting educated on the rules we are governed by. If they have individual needs, any and all training in that area will be at the expense of your free time."

"May I ask why this is necessary?" Marcus demands of Devlin.

"If you haven't figured it out by now, Restraint and all of its membership are under review. If we don't get this resolved, you're dissolved. You will be banished from the BDSM Lifestyle Authority. This is not a joke, gentlemen. This is for the good of the organization. The majority voted to just cut you off. They assume if you weren't a part of us then the media would follow you and leave us to our coveted privacy. I disagree. I think once they find a story they will never leave. You're lucky I spoke up for the review, because without me, you would've been disbanded."

Marcus leans his forehead on the table and pounds over and over in frustration. This is a testament to his lack of control, as well the type of relationship he had in the past with Devlin. The Marcus I know would never show this level of vulnerability.

"Dev, what's the real reason? It isn't about our membership boom or lack of training. I can believe that privacy is a real issue with some of the membership being in higher government with dirty secrets of their own. But what has been happening is not big enough to go on a witch hunt."

"I'll be honest with you since we're brothers under Master Fontaine. It's the fact that you have a mole leaking information like a sieve. It's obvious that someone has targeted your family and it's spilling over into our organization. We need to find this fucker. Ms. Whittenhower's exposé was the cherry on the shit sundae. Even if you get the membership weeded down and train fifty members to be the best of the best, it won't matter."

Hands balled into fists against the tabletop, Marc is about to lose his shit. "Why are we doing it then?"

"I appeased the masses during our last meeting by saying I was coming here to offer help to organize Restraint and its membership. But the sad reality is that I'm here to investigate who is leaking information to the media. It's not just info on your members. It involves every chapter world-wide. No way could Adelaide Whittenhower pull that off. The riots that are impacting your club are happening elsewhere as well."

In unison, Marcus and I breathe the word, "Shit!"

"Exactly, my friends," Devlin utters sadly. "Exactly."

Chapter Ten

I lean against the inside of my front door, completely exhausted. If we don't figure out who is leaking information, we're all ruined, and not just Restraint and its membership. I have a feeling if we ruin Maître du Jeu's BDSM cover, they will destroy us all.

I sigh heavily as I push away from the door and make my way to the liquor cabinet. I need a fucking drink– several drinks. Maybe a few hits of pot while I'm at it.

This never-ending night has only just begun for me.

Footsteps echo down the hallway and then enter the room as I pour a hearty amount of single malt into a lowball glass. "Tobias, is Monica here?" I ask without turning to look at him, guilt overpowering me because I feel like a hypocrite. I order Tobias to avoid all addictive substances, and here I am doing the opposite.

I pour the scotch back into the decanter, and then lock it back into the cabinet, without a drop passing my lips.

"Yeah, Dex," Toby murmurs softly. "Monica has been reflecting on her actions, as you told her to do." His pale blue eyes light on the liquor cabinet. "Sir, if I may? There is a difference between an addict and a person who drinks once and a while."

"There is no difference if the motivations are the same– to numb, to forget. That will turn a recreational drinker or drug user into an abuser. To drink red wine because it complements your steak is another matter entirely."

"Yes, sir," Toby agrees, and it's not because he feels that's the only response he can give. He recognizes the difference between use and abuse because of all the addicts in his family tree.

"Send for Monica, and then move her belongings to the guest bedroom," I order Tobias, refusing to meet his curiously sympathetic gaze.

"You're doing the right thing, Dexter." Toby ducks out of the parlor, but then he comes right back. "For what it's worth, I know how lost she feels. Monica was calling out for help, not trying to push you away."

"That's why I'm about to do what I'm about to do," I ramble, mind spinning out of control. Tobias quickly goes about doing as I asked, with no further commentary. Minion chirps, chasing after her owner in a zigzag formation down the hallway.

Head bowed, palms holding me upright as I lean against the liquor cabinet, I can't force myself to look as Monica enters the room. I'm unsure I can go through with treating my girlfriend as a piece of property. But in order to retrain how she feels about herself on a visceral level, she must be broken down to her baser form. I inhale deeply and hold it for a very long time before I let it out.

"Master," Monica whispers, the word warping into an agonized whimper.

Unable to stop myself, I watch as Monica debases herself by crawling on her hands and knees toward me. Dark hair damp from the shower, with a conservative nightgown covering most of her skin, she is hiding herself from me the best she can. At the pitiful sight, my throat goes dry, my eyes prickle with unshed tears, and my heart breaks. My fingertips curl into my palms, longing to pick Monica up and comfort her.

"Sit on the sofa, Monica," I order in an emotionless voice. She does as she's told, moving quickly but in jerking motions, as if her muscles ache. I sit in the chair opposite the sofa, since there is no way I could sit next to Monica and not offer her comfort.

Who am I kidding? I need Monica's touch as much as she needs mine. Tonight has left us both raw, and our minds, bodies, and hearts are calling out to soothe one another. But that is not going to happen this night.

"I made a mistake early on in our relationship. I treated you as a girlfriend– my equal. We were equals then, but we are not equals now."

Monica's death knell draws my attention. Low and deep, mournful, she keens into her hands as she sits on the sofa. Her skin holds a sickly pallor, yet at the same time it's bruised, and in some places the flesh is rubbed raw.

After fighting her self-hatred, having the stupid courage to cheat on me with Dalton, but being brave enough to face me in the aftermath instead of running away… Even at her worst, Monica is more beautiful to me than any other female. It's just too bad that she is too blind to see what I see, both inside and out.

"We are not equals, Monica. From this moment forward until you are finally able to take care of yourself, I am your master. You will obey me in all things, or suffer the consequences. Do you understand?"

"Yes, Master." Monica's words flow from between her fingertips, palms hiding her face from my view.

"I treated you as a girlfriend, but in doing so I allowed you to change me. You controlled me by making rules for us to follow as a couple. I complied because I love you. I undermined my own authority to your detriment. I was under the impression you and I were building a life together as equals, and it is my fault that I was too blind to notice the struggle you were having."

Avoiding my gaze, Monica sits on the sofa quietly bawling. As her master, as her boyfriend, as someone who loves and cherishes her, it's my job to make the tears stop. But I won't– Monica needs this reality check. Sometimes tears cleanse the soul, no different than the catharsis a masochist reaches with the help of a sadist.

"Rule change, Monica. We tried it your way. We were to be monogamous. I wasn't to train anyone new, nor was I allowed to practice my God-given gift of sadism with anyone other than Tobias. You, a self-professed submissive, were controlling me, the lone dominant in the house. After I abided by all of your requests, you betrayed me by breaking your own rules.

"Since you think so little of yourself, it's time I treat you as you see yourself. You have officially lost your right to make any decisions. No matter how big or small, you are to come ask me for permission, even if it's to use the bathroom. You're sneaky. Devious. Self-harming. You can't be trusted, Monica. I can't trust you, and you can't trust yourself."

I had never collared anyone before Monica, not even Tobias. The collar Monica previously wore when we first began our relationship was a bejeweled choker– a gift of jewelry, not a commitment. This time I use something more durable, less intimate, with the heavy weight a constant reminder of the situation she placed herself under.

Removing the collar from my jacket pocket, I walk over to Monica and gaze down at the shocked yet mortified expression on her face. Leaning down, my fingers brush her hair from her throat, leaving a perfect canvass for the collar. With deft movements, I buckle the black leather around her neck, fingers skimming along her skin. That small amount of physical contact almost brings me to my knees.

"Did you know, without fail, what you fear the most you create? You feared that you were inadequate, that I couldn't possibly love you, and that I will think less of you when the true Monica is revealed. You think yourself ugly inside and out. Truth?"

Eyes glued to my shoes, with her fingers reverently touching the collar surrounding her neck, Monica breathes, "Truth, Master."

"Your fear made you think so little of yourself that you stooped to a level you thought I wouldn't forgive. You gave me a test that was destined to fail, all so you could validate your self-hatred. In essence you manifested your own fear. Truth?"

"Truth, Master."

"Now I see you as weak and unable to make your own decisions. You pretend to eat the food I make for you, and then you vomit into the toilet when I turn my back. You exercise until exhaustion. You are anorexic and bulimic. I am not judging. I am stating facts. You are sick in the body, mind, and spirit. Truth?"

"Truth, Master," Monica gulps out. "It's a compulsion. I'll look in the mirror and see the skeleton I've made of myself. But then I will see a pretty girl walking down the street, with a smile on her face and expensive clothes on her back, and I know she's never had to work for anything in her life. Blonde, blue-eyed, curvy hips, with a firm behind, and large breasts. She can have anything she wants, go anywhere she wants. No matter how hard I tried, I was never good enough. But she's beautiful with a good disposition, so she made her father happy. Then the pressure builds, and the only way to release it is to vomit. Then the remorse and shame hits me. I have no control over how I was born to be ugly, but I do have control over what I do or don't put into my hideous body."

"You've lost that right as of now," I remind Monica, but not unkindly. "I do understand what you're saying, Monica. But it is unhealthy, even you have to admit that."

"Yes, Master."

"You will learn food is for sustenance, not for vanity. If you don't eat, Minion starves."

"Master?" Monica gasps, aghast at my suggestion.

"I will feed you as Toby does our pet. Unlike you, Minion is smart enough to catch mice and birds when she is hungry, while you will allow your body to cannibalize itself. You gain power from weakening yourself. So if you don't eat, Minion will be denied. Our cat will not be fed until every morsel of food that passes your lips has digested to nourish your system."

Monica's glare burns a hole into the tips of my shoes. I bite back a chuckle, knowing Monica is too softhearted to harm an animal. I wouldn't actually do as I threaten, but she doesn't know that for sure.

"Our family will also be taking a field trip to Transcend to work in the soup kitchen. Food is life, my dear. It is not a struggle for control. You will cook the food from scratch, then you will serve it to the homeless. You will see just how very important the food is that you waste every time you puke it back into the toilet. You wish you were a blonde, blue-eyed girl who is coddled; imagine being a homeless veteran who served our country, and you're starving to death but not by choice. We are going to re-educate you and you will learn, or you will suffer a lifetime of having no freewill."

"Yes, Master." Monica's voice is tight, defiant, but I know she will do as I bid. She'll hate every minute of it, and the thought is making the beast in my pants fill with blood.

My next words give me a straining erection. "Monica, your will is mine. Your thoughts are mine. Your inner dialogue is mine. Your pleasure is mine. Your pain is mine. You are mine in every sense of the word. I own you."

I walk from the room, mind sickened from the pleasure I derived from finally owning someone. Once I've passed the hallway, I take the basement stairs two at a time, running from Monica.

Once I enter my soundproof home dungeon, I scream– I scream as a dying man taking his last breath. I scream until no sound flows from my throat, my vocal cords reverberating from the assault.

I have to treat a woman I love and respect at the level you'd treat a dog. No matter how many times I repeat that it's for Monica's own good, that she needs to learn her self-worth, it seems wrong that the only way to accomplish it is by removing all the worth she has left.

My wish for our future is a partnership with each of us holding our own. I love playing with Monica in the dungeon and making love to her in our bedroom. I have Tobias to fill my sadism needs. I don't want, nor do I need this type of relationship with Monica because she isn't a masochist.

I wanted a true partnership– a meeting of the minds. I now realize that Monica needs me to dominate her to feel whole. I've fucked this up, and I just hope I'm fixing it before too much damage has happened, both to our relationship and to Monica's mental health.

Chapter Eleven

My plan solidifies as I head back into the living room. I feel a little better after screaming out my frustrations, ensuring I won't take them out on my girlfriend. Monica is exactly where I left her, only I find it hard to believe that she is crying even harder.

"Have you bathed?" I keep my voice level. Calm.

"Yes, Master." Monica sniffles as she answers. Both looking and sounding relieved that I haven't abandoned her.

"No more crying, Monica," I order in a rough voice from screaming. "I want details. How clean are you?"

"Yes, Master, no more crying." I watch as Monica shores up her confidence, sitting up straighter and holding her head higher. Good. That is a very good thing indeed. "I've showered and bathed. I've used three douches, trying to remove all traces of Dalton from my body." Her voice sounds as dead as the desolate look in her eyes.

Heart stuttering, I'm taken aback. "Did you allow Dalton to go inside of you?" Because of the spread of disease, the possibility of pregnancy, and the intense intimate connection of spending inside a woman, I've never had the pleasure with Monica. Even in a monogamous relationship and with her on birth control, I've never been bare inside her. I've never been bare inside anyone. If Dalton didn't suit up, he better fucking hide because I'm going to go reaper on his ass.

"No, I made Dalton wear two condoms," she admits readily.

I release the Zeitler patented sigh in relief. Douchebag Dalton lives another day. "Did he use his mouth on you?" I find the act of licking a woman an intimate experience. I only do it with those I'm closest to. The thought of Dalton's mouth on Monica makes me see red.

"No… no foreplay," Monica whispers so softly I barely hear the words. I hold her eyes to give her the strength to continue speaking. "He tied me, beat me, and then fucked me." She sounds so despondent that I want to hold her.

My resolve breaks, and Dexter the boyfriend overpowers Master Dexter. "Why, Monica? My God, why?" I drop into my chair and pull my fingers through my hair roughly. I want to yank it out at the roots out of sheer frustration. "Why did you do that to yourself? Why?"

"I...I...I..." Monica stutters, my passion shutting down the submissive side of her nature that wishes to obey me, leaving her confused and floundering.

I gaze at Monica, both as her boyfriend and master, and try to lend her my will. I try to project that she can trust me no matter what. I won't judge her or punish her. As someone who loves and cherishes her, it's my job to keep her content, keep her safe from harm, even if she is the one harming herself.

My Monica slowly filters into those brown eyes, giving her life as she works through the haze of her mental pain. "You could say... You could say that I've finally hit my rock bottom. I have a problem I'm unable to overcome. You're not the first person who told me I'm too negative about myself. I'm smart enough to recognize how it began and what triggers it. I'll see a pretty girl, and then I won't eat because I'm fearful I'll get fat. But the girl is always bigger than me, so why do I do it? Shouldn't I want to eat more to look like her? Gain weight, buy different clothing, and dye my hair. It doesn't make sense, yet I'm still compelled to do it. I'm self-punishing. Any fool can see that."

Silent, I project calm so Monica will continue without me butting in. I need her to understand that not only am I listening, that I *hear* her. She needs to sense that she can trust me with anything she has to say. While I'm calm on the outside, on the inside I'm an emotional storm brewing. I want to bundle Monica into my arms and take the pain away.

"Dalton was just another form of self-punishment. When I go to sleep at night, I wonder why you love me. Then I wake up thinking those same destructive thoughts. I can see how much you love me, but I can't fathom why." Looking down at her hands, Monica's next words kick me in the teeth. "Dalton looked at me how I see myself. Nothingness. Just a waste of oxygen."

On auto-pilot, I hand Monica a tissue to stem the steady flow of tears gliding down her face. She isn't telling me anything I didn't already know, but she needs to admit it out loud to believe it.

"I knew what Dalton was doing from day one. Three months—for three months he conditioned me. He made me doubt myself, made me doubt you, yet made me feel special. Today I finally gave in. Instant gratification. I liken it to if Toby had a relapse."

"You're probably dead-on with that analogy," I mutter more to myself than to Monica.

"As soon as I was tied up, Dalton started telling me how I was worthless, but it was like he was telling himself instead. In my head, we felt like the same person. Both of us hating each other and ourselves. At the time, I thought my rock bottom was when Dalton said you'd never want me again after he soiled me. He said he timed it for you to find us… you seeing me like that was my rock bottom."

I feel worse than I did before, and I didn't think that was humanly possible. "You're not ruined for me, Monica. You weren't a virgin, and I place no currency in that. I've been with other people, and I personally know the other people you've been with. I've watched you have sex with both Cortez and Katya. It was your low self-esteem that put the monogamy rule into place in our relationship. My being okay with you sharing your body wouldn't have been because I didn't love and want you. It would be because I want you to be happy. Sex and love are not mutually exclusive for our lifestyle, you know that. Dalton played to your weaknesses because I failed you. But I will never fail you again."

"Master," Monica whispers, terrified of insulting me. "Only I'm to blame for my own actions."

"And you're not capable of making good choices, so therefore you are exempt from their consequences. If you make a mistake, it is because I failed at educating you, protecting you, and caring for you. From now on, you have to not only ask before you act, you have to think to yourself, '*how would this reflect upon Dexter? Would he feel like a failure because I hurt myself?*' It's no different than watching out for your children by telling them no when they want to play in traffic. I'm not punishing you, Monica. I'm saving you from yourself. This is your new reality."

I stand and offer Monica my hand, and she immediately takes it. I'm so starve-gutted for the touch of her skin, that when her fingers twine with mine, I almost moan. My knees weaken and perspiration beads along my spine, but I make sure Monica doesn't notice.

I walk Monica to the guestroom, because any man with an ounce of self-respect will not sleep with the woman who just betrayed him. I love Monica and I need her, but she disrespected me. By acting as if nothing happened, by cuddling up to her while we sleep at night, it would mean I disrespect myself as well. Monica has to earn back the right to share my bed, my trust, my respect, and my heart.

Boundaries must be maintained, or else all hell breaks loose.

"This will be your room until you learn self-respect, until you remove the self-hatred, until you are mentally stable to be independent."

"Yes, Master." Monica sounds heartbroken, but the intelligence blazing from her eyes gives me hope. She looks around the utilitarian guest bedroom that Toby's brother and sister shared last time they visited.

"In disrespecting yourself, you disrespected me. You and I are mutually exclusive now, Monica. What you do to yourself, you do to me. You will not be treated as my girlfriend. You are now mindless property. I will not talk about feelings with you, except to discuss your own. I may not even hold a proper conversation with you, as one does not communicate with someone who is unable to contribute to the conversation. As you learn and grow as a human being, you will be given basic human rights back. If you prove you trust me, I will trust you. You have a long road ahead of you, Monica."

I read Monica's face as she comes to terms with her predicament. I wonder if she realizes how her entire life has built to this very moment. Her fear of inadequacy led her to me, forced me to retrain her as a human being.

I cup Monica's fragile neck in my hands, tempted to just squeeze the very life out of her and end this torment. I stare into her brown eyes and I'm overwhelmed. My fingers trail along her jaw until her head is cradled in my hands, stroking her eyelids with my thumbs.

Allowing us both one last kiss, my lips greet hers tenderly, releasing all the love and adoration I hold for her. Parting, her tears linger on my cheeks.

"This is the last time I will say this for a very long time." I almost cry the words. "I love you, Monica," I whisper across her lips. I will not say those words again unless and until she has the courage to say them to me in return.

I turn and walk into the attached bath because I need the privacy. I cry, shoulders rising and falling with my silent sobs. I say goodbye to the life Monica and I have built over the past three years.

I mourn.

Trust is broken. Illness changes us. You adapt, and then move on. I just hope that when this is over, we move forward to a better way of life. It's too scary to contemplate what may happen if I fail Monica. She will be irreparable.

It's time for tough love, but I don't have to be cruel. I'm going to miss telling Monica my feelings, sharing portions of my day with her, looking for support, guidance, and a shoulder to cry on. I will miss the sensation of *I love you* falling from my lips.

This motherfucking hurts.

I hold the belief that everything happens for a reason. God sent Monica to me because I'm the one who can fix her injured soul. I can complete her.

Please don't let me fail her, I pray as I walk back into the bedroom.

"Pull down the sheets, get undressed, and lay down. I need to tend to your skin." I order in an emotionless voice, expecting to be obeyed.

A wince ripples across my skin when I take in the bruises blooming on Monica's body. With Dalton on my mind, I revisit the bathroom to collect supplies. Training: we all need to be retrained. Even Dalton, a Master of Restraint, took advantage of Monica because his emotions were driving him. Every bruise on my woman's body was meant to be dealt to his flesh. As a sadist, I can spot a masochist from a distance, and Dalton is even more tortured than Tobias was when I met him.

When I return from the bathroom with aftercare supplies in my arms, I find Monica lying naked on the bed as requested.

I could count the bones in Monica's emaciated flesh. There are rope burns at her wrists, some wounds had bled and scabbed over. Bruises mar her breasts, thighs, and I even notice one on her cheek.

"How did that happen to your cheek?" I ask calmly, trying not to frighten her.

"Dalton was angry when he didn't get a rise out of you, so he hit me because I wasn't as important to you as he assumed." Her voice breaks, but she holds the cry that is building. Good girl. I told her not to cry because the sound was wrecking me.

I feel sick that Dalton touched my girlfriend, but furious that he harmed my property. A girlfriend should be independent and live their life separate of their boyfriend. They make their own decisions and live by the consequences. But a submissive is property. Their only choice is their master's choice. You can cheat with a girlfriend, because that is her decision, but it's theft to touch someone else's property. My mind has already changed my view on Monica.

Dalton touched who I own.

It sounds sick even inside my own head, but I feel a stronger connection to Monica than I did earlier today. Her life is dependent on mine.

I gently apply salve to Monica's inflamed skin. As I rub lotion into her sore muscles, I have to remind myself that I'm just caring for my property. It's not about emotions. It's just taking care of your investment. But that doesn't change a damned thing. I still love the way her silky skin slides beneath my fingertips and palms. I love the sounds of pleasure spilling from her parted lips. Hell, it has me panting right alongside her. I should be angry as hell, not ready to make love with her– to reconnect.

Fingertips lightly resting on her skin, I part Monica's thighs. I worry that Dalton was too rough, and that small glimpse of his flaccid cock concerned me by his size. Monica is extremely tight because she is a small-framed woman. I've torn her a few times when passions arose.

Monica's bare nether lips are red and tender. I slowly part them with a fingertip– a hiss whistles past my clenched teeth. She's rubbed raw, and I notice a little blood on her.

"What happened?" I try to mask my worry, but a tinge slips passed.

"I didn't want Dalton on me, so I scrubbed myself clean." Monica's shame slams into me so hard and fast, I almost fall off the bed. "I knew you wouldn't touch me if he was still on my skin."

"AH!" Lord, grant me the strength to get through this shit. I rub my face, trying to think how to fix this. Monica's acting like a victim, and she is– she's a victim of her own self-loathing.

I reach over to the nightstand to grab a bottle of lubricant. It's the only thing I can think of to moisturize her area without hurting her. I pour a large amount on my fingers and slowly smooth it over her abused skin. She whimpers from the pain and squirms from the pleasure. I slide one finger inside of her, checking for tears.

Monica is okay on the inside. But what worries me more is how all the damage she sustained is self-inflicted.

"This body is mine." I don't raise my voice in anger. Each word from my mouth flows lower and lower. "Do you understand?"

Monica's, "Yes, Master," is breathy because I'm still manipulating her body with my fingers. "This body is yours."

"Good. This is mine, but you *will* take good care of it for me," I warn in a raspy voice.

I can't help myself, seeing Monica spread out for me in pain, I bend down to suckle her clit between my lips. My tongue curls, questing lower to press inside her body. A moan of ecstasy rumbles past my lips as her flavor explodes on my taste buds.

Monica's body is mine, and I want it to feel pleasure. When she feels pain, I feel pain. When she feels pleasure, I feel pleasure. But I won't use her tonight. It would be cruel to the both of us. We're used to making love or playing. The betrayal is riding too close to the surface to be that intimate with one another.

Right now, the only thing I want in the whole wide world is for Monica to come against my mouth.

With a fingertip, I slide the hood off her clit, exposing the bundle of nerves beneath. Curling my tongue, I press directly on the swollen nub. I swirl in circles as I add a finger inside her. Never wanting to truly control Monica as a master demands of a submissive, I allow her to moan and move fluidly against me.

The caveman inside me howls in victory as Monica climaxes against my mouth and around my finger. We've waited all night to mark her as our own, to show her no one can give her the pleasure that we can.

She moans my name, but I allow it because I love the sound as much as I love the sound of her name falling from my lips. Starting tomorrow, I will have no name other than Master or Master Dexter, until she earns the right to simply call me Dexter.

As Monica's aftershocks wane, I stand up and tuck the covers around her. I stare down at her big brown eyes gazing back up at me filled with trust.

"When you get up in the morning, I will have a list you must follow. It will contain everything from what you're to eat to what chores you have to do after work. While you're at work, you will mind Katya. Both Katya and Tobias will keep an eye on you. You are not to be alone in the bathroom for two hours after eating. If you throw up, hide your food, or refuse to eat, Tobias will not feed Minion, no matter how hard she may yowl. Understood?"

"Yes, Master."

My eyes slip shut, fortifying my will. I've come to a conclusion: just do the total opposite of anything I really want to do. I want to make love to Monica, so I won't. I want to crawl into bed with her and hold her all night, so I walk away and sleep alone.

"This body is mine," I say as I run a hand down the length of Monica's body through the blankets. "Take care of it for me." I rub her temple as I speak. "This mind is mine. Do not think negative thoughts about my body and my mind. Nurture this body and mind as you would my soul."

I walk away before I lose my nerve and crawl into bed next to Monica.

Chapter Twelve

"Hey, Dex!" Katya appears in the doorway of my personal room here at Restraint. "Nice," she drawls as she takes in my new décor. I laugh over how I've turned my sanctuary into a school room.

All of my BDSM equipment is pushed to the corners of the room. A teacher's desk and chair are at the head of the space, with student desks in the center. I did keep a few Victorian settees for my own comfort. Between Devlin demanding it, seeing Marcus lose emotional restraint in the meeting, and Dalton punishing Monica as a way to punish himself, we all need a refresher course in BDSM.

"It's a welcome sight to see a friendly face around here." I straighten up a few of the new additions to my room, smiling to myself. "Everyone seems to be losing their shit. So, what are you up to, Kat?"

"I just finished my five minutes in hell with the Devil." She sits primly at a desk and clasps her hands on the top. I laugh at the innocent expression she flashes me. Katya is innocent no more. However, she was an apt pupil, and she looks adorable seated at a school desk.

"It seems I'm a person of interest." Green eyes roll back flippantly. "We all read Adelaide's torrid tales from Wintercrest Asylum because it was filled with shit about us. But did you know there is an underground publication called *Generation Next*?"

My ass rests on the edge of my desk. "I did not. Do tell."

"Generation Next exposes members from all over the world, especially those who wish to remain anonymous. The Devil is trying to blame this shit on us because it doesn't involve anyone from our area."

Pointing at Kat, "Publisher," I taunt.

"Ha-ha, Dex," Kat mock laughs. "It's some really juicy shit, too. So Devlin's interrogation only made me want to subscribe." An evil smirk plays along her lips. "It's such a guilty pleasure, and I mean *really* guilty."

"How guilty?" My curiosity is piqued, because I have a feeling this is moving past the BDSM Lifestyle Authority and into Maître du Jeu territory. If that is the case, we all need to be terrified.

Generation Next has to be shut down.

"Criminally guilty. There's even a website that you can subscribe to. Some sneaky bastards are making a ton of money off this. I have no clue how they get their information, but it clears us and makes us suspects at the same time. We definitely have a leak here at Restraint, but how the fuck would they know what's happening on the other side of the country?"

"If that's the case, we won't lose our chapter then. The entire organization would have to fold up since it involves all of us." This intrigues the shit out of me because I want to find whoever is stealing our information and whip them until they have atoned for their sins.

"Yup, I have no clue who's doing it, but I want to get my hands on that publication." Her eyes twinkle with mischief. I can see the wheels churning in her head because she runs Edge Publishing for Ezra.

"I'm guessing you don't mean to read it." Ironic laughter bubbles up my throat. "They would fry us if you bought the rights to it."

"Once a publisher. Always a publisher." Katya's snickers mischievously. "I didn't say I was going to do it. But a girl can dream, ya know?" she sighs wistfully, picking that trait up from a Zeitler. "So..." she draws out while smiling at me. "I hear you're having some trouble with our girl. This morning, Mr. Blue Eyes handed me a list Monica was to obey, but he wouldn't crack when I tried to get him to explain. What's up?"

"Tobias is a good boy, isn't he?" The warmth in my voice shifts as I give Katya a replay of the events over the past few days. "Right now my girlfriend is my property, and I hate it."

"I've waited for this to happen. I'm not giving you an '*I told ya so*', because I understood that you loved Monica as more than a toy. Ya know, the first time I met Monica, I could see inside her? I didn't even know what I was at the time. I just saw how she felt about herself. The stronger I honed my dominance, the more obvious it became."

"I recognized it, too. But I was stupid and thought love would repair it. I was too blind to see how it was getting worse until it was too late. I will retrain Monica to see herself clearly, I just can't guarantee our relationship will survive."

Kat leans forward to squeeze my hand. "It will. I know it will," she says with conviction. "I have confidence in you, Dexter, or I wouldn't have sent Monica to you to begin with."

"I've failed so far…" I flash Katya a loaded look. "But I don't enjoy failure, so it will not happen again."

Snorting, Katya laughs at me. "Monica needed someone strong enough to dominate her. But not for the reason everyone thinks. She said all the doms always thought she was a domme, or too strong to handle, that she wasn't truly a submissive. They were right and wrong. Monica has no urge to dominate anyone, and she has to be forced to submit."

"So I've learned over the past three years," I mutter dryly.

I earn a disrespectful eye roll. "What Monica truly needs is a master strong enough to dominate the one inside her own mind." She taps her temple. "Are you strong enough, Dex? Can you break her internal walls and defenses? Can you break the shield she carries always, whether it's her hairstyle, clothing choice, or her bitchiness? None of that is the real Monica. Can you help Monica find the real her, leaving her feeling fulfilled, wanted, cared for and taken care of? I want the best friend I see hiding deep inside."

I turn from Katya and wipe the stray tear that betrays the waves of emotions wracking me. "God, I hope so, Katya," I whisper roughly avoiding her gaze.

"I know you will, Dexter, because you love her." Her confident voice warps to a teasing tone. "Just wait. Dalton banging your girlfriend in your private room will probably be in the next issue of Generation Next."

"Ha-ha-ha," I mock laugh, patting my knee like it's hilarious. "You can be such a sarcastic bitch. You know that, right?"

"You love it," she says smugly with an evil grin. Pinching her fingertips together, "Admit it, you love me, even just a teensy bit." Her face sobers, changing to seriousness. "You can come to me to talk. We're friends first, Dex. I mean it. If you need a hug– take one."

I reach out and take one.

Katya holds me tightly, patting my back in soothing circles, as I cry cathartically.

Chapter Thirteen

Greta Wilson, the mocha-skinned, punctual, and strangely dressed trainee– probable member of Maître du Jeu –arrives as I'm putting the finishing touches on my private room.

Written in black ink on the dry-erase board: *Master Dexter says to open your ears and shut your mouth.*

I gesture politely to the student desk Katya vacated a half hour ago. "Please, have a seat."

Greta takes to the desk like she's used to it. Her khakis and floral blouse fit right at home just as long as you don't notice the kink equipment that borders the room and my red, purple, and black velvet furniture in the back.

I pull my chair from behind my desk, placing it in front of Greta. "Thanks for being punctual. It means you take this seriously, and I appreciate it." Maître du Jeu warning bells are pinging in my brain, along with Generation Next, and Devlin Conrick informing us that the BDSM Lifestyle Authority has a mole Restraint is most likely harboring.

"So, tell me a bit about yourself, Greta." The woman is gazing at me with open, honest hazel eyes. "What do you do for a living?"

"I'm an elementary school teacher. I teach third and fourth grade math." Greta answers as if it shouldn't matter what she does for a job, a defensive air in her tone.

I can't help it, I bust out laughing, causing her to instantly get pissed at me. Her round face has a scary scowl that would definitely get the kids in line, but never a dominant male.

"Sorry… sorry. It's a school teacher sitting at a student desk that is funny. I'm an IRS agent, so I can't judge. We all can't have cool jobs. But, hey, we both like math, so we actually have something in common." I try to smooth over Greta's visible annoyance.

I'm surprised we have anything in common. I'm wearing leather pants and a mesh shirt, and she looks exactly like an elementary school teacher with her mom clothing, her hair pulled up in a bun, and her no-nonsense demeanor. I will say, I wouldn't mess with Greta if she were my teacher. Looks aside, she's a bear.

"Obviously, you know my name is Dexter Hayes, but you will call me either Master Dexter or sir. There has to be a bit more to your life than being a teacher. Enlighten me, as it's of utmost importance to ensure the privacy of the members of this establishment."

"Master Dexter," she tests the feel of the words on her tongue. She nods when she finds it agreeable. "I have no family. I live alone. I teach school. I want to be trained." Greta is extremely succinct, which is a trait of a dominant person. But it's also the only way not to catch yourself in a lie when you're feeding someone a line of bullshit.

"Please, elaborate on that. Pretend this is an interview, Greta. Because it most certainly is. I need to feel you out, and you giving me one-liners is not helping your case any."

"Fine." She pats her hair to make sure that nary a hair is out of place. "I was trying to avoid this, but I guess there is no way around it."

Interest piqued. "Way around what?"

"I was attacked in my home about three years ago," is said in an emotionless voice.

I've been around rape survivors, and Greta is not one of them. It's a sob story to buy my sympathy. "And that is my problem, why?" I sound like a sonofabitch, but my bullshit meter is overflowing.

Mocha skin blushing in fury instead of paling in remembrance, Greta turns defensive. "Therapy doesn't work, and self-defense training doesn't help. I need to feel in control again. I didn't go to the police because the person who hurt me was sent to jail the next day. I read the papers. I know his other victims found solace here. I want to see if I can as well."

I'm instantly transported to the past, mind blanking to anything else. I've only met Ray Hunter once– handcuffed and being led to a squad car at Shadow Haven during Aaron and Kayla's wedding reception. But Ray has affected me for much longer than that.

I was with the family when Ezra was taken. Diane froze in pain. Marcus lost his shit. A teenage Cortez was completely inconsolable, as he ran around Shadow Haven, unlocking windows and doors, going as far as to break them. He wasn't a tiger trapped in a cage.

He was trying to open the birdcage to allow the bird to come back home after taking flight.

I was with Marcus when Cortez and Aaron were taken, and had to restrain my cousin against self-harm. Days later, without any sleep or sustenance, I drove Marcus to Pennsylvania to pick the boys up at the hospital where they were taken after the abduction.

As a family, we suffered with the aftermath. I trained Ezra as a way to deal with his pain, using BDSM as a positive outlet. The invisible scars infect everyone in my family, everything they do, and how they perceive the world.

Having our private pain exploited yet again, creates a fresh wound.

Raymond Hunter is not unfamiliar to me. Rape? He's done so many times before. Rape Greta? I highly doubt that, because that is not his signature. Raymond Hunter only allows his victims to live if they are of his blood or will propagate his family tree. If Ray had raped Greta, she would have never lived to tell the tale.

But the woman knows too much– too much to be a reporter – but enough to either be a contributor to Generation Next or a member of Maître du Jeu. After a lifetime of dealing with the nameless, faceless Boogieman, I play along, refusing to make a stink that would harm my family any more than it's already been harmed.

"Greta?" I say her name as a question, because now I even doubt that. Faceless. Nameless. Greta can't harm us if I keep an eye on her, giving me a face and a name. "I apologize for zoning out. I gather you are speaking of Raymond Hunter, and as you've probably uncovered, he has torn my family apart."

Completely emotionless, Greta rattles off the account of her assault. "Ray Hunter raped me. He entered my home while I was sleeping, tied me to my bed, and then brutally raped me. When I recovered enough to go to the police, he had already turned himself in for assaulting the two women at that wedding. There was no need for me to lose any more dignity by telling my story. Now I need to feel safe and in control of my life."

"I'm sorry, but I can't help but notice how unaffected you sounded as you revealed something so private." I tread carefully. "Powerlessness is an emotion all assault victims experience, so I can understand wanting to gain your power back. But it concerns me how you have such emotional restraint without the aid of therapy or a positive outlet. It comes across as either rehearsed or apathetic. I fear allowing you anywhere near a submissive, because you'll release all that pent-up anger on their person."

"Believe me or not," Greta snaps, hazel eyes sparking fury. "Do you need intimate details about Ray? He's as pale as a ghost, almost albino in appearance but has light brown hair. His gunmetal eyes are no longer sane. He's tall, exactly six foot, and thin yet strong. He's in his early fifties. He comes off as very charming, but turns on you quickly. None of that was in the papers."

"No, it wasn't. But it tells me nothing that I didn't already know," I mutter more to myself than to Greta. "Why did you decide to seek out Restraint and BDSM training as a way to cope with your alleged rape?"

"Alleged?" Greta scoffs, but the sound is hollow. I know deep down that she does know Ray Hunter but that he's never laid a hand on her. Ray is sick, calculating, but he does have total self-control. Ray raped whores, and then murdered them when he was finished. Diane and Katya were different because he wanted to expand his genepool– a genepool which is complete with both male and female descendants.

One look at Greta's plump, brown body, and I know she's been coddled to within an inch of her life. Her entitled attitude is proof positive of that. She's as far from a whore as I am.

"As you suspected, I am not a moron. I was able to piece together who Ray Hunter was from the papers. I read about Ezra Zeitler and his spouses. How he is the owner of this establishment. After what happened to me, I searched for anything dealing with this. I read Adelaide Whittenhower's Mistress & Master of Restraint, and it led me to you."

Looking Greta dead in the eyes, I say something that I will regret later. "Fine, we'll just play pretend." Frustrated, unsure how to proceed, my fingers comb through my curls, snagging on snarls. "I have no choice but to train you. Beware, I will test your limits. But know I'm not one to act out of haste or spite. So even if I believe you're feeding me a line of bullshit that most people would buy in fear of looking like an asshole, I will treat you with respect."

Relaxing her rounded shoulders, Greta doesn't even argue. "That is all I can ask. Just give me a chance to train. That is all I want."

"And that's all you'll get," I warn. "But if at any time it comes to my attention that you're here for any other purpose, I will drag your ass from my club and not give you a backward glance. Understood?"

"Understood, Master Dexter," Greta says respectfully.

A loud knock on the door signals the rest of our group has arrived.

"Greta, your training begins now."

Chapter Fourteen

I open the door for my merry band of deviants, and laugh at their vast array of expressions. They look at each other, trying to figure out why I called them together. I step aside and stand at the head of my room.

Our classroom has a Victorian theme– a red and purple velvet-draped bordello with torture devices bordering the room, with many desks situated in tidy rows in the center of the space.

"Please, take a seat at the desk that holds your nameplate." I smirk as they scurry around the room, checking out nameplates, and complaining about who they are seated near like they are in junior high.

Judging by my outward appearance, I'm bored. But inside I'm laughing hysterically at how cute they all are. At first I was put off about this situation even though I love to train a good student. Now I'm excited and giddy at the prospect of having a roomful of students. I may look stern right now, but I'm grinning like an idiot on the inside.

I turn around and write *SIR* on the dry-erase board I had installed. I glance back at my students sitting so studiously in their assigned seating. I had removed all the comfort items from my room, moved all the toys to the outside walls, and added desks. I pushed one of my settees to the center of the rear for when the principal comes to take my evaluation. I can't help the smile that breaks across my face as I envision Devlin's six-foot-seven-inch frame on the delicate sofa.

"I'm sure you're all wondering why Restraint's dungeon is closed for the night and why you were summoned here. I will explain, and then impart some necessary information."

A mix of '*sir*', '*Master*', '*Master Dexter*', and '*Yo, Dex!*' flows throughout the room.

"I know you've all been to see the man you've dubbed as the Devil. Devlin Conrick is here for reasons I cannot divulge. Please respect Devlin to his face, and do so behind his back. He's a decent man. Devlin and Marcus trained together under Master Fontaine."

"Isn't Olivia Fontaine a woman?" Kris blurts out. "A very hot woman, but a woman just the same."

"I'm Master Syn, remember?" Syn ribs her own friend. "It's an honorific that isn't gender specific."

"Any asshole who dares to call me Mistress Queen or Master Queen will be ignored. I'm no one's mistress in any sense of the word, nor am I a woman who has to use a male's honorific to stroke my ego."

"Hey!" Syn snarls. "For a feminist, you talk in circles."

"I rather like Mistress Kat." Katya offers everyone a saucy smirk.

"You would," Syn snarls.

"Don't slut shame!" Kris and Fate shout at the same time, when anyone else in their right mind would keep quiet when it comes to the Petite Sadist.

"Mistress doesn't mean what you think it means," Katya mutters. "And I'm not a slut."

"You like sex." Kris comes to Kat's defense before Syn can tear into her. "No harm in that."

"Yes, there is harm in that," Regina adds in. "Kris, your vagina is not a clown car."

"I can attest to the fact that Kristal's vagina is not a clown car." Alex forces the words out through his laughter. "Oh, Queen of my girlfriend—" he shakes his head left and right, black hair swinging around his jawline. "—or whatever your existential identity crisis wishes me to call you today... but you'll always be Reggie from the block to me, sweetheart."

Regina tries to stop Alex. "Shut—"

"Kris is my girlfriend, and I'd appreciate if you'd give her some respect. At least in public. Fucking doesn't alter whether or not you're a good human being. You girls need to remember how your pussies are not exactly uncharted territories— charted by the same explorers. Explorers who are praised for fucking every person in this club."

"Yes!" Kat shouts, pointing at Alex. "That is why you're my bestest buddy!"

Reaching over to high-five Kat, "I'm feeling ya, girl," Alex the dope dealer teases his favorite client.

"Can we just not go there?" Daniel Whittenhower III begs in a soothing voice. Niel's freckled cheeks are crimson, making his strawberry blond haystack look even redder. "I'm seventeen, so sex isn't that foreign to me, but hearing about your sex lives is making me want to upchuck my dinner."

"Why is there a child in the room?" Suddenly Dalton gains a conscience. "In *this* room, with *these* people. There should be laws against this."

"I'm one of you," Niel mutters, easily offended. The kid is built like a tank. Short and stocky, formed to protect. But he has the mind of his mother and the demeanor and voice of his father. The kid is probably the smartest and most cunning yet easily hurt person in this room.

Walking down a few desks, I pat the kid on the shoulder, feeling comforted just by being in his presence. "You are. Marcus and Devlin both wanted you to be here. But I will make sure sex is not spoken of in this room, for obvious reasons."

Relieved, Niel's thick shoulder relaxes under my touch. "Thank you, Dexter."

"Anytime." I stalk back to the front of the room. "BDSM is not about getting your rocks off in a kinky way. That is for those who play around in their bedroom because they're bored. BDSM is a discipline. Clearly I'm doing the right thing by refreshing your very short attention spans as to what our lifestyle truly means."

"You're going to trap us in here all the time, aren't you?" Kris looks around the room, eyes downcast and angry. "We're all here except for The Master of the Universe, his precious boys, and Aaron and his two curvy pieces of ass. That's not fair because it's probably their fault in the first fucking place!"

"I'm here, aren't I?" Kat points at her chest. "Don't be pissed at Dexter. You know damn well Ezra had a hand in who didn't have to be here."

"I'd call that favoritism, and a reason to chew your husband's ass out when you get home," Monica teases her best friend, and I'm relieved to see life in her gaze. She grips Toby's hand. "The teacher's pet and I will do what we're told."

"Suck up!" Kat flashes Monica a huge grin.

"Jeez, I seat you at a desk and you turn into children. Settle down, boys and girls." I roll my eyes as I rest my ass on the edge of my desk. "We have to be here– get over it." I press my fingertips together. "Truth be told, we are this close to being removed from the BDSM Lifestyle Authority and losing our membership. We'd be relegated to playing in our basements again, and having the authorities shut our club down for not having the proper permits that will be wrenched away from us."

Pausing, I wait until the rumble of panic waves through the room.

"Our resolution was to offer more training. We need another strong dominant who can be certified to train fellow dominants, and a submissive strong enough to train fellow submissives. Plus, we need to refresh everyone's memories, so when we see something not right, we will instantly put a stop to it. BDSM offers too many loopholes for abuse."

"When I see bad shit happening on the main floor, I never know if I should collar someone," Kris says in a panic. "I'm not a dominant, but I know what's right and wrong from the submissive side of things. We need this. Our dungeon monitors let too many things slip between the cracks."

"Agreed." My eyes flick from Kristal to roam around the room. "Firstly, when we're in this room, or on field trips–" A few snickers erupt. "You all will call me Master Dexter or sir. I may be your friend outside of this room, but inside it I am your trainer. Understood?"

A collective 'SIR' echoes throughout the room.

"This is Tobias Kline," I say of the young man that has been in my service for almost four years. "Tobias, I want to reward you for all of your hard work and dedication. I know I can trust you infallibly. Toby, you are our first submissive trainer. It will give you the proper respect you are due. I understand that by rights, a submissive is always considered beneath a dominant, but I want you to work beside our newest dominant trainer– as equals."

Tobias doesn't speak. He just gazes at me in utter shock with unshed tears glistening in his eyes. I can't help myself– I pull the young man into an embrace and squeeze him tightly. With a whisper, I let Toby know how much he means to me. "I'm so proud of you. I don't know what I'd do without you."

Pulling away, I explain my reasoning. "We have an influx of new members from all the media attention. They are without experience, and they're training their subs the wrong way. Ignorance begets abuse. It's a checks and balance system. A dominant can't pull the wool over a properly trained submissive's eyes."

"Last week, I had to toss some douchebag out of the dungeon and have Alex hold him until the police showed," Kat informs us all. "He was a member for less than a week, and yanking girls from the main floor. He got off on girls who thought reading about non-consent was hot. But reading and reality are not the same thing. They were saying no, using their safewords, and he was ignoring it because of a five second conversation about their reading tastes. The ultimate in victim shaming."

"Begging until I was blue in the face," Regina jumps into the conversation. "I told Ez how I want it to be against the rules for anyone to enter the dungeon who isn't a member. If they cross the threshold, they need to sign a waiver. Not have some idiot who paid a fee have free reign, culling prey from the herd."

"I agree. Which brings us to my next announcement. Whitt?" I gesture to Pretty Boy Whittenhower.

After receiving a mouthed, *"Dude, what'd you do?"* from his nephew, the young man slowly ambles up to me, testing my patience. Whitt smirks at me, letting me know he's just playing around with me.

Whitt is very childlike, almost innocent. At twenty-three, he has never lost his playfulness, same as his father never has. He isn't being malicious, just mischievous. I need someone like him in the class to lighten the mood. He's also strong enough to become our ultimate master someday, but his jovial spirit and loyalty will never go against Marcus.

"This is Master Daniel Whittenhower II." I extend my arm like a game show host to present the tall, lanky man. He's the boy next door in every sense of the word: blond-haired, blue-eyed, European ancestry, and so sweet he gives you a toothache.

"Whitt, you're our newest trainer to lighten Marcus and my loads. You and Tobias will be working in conjunction with one another. I chose you because you're laid back, patient, and very easy to get along with." I turn to face everyone. "Class, don't let this pretty mug and sunshine smile fool ya. Master Daniel is a strong taskmaster. If you make him proud, he will be your best friend. If you piss him off, he will be your very worst nightmare."

"Thank you for the honor and the privilege, sir." Whitt shakes my hand with great enthusiasm, genuinely surprised. "I will do anything to undo the damage that my sister caused. I can't apologize enough."

"Ah, Whitt." I quickly glance to Niel to draw him into the conversation. "No one blames you or your family for Adelaide's actions. She dragged you through the mud with the rest of us. You deserve this, and I'm pleased to work beside you again."

As Whitt walks back to his seat, I decide it's time to introduce the woman getting sideways glances from the class. "Greta Wilson, please join me." Her expression is serious as she approaches me, with her confidence level almost bordering on arrogance.

"Class, this is Greta. She'll be training with us from now on. Unlike the rest of you who had to be referred to me by a previous member, go through an extensive vetting process, and pay your dues– in more ways than one –Greta approached me last night, demanding to be allowed in our training program."

"Demanding seems a bit strong, Master Dexter." The woman has the gall to chastise me for my choice of words. "I felt it–"

"Tonight during our interview, Greta informed me how she was Raymond Hunter's last victim–"

"Hey!" Greta cuts me off, sputtering with fury. "That's private!"

"Bullshit!" is coughed into a curled fist. *"What is she playing at?"* *"Seriously?"* I cut off the rest of the unsavory commentary from the peanut gallery of people who actually know Ray.

"I suggest you treat Greta with the same level of respect you give one another." In other words, none. "Allow her to train, and step forward if you see her doing something wrong." *Not in BDSM terms* goes without saying.

"It's nice to meet you, Greta." Alex of all people is the first to shake her hand, and I try to figure out if they know one another already. With Jamie being someone important in Maître du Jeu, Alex is in the know. As a Master of Restraint, even I can't decipher their body language as they greet one another.

"Nice to meet you, Greta!" Kris chirps from her seat. "You have such lovely skin. You're not bi by chance, are you? Lesbian?"

"Kris!" Fate slaps at her roommate's arm. "Leave the lady alone. Not everyone is a conquest."

Syn's hooded eyes take in the newcomer, inspecting every inch. "Welcome," she says when she finds Greta satisfactory.

"Thank you," Greta says politely as she retakes her seat, but I can feel animosity wafting toward me from the woman. She's definitely not stupid, catching on that I was informing the class how I felt coerced into allowing her to join us.

"Monica?" I call, and she rushes forward with an expression of confusion. I haven't seen her in almost twenty-four hours. I did check on her constantly, she just didn't know it. She was a good girl and did everything on her list with Toby and Kat's supervision.

Minion is well-fed.

I've missed Monica so much I ache– the little things like calling her up and telling her about my day, and sharing details I'd never share with anyone else. I miss my partner in crime.

I smile at Monica and take her hand, wrapping my fingers around hers and marveling for the billionth time how our hands are exactly the same size. I feel the tension leave her body as our hands connect. Good, I must be her lifeline.

"This is Monica James. She is mine in all ways," I announce with pride, ignoring Dalton flinching a few seats away. Shame and guilt– a masochist's currency. I kiss Monica on the forehead because I just can't help myself. She leans into my touch, but doesn't try to touch me back, knowing I haven't granted permission.

"Monica, you will be used to train other submissives by example. I don't feel comfortable touching anyone else. While Tobias may join Whitt or me while training both dominants and submissives, you will only join me. I can't trust you to heel only at my command. Understood?"

"Yes, sir," Monica replies immediately, no inflection of hurt in her tone. "Tobias knows your word is law, and no one else has any influence over him. But I have yet to learn that. When I do, I will become more useful than I currently am."

I feel hopeful by the fire burning in the depths of Monica's eyes. Maybe this plan will actually work. She will learn there is no value in demeaning herself. Just as Tobias has learned to trust his gut-instinct, how *his* word is law if he doesn't feel comfortable with me controlling aspects of his life. I love taking care of a submissive, but I want them to use their freewill. I refuse to be a slave's master.

Every living being on this planet deserves respect. The only time anyone should have total control over another being is if it's for their best interests. Parents allow their children freedoms to learn and grow, and it's no different than a master to their submissive. There is no value in a person who can't think for themselves. They don't strengthen the team; they weaken it.

A person who takes a slave is a person with no sense of self, leeching off another human being to fill the void inside of them.

"Please retake your seat, Monica," I order softly. "We're going to play a little game– the opposite game. After hearing your earlier crosstalk, we need to see how the other half lives, use our neglected empathy. You guys need to loosen up and lose yourselves a little bit.

Right now a few of you are hiding behind your images while judging others for theirs."

"Can we point fingers?" blurts from Kat. Her verbal filter dissolves under the weight of how no one has ever truly accepted her, even after four years. "Shit! Sorry, Master Dexter."

"Forgiven." I wink in Kat's direction. "Daniels two and three, I need you to dress as if you don't have a roman numeral after your name. Maybe add some leather or style your hair differently. You need to add some bad boy to your corporate image." Whitt flashes a naughty smirk, while Niel looks terrified. "You're both still kids; act like it. Live a little."

Niel's green eyes flick around the room, and then down at his navy and gray pinstripe three-piece suit. "Um... what about my Hillbrook uniform?"

"I've got your back." Whitt thumps the poor kid upside the head while snickering, acting and sounding just like his father used to.

"Tobias, I want you to pick something out for yourself. Go to the store and buy something that isn't in your closet. Make it something that has always caught your eye, or the opposite of what you've always worn. Don't change the hair, though. It took me forever to get that hair looking so healthy and pretty. It would be a shame to muss up your golden waves."

"Yes, sir." Blushing, Toby mutters while looking at his hands folded on the top of his desk.

"Monica, you're getting a makeover. No more hiding behind pencil skirts and tightly bound hair. You don't think you're pretty, so you hide yourself. Katya is taking you shopping after work tomorrow– mind her. I want you to look as sexy and beautiful as I think you already are."

"Oh, I'll get our girl sexy," Kat promises in a salacious voice. "I know exactly how our girl looks when she loses control." Monica, Kat, and I all blush simultaneously.

"That's a memory I'll cherish until the day that I die." Uncomfortable laughter fills the room with a few derogatory remarks being sputtered. I clear my throat roughly. "Greta, you're going shopping with all the girls, too. No more hiding your sexuality behind khaki and floral prints. I understand you work at an elementary school; both Monica and Katya are professional women as well. Kat will know what to pick that accentuates you as a woman but is still classy without being frumpy."

"Yes, sir," Greta replies. The anticipatory gleam in her hazel eyes over being alone with all the women concerns me some.

"Now me– you'll have to see when you come into class tomorrow." I chuckle to myself. "Everyone must wear their new clothing all day, every day until I say otherwise. Got it?"

"Yes, sir," they say in unison but they don't sound happy about it.

"We have to meet for class every night at eight p.m. sharply. I'm sorry for the inconvenience this causes, but we have a lot of ground to cover in a short amount of time. I want to thank everyone for joining me tonight, and for behaving and obeying. You're dismissed." I turn to the interloper in our midst. "Sorry, Greta, but you have a date with the Devil. His office is two doors down– Devlin Conrick is on the plaque on the door. Just knock and go in."

"Will do, sir. Thank you." Greta's thin lips actually break into a vivid smile, like she's excited to meet Devlin. The smile is gone in an instant, but she was unable to control her reaction to the news.

I don't think I can trust anyone at this point. Either I'm being paranoid, or I should be feeling terrified.

"Greta," I call out before she flees my room. "Katya will find you when you're through and set up a time for shopping tomorrow afternoon."

"I'll walk you." Syn takes Greta's elbow like they're more than acquainted. "We'll tell Katya what time fits into our schedules."

I raise an eyebrow but don't comment. "If you live with me, prepare yourselves. We're going to have some fun of our own when we get home. It's been a stressful few days and we all need a release."

Tobias and Monica share a loaded look– part shock, part excitement. I chuckle at the pair, relieved to reward them in a way that rewards myself. Let's just hope Cortez's advice from yesterday was good.

Chapter Fifteen

I sit in my basement dungeon waiting for my masochist and my submissive to shower and prepare themselves for me. Sometimes I feel as if I have multiple personalities like Ezra. My tiny dungeon at Restraint has one style and this one another.

My home is a replica of my childhood home, so I added it to my room at Restraint as comfort. But I never wanted that to spill into my dungeon here at home. Instead, I use the industrial feel of Restraint's main dungeon with the soft comforts I always felt it lacked.

The soundproof walls and ceiling are dark gray. The black flooring is made of rubber like in a gymnasium. The rubber offers its own form of soundproofing. It's perfect for sensory deprivation– they can't hear you coming for them. It's also fun as hell to fuck on– the rougher the better.

Only two pieces of furniture are in the space. A round bed raised on a platform and a chaise in the corner to use as a voyeuristic vantage point. Both are wrapped in thick plastic for easy clean up.

The rest of the basement holds some of my favorite tools of the trade. Two St. Andrew's crosses are on display at center stage in the basement– Toby's favorite. A spanking bench and a swing are off to the side for Monica's pleasure. My tools are proudly displayed on one wall– the shelving and hooks create neat, tidy rows.

I guzzle a bottle of water as I wait. I never drink alcohol before I play. I have to be in total control of all my faculties. My favorite activities ride the edge of abuse. One slip, or too much pressure, and I could bring long-lasting harm or even death to my submissives. Tonight, this is especially important because it's the first time I will take two subs at the same time.

I've dreamed of the scenario for years on end. After cutting the ties binding me to Monica's rules made out of jealousy, insecurity, and self-loathing, I'm free to do as I wish. Taking everyone's best interests at heart, I'm rewarding all three of us tonight.

Monica pads silently across the floor and kneels at my feet. I pet her unbound, damp hair and press her face against my thigh. I stroke her for my own satisfaction. I allow my hand to roam anywhere it wants. She's nude for my enjoyment and I caress her small breasts, reveling at how her nipples pebble in reaction to my touch. I murmur approvingly when she presses her breast farther into my hand.

Monica was never one to initiate affection, being too insecure but also not trusting me. She was deaf to my words of adoration, too blind to recognize my signs of arousal, and too distrustful to believe either.

I've asked Monica in the past why she wouldn't touch me unless I asked. *"How am I to know you want me to touch you?"* I would respond with, *"It's not whether I want your touch or not, it's about you touching me because you wish to."*

It's never made sense to me why women think the way they do, especially the self-conscious ones. If I didn't want Monica, why would I be with her? Shouldn't that be invitation enough? But it wasn't. I'd have to beg her to reciprocate, and even then she still didn't quite believe that I wanted her hands on me.

Men don't ask. A real man doesn't force or take, but they know how to read their woman so they can touch without begging for affection. If I wanted to hold Monica's hand, I did. If she wanted to hold mine, she wouldn't.

I wanted an equal partner, not someone who wouldn't think for themselves in fear I wouldn't agree. As an alpha male, I do want to take care of my family. Play to their strengths, especially when it comes to my weaknesses. But I need to know they will be there for me when I am down. I shouldn't have to beg for simple affection.

It guts me to see someone as strong-willed as Monica reduced to an indecisive, self-loathing creature. With my strength, my intelligence, my power and influence, it is my job to raise my people higher, not shove them down so I can bloat my ego.

There may be a time when I need them to shoulder my burdens. But if I didn't teach them anything, they will be siphoning whatever strength I do have left, destroying us all.

Drawing me back from my thoughts, Monica rubs her cheek against my thigh. My body ignites with such a simple gesture of affection.

My God, this is what it feels like to have Monica touch me without requesting it first.

My cock fills so fast, I feel faint from the blood loss to my brain. I reach down and adjust the beast until he's no longer choking on the seam of my pants. Just the feel of my hand brushing against my dick, and her face stroking my thigh, renders me breathless.

Spreading my legs farther apart, I issue a silent invitation that she would usually ignore. Monica slips between my thighs within seconds. Her small hand fists my ankle and holds on as I play roughly with her nipples.

We stay like this for a few moments. Monica rests her head between my thighs, caressing me with her cheek as I fondle her breasts. I hum my pleasure underneath my breath.

Monica abruptly turns her face to the side and bites my cock through my pants. Hips rising off the chaise, I hiss between clenched teeth. My skin runs with goose bumps, pressure builds at the base of my spine, and pleasure coils in my stomach.

"Ah– good girl," I praise in a raspy voice. "I love it when you touch me freely. How proud you make me when you cross your own boundaries." I pet Monica's head with obvious adoration. Chuckling, I admit something no man my age ever would. "You almost made me cum in my pants."

Usually Monica would freeze up at this point, afraid that she crossed a boundary, or that her touch wasn't welcome. But she surprises me again when her little pink tongue flashes out to lick a long line over the bulge of my pants, leaving the leather shiny with her spit.

Eyes beginning to slip shut, I whimper as her hands tighten on my ankles and her teeth graze over my cock.

Movement draws my gaze up. Tobias is sitting on the edge of the spanking bench looking to the floor, unsure if he's welcome to watch. I've never played with them at the same time, but I've also never allowed them to watch as I played with the other.

I'm not big on voyeurism. Oh, I love to watch. I just hate being the center of attention. I feel that a scene is between the participants, just sadist and masochist– a true connection.

My voice is surprisingly tranquil and passive. "Tobias, would you like to play with us this evening?"

About a year ago or so, I gave Tobias more control over himself. I began by giving him *A* and *B* choices. Then I added choose your own choice. Now I have Minion as a pet, even after I told him no. Tobias is submissive in nature, but that doesn't mean he doesn't know what he wants. That is a misconception of the bond between a submissive and a dominant.

I'll never forget the night I met Tobias– I remember it as if it were only yesterday. It was also the same night I met Katya. Tobias intentionally messed with the small female, hoping she would give him something he couldn't name. He'd seen that spark inside Katya that would meet his needs.

Tobias hit rock bottom as I whipped him bloody in punishment. I could see his need and confusion warring with his shame and guilt. He was using drugs, not taking care of himself, unable to put his needs into words, and allowing his family's burdens to weigh heavily on his soul.

Tobias fell hard that night. I held him as he cried out his anguish, confessed all of his sins, and then I took him home like a stray puppy. I never regretted my decision. I saved his life. I've never doubted my belief in a higher power after watching Tobias heal. Just as I'm positive Monica was heaven-sent as well.

Tobias turns bashful, just as I knew he would, but he no longer denies his needs and curiosities. "I would very much like to join you, Master."

"I won't ask you if you wish to play, Monica. Only women who know their true value get a choice. Until then, I will choose what I know you secretly want but don't have the courage to voice."

Regretfully, I pull Monica from my lap, loving the way she was stroking me like a well-contented cat. "Tobias, take the cross on the left. Monica, you take the one on the right."

Shock crosses their features. There is no greater intimacy than that between a sadist and a masochist. Other than working Toby in front of Katya and Ezra once, I've never worked Tobias in Restraint's dungeon. Tonight is the first time Monica will ever witness the intimacy between Toby and myself.

Without hesitation, both face their crosses and wait for me to buckle them. If I wasn't already hard enough to pound nails, the sight of Tobias and Monica side-by-side against their crosses would do it.

My cock jerks in my pants– the intense throb beginning. The throb that always occurs when I indulge in the act of gifting pain to a true masochist. It becomes so powerful, that when Toby reaches emotional release, my cock explodes without touch.

I smooth my hands from Toby's shoulders until I meet his wrists. I touch him with affection. There is nothing sexual between us. It has never been, nor will it ever be. It's just the sensation of touching someone you hold a deep emotional and mental connection with. There is no way you could go through something so soul releasing and not form a bond.

I grab Toby's hands and settle them on the pegs I installed at the top of the cross. He grips the pegs as I strap his wrists with the padded leather straps. This is for his protection, not out of any need for restraint. I can't allow him to move for fear of injuring him accidentally.

I slide my hands down Toby's slim back, rounded ass, and firm thighs, until I reach his ankles. An outside observer would think I'm taking liberties. I'm not. I'm checking for tension and trying to relax him with my touch. A cramp isn't the kind of pain we are looking for, and it would cause me to stop the scene and all would be lost.

After strapping Toby's ankles to the cross, I stand upright, giving his calf a squeeze to let him know he's secure. I watch the tension melt from his body as he hangs on the cross by his wrists and ankles. Only his hands gripping the pegs belie his relaxation.

Nudging the leather collar, I remind Monica how I'm in control and she has nothing to fear. I will take care of all of her needs so that she may take care of her mind and soul. I kiss the back of Monica's neck. Watching a shudder roll up her spine, I moan into her ear.

The throbbing in my cock picks up its pace, signaling it's almost time to start. I won't last long tonight, not with both of them on display for me. I nibble, caress, and lick over the landscape of Monica's back as I secure her to the cross, her soft moans egging me on.

As I kneel at Monica's feet to secure her ankles, the pressure of my pants against my engorged head makes me gasp in pain. I palm the front of my leathers and hastily yank my fly open, setting my erection free. I sigh out in combination of relief and pleasure as air caresses my scorched flesh.

Any second, I'm going to fucking explode.

Monica's musky scent draws me like a fly to honey. I see it glistening in rivulets down her inner thighs. There is no way I could ever resist the taste. I spend a few moments licking her clean as she cries out above me.

The intense pressure builds with each small taste, with every whimper from her parted lips. When my balls tighten painfully, I fall backward onto the flooring, thankful for its padding or I would have bruised my tailbone. I pant against the need to come. With each ragged breath drawn, Monica's scent flows deeper into my lungs, as air passes my lips and tongue coated with her juices.

"Fuck," pours from my mouth in haste. I hop to my feet, ignoring my screaming erection. I yank my leathers closed on the demanding beastly fucker. *You'll get your release soon enough*, I coax him to be patient.

I grab a small paddle from the wall– Monica's favorite. I have to work her up to the level of pain that Tobias and I require for release. I've never used anything stronger than a cane on her, but tonight my pain slut will feel the bite of my whip. Not out of anger, frustration, or punishment over Monica's misdeeds, but because she needs to repent.

The rhythmic motion of the whip lashing out will force Monica to release the guilt and shame associated with her time with Dalton, and hopefully some of her insecurities will float away.

Just the thought of wielding my whip against Monica's flesh has pre-cum pouring into my pants. I palm my bulge, moving it around until I'm more comfortable and no longer trying to burrow out of my leathers to get at Monica.

I flick my wrist, exacting the perfect amount of force on the paddle against Monica's back. I redden the area where the untrained Katya left her mark behind. I lay mark after mark on Monica's skin, reddening her entire back as she gasps and moans for more.

Without thought, I toss the paddle behind me, and hear its thump on the rubber flooring as I lick along Monica's spine from the crack of her ass to the nape of her neck. She flexes in her restraints and cries out in pleasure.

I smack Monica's ass with the palm of my hand, enjoying its jiggle and she goes lax beneath my touch. "You please me so much– never doubt that." I breathe into her ear, and then smile against the side of her neck when it earns me a moan.

I look to Tobias, finding him out of breath from anticipation. The sounds of the paddle amped up his needs. His entire body is beaded with a sheen of sweat. Without hesitation, I roughly fist his beautiful locks and use it to turn his face toward me.

"You like having Monica here with us, don't you? You love hearing her moan as much as I do." I breathe across his face. "Admit it?"

Breathlessly, almost pleading, "Yes, Master."

"Tell her." I order, yanking Toby's hair until he's facing Monica. "Tell her how much you appreciate her."

"I enjoy your company, Monica." Voice thick with sincerity, "We make Dexter feel complete. I wish you could see yourself clearly so that we wouldn't have to worry constantly. It's never-ending, and Dexter and I can't take it anymore."

I pat Tobias on the head for being open and honest– for putting tears of reality in Monica's eyes.

Stepping away, I grab the length of leather that is an extension of my hand. Marcus gifted it to me when we began our BDSM journey. With slow, controlled movements, I stalk back to my waiting subs with my favorite tool in my hand. I watch Monica's large, brown eyes widen even larger when she takes in the whip resting in my palm.

Yes, Monica. I believe it's time you become acquainted with my little friend.

Tobias puffs out a few gasps as I stalk toward him, back rising and falling rapidly in anticipation. He's excited and aroused over the fact that he's finally going to feel the pain he's dreamed about all week. With so much going on in our lives, we haven't set foot in the basement in far too long. Tobias truly is addicted to the flick of my wrist.

"Face your crosses, boys and girls." I tease in a voice belying the violence contained in the palm of my hand. "No peeking."

I have them look away for two reasons: I don't want to injure their faces or eyes and I want them to anticipate my gift of pain.

With the flick of my wrist, I crack the thirty inches of braided leather on the rubber flooring. The only downside to having a cushioned floor is that the sound isn't as impressive or ominous. Restraint's slate tiles produce amazing sound quality as the cracker hits the smooth surface.

I toss the handle a few times, settling it in my palm. The handle is proportioned perfectly for my grip. It has fingertip grooves worn into it from my continual use.

I always crack the whip until Tobias stops flinching at the sound. It's never the same amount of times, depending on both of our moods. I don't want it to become obvious so I always do it a few more times to create a sense of surprise.

I coil up the leather tightly. Then with the flick of my wrist, I set a perfect line against Monica's back. She yelps in pain and surprise, and Tobias joins her. He thought he'd get the first blow, as did Monica.

Neck arched, teeth clenched, I breathe through the pounding need in my cock as it throbs in time with my rapidly beating heart. I flick my wrist again, taking Monica across the shoulder this time.

Tobias tenses as Monica releases a mournful scream. I mustn't allow them to believe they are taking even turns.

Flexing my sadism has never felt this intense, this intimate – compounded by the two most important people in my life. The blow's shock is what has my dick burning for release. Teeth gritted, I palm my balls as they tighten, threatening to shoot my release up the shaft of my cock. I inhale through my nose and breathe out my mouth until I'm finally able to regain my control.

I flick my wrist again, leather marking Monica across the top of her thighs. She screams bloody murder at the ceiling, causing a glorious smile to pull at my lips. It may hurt like a bitch, but the marks will fade quickly. I've never broken skin– not once.

Dealing pain is my passion…

Sadism is my gift.

Without a mental command, my whip lashes out to reach Tobias. The force exacted is stronger than all three of the hits Monica cushioned. I continue to alternate blows between them. Sometimes one takes four hits in a row and the next only one, all varying levels of pain. I don't allow any form of a pattern to emerge. The element of surprise is half of the experience.

The base of my neck tingles as my scalp tightens in pleasure. My nerves sing, coming alive as my flesh feels the bliss my mind conjures. My cock weeps with every blow, drawing me closer and closer to climax until I can no longer ignore the sensation.

The combined cries and moans of Monica and Tobias are my undoing. I come from the top of my head and the soles of my feet— the two forces meet in the center of my body to explode out the tip of my shaft. Neck arched, I scream my pleasure to the ceiling.

Sated, I rest my forehead against Monica's abused back and lay my hand on Toby's hip, fingertips flexing and slipping in his sweat. The aftershocks rolling through my body increase as I feel Tobias tense for his own release. I have no clue what Monica is feeling at this very moment, but Tobias and I are one on this. We both experience a full-body release as our minds try to absorb the endorphins flooding our systems.

For many moments, I lean cradled against their backs as my climax subsides. Breathless, we pant together, reforming into a new version of ourselves.

I unleash Monica from the wooden structure first, because I have no clue how she will react to the torments she just endured. Her back is red, but no skin is broken. I did an exceptional job on her, and she proved how courageous and fierce she truly is.

Palms resting lightly on her shoulders, I turn Monica to face me so I can get a reading on the emotions she's unable to name. Her eyes are glazed, pupils blown, face and chest flushed rosy red, and her mouth is parted on a pant. The tip of her tiny, pink tongue peeks out of her full lips to moisten their surface. I harden instantly at the sight.

With little effort, I pick Monica up and carry her to the bed. I lay her out before me, eyes inspecting the landscape of her flesh. Her expression is dazed as if high, like she finally took several hits off my bowl.

Running my hand up her inner thigh, I test to see if Monica was aroused by the session. It's an unrealized dream of mine that someday Monica would come to love and crave my ministrations. I touch her knee, preparing to slide my fingertips up her thigh, and I'm rendered shocked. My Monica is saturated down her thighs, past her knees, all the way to her calves.

I gaze into her blurry eyes and smile. "Did that make you come?" The words roll off my tongue in a seductive purr, causing Monica to shudder. "Did you love the crack of the whip? The flick of my wrist?"

"Yes, Master." Voice low and sultry– a sexual cadence she's never uttered. "Thank you," she sobs, almost sounding relieved.

I have to leave the bed in order to distract myself from the pressure building inside my body, from the need my mind is screaming for the woman spread out before me as an offering. I unleash Tobias while simultaneously inspecting his back. Perfection.

With deft movements, I turn Tobias to face me, resting his marked back on the cross. His clear blue eyes are glassy with contentment. Reaching to the side, I fetch a towel to wipe his release from his body. Unbidden, Toby hardens under my touch. It's not the first time that it has happened, nor will it be the last. The automatic reaction has nothing to do with me. It's just his heightened nerves relishing the sensation of skin-to-skin contact. I am thankful that he ripens for me. I need him to be ready for what comes next.

I lead Tobias to the bed and lay him next to Monica– who hasn't moved a single inch in the past few minutes. I chuckle at the sight of them lying so contently because of the pain and pleasure I provided.

It's a job well done.

"This is a once in a lifetime opportunity. We have to erase Monica's emotional trauma, to remove her shame, and replace it with something positive. We also have to satisfy Toby, so he doesn't have to steal a wank from a bi-curious guy who uses sexual pleasure to gain friends." I mutter wryly, on the verge of laughing.

Without asking for permission, I rip open a condom wrapper and extract the ring of latex. I grip the base of Toby's cock and roll the condom over his hard flesh, then I make sure that the reservoir tip has room for his spendings. I try not to get skeeved out about what I'm doing or why I'm doing it. If it were any other man lying here and letting me roll a condom on his cock, I'd freak the hell out. But Toby isn't any other man.

He's mine.

Grinning, I gesture between them. "Whichever one of you can move, mount the other. I want to watch as you take your reward for being my favorite people on earth. You deserve comfort, affection, and intimacy."

Tobias rolls his glazed eyes up at me. Shock and awe are clearly written in his facial expression. Thighs flexing with want, he can't move because I whipped all the energy out of him. I struck him ten times harder than Monica.

Monica gazes up at me from under the thick lace of her lashes. I watch as she struggles to trust me versus doubting whether or not this is a trap –a test she would have given me in the past. Fortifying herself, she draws from the last of her energy reserve to pull herself up to her knees.

Smiling with pride and adoration, my heart swells with love I didn't think it was possible to contain. Monica is finally trusting me completely. So in a way, this was a test Monica needed to pass, but unlike the trap she had sprung for me.

It's time to replace the memory of Dalton violating Monica in all of our minds. It was disturbing on many levels. It was a combination of cheating on me, why she chose to self-punish, and the desolate look upon her face.

With Toby, we will overwrite it. Monica must enjoy someone who she trusts and is comfortable with, someone who will enjoy her in return. Not as an agenda, but for friendship and intimacy. Monica needs to learn that sex has many reasons: love, friendship, connection, comfort, and need. It should never be used as a weapon wielded with precision to self-harm.

With my help, Monica rises on top of Tobias. He moves as much as he can to allow her easier access to his body. I fist his firm cock in my hand, causing him to moan and wiggle around the mattress. Toby hasn't had more than a quick pity handjob from Alex since Heidi. Standing his cock upright, I hold him steady for Monica to impale herself. I'm thankful that he isn't a large male. Monica is on the small side and I want this to be comfortable for the both of them.

Slowly, Monica lowers herself onto Tobias until she meets my hand. She sighs a sound of relief when he's seated deeply within her. I know that neither Monica nor Tobias see each other as sexual beings. This helps me as I willingly share my lover for the very first time. As I listen to Monica sigh in pleasure, I can see myself sharing her freely as long as she and I discussed it like mature adults. In the end, it would still be me giving the pleasure, as I am now with Monica and Tobias.

Sitting contently on the side of the bed, I rest a hand on Monica's hip to help her move in a steady rhythm. Tobias is so relaxed that he just lies there as she slowly rocks against him. He rests his palms on her thighs and gazes up at me softly. A wry, mischievous smile plays along his lips as he watches me watch them both.

Monica's back is spectacularly marked from my whip, muscles writhing as she rolls her hips in a wavelike motion atop Tobias. My eyes light everywhere, flicking between their faces, where their bodies join, how their muscles move and flex, and to their mouths were songs of pleasure flow.

It's only minutes later when Monica starts to release breathy pants in a way that signals she's on the edge of release. Beneath my palm, I can feel her body losing its last vestiges of strength.

I'm overcome with pride and hope as Monica uses her body in the way it was intended. She gives herself freely over to the sensations wracking her from head to toe. She isn't self-doubting, or abusing, or unsure of herself as she sensually takes Tobias. Someday she may believe deep-down at her soul's depth what everyone else around her has always known– Monica is an amazing, intelligent, beautiful person. The only thing she is lacking is self-confidence.

Whimpering, Monica's body starts to jerk in involuntary spasms. Tobias arches his back off the bed, lifting his hips into hers as he cries out his orgasm. She joins him with a deep, guttural groan from her chest.

Mentally and emotionally connected with Monica and Toby, upon hearing the combination of their animalistic cries, my body fills with pressure, to the point it forcefully releases itself in the form of an orgasm. My hand tightens on Monica's hip as I ride out my small climax. Her sated body finally loses its battle to stay in motion, and she falls sideways onto my chest. She curls around me, holding me tightly to her body.

I look over to Tobias, and he's lost his fight as well. Whether he's asleep, or his climax was strong enough to knock him unconscious, is anyone's guess.

I reach down and unfasten my pants. I came inside them twice, and sleeping in wet leather is not a wise decision. I manage to shimmy them down my hips before I, too, lose my fight with the sandman.

Chapter Sixteen

I walk into the front door, and then through the main floor of the club, arriving at Restraint to put in my time training the masses and looking for a mole. As I'm typing in the door code to enter the dungeon, it opens from the other side, surprising the piss out of me.

My cousin laughs at the girly sound he yanked out of me. "You're petite and kind of cute. I wouldn't make that sound around too many men. They'll take you for a prissy little girl."

"Ha-ha. Fuck you!" I enter the dungeon and come up short when I see that it's too empty for this time of night. I arch an eyebrow in question. "Now, what do we have here?" I gesture to the empty dungeon that is usually teeming with deviants.

"Conrick is having a little gathering." Marcus can be an ass when he has a secret. Just like a submissive, you have to spell it out to get him to answer. If I don't ask the right questions, I'll never get the right answer.

"Don't ruin my good mood by making me be literal. Just answer why Conrick emptied the dungeon and is having a meeting."

"You take all the fun out of life," Marc mutters, tan skin tinged pink because he was caught in the act of being a douchebag. "Another issue of Generation Next was released."

"Really?" My footsteps falter as I walk through the dungeon, coming to a complete standstill.

"Really." Marc's eyebrows rise in the center, making him look like a little boy sharing a juicy secret. "Generation Next published a story on Devlin. Oh, and get this–" Marc starts to howl a deep rumble of a laugh, causing his curls to flop around his ears.

I watch impatiently as Marc calms his ass down. I tap my fingertips against my leather-clad thigh, counting backward from a hundred. Yes, an accountant never leaves numbers at the office– we're all OCD when it comes to digits and deciphering.

"So, a large article hit the front page of Generation Next, right alongside Conrick's– Dalton. So we're obviously on the BDSM Lifestyle Authority's shit list again."

"What do you mean? Dalton?" I cringe on the inside. I have a feeling I know where this is headed, and I fear my dirty laundry has been printed for public consumption.

"Well, the article on Conrick is about his past transgressions, every one of his triggers, kinks, and sexual partners. But it highlighted how he's been interrogating Restraint's membership and trying to run the show."

"Truth," I murmur, nodding my head in agreement. "But I do like the fellow."

"Me, too," Marc admits reluctantly, which means there's a story his pride refuses to share with me. Jealousy hits me out of nowhere– I bet Jamie knows.

"Dalton's article was all about how he preyed on Monica to upset you. It was bad, Dex." Compassion and pain etch across Marc's features, confusing me. "Whoever this is cares a great deal for Restraint. I would also say they're very close to Monica or you, because they were very sympathetic. I don't understand it, but it makes us look guilty as all hell."

My fingertips move to tear at my ringlets out of sheer frustration. "Shit! What do we do about this?" I give another sharp yank, the pain clearing my head.

"Nothing we haven't been doing already." Marc says with a shrug. "We need to figure out who the leak is. But I doubt that they're the ones who are publishing Generation Next."

"You think there is more than one person targeting us?" My feet start toward the back hallway leading to the private rooms and meeting room.

"I believe there are three forces at work. Whoever is writing books for Adelaide and the leak are obviously against us, while whoever is publishing Generation Next is for us. Which makes our family the number one suspects. They're publishers, and Monica is Cort's ex-submissive and Katya's best friend. You're like a brother to me. Devlin is hurting us, and Dalton targeted you and Monica, so they were smeared on the cover of Generation Next. Not to mention that Restraint was created by me, you, and Ezra."

"I'm doing all I can," I grumble helplessly. "If you hear anything, let me know. If you suspect anyone, send them my way."

"Will do, cousin." Marc clasps my shoulder, giving a firm squeeze. "I stopped you because I needed to warn you how Conrick is on the warpath again. So beware, because tonight is a '*do whatever the fuck you want to do'* in the dungeon while Conrick studies us kind of night."

"Fucking lovely," I snarl, sounding like Syn. "You know how much I hate an audience."

"Cort and Ezra are dragging in our sofa from our private room for all of us to sit on. I warned you so you'd know whatever you do is being judged by Devlin."

"Thanks," I mutter dryly.

"This is necessary but inconvenient. I don't like seeing anyone smeared in the media. Dev and I trained together under Master Fontaine. So, I trust him, Dex. He's worried and that worries me. Hell, I even feel bad for Dalton."

Chest puffing up, I spit the words at my cousin. "I don't feel bad for that fucking asshole."

Marcus waves a hand, cutting off my string of vindictive swear words. "I have to talk to you about something else. You'll be really proud of Monica. She avoided all of Kat's advances today. While shopping, Katya tried to take Monica with her hand, and Monica told Kat no."

"Really?" Surprise colors my words. "They may be best friends, but no one can ignore the fact that Monica is in lust with Kat."

"Monica did damn well today by not bending to another master's will, Dexter." Marc flashes me a smile. "She said she wouldn't betray your trust ever again. Kat lied by telling Monica you said it was okay, and Monica still said no. She said you'd have to give her permission directly."

"She said that?" My lips twist up into a smile filled with pride. "I've been so worried over how anyone could manipulate Monica and warp her sense of self. Her father is a good man, strong and domineering, but he messed with her confidence, and I fear others having an influence."

"Don't," Marc assures me. "Don't fear. If Katya couldn't influence Monica, no one else will ever be able to. Now Monica trusts you'll always be with her no matter what, because of the fact that in the face of her betrayal, you took care of her and your love never faltered. It's what Monica needed. While she shouldn't have tested you, your reaction reassured her."

"Thank you," I whisper reverently. "I needed to hear that."

"That's what I'm here for, cousin." Marc pats me on the back affectionately. "I already let everyone into your room. Katya took the entire class shopping."

There is no laugh more evil than the one Marcus produces.

"Field trip!" I can't help but join the evil bastard in amusement. He was wicked to grow up with.

Marcus is the master of our BDSM Lifestyle Authority chapter for a reason. He knows our currency without us ever telling him what it is by mastering reading body language and understanding the human condition. This is exactly why the couch is being brought into the dungeon. The strongest of us will sit upon it and study everyone else, looking for the person who is betraying us all.

"Go check out our students and drag them in here. I wouldn't want to piss off the Devil if I were you," Marcus warns, causing me to retreat to my room and the awaiting trainees.

Sneaking quietly into my room, I take a good look at my trainees. Katya leans next to the chalkboard in my usual spot. She stares the trainees down while a smile plays along her lips. She enjoys being in charge, and has the confidence to truly lead.

"Enjoying yourself?" I ask as I kiss Kat's cheek.

"Immensely," she replies with a toothy grin.

"I hear Monica made some progress today," I whisper in Katya's ear. Kat nods at me and smiles. While curling my fingertips, "Come," I command Monica to join us. She immediately jumps from her seat and approaches us with caution. She worries her lip between her tiny teeth.

"Is there something you wish to ask of me?" I question Monica in a grave voice, but on the inside I'm teasing her.

"Master," she whispers, sounding breathless. "Kat requested my pleasure today. I'm sorry if you wished for me to give it to her, but I need for you to give me permission directly before I will play with her again."

Monica's big, brown eyes are glossy with unshed tears, fearing she's disappointing me. She truly is between a rock and hard place. I can't help the grin that splits my face– such a good girl Monica is being.

"Do you want to play with Kat?" I ask Monica, suddenly serious. I want her to own her decisions. I don't want her to push them off onto me or anyone else. She must have confidence in her own needs and wants.

"Yes, Master." Monica casts her eyes down in a bashful manner, and my smile broadens at the sight.

"If at any time you wish to touch or be touched by Kat, you have my permission as long as I have the honor of witnessing it.

Your needs belong to you, and it's not my place to pass judgment on them. Just be respectful by not breaking any promises or our trust."

"Yes, sir," Monica whispers, visibly uncomfortable.

I tip Monica's chin with my fingertip, raising her face so I may kiss her lightly on the lips. I always marvel at how amazing it is to kiss someone who is the exact height as me. It holds its own intimacy that can't be duplicated. A man as small as me has a hard time finding lovers that are shorter or close in height.

"Let me see how you're dressed." I speak across Monica's lips. Stepping away, I twirl her in a circle for my enjoyment.

No more pencil skirts and white blouses. Monica can't pull off the naughty librarian look. She ends up looking like a boring editor, which is exactly her plan. She hides out in the shadows, secretly upset that no one can see her. Monica is the creator of her own insecurities.

Now Monica is wearing a copper-colored scoop neck blouse, which accentuates how tiny her waist is while showcasing her breasts. The swingy, patterned skirt adds a curve at the hips and ass. As I pull Monica to a stop, the skirt keeps wrapping around her waist and thighs. I catch the slight curve of her ass from the movement– no panties.

"No panties or a bra?" I arch a brow in question in Katya's direction, while my eyes are glued to Monica's nipples beading against silk.

"Monica's breasts are perfect for going braless." Pale face flushing, Katya's next words are thready with lust. "Hell, Dex, I think we both would like easy-access under her skirt."

A shy female submissive is Kat's downfall. Monica is hitting all of Katya's triggers right now. She's rubbing her thighs together in a cute, horny way. I snicker at her obvious discomfort.

"Don't ever think no one is hot for you," I warn Monica while pointing between Katya and myself. "You look gorgeous with your hair down and all that smoky makeup. The only thing hotter than confidence is the '*just fucked*' messy look on a woman. If you wear your old clothes ever again, I'll have to punish you in our basement."

Finally! Monica's lips quirk up at the corners, truly trusting and believing my words. The vulnerability and courage clenches my heart.

Voice turning deep and sultry, "If I beg, will you do it," Monica flirts with me. *Monica is flirting with me.*

Eyes popping out of my skull in shock, I automatically run my palms down the front of my athletic-cut shirt. My nipples bead against my palms, eager for affection and attention.

I wear three-piece-suits seventy percent of the time. I wear leather pants and nothing else, not even shoes, twenty percent of the time. The rest of the hours in a day, I'm as naked as a baby. I haven't worn jeans and a t-shirt since I was a young man.

I smirk as my fingertips rasp over the writing on the front of my shirt. *If you beg nicely I'll crack my whip!*

"You do look positively edible, Dexter," Katya purrs, a flush creeping over her pale skin.

"Hmm… perhaps Monica will feast later on. That is if she begs properly." I tease both girls. The crimson flush on Kat's face tells me it's not me she's envisioning Monica feasting upon.

"Ladies and gentlemen, come up to the front of the room where I will inspect your new images. When I'm finished, please stand in the hall next to Mistress Kat."

Katya, who usually wears leather at Restraint, is wearing a white dress and nothing else. She and Monica leave through the open door and wait patiently in the hall. The rest of my trainees amble forward to line up in a tidy line, awaiting their inspections.

Tobias is first in line, wearing more than a blush and a silly grin. Tobias was in a pair of dirty jeans and a torn and grubby jacket when I first met him. He had a smell about him that was sickly. For the past several years, he has worked as my assistant from our home and is ready to graduate from college, so he usually wears workout clothes or khakis. Now he's dressed in a pair of tailored pants and a crisp white shirt. He looks like he could be a junior executive in any of the high-rises in the city. Instead of the clothing wearing him, Tobias is wearing the clothes, completely comfortable in his own skin and the image he projects.

"I may have to bring you to the office before your internship starts. The ladies will go nuts over your hair," I tease, ruffling the golden locks.

"Thank you, Master." Toby's bashfulness is replaced with confidence as he exits the room to join the others in the hallway.

Kristal approaches me grudgingly, dragging her pretty shoed feet, with Fate trailing her an inch behind. Kris likes to dress as a hard-ass bitch: tight leather pants and only a vest to cover her perfect breasts. Her hair is always colored and spiked wildly. She's covered in vibrant tattoos etched across her skin by our Pretty Boy. But, tonight, Kristal wears a floral sundress that shows off her golden skin. Her short hair is smoothed down to frame her face, albeit still colored blue and purple over her warm brown locks. She is dragging tan leather sandals on her feet. She looks cute and innocent if you can avoid looking at her tattoos and into her pissed off hazel eyes.

I chuckle at her discomfort. "Don't you look as pretty as a flower." I bait Kris, and she snarls *asshole* underneath her breath. I tsk-tsk her a few times and point to the door. "You guys switched closets, didn't you?" I turn to Kristal's housemate and longtime friend, Fate.

Angelic Fate is poured into Kristal's usual clothing. Flawless, creamy skin is showcased by black leather. Always covered in innocent dresses and business suits, I'm utterly shocked at Fate's tight breasts peeking out the top of the vest, and her firm, round ass filling out the pants.

Mouth suddenly dry, I pick my jaw up off the floor. "Looking fierce, Ms. Simpson. Fierce. The resemblance to your sister is obvious now."

Fate smiles at me, her blonde ponytail swinging around her shoulders. "Thank you," she says kindly, and then takes her leave.

Greta is next to approach me. By society's standards, she is a large woman and she carries it well. If I were her, I wouldn't drop a pound to satisfy those fucktards. Her large ass and thighs are encased in a pair of fitted black slacks. Her full breasts are covered by a purple blouse that is straining to contain them. The royal color looks fabulous with Greta's darker skin tone. The ease in which Greta wears these clothes, informs me this is how she usually dresses. She knows she's a big girl, and she celebrates it on a daily basis.

I'd bet Greta is the hot teacher at school, and those frumpy clothes were part of her lie to gain entry to Restraint. It makes me trust her even less. But I have to respect her, because whatever Greta is doing, she has her reasons, even if they cause me problems.

"Wow… Greta, you look fabulous." I mutter in astonishment, mind replaying the pleated khakis and grandma blouse she wore the last time I saw her.

"Thank you, Master Dexter." Greta grants me the same respect I grant her, even if she is invading my club. She can't be Generation Next because we don't know her. She can't be our mole, because she was just admitted to the membership. I have no idea why she is here, but I suspect I'll be finding out soon enough.

Alex approaches me with a huge grin on his face. He's always dressed as his clients and patients– jeans and t-shirts. You can't tout your wealth while working at a community outreach program. Alex's Native American ancestry gave him a unique bone structure and silky inky-black hair, which swings near his sharp jawline.

I've enjoyed Alex since the moment I met him. Marcus kept him away from Restraint for almost a decade, for reasons he never explained. But I've known Alex all that time from visiting Jamie and Alex's Brownstone.

"Dexter." Alex's greeting is smooth, and his blue-green eyes are filled with mischief. I just shake my head at him over and over again while laughing.

"I'm beyond flattered. Seriously flattered." Alex is dressed as me, poured into a pair of black leather pants and nothing else. I ignore the fact that his six-foot-tall frame looks damn fine in those painted-on pants, lovingly cupping his bulge and ass. No doubt sprayed with baby oil, Alex's hairless, lanky torso and chest are glittering in the light.

"Go," I laugh, pushing Alex from the room. "Just go."

Queen and Syn greet me as a pair, neither looking pleased. "Why aren't you participating?"

"Dex," Regina has a way of making my nickname feel like a slap to the face. "Really? Do I look like I have time to play dress up?" She lifts her arms, showing her jeans and t-shirt. Contrary to the clichéd dommes, Queen dresses like she does when she's working. "Restraint is going to shit. I have to run Empowerment and I have a family to take care of. Where in there do I have time to play dress up?"

"Regina," I caution. "We all have shit we have to do that we don't like. But it would have taken you five minutes to pull something out of your closet, when you had to get dressed anyway. You're just being stubborn."

"No one will listen to me," Regina mumbles as she leaves the room. Then loudly filtering in from the hallway, "So I'm not going to listen to you."

"Ez is out of control right now," Syn warns me. No doubt this is why Regina is being so confrontational. She runs Restraint for Ezra, and he's tying her hands behind her back, so to speak. "You didn't actually expect me to don a dress and heels, did you?" Syn demands.

Syn's wearing leather from her ankles, to her wrists, and to her neck. I know the canvas beneath is covered in Pretty Boy's artwork and metal piercings. Syn's pixie cut, blonde hair is dyed ebony, and her vibrant blue eyes are covered with violet contacts. She has metal implanted all over her face, erasing the sweet little girl she used to be.

"No, I expected you to ignore the request, not believing for a second you could grow past what you are now." I sigh, looking above Syn's head. The girl is barely five-foot-tall, yet she can hardly be ignored, but I manage to do so now.

"Veiled insults?" Syn stares me down, but I'm shocked she's not pissed. The woman takes offense if you tell her to have a good evening. "I never thought you'd be so passive-aggressive."

"Syn calls you out for a veiled insult while issuing one of her own," Whitt murmurs, coming up to me as Restraint's antagonist finds her way to the hallway. "How very Syn."

Last up are the Daniel Whittenhowers, minus the first. "Whitt, you amuse me as always." Tall and lean, the boy-next-door is wearing sweatpants, a hoodie, and a baseball cap.

"Well, this is more comfortable than a suit." Palms gliding over his torso, Whitt looks down at himself with a glimmer of humor sparking in his eyes. "Father has never allowed us to dress this way—you know from birth he had us in suits. I may adopt it permanently." Winking, he chuckles underneath his breath at the looks of horror that cross his nephew's and my face.

"Dim-Whitt, please don't. You're far too pretty to dress like this." I cringe in mock disgust. "Dimby-Whitt," I say to the youngest Whittenhower, giving them each a silly nickname.

Young Niel is the heir to the Whittenhower dynasty. He's the first and only born son of the deceased eldest Whittenhower son, Grant. Now Daniel I, only has a married daughter, Katherine Preston, and our baby boy, Whitt. The family's youngest daughter, Adelaide, the bane of our existence, is at Wintercrest Asylum. The Whittenhower title was stripped from her when she wrote the tell-all book, The Mistress & Master of Restraint. Now if we could just figure out who gave Ade the information about us, we would be one step closer to losing our six-foot-seven babysitter.

"That's not very nice," Niel grumbles, freckled skin turning pink. I only teased him so I could hear his smooth voice warble.

Niel's wearing an old-school tracksuit. I see a theme here. Must be there isn't an athletic bone in the Whittenhower family. Either that, or they were made to pursue mental hobbies– such as dominance. Any member of the family born with a submissive nature is consumed and digested, which is why Niel's father, Grant, is sadly not standing with us today.

"Since I've helped change your shitty diapers, I think that gives me the right to call you anything I wish. You'll forever be Dimby-Whitt in my eyes, son." Chuckling at the blush creeping up Neil's cheeks, I muss up his haystack strawberry hair. Not that I could make it any more tangled– someone needs to teach the teen how to fix it.

"Come on, Dimby-Whitt. Let's see how you like your first trip to the dungeon." The little bastard is almost half a foot taller than me, but he allows me to drag his ass from the room. He grins at me with an infectious smile showing off his dimples. Sometimes he looks so much like his mom, but the majority of the time he's Whitt and his father's doppelgänger.

Chapter Seventeen

I feel a tad like the Pied Piper of Miscreants as I stroll into the dungeon with everyone at my back. The Zeitler couch and loveseat are arranged in the dungeon to accommodate all the guests. Marcus, Ezra, Cortez, and Devlin are squeezed on the couch while their interviewees sit on the loveseat: Aaron and his wife, Kayla, and their lover, Heidi.

Deciding I should be privy to their conversation, I sit on the arm of the couch next to Marcus, while everyone just mills around, not sure why they are here.

"Why do you have two women?" Devlin asks Aaron, receiving a glare in return.

"Don't go there," Aaron warns, like he already knows Devlin well. "That is none of your business. You know damn well the three of us have nothing to do with Generation Next. Why would I help publish a book that included *my* name? Why would I destroy the very system I am a part of? Why the hell would I create riots that *I* have to clean up? I saw the assholes with my own two eyes, so step off, Dev."

Ignoring Aaron's outburst, Devlin changes his tactics. "Heidi? How many days a week do you spend at Restraint?"

Peach skin flushing, Heidi's eyes seek the floor out of deference. "Never more than two. My mother watches my son on Saturday nights, but sometimes that doesn't happen. I work the day-shift at Dominion General, and I spend my nights with my son. While Wesley is at debate club, I'll pop in here to say hi." Her eyes seek Devlin's, imploring him to believe her. "I don't have time to waste on whatever havoc is happening."

"Why are you here right now if you can't find the time to get away?" Devlin turns into a puke. Maybe he's a lawyer by profession. I'll need to get my hands on the newest edition of Generation Next to find out.

"You forced me, so I had to lie to my mother," Heidi bites out, turning feisty. "She doesn't agree with what I do here, so I had to tell her we had a staff meeting at the hospital and I'd be home before

Wesley had to go to bed." Standing from her seat, Heidi surprises me. "My family is well-connected, and I have a lot to lose if my name is published. Understood?"

Aaron and Kayla's faces are transfixed as they watch their lover cross the dungeon to exit into the main floor of the club. "Dev, you know dang well Heidi isn't doing any of this," Aaron grumbles, but never looks away from where Heidi exited.

"Kayla, please tell me more about your duties at Edge Publishing." Devlin crosses too many lines. "Do you have the knowledge on how to publish a pamphlet?"

"Fuck you!" Aaron bellows at Devlin, yanking Kayla up as he jumps to his feet.

I'm surprised how Ezra isn't stepping in. If anything, the pale bastard looks mildly amused at how Aaron is behaving. The curl of his lips almost looks proud.

"Please sit and answer the question," Devlin demands in an authoritative voice, brooking no room for argument.

"Sir?" Kayla says softly, squeezing Aaron's hand to calm him down. "Aaron and I are needed at home now. We have to watch the children, because clearly you're going to be bothering their parents for a long while." Kayla stares at Devlin with guileless eyes. "I don't know who is doing this, but we all know it isn't me, so quit wasting my time and your own." Tugging Aaron, Kayla acts out of the ordinary. "C'mon, behave."

"Devlin?" Cortez leans forward, looking around Ezra, who is separated them on the sofa. "Stop your witch-hunt for the evening. You're barking up the wrong tree, and you know it."

"One more," Devlin mutters brusquely, gesturing to the newly vacated loveseat that has my name written on it. "Young Daniel Whittenhower the third. Please take a seat."

The kid recoils as if struck. "Me?" Voice breaking, Niel ambles up to the sofa. He curls his thick fingers into fists against his thighs, but not out of violence. He's trying to hide his shaking. "Until last night, I've never set foot in Restraint, and it was through the backdoor. My family isn't too keen on me being here, but they understand how you demanded my presence."

Breaking into his conversation with Queen, Whitt stalks over to sit next to Niel. "What's the meaning of this?"

"Daniel, do you prefer to be called Niel?" Devlin seems genuinely curious.

"Yes, sir," Niel croaks out, ruining his perfect voice. "I'm not Grandfather's clone."

"So you admit you are rather…" Devlin waves his large hand about, coming up with a word. "Rebellious? You don't like how things are structured and you wish to implement your own changes?"

"Sir?" Niel shifts on the sofa, body seeking Whitt's for comfort. "I was born to lead an empire. I study year-round, day in and day out, and after dinner I have to learn how to run Whittenhower Enterprises."

"So you admit you are intelligent enough to gather knowledge and publish Generation Next?"

"I admit I'm more than capable, but I didn't admit I *am* Generation Next." Niel volleys back, years beneath the elder Daniel Whittenhower has taught the kid how to handle Devlin. "My grandfather sent me to Marcus for BDSM training because he said my father was too soft, and he wanted to make sure that was removed from my spirit. He also said I needed to hone my emotional control after what happened to Aunt Ade. I'm being groomed to lead this country in my Uncle Kent's footsteps. The mistakes of those before me are taught to form me into a better, stronger Whittenhower. Do you honestly believe I would destroy my family's legacy on a scandal rag?"

"Jesus, kid," Devlin breathes out in awe. "You sound like a goddamn zealot!"

Marcus and I share a loaded look, both of us holding our smiles at bay. Devlin didn't pay a lick of attention to Niel, too concerned with the words he spoke. Niel is sweet, his voice flowing like honey, but his manipulative powers rival Ezra's. Unless the kid loves you or respects you, he's terrifying.

Niel may be a Whittenhower, but he's also his mother's son.

"I've been spoon-fed that rhetoric since birth," Niel grumbles, causing Whitt to bark a laugh.

Leaning forward, Whitt proves he's more than just a pretty face. "I'm one of those genetic mistakes Niel is speaking of, so all I've earned is my namesake's ire."

"I'm not stupid," Devlin informs us of something we already know. "You have more time on your hands than you will admit. What is this I hear about you dating Ava Zeitler? Are you sexually active?"

Everyone on the couch freezes, except for Devlin. I don't dare look sideways, but I can feel rage wafting from Ezra toward two targets: Devlin and Niel.

Stopping a charging Katya– "That's it!" Whitt jumps off the sofa. "Are you just trying to piss us all off so we'll fight amongst ourselves? It's not going to work. All we'll do is hate you more."

Shifting on the sofa, Devlin wears a smug smile, as if our behavior proved his theory correct. "I believe you've run out of my secrets to publish in Generation Next."

"If you plan on doing anything sexual in this room, I'm taking my nephew out of here," Whitt threatens."

"Yes, we will be. I need to see who interacts with whom and how," Devlin answers readily. "Young Daniel isn't so innocent. While others were exposing me, I was exposing them. Son, does your girlfriend's parents know she sucks you off?"

"Niel, now!" Whitt commands in a booming voice, and the kid scrambles up in a second. Pointing while shouting, "My room– NOW!" The big kid runs from the dungeon and down the hallway as if the Devil himself were chasing after him. Whitt follows at a casual pace, no doubt calming himself before they're alone.

Marcus and I turn to watch as Queen peels herself from the wall to follow Whitt and Niel down the hall.

"Are you through?" Ezra asks Devlin. "Whatever my daughter is doing is none of your concern. Let the children be children– don't ruin innocent sexual exploration as if it's disgusting."

"You don't care?" Black eyebrows hitching so high they meet his bald head. "Ava's still a kid."

"There isn't anything about our daughter we don't know." Katya snarls in a cold voice as she moves to stand behind the sofa, directly behind Ezra. Her fingers clench her husband's shoulders, nails biting in. "If you mention my daughter again, particularly in a sexual manner, you will be removing your testicles from your throat."

"Meow." Marcus laughs uncomfortably, calling Kat off Devlin. "I'll have to clip your nails."

"You'll regret that if you try," Kat issues in a deadly voice, treating Marcus as if he were beneath her, which is why she has a hard time making friends in Dominion.

"Kat?" I know how to reason with her. "The loveseat is empty. I think it's calling you and your spouses' asses. You can glare at Devlin from over there."

Still angry but insane, finding the uncomfortable situation amusing, Ezra extracts himself from in between Devlin and Cort. His gray eyes dart to Cort, then to the sofa, ordering the man to move.

"Dev?" Ezra takes a seat, showing no emotions while looking politely at ease. "Why are you attacking the children?"

"Children?" Devlin scoffs. "At almost fifteen and eighteen, they're just like their parents, only smaller." He eyes Ezra warily. "You were terrifying at twelve years old, if what I have heard is not rumor but fact."

"Factual– absolutely." Ezra's beaming with pride while scooting down the loveseat so Katya can sit between him and Cortez. "Ava is most definitely her parents' daughter."

"I'd suggest a subject change," Marcus says conversationally. "Ezra will take great joy in listing the ways my granddaughter is just like him, and we don't want to freak Katya out."

Nudging Marcus in the shoulder with my elbow, I shove him down the couch so I have a place to rest comfortably without being near Devlin. Sighing as if put out, Marc shifts just enough so my ass fits because he doesn't want to be near Devlin, either.

"I still have a few interviews–"

"Interrogations, you mean?" Marcus interrupts.

"All else aside, I will find out who is smearing me on the front page of Generation Next, as well as Master Dalton."

At the sound of his name, Dalton turns shady, trying to shift out of my view by hiding behind the large black and red padded stocks. The douchebag wants me to beat the shit out of him– I can scent his masochistic needs riding the air. It's like he's subconsciously trying to attach himself to the bench and place his head and hands in the stocks, while putting out a mental signal for me to clutch my whip.

I'll make Dalton ask for it, then I'll deny him. I won't help him unless he begs.

Devlin continues on. "Tonight I'm merely interested in who interacts with whom and how."

"Yeah, how's that working out for ya?" Cort mutters snarkily while rolling his gray eyes so far back into his skull I worry they will never return. "You just gave them a heads-up. If anyone was working with someone else for nefarious reasons, now they'll really show us."

Syn's snort echoes around the dungeon, all the way over from the spanking bench, where she's longingly stroking the vinyl with a riding crop while eyeing Tobias. That snort was the nicest compliment she has shown Cortez in a decade and a half– back when they were best friends taking Hillbrook by storm.

"Well, this has been fun." Marcus rubs his palms on his slacks, leaving behind a faint perspiration mark along the top of his thighs. "But I better go check on the young lad. I wouldn't want him to harm Daniel and Regina."

Ezra, Kat, Cort, and I share a laugh at Devlin's expense as Marcus pads through the dungeon, down the hallway, to enter Whitt's private room. Poor Devlin doesn't understand how Niel truly is. By the time the kid leaves here tonight, everyone in that room will be wrapped around his pinky finger– Marcus especially.

"Gingers have no souls," Kat cracks a joke at her own expense, causing us to laugh harder.

"Master?" My eyes react instantly to the sound, finding Toby standing directly between Syn and me.

"Yes, Tobias?" I look a question at him, already knowing the answer.

"Syn wanted to know if we could play together." Bashful but confident, Toby is growing into a fine young man.

"Do you wish to join Syn?" My mind flashes back to when Toby asked if Syn had faith, and how he would like to speak God's Word to her if she were a Protestant. Odd, the relationships we forge.

"Yes, sir," Toby answers without hesitation. "Pain– no sex."

"Very well," I allow. I lift my eyes to seek out my protégée. "Syn, Tobias can have light pain only, as I used him roughly last night."

With the tilt of her chin, Syn's opening the stocks for Toby. My heart rate increases by double, never having shared Toby before. But I do want him to experience a vast array of things, hoping he'll find his true calling.

"No sex?" Ezra's white eyebrows knit together in the center of his forehead. "Is Toby even straight? I can never get a read on him."

"Tobias is straight," I answer without question. "He's young still and hasn't reached his sexual awakening. Religious doctrine has a way of stunting sexuality, as you well know."

"May I watch?" Alex leans over the back of the couch, getting into my face. "Can I? Can I?"

"It's your funeral," I mutter, trying hard not to laugh at Alex's enthusiasm.

"Now him?" Ez points at Alex as the grown man skips across the dungeon to spy on Syn and Toby. "He's not straight. He's not gay. He's not even bi. I have no fucking clue what Alex is, other than snoopy." A big grin splits Ezra's face, showcasing perfect, white teeth. "Hey, Dev? Maybe you ought to question Alex."

"You know I have," Dev grumbles deeply, then hides a chuckle beneath a cough.

"Look at him." Cort points at Alex, who is pestering poor Tobias by squeezing his cheeks. Toby is laying belly first on a padded bench, with his head and hands locked immobile by the stocks. Syn is staring at his exposed back and thighs while holding a riding crop. "He's probably going to try to give Toby a handy jay when it's all said and done."

"If Kris is a sex addict, then that makes Alex addicted to making his friends feel good." Ezra cocks his head to the side, looking at me while pondering some great universal truth. "What's the opposite of a sadist? I don't mean a masochist. But someone who gets off on making everyone feel happiness and pleasure."

"Alex is a rare breed," Devlin mutters with begrudging respect. "I don't think there is a word for it, actually."

Monica and Greta were having a pleasant conversation near us, but all of a sudden Monica looks betrayed. She swiftly walks over to the loveseat where Katya is seated, dropping to the floor near her. At first I'm confused, but then I realize that in order to sit with me, Monica has to be near Devlin, but it's also in perfect view of Toby.

"You don't like Toby playing with others?" I bite my lip from laughing. "He has to grow up sometime. The boy needs to find some friends."

"Knowing and seeing are two different things," Monica whispers, tears glistening in her eyes. "My God, Dexter." Voice warbling with agony. "What I did to you is unforgivable– to see it, to have it spread all over hell and back by Generation Next. I'm so sorry."

"C'mere," I coax, opening my arms for Monica to come sit in my lap. "You need to remember a person's actions speak of them, not who they are hurting. Toby is flexing his independence, while you were self-harming with Dalton, and neither of those things have to do with me. Compartmentalize."

"Oh, yeah," Kat grumbles, and the emotions infused in her words are suffocating. No doubt she is slowly learning Ezra's secrets, and it must be murdering her self-esteem. You can tell yourself until you're blue in the face that someone cheating on you isn't about you, but that doesn't mean in the quiet hours you believe it. Kat's ego must take a daily beating between Ezra and Cortez.

Monica slips into my arms, resting her head on my shoulder. More affectionate than ever, she begins playing with my hair. "I'm not the mole," she mutters to Devlin. "So don't bother questioning me. All of my secrets were published, too."

"I know." Devlin surprises me by sounding compassionate. "If it helps any, I believe Dalton has been beating himself up over his behavior."

At the sound of the douchebag's name, I gaze around the dungeon, wondering what everyone is up to. I'm shocked to see Dalton and Whitt taking Kristal. I hadn't even seen Whitt re-enter the dungeon. It's no wonder Alex wanted to go tease Toby and Syn while his girlfriend was taking on two guys at once. The pair have never joined forces before. Most people avoid Dalton like the plague– the masters especially.

Greta is standing in the center of the dungeon, watching the ménage with great interest. Kristal is standing but bent at the waist, with her dress pulled up over her ass and pulled down over her perfectly tattooed tits. Dalton is hanging onto her hips, plowing her from behind, while her mouth is wrapped about Pretty Boy's dick– that kid loves his cock sucked. I've seen Whitt get his dick sucked more than I have my own. But right now, he's wearing an odd expression of concentration on his face, like he's battling Dalton on who can hold out the longest.

A sharp squeak fills the dungeon, causing my eyes to seek out its owner. Submissive, innocent Fate is wielding the riding crop. Barely flicking her wrist, she swats Toby on the ass, squealing in shock when the blow lands. She jumps back immediately as if frightened, then she steps to the side to check Toby's facial expression. Toby's giggling at the ridiculousness.

"My turn!" Alex snatches the crop. "I want to try."

I watch for a moment to make sure Alex doesn't take advantage, but he hits even lighter than Fate. The three of them take turns lashing Toby, but I don't fear since the kid is giggling like a schoolgirl.

Queen exits the hallway with a scowl stretched across her face. But as soon as she sees the threesome, she laughs and looks excited. *"Very, very interesting,"* she mouths to herself.

"Where's the kid?" flows from my mouth but is echoed by everyone on the loveseat.

"They went out the backdoor– Marc's taking Niel for a one-on-one chat at the lake," she answers while walking toward Greta, probably to formally introduce herself.

"Who hasn't?" I shout back to her, laughing.

"Numerous times." "I have!" "Fuck, yeah!" echoes from Ezra, Kat, and Cortez.

"Hell, even I have." Queen wears a sardonic expression of remembrance. Moments later, she's giving the newbie a tour of *her* dungeon. Queen declared it was her dungeon a few years ago, and none of us have big enough balls to argue.

"The lake?" Devlin asks anyone who will answer.

"The Zeitler moat," I answer, surprised Marc and Dev hadn't had this conversation years ago during their year-long training in Las Vegas. "It's a small manmade lake. Our home used to be at the top of the hill overlooking it– before it was razed to the ground."

Sensing my mind going in a bad direction, Ezra takes over from there. "Whenever we do something wrong, Marc takes us to the lake for some one-on-one time."

"Marcus lectures the piss out of us," Cort tacks on. "He forces you to sit on the dock and listen without replying."

"Then he pushes you into the lake for a nice long swim, no matter what time of year!" Queen shouts across the dungeon. "I nearly froze to fucking death."

"I've been there when the lake was frozen over." Blush riding high on his cheeks, Cort covers his mouth to hide his grin. "The bastard made me get naked and lay on the ice, waiting for me to apologize."

"Did you get hypothermia?" Dev proves he knows Cortez well– I bet the bastard never apologized.

"Nah– Marc caved," Cort whispers, mouth twisted into a private smile. "Only I possess that ability."

Greta keeps tossing looks our way over her shoulder as Queen tells her the rules of the dungeon. I narrow my eyes, wondering who she's looking at. I peer around at our group and catch the interest in Devlin's gaze– it's not sexual, like he's hoping she'll look at him for some reason. But that isn't going to happen, because Queen and Greta part ways, with Queen observing the ménage with Greta joining the tickle-fest at the padded bench stocks for a turn with the riding crop.

Sex is riding the air, causing all of us to get heated. Kristal is gearing up for an epic climax, and judging by the primal sounds from both Whitt and Dalton, they are as well. I've never heard Dalton sound real– without a single porn rehearsed moan.

Monica is wiggling her behind in my lap, getting the beast in my pants at attention. Rubbing at my chest, she keeps accidentally on purpose hitting my nipples with her fingertips. I don't tell her to stop because she is exploring me, giving me attention and affection, without being commanded. Confidence is a fragile thing, so I know I can't tell her no yet, even if I don't want her to do it.

Pheromones affecting all of us, the loveseat is seeing some action. Kat shimmies her ass in between her spouses, gaining their attention. Each one turns to her with hunger etched across their faces, and then simultaneously attack the sides of her neck. The sucking sound is eclipsed by their combined moans.

Eyes held wide, Devlin mutters, "Holy shit."

"You wanted to watch the shenanigans in Restraint's dungeon," I remind him. "We don't have any espionage going down, no matter what you think. We just do what feels good."

"Yeah, I can see that." Devlin swallows thickly, Adam's apple bobbing. "Next time I'll find a friend."

"Monica?" I nuzzle the top of her head lovingly, needing her to leave me be before I blow my cork. "I have a reward for you."

Head popping up quickly, face flushed, Monica looks gorgeous right now. Pressing my lips to her ear to make sure no one else can overhear, "Kat needs you to do her a favor." Kat doesn't realize she needs a favor, but she's getting one. "Ezra's been misbehaving again. Why don't you teach him what he'll lose if he doesn't behave?"

Interest piqued, Monica's dark eyes glow with lust. "Like what?"

"Our Kitty Kat has never allowed a girl to pleasure her– do Kat a favor and start at her toes and work your way up."

No need for a reply, Monica is sliding from my lap to crawl across the span between the sofa and the loveseat. I'm not abusing my authority by telling Monica to touch Kat– there isn't a person in this dungeon who doesn't sense their palpable attraction to the other. Neither would want more than a taste once and a while, but that makes the taste even sweeter.

Unlike with Dalton, or any other man touching Monica for that matter, the thought of Monica touching Kat is driving me to distraction. I palm my bulge, fearing I'll make a mess inside my jeans.

Kristal's guttural scream draws my gaze. She's sandwiched between Dalton and Whitt, who are both fully dressed with only their cocks sticking out of their pants, but neither visible because they're hidden inside Kris. All three are kneeling on the hard tile floor. Dalton is behind her, thrusting violently and squeezing her hips in both hands. He closes his eyes as he tries to avoid the pretty boy's insistent gaze. Whitt is smoothly rolling his hips into Kristal's mouth, taking pleasure without giving any in return. Whitt's hands overlap Dalton's as he tries to unsuccessfully capture the other man's gaze in some type of battle of the wills.

I have no idea what is wrong with Whitt and Kris. Who in their right mind would want to voluntarily play with Dalton? Touch him?

Devlin is transfixed– my eyes immediately seek where he's gazing. My eyes flutter at half-mast and I begin to pant in need. The trio's sex parts are in perfect view. The hem of Katya's white dress, covers and then reveals her pussy lips with the movement of Ezra and Cortez's fingertips. She's spread wide, with a thigh hooked over Cort's and Ezra's. Her head lolls in ecstasy on the juncture of their shoulders, each of her hands working their cocks where they jut from their open flies.

The men devour each other's mouths above Katya's resting head, shiny tongues flashing in the light. Instead of focusing on her husbands' pleasures, Kat is distracted by Monica crawling across the floor toward her.

Katya's eyes lower, looking to her leg through the thick lace of her lashes. Brilliant green eyes blaze down at the woman sucking on her inner thigh. Katya whimpers in need as she telegraphs her wants to Monica with her gaze.

Katya's hand reverently strokes Ezra's cock, gaining both Monica's and my attentions. Kat's eyes pop wide open and meet mine in silent question. I wait for Monica to look over her shoulder at me, and then I give my permission with the tilt of my chin.

I don't wish to share Monica, but I'm more intrigued with how Ezra will react. The man is gay. There are no two ways about it. Gay. Gayer than gay. Ezra loves cock but knows Cort will murder him if he touches a man other than Cort. But that doesn't mean he doesn't love Katya, or that he's not sexually attracted to her. But it's in a way that transcends sexuality. Ezra loves and hungers for Katya on a cerebral level.

Sharing? It's not like I haven't been *inside* Ezra, for however brief it may have been. So the mature thing to do is watch with amusement as Monica creeps up an unsuspecting Ezra's thigh. With a tentative touch, Monica's tongue curls around the head of Ezra's cock while Kat jerks him off.

Ezra shouts to the ceiling, and I bark a sharp laugh of surprise– the muscles in my abdomen bunching painfully from the jarring movement. Ezra's fingers curl into fists as his mouth attacks Cortez with starvation. Sobering, my eyes are drawn like a magnet to Monica. She's enthusiastically sucking on Ezra's cock, cheeks hollowing and filling as she makes hungry, eager noises.

It pleases me to no end to see Monica leave all her of inhibitions behind, not worrying about who is watching or the ramifications of her actions. The fact that Ezra is not only allowing it, but reveling in the hedonism of it, makes it even sweeter.

Pulling his mouth free of Ezra's onslaught, Cort smiles fondly while watching the action. "Monica's the best at cock-sucking." Cort reaches past Katya to brush Monica's hair from her face, ensuring we all have a better view. He winks at me and smiles. "You were always such an eager cocksucker, weren't ya, beautiful girl? Have you ever licked a woman?"

"You know I haven't," Monica mutters, words slurring around Ezra's cock. She reluctantly pulls back. "We were together for four years, and you got off on me sucking you off while watching all the girls attack each other."

"Ah– our glorious orgy days." While said in a fond context, Cort's voice is strained with shame. "You'll get a taste tonight. You have no idea how much Kitten wants that pretty little mouth of yours on her kitty. She likes to pretend it's you when I go down on her. Will you do that for us, sweetheart? Will you make her fantasy a reality?" Cortez uses all the charm he exudes to put Monica at ease and turn her on. He knows how to work her after years of playacting being her master.

Monica seeks out Katya for direction. When their eyes meet, they enter silent communion– having an entire conversation with one look.

Out of everyone in the dungeon– Toby being gang-topped by four people, with Queen standing in the background monitoring, intense moans from our ménage à trois, and Ezra and Cort making out with Kat stuck in the middle, it's Monica who draws my undivided attention.

Her eyes are wild with lust and heat. Her body is beaded with sweat. Panty-free, her parted thighs glisten as her juices flow. Her big, brown eyes are wide as they plead with me to give her what she wants.

"Tell me what you need, Monica." I command, understanding Monica's insecurities and fears are getting in her own way. "Do you need me to push you over the edge?

"I want to taste Kat," she whispers bashfully, but at least she says what she wants.

"So do it." I lean back on the sofa, opening up my lap. I cup my considerable bulge through my jeans, showing her how I'm already aroused by her declaration. My cock throbs with the need to be inside her. "You have no idea how badly I want to watch you cause Katya to lose herself." I reassure her. "You *can* do it, Monica."

My eyes are riveted to the juncture of Kat's thighs as Monica's small face lowers in for her first taste. Katya is oblivious in her bliss as we look on in utter fascination. Not only is this Monica's first taste of another female, it's the first time Katya has allowed a female to top her. The pink tip of Monica's tongue slashed out in a long swipe along Kat's exposed slit.

The shocked female struggles to sit upright to get a better view of what's happening between her own legs. Kat's eyes are huge with wonder. "I'm thirty-six years old, and just gave Monica the last of my innocence," she mutters wryly.

None of us blink. Waiting.

"I've been a very patient Kat, girlfriend. It's time to lap up my cream." Kat releases a seductive moan, reaching to tangle her fingertips in Monica's chestnut tresses. Coaxing, Kat pushes Monica's face between her thighs, and then falls backward to rest on the sofa cushion with a deep sigh.

With Katya's legs hooked on Ezra's and Cortez's thighs, our view is unimpeded. I watch with pride and fascination as Monica slides her tongue along Katya's slit with slow, languid strokes. With a guttural groan, Monica leans forward to suck Kat's clit between her teeth.

Cort and Ezra restrain their writhing wife as Monica feasts between Kat's thighs. They each lean over to eat Kat's howl of ecstasy. Katya is devoured– mouth and tits being fought over by Ezra and Cortez, both of them guiding her hands to jerk them off, while Monica eats between Kat's thighs.

I can see a profound difference in Monica from just a few short days ago. She's never performed before an audience and had the confidence to enjoy it. Now she performs oral sex on her friend while we watch with rapt enthrallment.

Monica's small hand lashes backward to lift her flowing skirt above her ass to give me a peek at her glistening hair-free slit and thighs. Out of her mind with lust, she unknowingly gives Devlin a view, too. I smile with pride, cock going wild, trying to get at its favorite piece of ass on the planet.

Be patient, big guy. Monica's mouth will be on you soon enough. You'll be inside her before the night is through.

My cock doesn't calm, but the prospect excites him so much he oozes precum to dampen my jeans. It takes everything in me not to drop to my knees on the floor, and shove my dick into Monica, condom be damned. The need to claim her, mark Monica as mine, is the strongest compulsion I've ever felt. I'd fuck her so hard she'd scream her release against Katya's sopping wet pussy. In a soothing motion, my hand sneaks its way inside my pants to take my cock in hand. I give it a few pumps, and then I cup my balls and grip the base of my shaft to stop from coming.

Eyes darting around wildly, I glance at the rest of our party. Everyone looks heated by the scene playing out before them. Katya screams her release into Cort's mouth. Monica's moan vibrates against Kat's writhing body. Monica's fingertips grip Kat's thighs so deeply they indent the flesh. Ezra's groan joins the party as his release flows over Katya's and his fists– upon hearing his lover, Cortez loses the fight.

"Holy fuck." Kat laughs as if high, sounding just as she does when we're sitting in my parlor smoking weed. Her body loses all strength and slumps backward against the sofa. "Remind me again why I waited so long to allow a female to reciprocate."

Ezra's renewed moans draw all of our attention. Permission already granted, I watch in shock as Monica skims Katya's fingertip with her tongue, licking up Ezra's spendings. Then her small mouth latches onto his head, wrenching a grunt of shock from his throat.

With the trio blissed out on the loveseat, Monica crawls back to me on her hands and knees. More confident than ever, she unzips my jeans and then bats my hand out of the way. I'm hard-pressed to stop fisting my cock, fearing I'll pop my cork in an instant.

"Take all the time you need, Monica– touch me anyway you please." Unbidden, my mind creates pleasurable scenarios featuring my cock sliding between Monica's breasts, butting her in the chin until she opens to me.

Brown eyes glassy with want, Monica stares down at my cock like she's starving, and I'd do anything to feed her– to nourish her in every way. Without preamble, her tongue snakes out from between her supple lips to flick my head. Groaning in ecstasy, my precum spurts out across her lips, and she laps it up instantly.

My muscles clench violently, causing my dick to bob up for her touch. *Look at me– touch me!* it screams as the throbbing starts to build. The throbbing I only experience when I inflict pain. My mind luxuriates in the knowledge that this is a virgin encounter. Monica and I are far from being a virgin, but just as Katya had never allowed a woman to top her, Monica and I have never shared this level of intimacy in front of witnesses, nor has she ever topped me in any way. I lean back, eyes wide with wonder, falling deeper and deeper in love with this brave creature, finding every experience between us innocent exploration. Not even as a teen did I get to play with a virgin. I was a magnet for older, more experienced women, just as Marcus was. In this, Monica and I are on a level playing field.

I glance over to Devlin, suppressing a laugh at the expression of pure rapture on his face as he gazes at Monica exploring my length. Feeling the weight of her attention, my eyes flick to Katya, finding her wearing a similar expression.

My hips thrust off the sofa when Monica flicks her tongue against the tip of my cockhead, rimming the slit. I moan deep from my throat, clenching my fingers on the sofa cushion in a death grip. My hips undulate in the air as I writhe. I was so drawn by the act before me that Monica's soft touch has muted into the background, just a pleasant sensation that warms me. The feel of her wet tongue lapping up all my precum almost makes me lose it.

"Give me that sweet mouth," I demand, unable to not drive us forward when I was trying my damnedest to allow Monica the pleasure. "Suck me. Hard."

Mouth resting on my cock, tonguing my slit, Monica rolls huge eyes up to me, and then she wrecks my world with a confident, seductive smile. She's empowered by my unhinged reaction, and she should be. I'm totally under her thrall.

"Suck me, Monica," rolls out my throat. "I'll show you how good it can feel to be in control of another's pleasure."

Without any more foreplay, Monica sheaths my cock in the warmth of her mouth. She turns into a self-possessed woman at my feet. Even as she kneels before me with my cock rammed down her throat, she is the one in charge. Monica didn't take a small taste; she took me to the hilt.

Echoing, I yelp to the ceiling while writhing uncontrollably, hips jackknifing off the sofa. Monica sucks me deep into her throat, better than any pro possibly could. Oh, my God... I'm coming like a twelve-year-old when he gets his first real feel of titty. I try to stay my orgasm. A Master of Restraint cannot come on the first thrust, especially with witnesses.

Shit!

I think of work and tax laws– anything to reduce the pressure building in my lower back and nutsack. My scalp tingles and my body beads with sweat. My toes curl as my thighs part, thrusting me farther down her hot, convulsing throat. I keen as I try to keep myself on a precipice of pleasure.

If I as much as blink, I will come violently.

Thrilled by my reaction, Monica groans loudly, reverberating against my sensitive flesh. She's taken me into her mouth until her lips meet my pubic bone. The wet, slick slide of her tongue as she traces my bulging veins has me thrusting madly in the air. On their own volition, my hands grip the back of Monica's head, pulling her deeper still. I can't stop my hands any more than I can the sensation building in the center of my body.

The gurgle emanating from Monica's mouth, along with the sensation of her throat convulsing around my cock, is my undoing. I grunt sharply as I spill down her throat. Large in both girth and length, I'm deeply rooted several inches past Monica's gag reflex.

God, the sensation of Monica's throat squeezing around me over and over– milking my climax is incredible. My entire body tenses and warms until I limply fall back against the sofa cushion.

"Jesus Christ," Cort hisses, voice sounding far away. "I see the family resemblance now. Dexter just took Monica the same way Marc always takes my throat. Shit! I just jizzed in my pants at the thought."

"What?" the single word is slurred, my endorphin-flooded system not allowing me to understand Cort. "What did you say?"

"You're hearing shit," Cort mutters, tan face a brilliant shade of red. "I said nothing. Don't forget your girl," he reminds me while a flood of laughter echoes around the dungeon.

"Aaaahh... Monica, get up here and let me taste myself on those hot lips of yours. That was an expert-level blowjob. Fuck..." My body loses steam. "No one has ever sucked me off like that before. No one."

"No wonder Monica and I got along so well," Cort is mumbling quietly in the background. "We suck cock the same way."

Face flushed, eyes huge, lips swollen and ruddy, Monica stands on wobbly legs after giving me the mouth-fuck of my life. She leans in slowly, unsure if I'll accept her kiss, and it worries me that we've lost all progress we've made.

Sensing the direction of my thoughts, "Are you okay with tasting yourself?" Monica eases my fears but shame is tinting her voice. "I had Kat and Ez in my mouth before you."

Never wanting Monica to feel shame over owning her sexuality, I use the last vestiges of my strength to wrap her hair around my fist, yanking her mouth down to mine. I groan into her mouth as the taste of my seed bursts on my tongue, combined with those who came just before me.

Fingers untangling from Monica's hair, they slide down to cup her small breasts. Exactly the size of my palms, I squeeze over and over again, enjoying how the soft, supple flesh gives beneath my grip. I grind my palm against the swollen pebble beading against my stroke, eating the resulting moan which bubbles up from the contact.

My free hand seeks out to reward Monica. I slip my fingertips along the inside of her damp thigh. She grunts when I make contact with her labia, opening her thighs wider for my invasion. My fingertips slip along her slit, slowly opening her lips to my touch. My fingers are coated, slickened by her arousal.

"God, Mon– you're so fucking wet." Fingers delving deeper, sliding smoothly along scorching hot flesh, I moan into her mouth. "You loved sucking my cock." I growl my demand. "Admit it."

"Yes, Dexter!" Monica rasps hoarsely, voice wavering with lust. "I love your gorgeous cock shoved down my throat." Monica finally takes ownership– a woman who knows what she wants and takes it is a huge turn on for me. My cock begins to stir to life again.

I grind my palm against Monica's clit as she rides my hand. Straddling my hips, she stops kissing me, simply leaning against my shoulders for support. She's so close to my cock, the waves of heat are burning my flesh. I'm a heartbeat away from impaling Monica– no condom for the first time in my life. With witnesses. Impossible, it's like she's reading my mind, pussy throbbing with need beneath my fingertips.

"You're so fucking tight, Monica." I hiss, part arousal, part pain from my fingers being clenched tight by her pussy. "I'm going to hold you down on our bed, and then I'm going to shove my cock into your sopping wet pussy to the hilt– no rubber. I'm going to fuck you until you scream, pumping cum into you until you realize you're the only person I give a shit about." The ferocity of my words vibrating against Monica's ear has her unleashing, shattering apart against my hand.

Monica moans deep in her chest, hips no longer writhing, stilling on my hand. I continue to rotate my palm in a circle as she clenches around my fingertip and her pussy vibrates to the beat of its own drum.

Holding Monica on my lap, my blurry eyes take everyone in. Devlin is lounging next to me, looking a bit lust-crazed and on the edge of release. Cortez, Katya, and Ezra are draped against each other, watching every breath we take. We have a semi-circle sitting on the floor off to my right. I chuckle as I imagine our group of miscreants playing *Duck. Duck. Goose.* Queen, Greta, Fate, Syn, Kristal, Alex, Toby, Dalton, and Whitt sit cross-legged on the floor, all waiting for more entertainment.

"You doing okay, Tobias?" I call out to the stud. The loopy smirk stretched across his face makes him appear to have been good and fucked on every piece of BDSM equipment in the dungeon. A few Cheshire cat grins glow back at me, no doubt because they gave Toby a helping hand tonight. "Job well done, eh?"

"Restraint is not like Kink," Devlin mutters to himself. "KINK is a bordello that caters to BDSM clientele. You're like a perverted, incest-infested family."

"I'll take that as a compliment." Ezra pulls an evil giggle out of Cortez.

"Men don't giggle," Devlin mutters, getting the joke but ignoring the connotations of it.

Tired, ready to call it a night, I get to the heart of the matter. "So, Devlin, what did you get from this experiment of an orgy we just performed for you?"

The *Duck. Duck. Goose* participants rise from their seated positions on the tile floor to glance between Ezra, Devlin, and me, begging for permission to leave. I flick my fingers at them to let them know they can flee.

"Alex and Kris? Man your stations in the club." Regina turns back into Queen by issuing orders. "Syn and Dalton, go home."

Ignoring everyone, Dalton heads toward the rear hallway to the hidden door leading upstairs to his efficiency apartment. Syn leaves, making her way to the Green Building across the street from The Edge Building. "Whitt? Take Fate home for me and await me there, please."

"Yes, dear," Whitt murmurs dryly, rolling his eyes. "I already planned on it." Resting his palm on Fate's back, he escorts her across the dungeon.

"Hey!" Queen calls out. "Warm me up something to eat. I'll be home in about an hour. Greta has some membership paperwork to fill out."

"Yes, dear." Fate mimics Whitt, flashing her housemate a big grin. "Drive safe."

Following Regina's lead. "Toby, please take Monica home. I want you both to share a meal with Minion, bathe, and go to sleep. It's been a long day."

Moving quickly, Tobias clasps Monica's hand, pulling my reluctant girl from my lap. I give her a fleeting kiss and watch as the gaggle of deviants begin to depart.

"We have kids," Katya has to remind Ezra, who is hard-pressed not to leave. "I want to see Ava before she goes to sleep. I believe we have to have a little chat with our daughter, remember?" she says cryptically, reminding Ez and Cort about Devlin's revelation about Ava and Niel being naughty together. "Hopefully Marcus didn't get there before us."

"Shit!" Ezra jumps up like his ass just caught on fire– fastest move I've ever seen him make. "I forgot Niel is still a kid even if he's built like a grown man. Marc will have him home before bedtime. Shit. Shit. Shit. He probably beat us to Shadow Haven."

Chasing after a fleeing Ezra, "Monster is in trouble," Cort sings, beyond amused, with Kat giggling at his back.

"Paperwork. Now." Queen orders Greta. "I want to get home to have a meal before I have to get back to work."

"Workaholic," I call out to Regina in affection as she enters the club, and earn a toothy smile for my efforts. I look to Devlin, wondering if he will speak freely now that we're alone.

"You know Marcus and I were trained under Master Fontaine at the same time?"

"Yeah, but I don't know any details. Marcus keeps those kind of things close to the vest... or he tells Jamie," I say to gauge

Devlin's reaction to the name. "Because he's been silenced and can't talk."

I know Jamie is a higher-up in Maître du Jeu, as is Ezra. But I don't know if Devlin is like me, an underling who doesn't know shit other than of its existence.

No reaction to the name Jamie.

A door opening has our private conversation coming to a standstill. Whitt runs over to me from the hallway, carrying a book in his hand. "I forgot I left this in my car. I thought this might help you in your search."

Reluctant to touch it, I take the hardcover copy of The Mistress & Master of Restraint from Pretty Boy's hands with great distaste. "Did you get the author to sign it for me?" I tease, leafing through the front pages.

"Nah–" Whitt's mischievous laugh sounds just like his father's did, and my heart breaks for the billionth time. "Didn't think of it."

"Thanks, kid," I mutter, pretending what I did as a joke didn't net me a find– Whitt snuck a copy of Generation Next into the book, no doubt what he actually wanted me to read. "I'll be sure to read it word for word. We may discover who the mole is just yet."

"Night, Dex! Devlin!" Whitt jogs through the dungeon, exiting through to the alleyway.

Devlin eyes me, trying to get a read on me. "Whitt's a good kid– I hope." Then he returns to the subject at hand. "There wasn't a single BDSM club in Dominion back when Marcus first became interested. Master Fontaine– Olivia lived in Dominion during her teenage years. The Fontaine family is a Hillbrook legacy, therefore Olivia was good friends with Diane Holden."

I try to hide my shock, but fail. "Ezra's mom? Marc's wife? Her friend is the head of the BDSM Lifestyle Authority?"

"Absolutely," Devlin says with a zealot-worthy level of pride. "Kink– our club in Las Vegas –it has belonged in Olivia's maternal line for generations. She hoped to pass it on to her own daughter someday." Contemplative, Devlin is silent for a few moments. "Very young, Marcus had some sexual issues he had to work out, and was probably too embarrassed to share them with you or your Jamie. So Diane sent him to Las Vegas in Olivia's care."

"Oh, I remember," I mutter wryly, leaving out how that was when Maître du Jeu started blackmailing me, using Marc's release back to Dominion as ransom. I won't even acknowledge the lengths I've sunk to to keep Marcus safe. I didn't earn my position as an IRS agent. It was gifted to me, where I've cooked more books than I'd like to admit.

"That's one of the reasons why I'm here. When training together under a master, it forms a bond– a brotherhood of sorts. I view Marcus as my brother. I can see how you all feel a similar attachment to one another."

"It does," I agree, knowing exactly what Devlin is hinting at.

"We must unearth your mole," Devlin utters with blunt force. "Even though I would love to believe otherwise, Generation Next is published by one of Restraint's brothers or sisters. I can feel it. My intuition is screaming."

"I don't know what to say," I mutter hopelessly, fingers seeking my hair to tug at the ringlets out of sheer frustration. "I hope you don't believe it's me."

"If that were the case, we wouldn't be having this conversation," Devlin cautions, but his next words chill me to the bone. "You've been watched for over four years. It didn't net the results we needed, so Master Fontaine sent me to help. My master is very fond of Marcus. She doesn't want to witness all your hard work torn apart. Marcus and your family have made great strides, by not only creating Restraint, but by building its membership into a family. Olivia wants her home away from home, here in Dominion, to put the BDSM Lifestyle Authority in a good light."

"Do you ever listen to yourself when you speak of Olivia Fontaine?" Cocking my head to the side, I stare at Devlin. As dark-skinned as he is, I just know he's blushing at my observation. "You said Niel was a Whittenhower zealot earlier…"

"I'm here to help, Dexter. Tonight was to see who has allegiances to whom and why. It was a very enlightening evening. While you all were flushed with lust, I was observing you as a whole."

"What exactly did you discover?" I ask out of sheer curiosity. "Who has been watching us for the past four years?"

"No– not yet. In good time, I will tell you and Marcus. But not until I'm positive. While I'm amazed at who I think are the creators of Generation Next, the persons responsible will be a shock for all of you. I'll keep my suspicions quiet until I have definitive proof.

"Generation Next and the insider passing on information to Adelaide Whittenhower is not the same individual." And with that, Devlin unfurls from the sofa to his nearly seven-foot impressive height, and then he strides across the dungeon to the exit.

Chapter Eighteen

I'm procrastinating– hiding –by sitting in my parlor, staring at the hardcover resting on my thighs. I want to sleep with Monica tonight. Falling asleep on the round bed in the basement last night felt like a mistake at the time, but I woke feeling better than ever, with Monica and Tobias seeming soothed by it as well.

Monica is staying in the guest bedroom, and I want her back in our bedroom. So I feel like a coward. Will I look weak if I allow her back in so soon after she betrayed me, when I don't feel like it was about me in the first place? Should I do what I think is best for all of us?

I'm a coward, because, for some reason, I think other's opinions of me should matter, which is why I won't open the Mistress & Master of Restraint book sitting in my lap to extract the newest issue of Generation Next. I fear how Monica and I were portrayed. Will the subscribers to the publication find me weak for still loving Monica?

Society says, once a cheater, always a cheater, so it should be the automatic end of a relationship. But there are subtle nuances to every relationship, rendering it not so black and white.

"Dexter, use those big balls of yours." I try to pump myself up. With a deep breath, I wrench the cover open, and then my fingertips snare the pamphlet-sized publication.

Generation Next
Your BDSM Lifestyle Authority Insider

Dexter Hayes & Monica James: targeted & attacked by Dalton Thompson.

Earlier this week, Dalton Thompson used his skills of persuasion to prey upon Monica's insecurities and weaknesses. Monica is a formidable person who needs a firm hand to make her feel feminine. She has a soft nature hidden deeply beneath a strong exterior– only those she trusts are allowed to see her in a vulnerable state. After belittling and lowering Monica, Dalton ensured Dexter would find him brutally having sex with Dexter's restrained girlfriend. In Dexter's private room– encroaching upon Dexter's territory while sullying his greatest possession.

Here at Generation Next, our hearts go out to the couple for their broken trust. We have faith that the relationship will not only be repaired, but will be more solid in the end.

Dexter Hayes is one of the original Masters of Restraint. Dexter, along with Ezra & Marcus Zeitler, created the club as an outlet for all those who were looking for release. He is a calm yet dominant man who works as an IRS agent.

Dexter shares his Victorian-Era-inspired home in Dominion's Crestview gated community with Tobias Kline and Monica James. Tobias is Dexter's foundling, a young man he healed turned college student. Upon Toby's graduation, he will be working as Dexter's personal assistant. Monica James works at Edge Publishing for the Zeitler family. In fact, Dexter is the unknown half of the Zeitler family.

The late Dexter and Rebekah Zeitler's son and daughter: Marcus Zeitler Sr. and Hannah Zeitler Hayes are Marcus and Dexter's father and mother, respectively. Marcus and Dexter lost their parents in a plane crash during their late teens, shortly after the loss of the Zeitler patriarch, leaving Rebekah to raise her grandchildren as brothers. With the death of their grandmother when the cousins were in their late teens, Marcus and Dexter were the sole heirs to a large empire.

Today, the Zeitler fortune is without a blooded-heir, with neither Marcus nor Dexter having biological children. Marcus adopted his son, Ezra Holden, when the young man was in his teens.

Only time will tell what happens with this twisted family saga. But we're pulling for Dexter and Monica to tie the knot and breathe life into a dying bloodline.

Dalton Thompson: who the hell are you?

Dalton is a Master of Restraint, albeit their weakest. There is a rumor around Restraint that the man is not as he seems. It's a long-time running joke over the man's theatrics when it comes to his song of pleasure, stating it sounds like a choreographed soundtrack to a bad porn flick.

We, at Generation Next, are under the impression that Dalton used and abused Ms. James as a way to get to Dexter, wishing to push the sadist to the brink. Dalton, a closeted masochist, is a coward who simply won't ask to have his needs met.

If you really want a beating, Dalton, all you have to do is ask. There is a line forming at Restraint, who are more than willing to dole out your douchebag punishment.

Generation Next has done an extensive, thorough investigation into Dalton Thompson's identity, if that is even his real name, and we've come up empty-handed. No past, no present, and without the prospect of a future if he keeps riling up the Masters of Restraint.

The only facts we do know: Dalton is a dominant male, a masochist, and a self-professed asshole.

Devlin Conrick: Restraint's in-house Devil

Restraint has a new marshal in town, Devlin Conrick— otherwise known as The Devil. The gorgeous, intimidating, deadly second-in-command of the BDSM Lifestyle Authority showed up at Restraint and has them swarming like an angry wasp nest. Devlin has ordered shape up or fold up!

Sorry, folks, if the Masters of Restraint don't start acting like good submissive boys and girls, the mean panther is going on the prowl. I bet Devlin is even hotter when he bares his teeth and growls.

Meeeooooowww

Personally and professionally, we will do everything we can to keep The Devil in town. One of the main reasons he's stalking Restraint is because of our publication– Generation Next. We feel so special! The main reason is Adelaide Whittenhower's exposé– The Mistress & Master of Restraint. A little birdie went tweet, tweet in our ear. I hear we have a part two on the horizon. Those poor bastards who want to remain anonymous are running scared, so they brought The Devil to our doorstep to protect their dirty secrets.

Generation Next will stop at nothing to remove your anonymity, you cowardly bastards! You fucked with our families and we will fuck yours back– BDSM-style!

We sign off as usual…
Adelaide Whittenhower, may you rot in Hell!

Please visit www.generationnext.com for subscription details.

May dominance and submission feed your needs. Happy controlling and kneeling, boys and girls.

Devlin Conrick is correct. Generation Next is one of Restraint's own. I understand why he was so off-kilter this evening, pushing us past our boundaries. I've been sitting here for the past hour, fearing whatever was written about Monica and myself, and it was written by someone who absolutely holds us in high regard, even with affection. Obviously whoever created Generation Next is close to us, even loves us.

With that thought, I tuck the pamphlet into the hardcover book and lock it safely away in the liquor cabinet with the rest of my dirty secrets.

Generation Next and I are on the same team. Whoever the hell they may be, they won't call me weak or a coward– they will not judge me for not punishing Monica for her self-harm. Yes, I am hurt by her actions, but I don't feel like punishing myself by avoiding her to prove I am a manly man.

I've got a gigantic cock– I don't have to prove my masculinity to anyone.

The only person Monica betrayed, showed how little she loved, was herself. I will not pour salt into her wounds by not giving her the love, attention, affection, and devotion I feel.

After my shower and a quick detour to my study to subscribe to Generation Next's digital publication, I stalk quietly into the guestroom.

A small frame is bundled underneath the covers. I sit gingerly on the edge of the bed, not wishing to disturb her.

My emotions are all over the place as I remember how it felt when I first took Monica as my submissive. After Katya's initiation ceremony, Monica and I returned to my private room, and we never looked back.

Back then, Monica was curled up on my settee just as she is now on our guest bed. She was breathing softly with a quiet snore that I found absolutely adorable. I sat on the side of the settee and imprinted every inch of her skin into memory. She had turned me on like no other during her scene with Katya. I was enthralled at how responsive to pain she was.

Monica was brave then, and is braver now.

After a lifetime of searching and coming up empty, I thought I had found everything I was looking for in a submissive– no, not just a submissive. A wife. Someone who I would spend the rest of my life with and fill that minivan with tiny versions of us.

My grandparents had nothing but each other, working a lifetime to build security for their family, but never failing to realize none of it mattered if they didn't have each other. It's the sense of completion Marc's and my parents didn't inherit, but it skipped a generation and the need for partnership hit us twice as hard.

I'll never forget how Monica woke slowly and blinked the last vestiges of sleep away. She opened impossibly large brown eyes, and I was caught in her web. I knew then that I would do anything to make this woman happy, and I tried to the detriment of my manhood, our relationship, and her self-esteem.

I rub the ache in my chest from the heartache I've caused us both. I was hopeful as I stared into those bottomless eyes, looking toward our endless future. I fell in love with Monica in an instant–

but more so than just the idea of what our lives could be. I knew it would be work, and I accepted the challenge with open eyes and an open heart.

After Monica woke, she slowly slid to the floor and knelt on her knees before me and whispered *Master* in a shy voice. My heart exploded and my cock erupted at the sound.

I had pulled the collar from my pocket and presented Monica with the physical embodiment of our partnership. I wasn't owning Monica– I was giving her something tangible to touch when doubt inundated her thoughts. With a fingertip, she'd always know I wanted her, needed her, and was with her.

A collar is no different than a wedding band, but too many married people forget the symbolism. The jealous half of the couple sees the ring on their spouse's finger as a talisman against adultery, while the one wearing it feels it a form of punishment– neither mature enough to enter a lifelong commitment. Whether a ring, a collar, or a verbal promise, it's about the comfort in knowing you're not walking through life alone.

Believing is half the battle, trusting is the other. Without either, all you have is a piece of metal and a broken relationship.

Monica didn't have her collar when she cheated on me. I don't fault myself, nor do I truly blame Monica. I believe Dalton played to Monica's insecurities, when she didn't have tangible proof that I was with her, and it was a good thing. It taught us both how we didn't need something physical if Monica felt it on the inside– believed and trusted that I was always with her in spirit.

Over and over, I've passed Monica's tests. I proved there is nothing she could ever do to push me away, and now she finally believes it.

Monica had burst into tears as I collared her so many years ago. The platinum necklace had a charm dangling from the center of her throat– an intertwined D and M overlapped by an H. A promise she was my future.

After Aaron and Kayla's engagement party at The Edge Building, I knew who Katya had chosen to give me as a submissive. Afterwards, I'd spent endless hours researching Monica, to the point it was borderline stalking.

I'd commissioned the necklace to resemble a collar shortly before Katya's initiation ceremony. A dominant presenting a submissive with a collar is tantamount to a marriage. With absolute certainty, I knew as I clasped the necklace into place around her vulnerable throat, that I would marry Monica one day and it would be the happiest day of my life.

A week before Monica's betrayal, I had removed the collar to take it to a jeweler for repair. I had just retrieved the damn thing the afternoon I found Dalton rutting on Monica in my private room. It was almost a cosmic joke.

I'm hopeful for our future now. Monica denied Katya's advances, even with the love of friendship and the hunger of lust between them. If Monica can deny Kat, she can deny anyone. The confidence Monica displayed in touching me without my asking, and in doing so in front of witnesses. By the tumultuous emotions I'd felt as I watched her have sex with Tobias. Lastly, it was how she preened before us when she went down on Katya, swishing her ass at us like a proud bird. The cherry on the amazing life sundae is how Monica found release from the flick of my wrist.

I'd feared tapping into Monica's masochistic nature, only to realize we were the perfect counterbalance.

I will never shame Monica for her actions, instinctively knowing she'll never judge me for mine. Neither one of us are beyond reproach, both of us flawed sinners. Life is too short, too damned short, to not reach out and take whatever the fuck you want, consequences be damned.

I reach over, hands scooping the small bundle from the bed, and then I press her sleeping form to my chest. I carry Monica to *our* bed– exactly where she belongs. She doesn't wake, just keeps quietly snoring against the side of my neck.

I pull the blanket from around Monica and crawl underneath beside her. I wrap myself around her, loving how we are nearly the same height. I nestle my face into the crook where her shoulder meets her neck, inhaling her sweet scent– heaven. Home.

Slowly stroking, feathering a touch as to not wake her, my fingers skim along her nude body. Swirling a fingertip around her soft nipple, I barely suppress a chuckle as it beads for me even in her sleep. Pressing closer to her back, needing to feel connected, I wiggle around until my cock is wedged between the cheeks of her ass.

Reveling in the heat from her body, I groan from the intense sense of contentment that washes over me. "I've missed you so much," I breathe against the side of her throat, squeezing her tightly.

Monica stirs a bit, but doesn't fully wake as I lick a wet path up the side of her neck. My body runs with goosebumps as I stroke her skin with my tongue, fingertips, and the rocking of my cock. Not having enough contact, I reach between us to adjust the angle until my erection is resting against her slit instead of her crack. I rock a few times, groaning when I slide between her moist lips. Even in her sleep, Monica creams for me. Shifting my hips, my cockhead grazes over her clit several times, my eyelids growing heavy from the exquisite sensation.

Monica begins to pant as hard as I am, even though she's not completely awake yet. I continue to swivel my hips, passing my cock through the warm wetness of her slit, while my fingers latch onto her distended nipple. I move faster with each thrust, nearing my release. I won't let go, wanting to stay on the crest of my orgasm.

"Dexter?" Monica moans, recognizing me even when half asleep. I almost lose control hearing the reverence in her tone. Moving faster, gliding my cock along her folds, my precum combines with her juices. My bare cock has never touched anyone anywhere but hands and mouths. Never before. Knowing my bare skin is against Monica's, our fluids mixing as one, is almost my undoing.

I bite back a moan by gripping Monica's shoulder with my front teeth. She hisses out a breath and arches her back into me as I mark her. We move together in a primal dance as my inner caveman screams his victory. He knows I'm finally going to give into his demands and make Monica mine in all the ways that count.

Gripping Monica's hair, I yank her head to the side, gaining access to her sweet lips. Mouths connecting feverishly, I can still taste the remnants of her earlier passions. A moan is torn from my throat at the flavor of not only Katya and Ez on her lips, but me as well.

"Just so you know, eventually I'm going to fuck Katya–completely annihilate her pussy with my huge cock," spills from my lips without thought, shocking the hell out of me. "How do you feel about that, woman?" I yank Monica's head back farther so that I can see into her wild eyes.

"Yes..." she pants breathlessly, body quivering against mine. "God, I hope you'll let me watch."

"You'll join," rasps in a command. "You'll both lie together in the missionary position, so as I fuck one, you'll rub your sweet pussies together."

Monica doesn't need to answer; her body language does all the talking. Her entire body shudders as she envisions Katya and herself being fucked by me, moaning her agreement against my lips.

"First, I'm going to make love to you." I whisper my intention as I move Monica's leg so I can roll her onto her back. I settle at the juncture of her thighs, hissing as if in pain when her heat burns my throbbing cock.

"No barriers between us again, Monica." I warn a split-second before I thrust my length inside her pussy– raw and bare for the very first time in my life.

It's nearly my undoing, the heat of her, the tight suction of her walls as they constrict around my cock, trying desperately to milk me dry. Monica's always so damn tight. She's a fraction smaller than normal-sized, but I'm way larger than average. Combined together, it's always an instant need to release the second I enter her.

Monica makes me feel like an inexperienced boy– I laugh because that isn't necessarily a bad thing.

"Oh, Dexter, don't stop," she moans as I roll my hips into her.

"Does it feel better skin-to-skin, baby?" I swivel in a way which guarantees an instantaneous release for her– my cock rubbing at her walls and my pelvis grinding at her engorged clit. "Incredible."

"I'm so close," rasps heavily against my ear. Monica's arms squeeze me tightly, never wanting to let me go. Her legs wrap around my hips, drawing me deeper inside of her. She's no longer inhibited– finally taking what she wants without asking if I want to give it. Voice pleading, "Cum inside me, Dexter," she wants definitive proof I believe we belong together forever.

STDs were only one reason I never rode anyone raw– with my wealth comes great responsibility, and I couldn't risk an unwanted pregnancy, giving some woman power over Marcus and myself.

Monica isn't some woman. I yank her hair, keeping us face-to-face. Locking our eyes with a silent command, I kiss her lips as I rock my hips. I will Monica to open herself up to me in all ways as we make love.

Our bodies glide slickly against one another from our sweat and combined juices. Our legs are as tangled as my fingers in her hair. My left hand wraps around her throat, restraining her. Her body language speaks volumes– the vice-like pressure has her hot cunt quivering around my cock. I squeeze just a bit more to collar Monica with my fingertips.

Our breath mingles as we gasp our combined pleasure against each other's lips. My muscles seize, scalp tightening, toes curling, skin prickling with gooseflesh as force builds at the base of my spine to radiate throughout my body. All the blood in my veins is drawn to my center, building the explosive pressure for release.

Monica's garbled moans vibrate against the palm of my hand as I apply more pressure against her throat. I'm not sure if it's the beat in my cock or if it's a beat inside her cunt, but the pounding starts the same as it did when I was thoroughly whipping Monica on the cross.

It's the sensation of my mind converting mental pleasure into a physical form that can be expressed. It's the kind of incredible pleasure that shoots out the tip of my cock without being touched.

The cerebral and the physical have joined forces to create the mother of all orgasms.

Never in my life have I felt the sensation outside of the dungeon, and never while making love. Both have held separate identities inside of me: one type of orgasm for sex, and one for gifting pain. The two combine in a deadly mix that I'm not sure I can ever recover from it.

With our eyes locked, connecting us as one, I arch my neck to scream my release. Gripping tightly, the walls of Monica's pussy suck my seed deeper inside, into the place I could never reach otherwise. For the first time in my life, I swear at myself for making her take birth control.

Lust-fogged, love-drunk, pleasure-high, I reach clarity. I never realized how badly I wanted to procreate until this very moment. This morning was Monica's last pill. The caveman screams his victory in hope for future conception. My cock spurts endlessly as if thrilled to shoot its seed for the first time inside another being.

A sudden snap– an unbreakable connection formed. My breath hitches as I stare into wide, brown eyes and realize she feels it, too. "Dexter," Monica slurs in a voice tinged with fear.

"It's okay. I have you... You're safe." I croon to Monica, masking my confusion. After tonight, I finally understand Ezra–Cortez. Once the connection has been forged, you'd allow your other half to destroy your life. No matter what, you'd do anything to feel the pain because there is a sick level of pleasure to it. But I refuse to allow this union to become tainted like Ezra's has been.

"I love you with all of my soul, Monica." My fingers untangle from her hair, reaching for something important off our nightstand. I draw my hand back and place the object around Monica's throat.

Gasping for breath, completely in shock, her hands fly up to touch the cool metal. I watch as tears stream down her face in a torrent. I smile reassuringly because they're happy tears.

"A reminder for when you forget how you're mine and I'm yours. Forever– no matter what obstacles form in our path, we'll hurdle them together. We don't need a physical representation of our partnership, because we both can feel the bond between us as if someone has threaded our souls together."

Confused, Monica's fingers skate across the thick necklace, asking a silent question.

"This collar is a promise that I will never break. You can always come to me, Monica. You can talk to me about anything, and I will never judge or shame you. When you feel overwhelmed, I will be the one to unburden you, and I expect the same in return."

With the flick of my fingertips, I snap the lock into place at the nape of her neck. Monica gazes up at me in wonder, as if she never expected me to forgive her, let alone continue to love her.

"Marry me, Monica– be my wife." I don't ask or command. It's a relief to finally utter the words I've wanted to say since our first night together at Restraint.

"God– I never thought…" eyes filled with tears of shame and regret. "I don't know if I could have been so confident. If you had done to me what I did to you, it would have killed me."

"I know," I whisper softly. "But I'm not you, and you're not me. We're a perfect balance of flaws." Gazing down at her, our bodies still connected, my thumb clears tears from her cheek. "Say yes, Monica. Don't make me beg, because you know I will."

"Yes! God, yes! I love you so much." I watch a change come over Monica. Her eyes close me out. She worries her bottom lip between her teeth, and begins to stammer. "But– what about my issues?"

Unbidden, I huff a laugh. "We'll be a work in progress. Each day will be better than the last. We're not immortal. We don't have the luxury of waiting forever to become perfect. While a happy life isn't a guarantee, my love for you is."

"I believe you," Monica murmurs, and I believe her too. "We'll just have to settle for being perfect for each other."

"I'm ready to make love to my wife for the very first time." Shifting inside of Monica, I prove I'm *all* man. "I know we aren't married yet, but in my heart we were the moment I fastened your collar the very first time."

With slow ease, I make love to Monica in a way I've never experienced. It's sensuous and sweet. It's everything innocent I never got to be.

At a young age, I was taught how to fuck by socialite cougars. My ruthless parents were still alive, dictating my actions like evil puppet masters. My first time was at a charity function with a thirty-five-year-old woman when I was only fourteen. Marcus walked in, freaked out, and swore he wouldn't have sex until marriage. Something snapped inside of me, and I ended up being traded about by the elite while Marc was auctioned off to Diane Holden for marriage by his own father.

Used for the size of our wallets and cocks, Marc's vow didn't help him any once he was trapped in Las Vegas, nor did my twisted education. Later, we formed Restraint to cure our issues. I learned the art of kinky sex from all those who strolled through Restraint's dungeon. But I never learned how to make love until this very moment.

With Monica beneath me, I marvel at the feel of completely connecting with another being. I now know the joy of forming a bond in all ways, not just sharing a few moments of stolen physical pleasure that fade as quickly as an orgasm.

Chapter Nineteen

Head propped on the armrest, with one thigh hooked over the back, I lounge on the sofa that still resides in the dungeon, waiting for my class to begin. I'm just on the edge of sleep because I spent all my time inside Monica last night.

If they plan on moving this sofa, they'll have to carry me, too. We need to have a meeting on revamping the dungeon. I'd deny it, but I secretly love playing decorator– everyone needs a creative outlet, and marking flesh doesn't have long-lasting results. Then again, everything can't look like my grandmother's parlor. It's a good thing bordellos stole the style, because it fits in with the BDSM theme. Imagine velvet draped on everything. Red. Purple. Black. Leather everywhere.

"Mmm…" I purr, mind already placing an order. Marcus felt that the dungeon should have an industrial feel, while I protested that it was a BDSM dungeon, not a snuff film. Ezra was the tie-breaker, obviously the crazy sided with Marc.

We should at least have some seating for comfort's sake– big, fluffy velvet floor cushions, which would be great for kneeling during blowjobs. Why do the submissive's knees have to hurt? I'm a sadist, and even I don't understand that bullshit. I want Monica to be comfortable, because I want her to choke on my cock, not wince from her knees grinding into slate tiles.

I have a custom red and black padded St. Andrew's cross on backorder that would look great in the rear corner. Whitt keeps requesting a spot to build a wall with a pulley suspension system so he can truss up his submissives. Kris designed a blackout cage that has access to all the necessary body parts but leaves the victim completely motionless and blind and deaf to who or what is touching them. The look of rapture on Kristal's face when she described the device had me a heartbeat from coming in my leathers. Whitt was so turned on, he had Kris suck him off– as I said, I've seen that kid's dick more than I have my own.

The ultimate gloryhole. Restraint needs the blackout cage—padded with silk and velvet hole protectors so our cocks won't be chafed on raw wood.

"So unimaginative. Gray. Gray. Gray." I mutter underneath my breath, eyes lighting around the empty dungeon. "Everything is gray, from the ceiling to the floor, to the décor. Even the BDSM equipment is lacquered gray. Idiots are obsessed with each other's eyes like they're teenage girls. I'm going to have to start making everything brown from now on."

A ping from my cellphone signals an incoming message. Cramming my fingertips into my pocket, it takes some maneuvering to pull my phone from my tight jeans. My eyes widen when I read the message. *Generation Next.* I click the link on the message to see what could have possibly pissed off the publishers enough to make another posting one day after the previous edition.

Generation Next
Your BDSM Lifestyle Authority Insider

Marcus Zeitler: The Master of the Masters of Restraint

Egocentric, with a god-complex, Marcus Zeitler is known as the Master of the Universe. He's fast approaching his thirty-eighth birthday (history was explained in our previous edition). He is the last born in the Zeitler dynasty. As a young man, he walked in Marcus Sr.'s footsteps as a corporate raider, stealing other's hard work. Growing bored of controlling money so easily obtained, he studied law and rose in the ranks to become Dominion's District Attorney. His eye is set on a new prize: Judge.

Marcus Zeitler married young— an arranged marriage contracted when he was fifteen by his father, finalized at the age of twenty. With no love lost between them, heiress Diane Holden is thirteen years his senior. Upon their marriage, Marcus adopted Diane's fourteen-year-old fatherless son, Ezra.

Marcus Zeitler's public image is that of a handsome benefactor with strong family ties. We, at Generation Next, know the real Master Marcus. Outward appearances show him as a loving family man. Reality is that Marcus has no children of his own, and that has been a point of contention within his marriage. Diane Holden's advanced age makes conception impossible, after failing to beget an heir early on in their marriage.

What does a man do when his dynasty's future hinges on a bloodline heir? We'd like to know. Marcus is not a spring-chicken any longer and will have to name an heir to his vast wealth. What the public doesn't know, is that Marcus creeps around Shadow Haven Estates, breaking marriages. Behind closed doors, where he thinks no one can see or hear, Marcus is taking advantage of one of his wards. We, at Generation Next, will not sully the good reputation of this lost soul.

Shadow Haven is not a home befitting family. It's cold, lonely, and downright hostile. Diane Holden sleeps alone, while her loving husband sleeps down the hall near his adopted son and his spouses. Ezra already has an unconventional polyamorous marriage with his longtime love, Cortez Hunter– pseudonym: Cortez Abernathy – and his legal wife, Katya Waters.

Marcus is sneaking around with one of the three, but not the son nor the daughter-in-law. You do the math. The depravity lurking around Shadow Haven's long corridors is happening right under the noses of the three Zeitler children: Ava, Marcus Zane, and Azrael. Ava and Marcus Zane are the product of Ezra's genetics, while Azrael is the daughter of Cortez.

We, at Generation Next, want to know what Marcus thinks he's accomplishing. Does Marcus want his seed in the mix by creating another Zeitler child to run the halls of Shadow Haven?

How can so many people within a committed relationship make it work? They don't. The whispers behind closed doors and unvoiced resentments are building to an explosive finale. Who will be standing when it blows Shadow Haven to the ground?

Master Marcus Zeitler is the Master of all the Masters of Restraint, as well as holding the throne at Shadow Haven Estates. He demands his family do his bidding, or they are severely punished. Marcus thrives on pushing your limits past the edge. One day his throne will be usurped, and that day is rapidly approaching.

We sign off as usual…
Adelaide Whittenhower, may you rot in Hell!

Please visit www.generationnext.com for subscription details.

May dominance and submission feed your needs. Happy controlling and kneeling, boys and girls.

"That explains Cortez's comment last night on how I take head like Marcus." Shaking my head in disgust, I mutter, "You fucking idiot. Who did you piss off this time?"

Holy fuck, Marc is going to flip his shit. I smash the phone into my back pocket, wishing I'd never laid eyes on the blog posting. I pound the back of my skull into the armrest of the sofa. Not that it does any good since it's cushioned. I skim my hands down the front of my shirt, smiling at the small amount of comedic relief it offers. *Kneel* is boldly scripted across my pecs. I plan on wearing a new shirt every day.

I recognize the distinct heavy sigh just as an ass plants on the loveseat across from me.

"Bad day, cousin?" I crack an eyelid to look in Marc's direction. Leaning forward, his head is hanging in his hands. Marc's day is about to get worse. I'd called him to join me, planning on asking him an important question, so I might as well get to that before I drop the Generation Next bomb.

Without hesitation, "I asked Monica to marry me last night. I'd be honored if you'd be my best man." I struggle on the sofa until I'm in an upright position.

"Wow! I'd love to." Wearing a big grin, his eyes twinkle with happiness. "While it seems sudden with what just happened... why'd you wait so long?"

"Idiot." I huff a laugh, but then turn serious. "I have something to say to you before I show you something. Are you messing around with Cort?"

"Ah–" Marc sighs until his lungs are empty of air. "How'd you come to that conclusion?"

"Monica was giving me head last night during Devlin's show and tell session in the dungeon. Cort made some comments about how you and I are similar." Waiting, I watch Marc's frozen facial expression of innocence. When he doesn't answer me, I pry. "I always assumed you were straight."

Voice cold and deep, Marc doesn't move a fraction of an inch. "And if I'm not?"

Offended, "I don't give a fuck. We both know I'm straighter than straight, but I've done things with men for the sake of experience. But there is a difference between me putting a rubber on Toby's dick and having the kid you raised, who is now your pseudo-son-in-law, suck your dick. Are you fucking Cort, too?"

Marcus lunges from the loveseat, and I fear he's running away from me– I don't want to fracture our relationship when he's the only relative I have left. But instead of running away, he settles on the sofa next to me so we're not overheard.

"Fine, it's like ground zero of a battle at Shadow Haven. We're all furious with one another and doing a piss-poor job at hiding it. I'm being an asshole, Cort is being a bastard, Kat is confused, and Ezra's getting the brunt of it."

"What's going on?" I turn to face Marcus. "I tried to reassure Kat how Cort was doing what he always does to get Ezra's undivided attention, but she said it was different this time."

"I've tried to talk to Katya, but she doesn't trust me."

"With good reason," I mutter in an uproar. "You're cheating with her husband behind her back."

"Not behind Kat's back." Marc sputters, annoyed that I'm not on his side as usual. "It has been right in front of her face, even before she hooked up with Cort. It was one of the things they overlooked in their relationship to pretend it could actually work without destroying us all."

"Mr. Doom and Gloom, I see Ezra has been a positive influence on your personality," I mutter wryly, wondering where my cousin has gone.

"Ezra– the poor guy is nearly broken in half by Cort's tug-of-war. You know what happens when Ezra feels powerless." A shudder works its way down Marc's spine. "Listen–"

I wait, and wait, and wait, ready to listen, but Marcus doesn't speak. Impatient, I tap a finger against my thigh... still waiting.

Counting my own heartbeats, I reach the end of my patience. "I'm listening, but you're not saying anything."

"I'm trying to figure out how to explain," Marcus grumbles, so embarrassed even the tips of his ears turn red. "I'm ashamed of myself, okay?"

"Shit," I hiss. "Okay."

"The first time–" Marc shifts next to me like I'm not going to like what he has to say next. "The first blow job was a long, long time ago, and it's been happening ever since. It was about self-punishment. Like the bullshit Monica pulled with Dalton. Cort came to me after he found you inside Ez."

Freezing, stomach roiling with sickness, "You blame me?"

"Of course not. No one is to blame. It is what it is, but it doesn't mean it's not difficult to stop. We've tried over the years, like addicts. It's not about the release, or the act, or that it's Cortez and me. Now it's like a sickness we can't cure. When Cort feels lost, he self-punishes. He's more submissive than anyone would believe, with massive masochistic tendencies. He would kill me if he heard me say this, but his insecurities put Monica's to shame."

"Jesus." Scrubbing at my face with my palms, I try to erase what I just heard.

"Cort feels better after a few stolen moments with me, and I feel worse." Laughing without humor, Marcus sounds insane. "It's similar to you having to whip the piss out of Toby to make him feel whole, at the risk of harming your soul."

"I've come to terms with my sadism. I see it as a gift rather than a curse. I'm not hurting Tobias, so I feel proud of the service I provide."

"The sick shit we do for those we love..."

"You can't tell me it isn't–" I approach the subject hesitantly but decide to just dive right in. "Intimate between the two of you. There is no way emotions aren't involved when it's two people who've known each other since they were teenagers."

"I knew of Cort and Ez when I was fifteen, but I didn't meet them until I moved into Shadow Haven on my eighteenth birthday."

"I remember," I breathe, hating how helpless I felt that day. "Grandmother and Priscilla Whittenhower had us meet someone else earlier in the day, remember? Jamie was with us, too."

"It was the most important day of my life." The reverence in Marc's voice surprises me. "I was a readymade dad but still a kid. Cort and Ez were twelve, and a small part of me saw them as my equals, more so then than now. So yeah– I can't ignore feelings are involved, and that is why I feel sick every time we're through."

"What are you going to do?"

Marc's snorts turn to laughter– the sound taking on a malicious tone. "Pray to God Cortez finally grows up and figures out what he wants in life so I can move on with my own. With any addiction, the user and the drug are mutually dependent. In this case, I have no idea which of us is the drug and which is the user."

"You've made someone angry." I muse, things clicking into place with why Generation Next is furious at Marcus right now. With how despondent my cousin is, I don't dare bring up the blog posting.

"I've heard the newest rumor." Marc doesn't acknowledge from where, so I don't ask. My policy of not asking questions when I'm not ready to hear the answers is always the best recourse. "It's not a new rumor, by any means. It's been going around for the past four years since Katya joined us. How I'm going to knock Kat up to beget an heir."

"You need one– Ezra doesn't count," I remind Marcus. "Ezra and his kids can have all of our money, but we can't allow our grandparents' bloodline to die out. The Zeitler name has to be attached genetically, not legally."

"Diane started it," Marcus answers some unspoken question from inside his own mind, not hearing a word I'm saying. "She's the one spreading this shit about me wanting a kid with Kat. She's doing it to create a wider divide between Ezra and Cortez, pushing Cort at me while alienating Katya."

"Why? Other than being a fucking cougar, I've always respected Diane."

"Revenge. I wanted a conventional marriage, arranged or not. Diane did not. She wanted to marry for the security of our combined power and influence without any duties of a wife." Desperate, Marcus looks at me, imploring me to believe. "It's not true, ya know? Me wanting to use Kat how Cortez did. She's not a broodmare."

"How very gracious of you," I mutter dryly. I'm suddenly pissed off that Katya's fears are being proven correct. If Cort were to appear before me, I might turn violent on his childish ass.

An odd light shines in Marc's amber eyes– a spooked horse readying to jump off a cliff. "I have enough kids, biological or not. Diane's using our discord as a diversion while she poisons my family against me. I have to take it up the ass and smile."

"Okay," I drawl, trying to calm an unhinged Marcus. Is Diane the publisher of Generation Next?

"I've done bad things, Dex. Things I never thought I was capable of doing." Voice broken, eyes haunted, he threads his fingers in his hair and yanks.

"Shh..." I rub at Marc's back, trying to soothe him. "We're human, born of sin. We are flawed beings unable to reach perfection." I remind Marcus of our grandmother's religious teachings. "I've done many things I regret. You repent by learning from your mistakes by never repeating the actions." I try to comfort him, sensing he's about to fall apart. "So I'm positive it's not as bad as you make it out to be, Marcus."

"I did something unforgivable to Diane. Last week, I punished Cort because he wouldn't share a bed with Ez and Kat. He was being an asshole and I snapped. I put a device on Cort's face to hold his mouth open so he couldn't bite..."

Eyes held wide, I stare in utter shock at the man who was always the paradigm of virtue between the two of us. I fucked the heiresses while he waited for marriage. Aside from whatever happened in Las Vegas, because Marc would never share his secrets with me, he has never taken a submissive. Outside of his marriage, the only time there was mention of him having any sexual activity was during Katya's initiation when Ezra forced Kat to give Marc a blowjob. Never would I have thought Marc capable of having a fifteen-year affair with Cortez, but it helps me understand what actually went down at Kat's initiation.

I'm just now realizing I don't know my cousin at all, just as he doesn't truly know me. All I can do is stare at the side of Marc's face as he falls apart– we look so similar. I hadn't realized we were similar in our natures as well. Both of us willing to commit sins for those we love. I have bowed before Maître du Jeu to save Marcus while he bends his own ideology to save Ezra and Cortez from themselves, leaving both of us trapped by our actions.

Face gaunt– haunted –Marc sobs from deep within his chest, choking on his words. "The rumors are ruining us. None of them are true. I've never touched Kat, and she's only ever touched me during her initiation. I never touch Ezra with anything other than affection. I'm only trying to bring our family together. Cort needs to get over his issues to heal. I'm falling apart. Everything I've worked toward for the last twenty years is dissolving before my eyes."

Head resting in his hands, Marc's shoulders rise and fall as he sobs. The sound is killing me. I rest my palm in the center of his back, trying to calm my cousin.

With huge amber eyes peeking at me through his splayed fingers, Marc breathes, "I can't even tell the world about *her*."

"What?" My voice holds panic. "Her, who?" I whisper so softly, I fear Marc doesn't hear me.

"I have many secrets." Marc's insanity-filled laughter echoes around the dungeon, causing my heart to pound out of my chest. "Her. She's my dirty secret. My daughter– I have a daughter," he breathes, unable to keep the secrets from tumbling out. "Her. I have a lover who I wish was my real wife. I see her kids as I do Ezra, and I want more with her. I have to ignore them to protect them." Gut-wrenching sobs have me suffocating on Marc's agony. "I miss them. I need them. Nothing will be right with the world until I can publically recognize them as mine."

Hand stilling mid-motion in the center of Marc's back, I freeze in shock. "What?" is a breath of a sound– the sound of my world tilting on its axis. My heart bursts wide open as it breaks. "I have another cousin? We have more family?"

"You don't have to show me, Dexter. I can see the war raging across your face." Marcus slides down the sofa so I can't comfort him with touch– curled up into himself, he looks defeated. Broken. Lost. Ashamed. "I saw the damned post just before I came to you."

"I'm sorry," is the only thing I can think to say.

"I want our family to be whole," comes out as a whine. "I'm sick of feeling tormented and tortured by people who are supposed to love me. I'm nearing forty and I've yet to be allowed to live my own life. At fifteen, my life was already written out."

Speechless, I reach over to comfort Marc, but a hand pulls my wrist away. "I made him cry." Cort's tortured voice startles me. "I'll comfort him."

"I don't think Marc needs your type of comfort right now, Cort." With a firm yank, I pull my wrist from his grip. "I have no ulterior motives."

"I said *comfort*," Cort snarls at me. "Come, Marc." Cort pulls my broken, sobbing cousin from the loveseat, and I realize I do have ulterior motives. In his weakened state, I planned on getting the whereabouts of my cousin and claiming her as a Zeitler, whether Marcus wanted me to or not.

"Dex?" Marc's eyes plead with me not to ask, as if he can read my mind. "I know you have reservations about your marriage to Monica." The switch of topics is dizzying. "Don't worry about it. Compared to my life, yours is almost normal. If you love each other, you can work through anything." He tries to smile reassuringly, but fails.

Marcus manages to walk on his own down the hallway toward the Zeitler private room. Cort follows him a step behind, with his hand firmly on Marc's shoulder– steering him.

"Yeah, love's a bitch. It makes you bleed like nothing else." I whisper under my breath as the pair retreat down the hallway.

How do I forget what Marcus just told me? How do I just go on like nothing was said? For once, I'm on the side of the very people I'm supposed to be exposing. Generation Next targeted Marcus, but I can tell it's because they are as fed up with the secrets and lies as I am.

Generation Next is undoubtedly one of our own.

Chapter Twenty

"Okay, boys and girls?" I stand at the head of my room with my hands fisted at my hips. "I take it you didn't like the seating arrangements?"

The Whittenhowers are sitting on my velvet settee with Alex leaning over the back snickering in their ears. Kris is sitting in a chair pulled from Pretty Boy's private room– a black leather wingback with rings bolted in strategic places. Judging by the twisted scowl on Syn's pierced face, she and Kris fought over it, and she lost.

Everyone else is seated at desks, where they're supposed to be.

"We had a hard night," Whitt mutters bashfully, pale skin pinking. "Marc's lecture at the lake with Niel didn't go so well, so I had to spend all night trying to correct whatever brainwashing was done."

"I understand the need for creature comforts," I admit. "I rounded up Roarke to sit on the sofa in the dungeon so Ezra wouldn't put it back in his private room. Judging by the fact he had his laptop booted up with Farmville 2, he planned on camping there for the night." Suddenly exhausted, I rest my ass on the edge of my desk. "Tonight was meant to be a collaborative effort, but Master Marcus isn't feeling well this evening."

"Oh, snap!" Kris puts her palm over her mouth, like she didn't mean to say that out loud. "I guess he saw Generation Next, huh? The Master of the Universe pissed somebody off royally."

"It appears so," I muse, eyes closing slightly.

Movement draws my attention– Whitt raising his hand like he's a little kid in school, wiggling around in his seat like he has to go potty.

"Prankster," I say with affection. "What do you need, Pretty Boy?"

"I've already been over this with Marcus when it comes to Niel's training. If we include sex in any demonstration, Niel is to either go home or sit in my room. I don't want him subjected to it.

Someone was very angry last night," he stresses his underlying meaning.

"Fair enough. I agree. This part of tonight's class will benefit young Niel. But later we're going into the dungeon on a field trip, so you better call your driver to pick him up."

"I'm not a baby!" Stocky, with reddish blond hair and green eyes, Niel looks like an adult. But while pouting, he looks younger than he is. I assume he's pissed because he won't be in the dungeon, until he says, "I can drive myself."

"Not at night in this city, you aren't," Whitt protests. "Albert is already waiting outside for you."

With that settled, I turn to the chalkboard and write *Dominant | Switch | Submissive.*

"I thought it would be wise to explain the differences between these words and their true meanings." I look to the class, waiting for their affirmation.

"Yes, sir," comes out loud and clear from all but one student.

"Syn?" I command.

"Yes, Master Dexter," she says loudly with only a slight tinge of sarcasm. Sadist or not, Syn is a very nice person if she likes you. She just happens to be the most judgmental person on the planet, only seeing things from her point of view, with a total lack of empathy unless it's about her needs. I love Syn. I respect her more. But right now she's giving me shit because Whitt gave Kris his chair.

Someday Syn will learn the world doesn't revolve around her, how her opinions are only valid when it comes to her life, and she doesn't know everything. Syn and Cort are mortal enemies, their fighting stemming over the same person, with the exact same immature personality.

"A dominant is also known as Master, Top, Mistress, or Dom or Domme. It's up to the individual on what title they place for themselves. I personally use master, as do most of the masters at Restraint. Queen, for instance, hates the negative connotations of a mistress, so she simply demands that everyone call her Queen. In essence, she made her own title. It's all about respect, and none of it holds any bearing on your level of strength. It's just what you prefer. Any questions?"

"No, sir," echoes around the small room.

"Very good. You can ask me anything about anything at a later time, even if we've already covered the subject." I gaze around the room, seeing most everyone bored out of their skulls, with Niel soaking my words up like a sponge.

"Moving on to what it means to be a dominant personality. A dominant's first priority is the need to be in control of any given situation. This need is intensified in times of stress, but it is wholly inborn. On occasion, it's manifested through tragedy as a coping skill. You cannot learn dominance. You either are, or you aren't. It's also not something that just occurs in the dungeon or bedroom. It bleeds into every facet of your life, because it is who you essentially are. The dungeon is the place you release your pent-up energy that you stored over time. We all have different needs, and I will address those in a later class. Any questions?"

"What if you allow someone to dominate you?" Niel asks hesitantly. "Does that mean you're a submissive?" "No, there are three types for this reason. A dominant will always have someone stronger than them who will try to bend their will– be it in the dungeon, the bedroom, the boardroom, or in life in general. It's an annoyance, but it doesn't change the fact that the world doesn't revolve around us just because we think it should. Being dominant also doesn't mean that you won't need guidance, or help, or a partner. It's a personality type, and nothing more.

"Black and white... if you feel the need to be in control, then you're a dominant. If you feel the need to submit, then you're a submissive. If you feel the need for both, then you're a switch."

"Thank you, sir," Niel replies when I finish speaking.

"A switch has both needs. Usually they lean more toward one side of their nature than the other, but the need is still lying in wait. They are a very versatile personality type who can roll with anything that comes at them.

"Take for instance if a dominant personality doesn't get what they want." I point to a pouting Syn. "They can't handle it and shut down." I get flipped the bird and a grin in response. "Or if a submissive is put into a leadership role they feel they are unable to handle, they will shut down. A switch is least likely to fold under pressure."

"Hear that, you dominant fuckers?" Alex thumps his chest. "We're better than you. I'm a switch, bitch!"

Chuckling underneath my breath, I ignore the distraction. "More often than not, they are a dominant personality who submits to a loved one or friend to meet their mutual needs. Or as Ezra likes to say, a switch is smart enough to ask for help, while a submissive screams bloody murder and a dominant drowns because they're too proud to ask someone to teach them to swim in the first place."

"Are you calling half of us, including yourself, a blockhead?" Pretty Boy flashes me a grin. "I'm not a switch, but I'm not stupid. I know when to use an SOS."

"I'm generalizing. Katya identified as a switch, assuming her need for partnership meant she was lesser of a dominant, but it was just another facet of her personality."

Smiling sadly, Kat's green eyes aren't sparking with vivaciousness as usual. She had a bad night too, and it has me saying something I shouldn't.

"Master Cortez is actually a submissive, but don't you dare tell anyone." I allow the class to razz each other, shouting out derogatory comments. "Except his demanding nature is running rampant at the moment." I cringe at the thought of all of them at Shadow Haven, making each other's lives miserable. "Being demanding doesn't equate dominance. Being abusive doesn't equate dominance. The need for companionship, affection, and partnership doesn't equate submissiveness. Any questions?"

Niel's arm goes up in an instant, and a light bulb burns bright in my mind. I nod at the confused boy.

"If you're a switch, does that make you weak?" His fair skin blushes bright red, darkening his freckles. "Grandfather said my dad was weak, that his nature was submissive, and he chose my mom to make me stronger. Does that mean if a dominant and a submissive had a kid, it would be a switch?"

"It's simply personality, Daniel." I sigh, feeling horrible for the kid. His dad was not weak. "No one can genetically craft a personality. Being submissive doesn't make you weak, either. One is not better than the other. A switch is not weaker than a dominant, nor stronger than a submissive." I try to take the tortured expression off the boy's face. "It's just who they were born to be."

Now it makes sense how Niel and Ava get along. Ava's already challenging Marcus at her young age. Two dominant beings either fight each other until one of them prevails, or one bows out, submitting to the other. If Niel's a switch, it would be easier on their budding partnership.

"Submissives are also called a sub or bottom. Slaves have another distinction, which I will explain next. There is a stigma attached to submissives. People outside of the lifestyle see a dominant as strong and a submissive as weak. Hell, some dominants in this very room are under that impression as well.

"It takes a lot of strength to put your trust in another human being, and allow them to do all sorts of depraved things in hope of meeting your mutual needs. I have a lot of respect for a submissive. They are brave, faithful, loyal, trusting, and courageous.

"I couldn't do what they do, and they couldn't do as I do. It's a delicate balance between the pair– neither can find enlightenment without the other. This is why we train here at Restraint, because this leaves an opening for abuse. Abuse of power in any form is wrong. A dominant who abuses isn't in control at all. It's only the perception of control. To abuse, you are no longer in control of your own actions.

"A submissive is usually a person who holds a lot of responsibilities on a daily basis. They wish to relinquish control over to someone they can trust so they may relax. These people are independent of their masters. Contrary to popular opinion, they are not lazy, selfish people who only care about getting their needs met. They lead productive lives and are highly intelligent people. Any questions?"

"No, sir," echoes throughout the room.

"Slaves are submissive beings in the extreme. A slave isn't an irresponsible person, or weak either. They simply need to feel the comfort, security, and safety that total control by a master may provide. I met Tobias when he was lost, so I took total control over his actions as if they were my own. In time, with the trust he placed in me, he was able to trust himself, finding the world not as scary of a place. I don't believe in a dominant owning a human being's freewill, because that infallible trust can be abused, but sometimes it's necessary. A slave needs structure, boundaries, and every move they make in black and white, along with the consequences for every action they fail to meet. Any questions?"

"No, sir," the group replies obediently.

"That's all the lecturing for tonight. I have to check on something. Tomorrow evening, I want you all to come prepared to inform me why you are what you are with examples. If you can't explain it, then you can't own it.

"Please stay and chat while I check on something. I'll be back to take you to the dungeon. Except you, Niel– I'm sure Albert is waiting for you at the backdoor. I'll walk you out." I gesture to the door while issuing a warning. "Everyone else, don't leave my room."

"Dex?" Soothing voice suddenly sheepish, Niel waits until we pass the threshold. "Is it bad if I'm a switch?"

Raising my arm, I yank the unsure kid to my side. I give him a fierce squeeze, as if his dad himself was giving it to him. "Stop listening to your grandfather's bullshit. There was nothing wrong with your dad. Just as there is nothing wrong with Whitt for his true nature. If you are a switch, then there is nothing wrong with it."

"Grandfather would probably hate it, though." Niel breaks my heart. "He wanted me to be more like Mom. But what does he expect after ordering me around all these years?"

I pull Niel to a stop by the exit. "Daniel, you're seventeen. That has nothing to do with your personality, but no kid your age has their shit together. You need parents, and siblings, and friends, and a girlfriend. That was what I was trying to get through in the lecture, especially to Syn. Just because you're dominant, doesn't mean you don't need a support system."

"Yeah, I get that." Light red eyebrows knitting in the center of his freckled forehead, I pity the kid being born into the family he was given. "Mom would never ask for help. Whitt had to force her to accept it, even when it was for her own good."

"Exactly. That's the perfect example." I give him another quick squeeze, and then let him go. "Are you a switch? I don't know. But I do know you're the smartest kid I've ever met. You know your own mind and heart, and you don't allow anyone to change who you are. So just go with that– no need for a label."

I quickly walk the kid to the back entrance and escort him to the idling Town Car. I tuck Niel in the backseat while Albert gets behind the wheel. Whitt would be livid if something happened to the boy, but his mom would cut my nuts off and shove them down my throat if so much as one of his wiry hairs got bent. I'm rather fond of the Whittenhower prince, but not as fond as I am of my testicles.

During the hour since I last saw Marcus and Cortez, I haven't been able to get rid of the defeated expression on my cousin's face. His confessions keep ringing in my ears. I make the class wait while I check up on him.

I quickly type in the code to the Zeitler private room and enter as soon as the locks disengage. With automatic movements, I close the door, and then lean against it. Blinking repeatedly to clear my vision, I gasp in shock when the sight before me comes into sharp focus.

Marcus and Cortez are on the bed, tangled in an intimate embrace with the sheets twisted around their legs. Cort is lying on top of Marc and he's hungrily devouring my cousin's lips. Their breathy moans permeate the air, combined with the musky scent of sex. Marc's fingertips bite into Cort's ass as he pumps against the other man's hips. Whether they're intimately connected or not, is anyone's guess.

Hand clutching at my chest, a strangled sound is torn from my throat– my mind's way of coping with having a front row seat to their love-making.

What about Ezra? Kat? Whoever the lady is that Marcus is seeing? Marc called this addiction, self-punishment. This is not the same bullshit that Monica and Dalton pulled. This is straight-up, 100% adultery.

Both faces turn to me in a flash when they sense my condemnation. Cort's smoky eyes are clouded with lust and need, and Marc's whiskey gaze is glazed from pleasure. Clearly this twisted sickness is their version of make-up sex, and Marc is not in any pain at the moment.

"Um– yeah… I'm sorry to interrupt." Stammering, I rub my palms over my face, trying to erase the sight before me. It's not unpleasant. I always felt I'd be sick to my stomach if I walked in on Marc. "I just wanted to make sure everyone was okay. So… yup… ya both look perfectly happy." I mutter as I back away from the door so I can open it. "Enjoy the rest of your night."

Utterly speechless, they both nod in my direction, but don't move otherwise. I turn, opening the door, and flee the scene.

"That was a billion shades of creepy beautiful." I mutter to myself as I close the door.

They truly are beautiful. Their strong bodies intertwined, one golden and one bronze. But it wasn't their incredible bodies, it was the look of rapture on their faces. I have never doubted their love for one another. Nor do I doubt their love for Ezra and Katya, even though it's different types of love. It's the only reason they can hurt each other so thoroughly.

Chapter Twenty-One

"I'm back!" I call out as I re-enter my room. I had to take a few moments to collect myself before I came back in. Jesus, I don't know if I'm hot or cold after watching them together. Confused. I'm definitely confused.

"Field trip time." They all laugh at how ridiculous I'm being. "I know you've all been to the dungeon, but I want to go over a few of the contraptions in there. Pretty much everyone gravitates to one or two things, and never touches the rest of the stuff. It's always different depending on the person. Obviously the cross is my favorite, while someone else may only play with the bondage gear. I think it's best if we're educated on what equipment is for what type of play."

They all follow me down the hallway like good boys and girls. We're all so in tune with one another, it takes a moment to notice something is off. The absence of noise hits me first. The dungeon's usually very loud at this time of night. That's why I took the kid out the back way so he wouldn't witness anything. But it's eerily quiet, and I know it was packed in here earlier when I checked on Marc and Cort. I could hear its symphony of noises all the way at the end of the hallway.

A large crowd circles the rack, with no one lingering elsewhere in the dungeon. It's just a solid mass of bodies surrounding the wooden contraption, with a few people trying to force their way through. I can't see what's going on, and I have no idea where the majority of the members and their guests have run off to.

"Red," a low, painful moan echoes throughout the dungeon. I can tell by the garbled sound that it's through a ball gag. Red is the universal code for safewording out. I don't rush because that word ends all contact. The next moan of protest has me running across the dungeon.

"Let me through!" A man's panicked voice cuts through all other sound. "Move it, goddammit!"

"Out of the way, assholes!" Another orders in a controlled, forceful tone.

"Red," is gurgled again.

Pushing past me, "Dalton!" Alex screams as he sprints toward the horde. He'd know the sounds of Dalton's pain. Alex and Dalton trained under Marcus as partners.

When Dalton hadn't shown up for training tonight, I thought nothing of it. Even now, my distaste for the douchebag has a need to slow my feet so the asshole finally gets what's coming to him. No doubt, he's finally pissed off the wrong person. But my nature pushes me forward because I know that Dalton would never willingly submit, especially when it's not to one of our own.

With a cursory glance, I recognize none of the members circling the rack. I fight my way through, with two strangers at my side. When I breach the crowd, I stop dead in my tracks. The relief and trust in Dalton's eyes when he sees me weakens my knees, but not nearly as much as the condition he's in.

Dalton is strung up on the rack. His arms and legs are pulled taut, and I can tell by the way his torso arches up that he's strung too tight. His entire body has been used as a punching bag, and he's nearly unconscious. Actually, I think he passed out the second he saw me, sure in the knowledge I'd save him.

It took only a second to assess Dalton's damage and unfreeze me from my shock. But the rest of my crew never froze. Alex is beating the shit out of anyone he can reach. His previous life as a street thug erupts from the well-educated man. Even mild-mannered Tobias is holding a guy down so Syn can kick him in the nuts. School teacher Greta is doing more damage than Kristal, who's gone completely batshit postal. The biggest shock is Monica. She has a woman on the ground and she's bashing the woman's head against the slate tile. Whitt is unsuccessfully trying to untie Dalton because the throng is fighting back. The three riot instigators from a few weeks back shock me. Instead of fighting against us, they're helping us.

"STOP!" I scream at the top of my lungs, and all action ceases. "WHAT THE FUCK IS GOING ON?" I bellow my demand while hopping up onto the rack. I'm above everyone while shielding Dalton from any more damage.

"Tobias, lock the door. No one leaves until I have my answers," I threaten. "You," I point to the man Aaron called GI Joe. He'd been tearing through the crowd with cold efficiency. "Explain. Did you start this bullshit like last time?"

Surprise crosses his face. "No. I can't explain too much more in mixed company. We were in the club when a riot broke out. All the security came pouring from the dungeon, and I noticed the inciters charged in here. I was worried about anyone left in a vulnerable state."

Seething, practically livid, the man Aaron called the Magic Eraser is staring down at Dalton like he wants to commit mass homicide. "As we were running in here, that fuckface–" he points at an unconscious man lying on the floor. I hope he's only unconscious. "He yelled '*ShowTime*' as soon as the dungeon was clear. Then he and his friends grabbed Dalton and strung him up."

"How do you know Dalton's name?" My eyes flick between the Magic Eraser and GI Joe. I notice The Whore standing behind them, watery eyes locked on Whitt for some reason. "I watched you start a riot before."

"Don't ask questions when you're not prepared for the answers, Dexter," GI Joe warns as if he knows me personally, and that's answer enough.

"No one moves," I threaten. I hop down and begin working on Dalton's feet. The asshole who trussed Dalton up didn't even tie proper knots, making it next to impossible to untie him, which was probably the point. If your objective is to beat a man as a diversion, it doesn't matter what kind of knot you use.

"Syn, peek out in the club and see if the riot is over and if the men in blue have swarmed our asses for a sixth time. Then find out where our security went."

Whitt picks up Dalton, cradling him to his chest, and the beaten man moans hollowly. I actually feel for the asshole. He didn't deserve this– no one does.

"I'll take him to my room and clean him up," Whitt says as he starts to walk away.

"No," Dalton moans in a panic, fingers curled into claws against Whitt's shirt.

"Put him down!" the Magic Eraser demands, his odd, glacial eyes glowing with fury. "Now."

"Who the fuck are you? That's an answer I want. Right now."

"I'm Gunner," GI Joe answers readily while the other guy ignores me, running over to Dalton's side. "And the guy checking out your young man is Wil. I'd suggest you let him do his job."

Gunner's eyes linger on all the fallen bodies around the floor, most taken out by Wil.

"Hey, buddy." Wil's entire badass demeanor changes to gentle examination. "Dalton, look at my eyes and relax. That's right, buddy. I've got you. Look at me."

Whitt is frozen in shock, holding a battered Dalton in his arms while a man who looks about as innocent as a serial killer is stroking Dalton's beaten face. Not that Wil looks like a thug. That's the problem. He looks like an everyday Joe, but the intensity wafting off of him is terrifying.

Dalton's sharp intake of breath has all our hearts faltering. Then he's struggling to get away from Whitt, clutching at this Wil character, trying to climb into his arms. "Shh... Buddy, you've got to go get patched up. I'm not going anywhere– I promise."

"I'll take him to my room," Whitt murmurs gently, trying to walk without jostling Dalton.

"Nooo..." the sound is long and mournful. "No."

"I'll go," Alex tries to take the struggling man from Whitt's arms.

"Just follow me. What's up with you?" Whitt accuses Alex as they walk away.

"Dalton doesn't like to be touched, is all. He trusts me, not you." Alex's voice fades as he follows behind Whitt. "You might hurt him on purpose."

"Cops are here," Toby calls from the door as he's letting Syn back into the dungeon.

"Toby, send a couple in here. We have some trash to collect."

"Where'd Dalton go?" I've never heard Syn sound so panicked. Her eyes take in Gunner and Wil, and then the woman behind them. She's asking them, not me.

But I answer her anyway. "Whitt's room," has Syn sprinting across the dungeon and down the hallway.

"You again." I point to Gunner, because he seems the most rational. "Who were the instigators? Who fought them off? And who was fighting with us when we arrived?"

Gunner quickly points everyone out and pulls them into groups.

"Everyone in the big group." I gesture to the majority. "These three ladies will escort you to the backdoor. Remember the damage they inflicted. In other words, don't fucking touch them and leave out the door they escort you through."

I wait until Monica, Kris, and Greta return from herding the cowards to the backdoor. I breathe a sigh of relief when they return unscathed.

Arms crossed over their chests, eyes downcast, Wil and Gunner are standing over five burly guys who look like hired thugs. From a glance, you wouldn't think those two men would be able to take them on. Neither of them are big guys– they're more unassuming than anything. Gunner is wearing jeans and a t-shirt and a pair of flip-flops, for shit's sake.

My eyes dart about, getting a headcount of my people. Queen had followed Whit and Alex with Dalton, and then Syn joined them. Leaving only Katya standing to the side, staring at everyone like she's puzzle-piecing exactly what I am.

Monica and Toby are standing guard at the door, waiting to let the police in. While Greta, Kris and Fate are communing with the woman who was with Wil and Gunner.

"Who's she?" I point at the fragile blonde who has to be in her forties. "Why do you keep bringing her with you?"

"Lynn?" Gunner's upward inflection makes it sound like a question.

Exasperated, "Is your name even Gunner?" I can't believe a word out of his mouth. If it wasn't for the fact that Dalton actually wanted to be with them, not taken from them, I'd think they were the ones who beat the shit out of our resident douchebag.

"Gunner." The man steps forward to shake my hand. "It's nice to finally meet you, Dexter. I picked up the name Gunner when I was fourteen in military school. On my eighteenth birthday, I left for basic training and became a member of the United States Marine Corps. I've been back on American soil for exactly three months."

"What are you doing here?"

"Me?" Gunner points at his chest. "Retired thanks to a roadside bombing and nearly a year of rehabilitation in Germany. Now I'm back, trying to clean up all the Boogieman's messes with my partner here–" he points at Wil. "His name really is Wil. Her name isn't Lynn, but it's part of her name."

"Again, what are you doing here?" I repeat, losing my patience. Out the corner of my eye, I catch Katya giving 'Lynn' a funny look while eyeing everyone near her.

"Cleaning up messes," Gunner says without hesitation. He steps in between Kat and Lynn, not allowing her to inspect the woman too closely.

"Dex?" Kat calls, voice warbling. "You've… what the fuck?"

"Sparky?" Gunner stops Kat. "Move over there by Dexter's people."

"There's no way… no goddamn way," Kat sputters as she makes her way over to Monica and Tobias. "Do you see what I see?"

"We see nothing," Toby and Monica say in unison, meaning they see too much and have adopted my survival instincts. Kat is too curious for her own good. I refuse to even look at Lynn now.

"Why are you taking over my people?" My voice holds no weight, because I know the three interlopers in our mix are Maître du Jeu– not the BDSM Lifestyle Authority bullshit. They are *my* boogeymen.

"The riots began with one of your own, so we came in to stop them but couldn't. Tonight, we noticed that someone else had taken the ball out of your court and was playing to win. Dalton wasn't a diversion. He was the target."

"Wh–"

"Don't ask why," Gunner stops me in my tracks. "I need you to understand the gravity of the situation you're under. Restraint is ground zero for many things, most having absolutely nothing to do with you. Pretend Restraint is a stop on a game board, and all the pieces are piled on one square."

Slumping against the rack, "What good does that do me?"

"Wil and I are truly here to help." Gunner points to himself and the other man. "We have more to lose than you do– loved ones who are near and dear to us. We've been here every night since I landed in Dominion. How about we do something to keep us all safe? Allow us to work for you for real. Until tonight, we were stuck in the club, unable to protect you in this half of the building. You can be in charge as long as you let us protect you in return."

My arms fold over my chest, feet spread. "What do you suggest?" When I realize I'm mirroring the way Wil is standing, I drop my arms to my sides and shuffle my feet.

"Private security," Gunner answers in a heartbeat. "Not the security firms who keep coming up with excuses to leave you unprotected. Eh– before you ask. No, that was not me. Someone saw the bullshit going on down here and decided it would be a great diversion to cover up what they were doing– that's all. I've got it under control."

Voice filled with attitude, paying more attention than she should. "Does Devlin Conrick think you've got it under control?" *Shut up, Kat.*

Gunner looks over his shoulder at Katya, chuckling underneath his breath. "I've known Ezra and Cort since we were little shits together, Sparky. They will not be adverse to me making sure you and your spawn are safe."

"Cort might," Wil mutters dryly, but I can tell the icy-eyed fucker is laughing on the inside. "Devlin is–"

"Devlin," Gunner finishes. "While I respect him, he's a fanatic when it comes to certain people, to the point he becomes blind. My job is to be impartial. If my own grandmother was being a little stinker, I'd have to stop her. Devlin would let his grandfather hurt us and say nothing."

"Seriously?" Wil's voice pitches high in anger. "Don't go there. Never go there."

"My suggestion, you all go on your merry way, like you saw nothing amiss in the dungeon tonight. Perhaps a few of you will check on Dalton's condition. Tomorrow morning, bright and early, you'll meet with me. Since you trust Roarke, you can bring him along since he has an untapped resource of trained ex-cops at his beck and call. We'll get a reliable security force."

"It's just a club," Katya says for me. "Let's just do what Regina said, and close this fucker down."

"Sparky?" Gunner turns to Kat.

"Quit calling me Sparky!" Kat's face twists up into a scowl. "Do we all get codenames, or some shit? Like Lynn?"

"Oh, you wouldn't like Lynn's codename very much." Gunner's chuckle is mirrored around the dungeon, and I realize most of my people are traitors. "It's not about Restraint. You can close it down, but the people who are attacking each other still exist. They are attacking the unsuspecting for shits and giggles. It just so happens you're all in Restraint, and they can hit you all at once."

"Motherfucking Ez," Kat snarls, getting to the heart of the matter.

"Yes, it would be helpful if your husband wasn't insane, attacking his friends when he throws temper tantrums, but we expect nothing less. Something else is going on."

"What do we do with these guys?" I kick one of the guys in the foot. The five thugs are conscious and listening to every word we say. But unlike me, they look as if they understand what's actually going on.

"Ms. Fate's attackers went free within hours of being in police custody, so we suggest you allow Wil and Lynn to take these fine gentleman with them, and not ask any questions later. I'll stick around here, making plans for upgrading your security."

A door down the hallway slams shut. Every head turns to see who is joining us. Syn comes into view, wiping blood from her hands onto a wet washcloth.

"Dalton's resting in his apartment. Alex and Devlin are making sure Whitt and Regina don't upset him too much. He's terrified one of you will hit him when he's most vulnerable."

"Pretty Boy would never do that," I jump to defend Whitt. "Never."

"I know that," Syn actually agrees with me for once. "But Dalton's trust was broken, and he hasn't exactly been nice to anyone but Alex."

"I could pray with him if he'd allow it." Toby steps forward, vibrating with the need to help.

"Dalton's... um..." Syn's eyes cut toward me. "Dalton's Jewish, Toby. But if you want to sit with him, he wouldn't be adverse to you. You're too nice to hurt him on purpose."

I realize what's going on, and I'm insulted. "I will not hurt him, even after what he did with Monica. What the fuck, Syn? Are you our mole?"

"What?" A miracle happens, Syn laughs for the first time in a decade. She wraps her arms around her waist and laughs like a loon, sounding like her old self. "Jesus Christ, Dex. Dalton has been with us for nearly four years. I thought I should get to know him, asshole or not. He converted to Judaism because of his little sister. He's about as devout as Marc."

"Unlike me," I mutter underneath my breath. "I'm trying really hard not to look too closely, but the only people in this room who don't know what's going on are me, Toby, Monica, and Kat. So that makes me question everything. Are one of you the mole? Generation Next?"

"Neither," Gunner and Wil answer in unison, and Wil continues. "Generation Next is only bothersome to the BDSM Lifestyle Authority, which is why Devlin is so tenacious right now. But we don't care– they're harmless."

"Marc really shouldn't have pissed them off last night." Syn actually smiles. I've never seen her so– normal. Odder still, we've been invaded and have prisoners seated on the floor. "They haven't learned the valuable lesson on how everyone is a hypocrite– it's so precious." She stalks over to one of the goons who attacked Dalton. "You!" she points, seething. "Are a dead motherfucker."

"Yes, he is," Wil says coldly. Then his eerie eyes flick in my direction. "This would be the man who tried to rape Fate. You put too much trust in your police system."

"Come." Syn issues one word, and Fate, Kris, Greta, and '*Lynn*' all move. "We're going for a ride."

"Up!" Wil kicks at the feet of the five men seated on the floor. "I suggest you listen to her– out of all of us, she's who you should be worried about. So if you want to see the sun rise, pay close attention. Walk down the corridor, and don't try to run once we hit the parking lot."

"Wil, don't offer them false hope," Syn mutters in a cold and calculated voice, causing Greta to release a sadistic laugh.

"What's going on?" I demand.

Suddenly bloodthirsty, "Justice," comes from sweet, submissive Fate. She's seething with fury.

Dumbfounded, all I can do is stare at their backs as the dungeon empties out. After a few moments, my head cocks to the side as I watch the door shut behind them, not knowing what they are going to do, and I probably shouldn't look to closely as my conscience couldn't bear it.

Unfreezing from against the door leading to the club, Katya's words break the silence. "Anyone else feel like we've been played? Did you get a good look at Lynn? Realistically, she has to be in her fifties. I want the number of her plastic surgeon."

"I'd say it's good genetics." Monica is next to defrost. "So expect half of our membership to age well."

"I know, right?" Kat's green eyes are glazed with wonder. "They have to know. How could they not look at each other and just *know*?"

"Codenames, Sparky," Monica teases. "The Whore was a dead-giveaway. I expect they are doing some Magic Erasing out of their van. We always joked that Syn was an assassin by trade. Anybody get a gander at Wil's eyes? Remind you of anyone else we just met?"

"Where'd GI Joe go?" Kat looks around, acting as if Gunner turned invisible.

"Gunner took the doorway leading to Dalton's apartment." Toby finally unthaws. "My observation... Since Gunner and Wil couldn't get into the dungeon '*to protect us*' from ourselves, they sent Greta in their stead, knowing Dex is a sucker for a damsel in distress."

"Good catch!" Kat beams with pride. "We make a good team. Like super-sleuths."

"Dexter should have just asked us for help with his quest to catch the mole," Monica adds in.

"There is no mole." Tobias is the smartest of all of us. "We're all the mole in our own right, never realizing it. Devlin is too focused on the BDSM Lifestyle Authority to notice Restraint's entire membership is leaking like a sieve. It's got to be like this everywhere."

"It doesn't even have to be someone from one of the clubs." Monica begins pacing around us in a circle. "It could just be a friend of a friend of a friend. Like the telephone game. Kat and I could be overheard in the park while eating lunch, and if the right person heard it–"

"Like when I talk to my brother about what I'm doing with my time," Toby adds. "We're not releasing anything major, but someone who wants to know now has a thread to work from. The rest of the dirt is easy enough to dig up."

"I don't care if there is a part two of The Mistress & Master of Restraint." Kat joins Monica's pacing. "All my dirty laundry has been aired. I agree with Generation Next. If some of us are exposed, then we all should be."

"Whoever Adelaide is working for is very biased, wishing to defame their enemies." Toby begins the walk and think routine. "I believe that is Generation Next's true purpose. Balance."

"Stop!" I meant to shout, but it comes out as a wheezy gasp. "No more. You're all right, and you know it. But to know too much means you might be taking a ride in that van," I remind them while issuing a very important warning. "Trust me when I say you don't want to be on their radar. They will enlist your help when you don't want to give it because they know your currency. So for sanity's sake, let's drop this conversation and get the fuck out of here."

"Ahhh– Dex," Kat whines, and Toby mimics her. "I was having fun."

"Go have fun at home– torture some sense into your husbands."

Chapter Twenty-Two

I'm a mere mortal. When a man wants to forget, we use sex. It's just a fact of life. "I'm starving for you, wife," comes gravelly deep as I pick Monica up by the back of her thighs and thrust her against our study wall.

Fresh from the shower, Monica's wearing tiny shorts and a tank top. I love seeing her in something so mundane. It goes against the grain. Most men want to see latex and leather that barely covers the flesh. I see plenty of that on a nightly basis. Innocent clothing covering all the fun bits is more exciting for me. It makes me want to slowly reveal what lies beneath.

"I ache for you." I pant breathlessly as I rotate my engorged bulge against the juncture of her thighs. The past hour has been torture as I've tried to keep my mind on the important things. But something I saw earlier in the night keeps replaying on repeat in my mind– the way Marc and Cort moved together. It brought up the sensation of taking Ezra from behind. I love my future wife, and I'm nothing if not a straight man. But the experience of bending a man to my will and impaling him was nothing short of orgasmic.

My cock has throbbed and released precum in amazing amounts for the last agonizing hour of my life as I waited for Monica to get out of the shower. I'm in need of a warm, wet hole, and pumping into my palm is not good enough. I've been looking forward to spending some quality time with my soon-to-be wife.

I'm going to fuck Monica raw.

"You're awfully aroused," Monica laughs in amazement. I'm usually more suave and less obvious than this when it comes to seduction.

"I saw Cort and Marcus making love tonight. Even if it was the highest form of adultery, and I shouldn't have watched, it has me insane with need." I hiss in pain as my cock starts to beat to a sound only it can hear.

"Oh, God," she moans. "I would've loved to have seen that."

"It was priceless. And I'm not even sure if they were fucking, or if it was the world's hottest make-out session. Either way, I'm on fire with need. I will not take no for an answer from you tonight."

"As if I've ever said no to you." Monica trills a delighted laugh again. The sound of her happiness pushes my arousal to astronomical proportions.

Monica squeals a girly sound when I pick her up, wrapping her arms around my neck and her legs around my waist. I carry her up the stairs to our bedroom, every step pressing my bulge against her warm pussy. Groaning with need, I drop Monica ass-first on our bed. I stifle a chuckle at the giddy expression on her face as she bounces on the mattress.

I lock our gazes and issue her a commanding stare. She immediately freezes, eyes glazed over with need and breath leaving her parted lips in quick puffs of air. I flash her a predatory smile filled with teeth that will soon be sinking into her flesh.

God, I'm addicted to the power we hold over one another– a perfect balance of want and need. My dick starts to spurt inside my pants just from the thought, dampness sticking to my skin. I'm going to tear Monica apart tonight if I'm not careful.

I grab Monica's ankle, and then yank until her purple-painted toes are near my mouth. I nibble each tiny piggy as she tries to pull her foot from my grasp. She giggles from the onslaught as I tickle her with my teeth. Writhing on our bed, her laughter fills my heart with joy. This moment isn't about fucking Monica, or even professing our love. It's about playing, being free during an unexpected moment, and the great joy it brings your soul.

I drag Monica until she is lying face-down in the center of the mattress. I rub her small body until she quiets beneath my hands. I can feel the trust radiating out from her body as if it's a tangible thing.

Leaning forward, I fasten a braided-wire cable covered in vinyl– one most people use for a dog-run –to the eyebolt that's hidden behind the headboard. I've cut the cable to sixteen inches in length and added a carabineer to each end for quick release. I snap the cable on the D ring that's soldered to Monica's collar near the clasp.

"Now you're leashed, my pet," I purr salaciously into Monica's ear. My cock jerks in my pants from the sight of Monica lying prone on the bed while tethered to the headboard. It's so fucking hot. "You love being on my leash, don't you, pet?" My hand lashes out to smack her ass. Hard.

A heavy moan gurgles up Monica's throat, one that warps into words. "Yes, Master. I would tie myself to you in every imaginable way possible."

"Good." Even to my own ears, I sound very pleased with her response. "From this moment on, I give you no permission to speak unless I ask a direct question. Feel free to scream until you're hoarse. I'd prefer you to scream '*husband*' every time you feel the need to expel your breath."

My hand snaps at Monica's ass again in a strike that has my palm stinging. The sadist in me gets off on the sound of her screams as her flesh reverberates against my palm. This is the secondary reason why I wish for Monica to gain a healthy amount of weight. I don't want to touch flesh-covered bones. I want softness that moves beneath me while we make love. I want to watch the jiggle come to rest just as I'm readying to strike again. I don't want to fear harming her because she's too fragile.

I hit Monica a few more times to get my cock pulsing from the gift of pain. "I love watching your ass move beneath my smack. Don't starve this body in hopes to please me, or to assuage strangers who don't know you. Nothing pleases me more than a healthy amount of flesh to strike."

I yank Monica's girly shorts down, baring her ass to my vision. Her cheeks are blooming a bright shade of pink from the whacks. A possessive growl rumbles up from my throat as I take in the outline of my fingers on her skin.

Dropping to the mattress on my belly, my teeth nip at the tender skin. Monica shrieks from the sensation, so I do it again and again. Then I lave the marks with the flat of my tongue in soothing circles until she starts to wiggle restlessly on the bed. My hand lashes out to strike to the back of her thighs, and she immediately stills her movements.

"Good girl," I utter with pride.

Changing position, I straddle Monica's thighs. Gripping her ass cheeks in each of my palms, I pull the globes apart until she's laid bare before me. I lean down to glide my tongue along the crevice of her parted ass cheeks, rolling my tongue across her pucker, leaving her damp with saliva.

Fretting, Monica pulls on her leash, and I fear she'll hurt her pretty throat. "Shh…" I murmur soothingly. "It's all right. Trust me,

Monica. There isn't a spot on your body that I don't love the taste, scent, or feel of– inside or out."

Continuing to lick until Monica calms beneath my touch, I find a rhythm that takes me from the entrance of her pussy to the tight bud of her ass. I spread her arousal up to the tight ring for later. With my tongue spearing her cunt, Monica's body vibrates beneath me, begging for more. I follow the action with a long lick to relax her, then I pierce the tight ring of her asshole with my tongue.

Both of us getting way into it, "AH!" she groans loudly as I tongue-fuck her ass, working her muscles, opening her, relaxing her for later.

"Seeing the men together reminded me of how amazing anal felt– not so much how snug and hot it is, but the sense of power and trust when your partner is at their most vulnerable." With one last slip of my tongue, I lick a wet line from her clit to her tailbone. "This is your warning. I will deflower this tight little bud tonight before we're through."

Leaning upright, my fingertips grip the thin fabric of her shorts and pull until they rip from her thighs. My dick throbs from the intense sensation of renting fabric against flesh.

Suddenly impatient, I lunge from the bed and begin tearing at my clothing with jerky movements. Breathless, I kick my jeans across the room.

Gripping Monica's ankles, I arrange her legs until her knees are pressed beneath her small breasts, leaving her fully exposed in the doggie-style position. My fingers skim from her shoulders down to her wrists. She allows me to move her as a puppet master would his marionette. Placing her hands on the top of the headboard, I press until she clenches her fingers on the wood for support. Then I move her leash to make sure she can't accidentally choke herself.

Reaching beneath the mattress, I retrieve the hidden restraints. A leather strap is pulled beneath the backs of her thighs and buckled around her back. Monica is resting on her knees with her fingers holding her upright against the headboard. I like to call this the upright fetal position. Monica can't move a muscle because her hands are keeping her from falling forward and the belt keeps her immobile. The collar and leash will result in pain if she moves against my will. She is my doll with her ass and pussy on display for my pleasure. The expanse of her back, ass, and thighs is for pain.

Chuckling in amazement, a splat of precum hits my thigh in anticipation, sliding south in a wet line.

Patience.

I retrieve a Wartenberg wheel from the shelf hidden behind the headboard. With practiced ease, I lightly roll along her back, stimulating and enlivening nerves that have been asleep. I steadily increase the pressure until the fine needle-like teeth start to bite into her skin.

Monica is such a pride to behold. She doesn't even squirm in fear that I'll stop. She whimpers as the wheel leaves red spots in its wake. Her body beads with sweat and she licks her lips repeatedly. I roll the wheel along the tender, already beaten globes of her ass. She jerks in reaction, nearly choking herself in the process.

I quickly check the tension on the cable and find it perfect to torment Monica— to keep her in the here and now, not inside her mind with her insecurities. I give a tug, just so I can experience the sound of her sharp intake of breath. Another splat of precum hits my thigh, screaming that it's time for some pleasure of my own.

Rubbing my slick head along Monica's snatch, I marvel as she tries to still her pleas. She's drenched for me. My thighs stick to the back of hers from our combined juices. My eyes roll back when my head makes contact with her erect clit. It's so engorged, I know I could suck it like a cockhead.

With a forceful thrust, I enter Monica to the hilt, her tight cunt resisting me. Her shrill scream of shock and pain increases the insistent throbbing in my dick. Stilling, I count to one hundred before I can so much as breathe.

Monica always makes me feel like a virgin entering a virgin pussy. She's so goddamned small, my huge cock can barely breach her. I always have to force my way in, the muscles finally relaxing just before the finale. There is no amount of preparation that can avoid this. I can either use my cock or a dong to open her. The second time of the night is always pain-free for Monica.

Instead of resting inside of her all night, I know it takes force to loosen Monica's muscles. Time and gentleness only delay and prolong her discomfort. Gripping her hips, I pound into her violently, cock bottoming out way before I'm deeply rooted.

With every thrust, Monica is slightly choked by the leash. *Pant… silence… wheeze… pant… silence…* music to my ears as I ruthlessly hammer into her from behind. She tries to rear backward, begging for more.

Bending backward, I reach for the cane I placed near my feet. Flowing like lava, the buildup of anticipation enters my veins. I have dreamt of this moment since I held the object in my palm— what would it be like to fuck while beating my lover?

The whip has always been the tool I utilized, but it's impossible to wield while entering more than your masochist's mind. When I fantasize, I always imagine how explosive the orgasm would be to combine sadism with sex, to be able to inflict my gift during the intense pleasure of fucking.

THWACK... TAP... THWACK... The cane snaps as it delivers its punishing blows in swift succession across Monica's upper back and shoulders. It comes so fast that she cannot scream for each hit, warping the sound into a continual moaning. I attack Monica's shoulders with the cane, all the while impaling her so deeply my cock meets the resistance of her cervix. Her screams are cut off on the upstroke by the pull on her collar— choker chain.

My entire body thrums with pressure as it builds beyond the amount that it can withstand. I keen from the intense ecstasy that fills my system. I pull from the warmth of Monica's cunt just a moment before I fall from the precipice of release.

With quick, deft movement, I snap the carabineer free from Monica's collar to unleash her from the cable. Pulling her upright, I draw her flush with me— Monica's back to my chest. Lips seeking and eager, I kiss the side of her neck.

Monica gasps in my arms, her body scorching hot against my flesh. The element of surprise is our favorite game we play. I slam Monica's hands on the headboard again before she completely catches her breath. Then I smack her ass just for the pleasure of hearing her whimper in pain.

My cock is screaming for release, and I won't last but a minute with what I'm about to do with Monica. But it will be better for her if I don't last too long.

With shaking hands, I slide our combined juices along Monica's slit with my cockhead. She buckles against the headboard, moaning my name. I squeeze my sack so tightly it would bring a lesser man to his knees. The pressure forces a large amount of precum from my head. The spurt clops to her asshole, right where I aimed it. Using the moisture as a lubricant, without any preamble, I sheath my cock deep within the intense, tight heat of her ass.

"HUSBAND!" echoes around the room, vibrating my eardrums, as Monica writhes in pain in front of me— her version of shouting uncle or safewording out. The force of her hands on the headboard clangs it against the wall with her struggles.

I breathe rapidly out my nostrils as I try to regain my control. Her tight channel throbs and clenches my cock, rolling my eyes backward in pleasure. Shivers of lightning strike up my spine, urging me to thrust forward, but my love for the woman I am harming keeps me stationary.

Monica moans and goes limp beneath me as the pain warps into a sick and twisted type of pleasure only a masochist would enjoy. Holding still, I cannot move from the force of her muscles contracting around my dick. My balls tighten to my body as seed races up the length of my cock. I breathe through the urgent need. I will not cum until I'm ready– I will enjoy Monica's tight ass for more than a single stroke.

My fingers link in the back of Monica's collar and twist until it's as tight around her neck as her ass is around my cock. Every throb I mirror with the collar. I gasp in pleasure as she gasps for oxygen. I loosen my grip when I feel the strength leave her body.

I lash Monica with three more hard thwacks with my cane. I use her struggles for friction instead of thrusting my cock forward. The more Monica struggles, the more pleasure infuses my body.

Palm sliding up the column of Monica's throat, fingers wrapping tightly, I lift her back to my chest again. I meld our upper bodies together while my breath rasps roughly in her ear. I press inside her to the hilt, and then still our movements.

With absolute control over all of my faculties, I slowly tighten my fingers against Monica's neck, exacting slight pressure. Her ass clenches repeatedly on my swollen cock. Using her contractions to milk my release, I tighten my fingers in increments until I inhibit all breath from flowing across her parted lips.

Monica groans from deep within her chest as she struggles to breathe. The laxness of her body flees as she fights to survive. Monica thrashing in involuntary jerks against my dick has my breath hitching in my throat.

Body beaded with sweat and goosebumps prickling at my flesh, the buildup is instantaneous. I had maintained a steady foothold at the precipice during our entire session until now. The pressure explodes in a monumental release. My pleasure erupts in a garbled rush   from   my   throat. Monica thrashes against my cock as she joins my release– her moans cushioned by the hold of my palm.

We're suspended in time as my seed shoots in fiery eruptions deep inside her ass. Shuddering together, we experience the longest and strongest climaxes of our lives.

All strength leaving my body, we fall lax onto the mattress. I curl around Monica's back, still connected deep inside her.

"Thank you, Dex," Monica wheezes roughly, tugging my arms around her chest to cuddle with her. "I needed that tonight– I always feel closest to you during and after."

I brush tendrils of hair away from Monica's forehead to gain access to the mirror of her eyes. Her big brown, glassy eyes glow back at me filled with love and satisfaction.

"It was my pleasure." I gasp, trying to regain my breath. "Wife, I want you to arrange our wedding. I'll give you two weeks. Everything is your decision right down to the time and place. You can ask anyone for help. The only thing I wish is for our union to be legally recognized by the state. I want everything else to be your dream. Will you do that for me?"

"Yes, I can't wait until you're my husband, Dexter. I will make you proud of me." She rubs her cheek against my palm.

"You don't need to do anything to make me proud, Monica. Just be you. We both need this for different reasons. Maybe if we tie ourselves together in every way possible, you'll believe I love you no matter what– I want a wife who is confident of her place in my life. No more insecurities." I kiss Monica softly on the temple, and then drift into oblivion.

Chapter Twenty-Three

"I cannot believe you're actually eating bacon." I tease Monica, and I'm rewarded with a toothy grin as she bites into a thick piece. "It's so *bad* for you. Naughty and decadent."

Ding-dong. Diinnnggg-dooonnngg

"Somebody worked up my appetite last night," she murmurs salaciously, and my cock yaps like a happy dog because she's flirting with me.

"If you eat all your breakfast, I'll work up your appetite for lunch," I flirt back.

"Why wait until lunch, Dex?" purrs from kiss-swollen lips. "We could feed from each other in the bedroom… or on the table." She runs her fingertips along the breakfast nook tabletop in invitation.

My jaw drops open and my eyes bulge from my skull at Monica's newfound forwardness. Blushing, Tobias laughs at the gobsmacked expression on my face.

"Are you flirting with me, Monica? Hmm? I believe you are." The three of us laugh together, while Minion yowls over someone invading her territory.

Ding-dong. Diinnnggg-dooonnngg

"Somebody's persistent this morning. Lay off on the doorbell." I grumble as I shuffle to the door, with Minion weaving around my ankles. "Jeez, it's Saturday. Ya shouldn't bother a man's family on the weekend."

"C'mere, Minion. You're an inside kitty now." With the alien cat tucked underneath my arm, I'm grinning as I fling the door open.

"Mr. Hayes, or is it Master Hayes?" a nasal voice beckons as a microphone is pushed directly into my face by a gossip reporter.

Bright lights flash everywhere, momentarily blinding me. I curse underneath my breath for not checking the door before I opened it. Worse yet, is that I'm only wearing a pair of pajama pants and nothing else. I'm also at half-mast while holding a hairless kitten.

"Leave," I hiss to the throng crowding my wraparound porch. A news van with a big satellite on top sits in my driveway, and twenty or so media hounds are scattered in my front lawn. I'm being recorded by audio and video, and several photographers are snapping still-shots of me and my property.

Minion's back arches underneath my armpit, hissing and scratching the air. "Even my cat wants you off our property. This is not public domain. You had to enter a gated community, then you had to enter my driveway gate, and now you're on my porch. You're doubly trespassing."

"Dexter Hayes, we have a few questions for you," a female reporter demands as she elbows her way to the front of the pack.

"No shit. I'm sure you do," I mutter sarcastically as I step back to shut my door in their faces. A heavy booted foot wedges my door by the hinge. It's not shutting until that foot moves. I growl at the burly fucker who dared to touch my home, but I can't touch him with the cameras on me. I won't feed into their need for sensational news.

"Mr. Hayes, what do you have to say about the allegations leveled against your family?" The microphone makes an annoying reappearance, inches from my nose.

I shift Minion until she's straddling my forearm, legs swinging freely, because her hind claws were finding traction with my ribcage. "What allegations?"

"Is it true that your cousin is engaged in an incestuous affair with his adopted son?" The microphone is shoved against my mouth and lights flash as the camera man goes nuts snapping photos.

"Total bullshit," I spit with disgust. "First of all, that allegation is unfounded, and completely untrue bullshit. Plus, I'm pretty sure it can't be incest if you use the term *adopted* in the same sentence." I roll my eyes at the ridiculousness. "Marcus and Ezra are both grown men in their thirties. Aside from the legal implications, how do you father someone only six years your junior? Just leave my property. My assistant has probably already called the police on you."

"As an agent for the US government, do you believe it is appropriate to engage in hedonistic acts at Restraint? Do you believe it's appropriate to live in a polygamist relationship?"

"I determine if you've broken tax laws and regulations. I'm not a paradigm of religion. To each their own. I'm not my cousin's keeper." I pass the struggling cat to Toby, who's standing just out of their line of sight. "Marcus isn't in a polygamist relationship, by the way. It's actually polyamorous. If you're going to accuse someone, get the vocabulary correct. That is his adoptive son, Ezra. I believe they prefer the term triad. As for what we do at Restraint, it's no one's business as long as no one gets hurt."

Please don't mention the five goons who probably weren't breathing when they left the van.

"We weren't speaking of Marcus Zeitler. We were referencing your relationship with Tobias Kline and Monica James. You are an agent of our government. I'm sure tax-paying Americans wouldn't like their finances in the hands of an individual who has no moral compass. Who is to say you don't commit extortion, or aren't bribable?"

No one. Truth: I'm an IRS agent solely because Maître du Jeu wished me to be.

"Wow…" I drawl, enraged and hiding it. "I don't even know why I'm answering this, or where this is coming from." I shake my head sadly, disgust written across my face. "I'm engaged to be married to Monica James. I mentor Tobias Kline, and he's my personal assistant. I see Tobias as a son, so your allegation sickens me. You're at my home, on my porch, recording me for the record while accusing me of polygamy, extortion, and bribery. Yet, you seem to forget who you're speaking with. I am Dexter Hayes, and I haven't needed to work since I was in the womb. I chose to make my own way instead of spending the money that rests in multiple bank accounts. I've never touched it with the exception of investments and charitable contributions. If the American people have an issue with my personal life, then it won't affect my future. But, in the end, they will lose an honest person who's on their side when it comes to the United States government bleeding them dry of their hard earned money. I'm an agent for the little people, against corporate America."

"You're part-owner of Restraint, is this correct?" I'm going to break the microphone if it's jabbed at me one more fucking time. Why do reporters punch you in the face with the mic when they ask a question, when their hand never moved since they asked the last. The tip of my nose is going to be bruised.

I flash them a *no shit* look. "Yes, of course. That is a matter of public record." I flinch backward, awaiting the next question while protecting my nose.

The mic brushes my cheekbone this time. "What do you say about the riots and violence that have erupted at your place of business? It has left many injured, and lawsuits are being filed."

I knock the microphone from my face. "Do they teach you that nasty trick in journalism school? Microphone fencing?" I cover my face with both hands, preparing for battle. "*En garde!* Gross. At least put on a fresh cover. Think of the germs from the last schmuck you stalked touching me."

"Mr. Hayes, answer the question," another reporter demands, but his mic stays at chest-level.

"Truthfully? I blame you!" I point to the crowd of paparazzi swarming my property. "This is the shit that brings everyone to Restraint. Instead of a clientele who's looking for a good time, we get people earning a rite of passage for hitting Restraint. We get people who want to catch a sighting of one of the infamous Masters of Restraint. We get women and men walking into our club who treat us like whores, thinking we don't have the right to say no after what has been publicized about us. We get undesirables who want five minutes of fame by pulling crap at the club. If you'd stop stalking our homes, businesses, and jobs, we could find some peace. Don't believe the rumors you hear, the gossip you read, or the shit you spread."

"Should we be worried about the Zeitler children at Shadow Haven Estates?" The microphone is jammed into my face so hard it taps my nose and chin.

Eyes watering from my nose being hit, while rubbing my bruised chin, I demand. "Kindly remove your foot from my door." I stare pointedly at the big man whose boot is wedging my door open.

The asshole gazes back at me with utter defiance, and I mentally scream out my frustrations. I try to project a calm aura and stare him down, but I'd forgotten why they're called news hounds. His job is to push and push someone until they break. He will never back down, foot never budging until I do something newsworthy.

"Are you aware there is another book coming out by Adelaide Whittenhower? Mistress & Master of Restraint: The Collapse?"

"How presumptuous of Ms. Whittenhower," I mutter dryly. "Add arrogant to the list if she believes her first novel will collapse the structure we've put into place at Restraint."

A deep sigh of relief flows from my chest when I spot a familiar black SUV pulling up my driveway. I don't even get angry when he drives through my yard, rutting up the grass. I smile when Roarke jumps out and charges the crowd.

"Crestview security notified the authorities when you failed to stop at the gate. The police will be here momentarily. I suggest you leave before they arrive." The ex-cop is a mountain of muscle with the brains to use them. "Although, I'm sure Mr. Hayes would love to arrest you for trespassing, defamation, and harassment. Whatever monies levied against you would do wonders down at Transcend."

The boot immediately disappears with Roarke's appearance. He charges into my house, shoving me out of the way. "Jesus," Roarke pants breathlessly while leaning against my front door, worried they'll break it down. "It's a goddamn shit-storm out there."

"Are your brothers in blue really coming here?" I arch a brow and point at my sofa. When he flops down to take a seat, I flick all the locks on my door and engage the security system.

"Nah– we're spread too thin." Toby offers Roarke a bottled water because the poor guy looks beat. "Thanks, bub."

While Roarke recharges for a moment, I settle onto my grandmother's settee. Monica comes in fully dressed, prepared for battle in her work clothes on a Saturday. Two minutes later, Toby is sporting khakis and a polo. They both mean business.

"What you see out there is nothing compared to what's happening at Edge and Restraint right now. An entire block in front of each building is cordoned off. But nothing is as bad as what's going down at Shadow Haven and Whittenhower Estates. When I drove down the driveway at home, I passed five satellite trucks from all the major media outlets. Pretty Boy called to inform Ez there were that many and more at Whittenhower Estates."

"Toby? Go get me my office clothes," I demand, knowing he'll do as I ask.

"Good call," Roarke sounds relieved we're not wilting under pressure. "Somehow they got Queen's true identity this time around."

"Jesus Christ," Monica mutters, sounding heartbroken. "Everything?"

"Every-fucking-thing. Regina's going mama bear on them. Everyone's stuck at Shadow Haven, when I just barely got out so I could help. Whitt and Niel are locked in nice and tight at Whittenhower Estate. I just left there after evacuating Regina, Alex, and the girls to a safe location. Regina's house isn't a mansion, but with all of them living together, they got as much paparazzi as the Estates. The house was completely surrounded."

"I cannot imagine how this must be killing Regina." I bury my head in my hands. "There must be more to this, because the reporters were asking me things that I'd never caught wind of being published anywhere."

"Yeah–" Roarke hesitates to answer me. "All of our identities are listed, along with our places of employment, our addresses and phone numbers. Sorry, Dexter, this shit just got real."

"I'm not leaving my house, Roarke." I gaze at the liquor cabinet in the corner of my parlor. Is ten a.m. too early for a scotch? Probably. "I assume that is what the others are doing, scrambling to find secure locations. I built this house– I'm not moving."

"Obviously Regina had no choice, being that she lived in a single-story ranch house. Syn lives in The Green Building, and no one in their right mind would ever enter Stanton Green's territory and live to tell the tale."

"Yes, entering Dominion's mafia kingpin's domicile would be moronic," I mutter wryly. "Ah!" So many things just clicked into place. I always knew Maître du Jeu was mafia-related. Syn practically shouted she was in on it last night. I'd never thought twice about Syn living in Stanton Green's building, forgetting only those in his organization lived there. "I'm an idiot."

"What? What are you thinking so hard about, Dex?" Roarke looks decidedly concerned for my mental health.

"Nothing– go on. What's happening?"

"Resident hopping, basically. Trying to keep ahead of the media. We got everyone out who had no defenses put into place. Whittenhower Estates is a fucking castle, for Christ's sake. It can withstand anything. But I worry about Shadow Haven in the long-run. We already know it's penetrable with Ray Hunter storming it not once, not twice, but four fucking times."

"What do we plan to do? What contingency plans are being put into place? Who's running the show?"

"Marcus and I were discussing private security. No more firms. Ironically, we lost our contract with the newest set of security last night– as you evidently found out when you were cleaning up the mess in the dungeon. We're looking into ex-military and cops. We need hardcore honest types who can't be bought."

"Do you know Gunner and Wil?" Roarke flinches the moment the words flow from my tongue, which is answer enough. "How long have you known them, and can we trust them to work with us on this?"

Refusing to look at me, Roarke stares at the ceiling while answering. "My entire life." At first I wonder if he's lying, then I realize he's feeling guilty for lying to me to begin with. "In this, you can trust them."

"How very vague," Monica deadpans, picking up everything I've failed to explain in the past four years. Monica and Katya would make a deadly team.

"Dexter, you're the one who didn't want to be brought into this. Sometimes it's easier to deal with the boogeymen you can see instead of allowing your ignorance to get you hurt. But this was a choice you made a very long time ago, and I'm trying to respect your wishes. I'm not lying to you; I'm abiding by *your* rules of engagement."

"Fair enough," I allow. "Just tell me whether or not I can trust Wil and Gunner."

"Do you trust Ezra? Aaron? Jamie? Me? Syn?" Roarke says cryptically. "You should and you shouldn't. If you hadn't demanded that we leave you out of it, you'd understand what was going on, and it would be a help to those who are trying their damnedest to keep us all safe– safe from those who think they're protecting us when they aren't safe from themselves."

"Why does it sound like you're describing Ezra, right there?" Monica mutters, but then she laughs at how cloak and dagger all this bullshit is.

"Ezra's obvious. But perhaps most people operate like him but don't realize it." Roarke says the most rational thing I've ever heard. "Human nature dictates that we be selfish, narcissistic assholes, who are blind to our own faults, and we'll deny it even when it's right in front of our faces. Right-fighters who believe our opinion is right for everyone, even when it's wrong."

"Now you're describing Syn," I grumble underneath my breath.

"Gunner and Wil are impartial. So they spend all their time protecting us from the very people who need to be protected from themselves, particularly Ezra most of the time. But it's not our favorite crazy this time around. Everyone in the organization is a special flavor of crazy, and it's exhausting just surviving it."

"Lovely," I mutter wryly just as my text message alert pings. "You just explained why I said fuck no when they wanted me to be in the know. Leave my ass out of it, but tell me enough to keep my flesh intact."

Reaching over to the coffee table, I snatch up my cellphone. After unlocking it, I read the message from Marcus.

All hands on deck: Midnight. Dungeon. Be there, or don't come back. —Master of the Universe.

I look up to see Roarke checking the same message. Toby is standing in the doorway with my clothing slung over his arm and phone in hand. Monica's staring blurrily down at her cellphone. I guess Marcus isn't messing around this time.

Chapter Twenty-Four

"Damn!" I clap and laugh as I enter the dungeon. The Zeitler sofas have been removed, but what's in their place is fan-fucking-tastic. A large section of the dungeon now has seating for the entire membership. Sofas, chairs, and furniture of every style and design are arranged in a mishmash. There are even large pillows on the floor to sit upon.

"Nice…" I drawl, thanking my cousin for the big dais that is situated in the middle of the dungeon. "Are we getting a stripper pole, too?" I tease.

"Maybe." Marc blushes from the praise. "If you ask nicely."

I watch Queen with curiosity. She's fluttering around, taping index cards to the seating. I recognize my name on a velvet settee. "Ah, you bought us personalized seating. How quaint." I huff a laugh. "Where's your throne?"

"Jackass." Marcus pushes against my shoulder. "Go sit!"

Our settee only has notecards with Dexter and Tobias. Monica gazes forlornly at the floor. No way in hell am I making my wife sit at my feet.

I'm about to pitch a fit when Queen stalks over and shoves Toby and me into our seats. Smirking, she tapes a notecard to my chest, and then walks away. I look down with a chuckle.

Place Monica here.

"Gitcha ass in my lap, wife," I command, more than happy to have Monica in my lap.

I laugh wholeheartedly when I spot a throne with Queen's name taped on it. Next to the throne is a small loveseat. Kristal and Fate chat while watching their housemate's antics with amused smiles. Another throne has the Whittenhower prince's photo taped to it. I guess Niel won't be joining us this evening. Either tonight will bring violence or sex, so the kid isn't invited.

Alex and Whitt sit on opposite ends of an overstuffed leather sofa. Giggling, Kristal runs over and sits between them, then she attacks her boyfriend's mouth with great fervor.

Queen stalks over, tsk-tsk-ing over her hard work being ignored. "Move it, chica. I know you can read." She taps Kris on the top of the head with a stack of notecards.

Kris sulks back to her loveseat, and her absence reveals whose seat she had taken– Dalton. Why in hell would Regina put Dalton between Whitt and Alex?

The mood is light as our membership slowly files in and takes their assigned seats. Queen has made sure that everyone is sitting with their nearest and dearest with amusing consequences.

The Zeitlers are cuddled up in a double-chaise, making it impossible for Cort to be a pouty spoiled brat. Syn sits in a leather chair, happily all by herself. Our newest member, Greta, has an office chair. Devlin's sitting on a stool, dunce hat near his feet. Aaron has both Kayla and Heidi giggling in delight from their futon mattress on the floor. Roarke, sitting in a rocking gaming chair, keeps scooting closer– predatory eyes roving over Heidi in interest. Roarke will be on that mattress come hell or high water before the night is through.

Our new guard dogs, Wil and Gunner, minus Lynn, are facing off from opposite walls, making sure we aren't up to no good.

"Attention members of Restraint." Marc's deep voice draws our attention. "The majority of us are accounted for and present. I kept our gathering small. With the climate of today's events, I thought it best not to invite those who aren't in the know."

Marcus hops onto the dais and turns in a circle, taking in his kingdom and his minions. He smiles at us, and then releases the Zeitler patented sigh.

"I was lying in my lover's bed this morning–" a buzz of activity radiates around the dungeon, none of us knowing Marc had a lover, at least I hadn't until yesterday, and Marc said it was a woman, not Cortez. "We were discussing how best to approach this situation, creating a battle plan. Ironically, I received a call from my family that Shadow Haven had been infiltrated with paparazzi.

"I hurried to dress so I could join them, only to find a slew of paparazzi circling the home I was in. I wanted to maim, kill, and then panic. Instead, a very intelligent female said we needed to find the good in this. So, this evening is about us, because Restraint will be closed until further notice."

A sharp gasp of surprise is pulled from my chest, following on the heels of that is fury. I believe in the decision, but I'm angry that I wasn't consulted, let alone told prior to the membership, being as

I'm an equal partner in Restraint. I'm not the only one expressing their displeasure. A wave of anger rolls through the dungeon.

"We're lacking adequate security. I'm working on it. It may be a day, a week, or a month, but it will be resolved. Tonight we're going back to our original roots. In the beginning, this dungeon was for our personal use. Dexter, Ezra, and I would sit in here and bullshit. I think it's time we do that again. We're going to play show and tell," Marcus announces, and you can hear that he will not take no for an answer– he never does.

"I'll start." With an evil grin, Marcus starts to strip off his clothing, and I instantly close my eyes. I don't want to watch that. Until the Mistress & Master of Restraint was released, he never came in here without total anonymity. None of us have seen Marc in the nude.

"Bastard," I curse under my breath, causing Monica to chuckle against my chest. I thought I got the muscles and he got the height. I was wrong. Marcus stands before us on the dais in his birthday suit. He's tall and built. I curse the genetic lottery that gave me the proverbial middle finger.

"This is my show." Marc struts around in a circle, wiggling his ass and flopping his thick wiener about– that image will forever be burned into my brain. "Now I'll tell… this is our opportunity to put rumors to rest. When you take your turn, you may say and do whatever you wish up here, but you will take a turn," Marcus stresses, a threat in his tone.

"Ezra is my adopted son, and I've loved him from the moment we met. No, Ezra is *not* my lover, nor is his wife. Yes, I do engage in sexual contact with Cortez on occasion. To me, it's no different than strapping a masochist down and whipping them to meet their needs. There is a reason we do it, and it's private. Obviously it's in bad form to touch your adopted son's husband. Tsk-tsk," he teases himself.

"The ridiculous nature of the baby rumor." Marc hangs his head, shaking it back and forth in disgust. "NO! I do plan on having children in the future, but I do believe my lover would cut my nuts off if I knocked up my daughter-in-law. This has been my show and tell. Who's next?" He stares us down, looking for a victim.

Monica crawls from my lap and stands. Marcus beams down at her, while I'm shocked senseless. She slowly makes her way to the stage, then Marc grabs her by the waist and places her on the dais.

"Hi, I'm Monica James." Voice quiet, she gives a little wave. "No need for me to strip since I'm sure you've seen the show countless times. My '*tell*' is that I'm not really a huge bitch. Honest. My dad was a hard-worker, but very bigoted against anyone with money, or anyone who wouldn't earn their own way. You know, the type who will bitch and moan about his tax dollars going to waste? He'd also see pretty girls walking down the street and call them worthless cunts who leech off their husbands because they popped out a kid."

Monica looks down in shame, closing her eyes. "Dad's words– not mine. If anyone praised me for being pretty, or cute, or beautiful, Dad would bite their head off. I wasn't allowed to have frilly things– no makeup, no nail polish, no stylish clothing that showed off a figure, or trips to the salon.

"I was educated, with a heavy emphasis on my intelligence, but forced to pay for my own schooling– even my private middle school and high school, I had to repay when I began at Edge Publishing. Not that that was necessarily a bad thing. From the outside looking in, to expect more from your daughter than being a pretty face was very progressive thinking for a plumber. But see–"

Monica reaches down and begins opening the buttons on her blouse. "I am a woman." She parts her shirt, showing off a lacy purple bra. "And I do like frilly, girly things. I want to feel beautiful. But from an early age, it was hammered into my skull that that was a horrible thing."

With deft fingers, not showing the slightest bit of nervousness, Monica buttons her shirt. "When people see me, they believe my anorexia is because I thought I was fat and needed to be thinner to be beautiful. But that couldn't be farther from the truth– I wouldn't eat so I could become invisible. I did it to remove my feminine curves because they made me feel worthless. I buried the longing need to have a husband and children because that meant I was a leech on the system.

"The joke's on Dad." Monica laughs without humor. "Because while he was trying to empower me as a woman, he was denigrating everything it meant to be one. While he was refusing to help me with any task no matter how big or small, saying I needed to be self-reliant, his lack of nurturing was forming a Monica who would have never been born. A Monica who has a submissive side simply because sometimes she doesn't want everything to be about self– there is nothing wrong with wanting a partner. You can feel beautiful *and* be smart. You can be married and have children, *and* work away from home or at home. You can nourish yourself and appreciate what grows."

I wear the hugest grin imaginable as Monica hops off the dais and ambles toward me. The dungeon has fallen silent, many surprised at how we perceive people, judging them for their outward appearances instead of who they truly are. Clutching Monica tightly to my chest, I whisper, "I'm so very proud of you," a billion times over in her ear while the rest of the members do their show and tell.

It takes me listening to ten different stories before I understand Marc's diabolical plan. He's using this as a way to release our sins and to tightly bond us together in our time of trial. But the underlying reason is so delicate that I almost missed it. He's testing us. Every member is telling their secrets. If those secrets are released, then one of us is the mole. Whoever holds back will be suspect. I have no doubt that Marcus already knows our deepest and darkest shames.

Catching the tail-end of Pretty Boy's confession... "I have a crush on one of you." Whitt snickers at us from the stage, then he winks and jumps down, trailing a taunting laugh as he swaggers back to his sofa.

Queen stands in the center of the stage, fingering the bottom of her t-shirt like she's going to pull it off, but then she narrows her eyes. "Nah-uh, you guys don't wanna see my shemale body. So I'm just going to lay my shit on the table.

"I'm Regina Regal, but one of you named me Queen when they were only six years old. I'm married to one of you. I'm not a lesbian. My best friend betrayed us all. I'm a mother. I grew up in a one-bedroom walkup and I never knew where my next meal was coming from. I spent my days at Hillbrook with the children of Dominion's one-percenters, and my nights sleeping with a baseball bat tucked to my chest for safety. I've knelt down before a drug dealer and prepared to suck his cock to pay for my mother's pain medication while she was dying of breast cancer.

"The dealer became one of my best friends when he pulled me to my feet and said I was worth more than that. I might not have sold my body that day, but I did shortly thereafter. I use a boy's term of endearment because the term mistress makes me want to vomit. I was a married man's mistress for over four years but not for money.

"I've earned every dollar I have, and I have more money than all of you combined. I donate more money in a week then some of you will make in a lifetime. I'm not bragging. It is what it is. I could earn a trillion dollars, and I'll still doubt my worth, because once you're a whore, you're always a whore...

"Excuse me." Regina murmurs politely with tears in her voice as she walks off to her private room. Alex runs after her, and I can tell each and every one of us is trying to figure out which person Alex is in Regina's list of realities. Is he her husband? Did he name her Queen? Is he the father of her children?

I know the answer to every one of Regina's questions because it was Rebekah Zeitler's money that paid for her fancy Hillbrook education. I also know the man who made Regina his mistress never saw her as a whore. He may have been married to another, but Regina was his wife.

Alex was Regina's dealer turned friend.

"I'm not taking my clothes off, asshole." Syn growls at Marcus, baring her teeth. "I like this better. Whitt and Queen started a trend. I will say truths but not really give the truth."

Syn laughs, and it's genuine and one of the most intoxicating sounds I've ever heard. I know most of my protégées secrets, but she is a very private human being. I know who she used to be, and her persona of Syn, but not who she truly is. Syn's personal life remains a mystery. I can't wait to see how she spins this.

"My given name isn't Syn. A long time ago I was a sweet, innocent girl with blonde hair and big blue eyes. I was the product of an affair– my daddy's dirty little secret." Syn's voice warps with a thick West Virginia accent. "I grew up in a trailer down in the hollers because the snooty bitch my daddy married couldn't stand the sight of me, and my own momma couldn't claim me.

"My sister is a submissive, and she's sitting in this dungeon right as we speak. The incredible woman who just fled to her room used to play Barbies with me when I'd come home to visit my daddy and sissy on holidays. Reggie was always Ken." Syn actually winks, and then shuts off her diction.

"Sorry, Kat and Monica, but I'm not an assassin by trade. I've saved far more lives than I've taken," she taunts, and I pray to God Syn's joking about killing people. "I became a paramedic because I watched the man you all call Alex get shot in the chest. I put all ninety pounds of my weight on his body, and I couldn't keep the blood from gushing out... that changed me.

"I'm a sadist– the daughter of a whore and a deceased, adulterous, white-collar criminal. He was a hated man in Dominion, a scam-artist looking for a big score. But he was still my daddy, who I love and miss every day when I wake up to realize he is truly dead and gone. Life goes on, and nothing will change the fact that I'm a daughter, a sister, an aunt, a mother, and a wife."

Member after member plays show and tell. No one holds back as we try to figure out if one of our people will betray our trust.

"I don't want to be here," Dalton announces to no one's great surprise. Short and small, covered in layers of drab brown clothing, I want to charge the stage and reveal the real Dalton. "I love and hate my true master in equal measure. I know why Marcus is making us spill our guts up here. I may be an asshole, but I'm not your leak." He glares at each and every one of us. "So, I'll tell you my ultimate secret to prove it. I murdered my grandfather and his partner-in-crime in cold blood, and I'm proud of myself."

"Wow," I breathe. Either Dalton doesn't care if that information gets leaked, or he knows it won't because he's the one doing the leakage.

"Since you guys are being depressing with your woe-is-me tales of poverty and death, I won't add to the angst." Ezra smirks at us. "How about I give you some romance? We all know how much I love my wife, but I thought you'd like to know how I feel about my husband." He points at the man in question, and then fists his hand over his heart. "Cort, this is an apology.

"When you're twelve, the world is huge and exciting. Every small gesture is epic. Cortez was crushing on this girl named Faith, and I was crushing on him. Long story short, he eventually got the girl, but I got my guy forever." Ezra blushes and casts his eyes downward to the floor.

"Aww," all of us croon to Ezra's embarrassment.

"It was the summer Cort and I turned thirteen. We were running through the woods, hunting and stalking invisible prey. We called our adventuring in the woods surrounding Shadow Haven *The Hunter*. It was hotter than hell that summer, and Cort was always running around in a pair of swim trunks and little else.

"During The Hunter, I found out how much I loved chasing my prey. I hid behind a tree, and when Cort ran by, I tripped him. I tackled his ass to the ground. It was innocent play, wrestling around, and I liked it way too much." Ezra's pale skin burns bright in the dark of the dungeon.

"I thought Cort would kick my ass, but his reaction was the same as mine, so I kissed him. I stole my very first kiss, and to my surprise, he kissed me back. It was sweet and innocent, and you only get one of those in your lifetime, and I couldn't have dreamed of a better person to share the experience with. We've ruined each other, time and time again since that day, but nothing will ever take that kiss away..."

We all gaze at Ezra with misty eyes as he struts back to his seat wearing a huge shit-eating grin on his face. I realize Ez just manipulated the whole lot of us, but it was directed at Cort.

When Ezra is within arm's reach, Cort tackles him to the chair and devours his lips. The temperature in the dungeon reaches molten lava on the hotter than hell scale.

What I witnessed between Marc and Cort in their private room last night pales in comparison to Ezra and Cortez when they are at their worst. I'm too terrified to contemplate what it would be like for the pair if they were at their best.

"No," Ezra declares in his Master Ez voice, then extracts himself from Cort's embrace.

"Please," Cort begs, crawling over Katya to get at Ezra. Kat decides she wants Roarke's evacuated gaming chair. "I want you right now, so badly I ache. I'll even let you fuck me."

"Jesus Christ." Marc and Katya gasp in shock, clearly taken aback.

Cort's ass has always been on lockdown as an exit-only. He's offering up virgin territory.

"Too bad," Ezra murmurs, but he's smirking like a crazy sonofabitch.

I laugh at the genius of Ezra's plan. Finally he's turning the tables on Cortez. If you can't catch your prey by stalking them, you lie in wait and then make them beg you to chase them again.

"I'll wear you down, Ezra." Cort vows, and then he tries to take Ezra's lips again.

Pushing Cort off him, Ezra struggles. "I have no doubt about that, Cortez. You made me beg for a decade. If you think I'll give you what you want the first time you ask, then you don't know me very well. Master Ez is pissed at you, so no matter how badly I want to make love to you, you have to earn it first."

Always one to contradict himself, contrary to his words of rejection, Ezra grabs Cort and kisses him fiercely. They nearly roll off the chaise in the heat of their mutual passion— groping hands, clenching fingertips, rutting hips. Ezra waits until Cort is begging and pleading, and then he pulls away with a smirk on his face.

While Cortez is dazed and confused, Ezra yanks Kat back on the chaise with them, situating her between them as a buffer.

In this moment, Monica and I can feel Katya's pain. Ezra's not rejecting her. But just like with his contradicting words and actions, I can see why Katya would be in pain. I had teased Monica last night about trading in the reward offer and fucking Kat. I hadn't meant it, no matter how badly I'd love to play with her. But in this instant, I decide to do it.

Ezra and Cortez need to learn they have a lot to lose. Katya is not their third-wheel but an integral part of their union.

Marc points at me and mouths, *"Last man standing,"* while Monica and I seem to come to a silent mutual agreement about Katya.

I quickly make my way to the dais, wanting to get this done and over with after Ezra and Cortez soured my mood, more so than Dalton's admission of murder and Syn and Regina's pain-filled tales of woe. "Well, I can't top that." I point to Ezra's smug face, Cort's flushed skin, and Katya's expression of immense pain.

"I'm an open book, so I obviously don't have anything to tell. You've all seen my bare ass and my hard cock. You've witnessed me in every sexual position imaginable, so I have nothing new to show.

"I will make a vow instead. I promise to find the person who has betrayed our trust. It won't solve all of our problems. But if our secrets are secure, then so are we. I care for each and every single one of you, and I hope and pray to God that you're not betraying us. It would break my heart to lose one of you– even Dalton," I joke, making the man blush. "I mean it. May our bond be strong enough to take the impact of the shit-storm– the members of Restraint may bend, but we will never break."

Chapter Twenty-Five

Generation Next
Your BDSM Lifestyle Authority Insider

We, at Generation Next, strive to bring you the juiciest information possible. We have scanned the world looking for the most high-profile masters in the BDSM Lifestyle Authority. We adore the masters who own their lifestyle and do not hide behind their money, influence, and power. We hold high-esteem for the below-mentioned master. Someday, we hope to meet this inspiring woman.

Master Olivia Fontaine

*Master Fontaine's grandmother was the originator of the BDSM Lifestyle Authority. Her family began with a single bordello simply known as **KINK** in Las Vegas, Nevada. Their members-only club spread in popularity across the world, because participants in the lifestyle didn't want to hide in their basements any longer. They created the system of training that we still use today.*

*Master Fontaine, while a woman, refuses the term Domme or Mistress. She simply is referred to as **Master**. Do not call her by any other name, including her given name, unless you want her wrath to fall upon you. Master resides in Las Vegas, Nevada, with her seventeen-year-old daughter. Master retired as the head of the BDSM Lifestyle Authority one month ago when she named Devlin Conrick as her successor. He was promptly sent to babysit the fine Masters of Restraint.*

Generation Next contacted Olivia Fontaine via a telephone call. Generation Next enjoyed the lovely French accent she possessed, but we were promptly hung up on. No worries– we were not offended. We called back a few hours later, requesting a word with Master Fontaine's daughter. She was a joy to speak with, and offered up a fount of information.

Spyder– no last name. When asked why she had no surname, Miss Spyder replied with the following. "By my mother's account, it was Immaculate Conception. My mother refuses to say who my father is. So until I know who he is, I will not take a last name. Please call me Spy."

We are more than happy to call Spyder, Spy. We asked for more information on her father, more than happy to offer our considerable research abilities, because Generation Next is nothing if not thorough.

According to Miss Spy, her father was a trainee of her mother's, and that's all she was told.

Spy describes her mother with the term Vampy Kitten. She says that the woman never ages, that her fifty-two-year-old body resembles that of a woman in her late twenties or early thirties.

We were mystified by the agelessness of Master, so Spy immediately sent us a picture of mother and daughter. The picture was taken outside of the KINK club in Las Vegas. Spy was correct. Olivia Fontaine is stunning. At almost six feet in height and extremely curvaceous, we understood the vampire reference. Master Fontaine doesn't age, her skin is as pale as paper, her black tresses fall in thick waves to her waist, and her luscious lips are an unnatural shade of crimson. The emerald green eyes blazing from the image are captivating. She must stun her submissives with her gaze.

We asked Spy for permission to print her attributes since she is a minor. Spy is several inches shorter than her mother. She has the same pale skin, vibrant lips, and captivating eyes. Her inky black hair falls in impossible ringlets to her waist. But the resemblance between mother and daughter stops there. Spyder's unknown father's features are prominent on the young woman's face.

Our breath was taken when we studied the image. We informed Spy, how she does, in fact, have a father, and we know who he is. We did the research and can back up our guess with facts. I offered Spyder– surname not revealed –to join us at Generation Next. We would love to have her, and we feel a deep connection with her and wish to further explore our bond.

We sign off as usual…
Adelaide Whittenhower, may you rot in Hell!

Please visit www.generationnext.com for subscription details.

May dominance and submission feed your needs. Happy controlling and kneeling, boys and girls.

I wait in my private room at Restraint, reading the newest copy of Generation Next. It's no longer a weekly publication. Several times a day, information is released on masters and submissives across the country. Whoever the publishers are, they're respectful of members who embrace the lifestyle and attack those who hide. Today's posting is evident at how far-reaching the tendrils of Generation Next's information gathering extends.

The postings are gathered on a weekly basis and printed into a brochure-style pamphlet. Subscribers receive the publication every Saturday morning. I hold the impressive copy in my hand. The Fontaine story wasn't sent out during the blog blasts. I was surprised to see it on the cover, along with a blown-up, cropped photo of Olivia Fontaine.

Yes, stunning doesn't even begin to describe Olivia Fontaine. I can't believe Marcus and Devlin trained beneath this woman. She scares the hell out of me in the picture. Her force must be suffocating in person.

What's going to bring the Devil down on us is the new addition to the back of the pamphlet.

Waters-Edge Publishing ;)

This implicates both Katya and the entire Zeitler family. And what the fuck is up with the winking smiley face? I get that we're the mice to their cat, but I'm sick of being toyed with. We're not the ones who are printing this, and yet we're going to be executed for it.

I'm using my annoyance over Generation Next and the mole to avoid the butterflies tearing up my guts. I was ushered into my private room to await further instructions.

Monica's two weeks are up, and our wedding is happening somewhere outside this door. I was told to dress as per usual. I'm in my favorite leathers and a new t-shirt. **Submit** is scrawled across the front in muted black letters against the gray fabric.

"Cold feet?" a smooth voice flows from the open doorway.

"Nah– I can't wait to marry Monica." I reassure my best man. "I have no doubts. We were meant for each other."

"How is Monica fairing with her self-esteem issues?" Marcus asks as he sits atop a desk in the front row.

"Good, actually. I think that the stamp of ownership a marriage provides is reassurance enough that I love Monica no matter what. She no longer tests my motives." Shifting in my chair, I drop my feet from atop my desk. "How's your family life?"

I cock an eyebrow at Marc when he winces. "I can see the newest edition of Generation Next you're hiding in your lap, Dex."

If Marc is going to be candid... "Are you gay?"

"What?" Marcus sputters, completely taken aback by my question. "God, no. Why?"

"Why? You're really going to ask that? After what I witnessed in the Zeitler private room, then that bullshit Ez and Cort pulled during our dungeon bonding time... Seriously?"

"You're taking my measure?" Marcus breathes in a cold voice, nearly seething. "Today of all days?"

"I feel as if I don't even know you anymore, Marc. You were supposed to be the closest person to me, yet somehow our bond has broken."

"Don't!" Marc orders, voice heated with emotion. "Don't!"

Furious, I whip Generation Next across my desk, smacking him right in the face. "I'm not a fucking idiot. I figured out who your lover is, not counting the emotional and physical affair with Cort you're calling cathartic addiction. That's going to blow up in your face, destroying a marriage and your relationship with your *lover*. The only people who will be left standing are Cort and Ez, just as usual."

"Well, I'm glad that's out in the open," Marc mutters wryly. "It's amazing how being honest feels so... spectacularly *horrific*. Maybe I didn't want you to know these things because I wanted you to still love and respect me as a brother."

"I always will, flaws and sins and betrayals and lies," I vow. I reach forward, just so I can snatch Generation Next out of his hands. Only to whip it back at Marc's face like an accusation. "Spyder's your daughter."

"Olivia's not my lover," Marc spews immediately.

"I know *that*," I snarl. "I'm not a fucking moron. You named her after Grandfather's car. Spyder Zeitler is your daughter."

"Since that dang publication arrived two hours ago, I've been walking around waiting to be tarred and feathered, ya know?" Marcus gives up all pretenses of keeping his shit together, and comes around my desk to practically sit on my lap, begging for comfort I'm not ready to give.

"Spyder has always had my last name," Marc admits, bleeding shame. "It's on her birth certificate, as am I. Olivia is a cunt of the highest order– controlling, egomaniacal, and sociopathic. She's the type who eats the father after conception, and then eats any young who won't worship at her feet."

"A match made in heaven– you and Olivia. Half of her DNA is inside your daughter." I remind Marc just to be an asshole.

"It's not exactly an ideal situation." Marc creeps closer to me, begging me to touch him. "The conception wasn't exactly consensual." Leaning forward, he hides his face against my shoulder. "Not at all consensual on my part," he whispers against my neck.

"Jesus Christ," I cry, hands reaching to hold him. Marcus folds around me, nearly sliding into my lap. Quivering with stifled emotions, he uses me for support.

"I love my daughter, though. I gave her our name, and I made sure her big brother taught her the faith. Then later, since I couldn't care for Spyder, I took care of her brother when his mother tried to consume her young."

I pull away, annoyed yet again with Marcus. Unrepentant amber eyes gaze back at me. "Are you telling me Olivia's kid is running around Restraint somewhere? The kid she excommunicated from her BDSM cult in Las Vegas? And you're just now informing me?"

"You don't like answers," Marc reminds me. "So you don't ask questions… so I assume you don't want to know these things."

I try to push my cousin off me, but he tightens his hold. "Because of my delicate sensibilities?"

"Exactly. You're an ostrich with his head in the sand." I can hear the smile in Marc's voice as he squeezes me tightly. Finally he unlatches his arms from around me, and slides to sit on the top of my desk. "You can't be mad at me. Everyone is always mad at me, making me jump through hoops to please them. You're my constant. You'll never judge me for being who I am, so don't start now."

"I can't judge someone I don't know," I stress, betrayal lacing my tone. "You've got to realize there is nothing you could possibly do to make me push you from my life— you're acting like Monica was."

"I'm going to pretend you didn't just compare me to a woman— a submissive woman. The woman you're about to marry." Marc flashes me a smarmy grin. "I'm all for incest— but only as a spectator."

"Eww…" I grimace, and then issue a warning. "I want to meet my cousin."

"Good luck," Marc breathes, sounding hopeless. "Spyder's in Dominion, hiding out in The Edge Building, of all places. Olivia, Spyder, Bianca— Olivia's daughter-in-law. You met her at the meeting. Sweet, little brunette, otherwise known as the Ballerina Mafia Princess. Plus a male and three female submissives named Darcy, Di, Sandy, and Sebastian. The entire Las Vegas contingent arrived when Devlin did. I keep trying to get to my daughter, but Olivia anticipates my moves. I'm going to have our naughty Generation Next lure Spyder out for me."

With Marcus leaning heavily on my shoulder, "Tell me who GN is," I demand. With force, I push a clingy Marc off me.

"Nah—" Marc smiles blindingly with tears of mirth glistening in his eyes. "The reveal is too precious to ruin. You've got to figure this one out on your own."

"I've figured all of it out on my own. Would it kill you to be forthcoming for once?" I shout, flabbergasted.

"Nope, Generation Next has been spoon-feeding you this whole time." Marc is about as smug as smug can get. Still emotionally raw, he pulls me into a strong embrace and holds me for a few minutes. "I'm proud to call you family," he whispers against my forehead before he kisses it gently.

"Good God, what is up with you today?" Shuddering, I pry myself away from Marc and slip out of my chair. "All octopus arms."

"You know I cling to you when I'm scared, or I go find Jamie and use him as my teddy bear." Marc finally allows me to see how spooked he truly is. Older by almost a year, when we were kids,

Marc would run to me when he was scared. He'd climb into bed with me because I'd keep him safe. I've been doing that my entire life, even after he grew taller than me.

"What am I missing? Other than how anyone with a brain will put two and two together to equal you being Spy's dad?"

"Just wait until you see who's officiating your wedding." This time it's a whole body shudder, and the need to protect him doubles my heart rate. "Let's go get you hitched." Marcus pounds me in the center of my back with his clenched fist, barely keeping his shit together. We share a mutual strained laugh as we head down the hallway into Restraint's main dungeon.

Chapter Twenty-Six

With Marcus at my side, I slowly walk down the long corridor. Instinctively, I know our wedding will be performed in the center of the dungeon, on that dais Marc had constructed for unknown, now known, reasons.

If I didn't know Monica better, I'd think she made the preparations with just me in mind. But I do know her better. She sees our union taking place in the location we met as the ultimate conclusion. I agree; the dungeon is the perfect location for our wedding. Knowing that all of this was her idea, her decision, knowing I was in the front of her mind while she made her choices, it gives me hope for our future longevity.

Monica is submissive, but she only wishes to relinquish control on certain things. I want her to be in control of her own life, to make her own decisions. I will step in at a moment's notice if she begins to self-sabotage. But, overall, I want a strong, independent woman to be my wife and the mother of my children. She can bend to my will in the bedroom and dungeon, but I expect her to flex that will back at me in all other arenas.

I exit the hallway and breath ceases to pass my lips. A circle of our people are at the dais, centering on my bride, hiding her from sight. All of the Masters of Restraint, including Devlin Conrick, and our trainees are wearing initiation robes, with the submissives loosely arced completely in the nude. The black hooded cowls cover every inch of our masters, and I can only tell them apart by their stances and body structures.

Marcus hands me my cowl, and then puts his on while I struggle into my own. Preparing myself, I hold my cousin's familiar gaze, so similar to my own, as we lower our hoods over our heads. I catch a sly smirk stretch his lips before all access to his face is cut off. The hoods represent silence– we aren't allowed to speak once they're in place.

Marc's delicate fingers wrap around my wrist, and then he escorts me through the parting crowd until I am toe-to-knee with my submissive Monica.

My breath puffs from my chest in violent bursts as I lay eyes on Monica for the first time since yesterday afternoon, keeping with marital traditions of not seeing the bride. She's kneeling on the floor, naked as the day she was born. She isn't in the submissive kneeling position. No, she's abasing herself on the floor at my feet.

Deep brown eyes rolling up to connect with mine, her pink tongue flashes out to lick a swath across my foot from toe to heel in a long, wet line. It takes all of my control not to moan at the intense contact.

With practiced movements, Monica slowly resumes her kneeling position, and I'm hit with a flash of pride so strong I nearly fall to my knees. Monica is giving herself to me with no reservations in front of a large crowd. Her issues have no hold inside her soul any longer.

A tug on my fingers draws my attention away from my bride. I glance down to see Marcus handing me a leather strap. I follow the leather until it reaches the back of Monica's neck. It's attached to her platinum collar– a leash. Monica wants to fasten herself to me in every way imaginable at our union. I smile down at my bride with a combination of pride and amusement. In return, the seriousness of Monica's expression is frozen in place, but the shine in her eyes is giving away her joy.

A presence makes itself known, causing Marcus to stiffen beside me. My eyes flick away from Monica to land on Olivia Fontaine. Cowl covering everything but the tips of her toes and her fingertips, I instinctively know who is officiating our union.

"We are Maître du Jeu. Members of the BDSM Lifestyle Authority through KINK and Restraint. Today, we stand as a family as we witness the union of two of our own." The beautiful dulcet tones echo around the dungeon– the acoustics of the large room are perfect for the French accent of the woman officiating our service. "Submissive Monica Penelope James, please articulate your vows to Master Dexter Marcus Zeitler-Hayes," the sultry voice commands.

"Yes, Master," Monica begins, but I cannot abide by her kneeling at my feet when I expect her to be my equal in our marriage. I pull Monica's leash, until her eyes are nearly level with mine. Flexing my fingers around the leather strap, I will never relinquish Monica's leash to anyone but herself.

With a voice filled with surety, "Dexter, I will be proud to call you my husband from this day forth. I give my thanks to the higher power who led you into my life. You complete and fulfill my life and soul. Our connection is far stronger than any marriage vow could ever represent. I give myself wholly and completely unto you. My trust in you is infallible, and I promise to obey you on this trust alone. I will respect you unconditionally. I will remain by your side in sickness and health, for richer or poorer, until death do us part. I promise that every day will be more fulfilling than the last as we meet each other's needs completely." Monica's eyes fill with tears as she professes her vows to me. I wipe a few with the tip of my thumb and receive a feminine chuckle from my cousin's boogeyman.

"Master Dexter Marcus Zeitler-Hayes, please articulate your vows to submissive Monica Penelope James," the French accented voice commands me out of my haze.

"Monica, I will be proud to call you my wife from this day forth. With the trust you place in me, believe me when I say the ultimate truth– you are an intelligent, beautiful, amazing, entertaining, competent woman. Know this deep within your soul and do not fall back on past crutches you no longer need to use to survive. I will hold you up when you fall. When life becomes too complicated, all you need to do is come to me and I will take the weight off your shoulders. I promise to take care of your body, mind, and spirit as if it were my own. I want nothing more than your happiness, for your happiness is mine.

"We are deeply connected in a way where nothing can come between us. I promise to respect, honor, and cherish you every day for the rest of my life. I promise to stand by your side in sickness and health, because I will do everything within my power to heal you by making sure you are well-fed. I promise to stand by your side for richer or poorer until death do us part. I will do everything in my power to provide all that we need to survive. You and I will be shoulder-to-shoulder as we fight for what is ours. We are a team, a partnership in all things, until I exercise my right to veto power. I promise that I will not abuse my rights, but know that when I do, it is for your own wellbeing." The vehemence of my vows rolls through the dungeon with the righteousness that I speak.

The silence is deafening until everyone in the dungeon takes a collective breath, and then movement returns to our guests as we wait. Since I have no idea what comes next, it's as exciting for me as it is for them. Adrenaline courses through my veins, flooding my muscles with anticipation until I begin to shiver.

"Now for the rings," the feminine voice is filled with emotions I cannot fathom. I hear a few sniffles from beneath the hood of her cowl, proving no matter how formidable the woman may be, she's still a human being, no matter if Marcus believes Olivia to be the Devil incarnate.

The rickety sound hitting my ears first, a familiar rolling table is placed to the left of me. I smirk, knowing yet fearing what comes next.

"Master Daniel Whittenhower II, please join us," Olivia demands.

With smooth movements, Whitt leaves his section of the circle. I would recognize his lanky frame anywhere, that and the aura of kindness and playfulness that always accompanies him.

"Master," Whitt utters with reverence, bowing deeply.

"Young Master Daniel would like to offer you his services as a gift for your marriage," Olivia explains. "Your wife thought it best to immortalize your union with ink instead of a removable band of metal. I believe she is so smitten with you, Dexter, that she would tattoo her throat in a living collar in homage to you. I don't think that is a wise decision since she's a professional woman. But we all agreed on tattooing wedding bands on your ring fingers. Is this acceptable to you, Master Dexter?"

"Master, yes." I can't help the grin that splits my face. I've been trying my damnedest to reassure Monica all this time, not realizing I needed some reassurance myself. "I love the idea. Thank you, Master," I say with equal reverence as I bow before her.

Olivia lightly laughs at my adoration, no doubt the Maître du Jeu culprit who first began using Marcus against me as a way to make me pliant to their suggestions. On the precipice of distrust and begrudging respect, I watch as Olivia curls her finger around Monica's wrist, and then she places Monica's hand on the table. With deft movements, Olivia straps my wife securely for Whitt's ministrations.

I watch in fascination as Whitt exhibits his true talent. The ignored heir to the Whittenhower kingdom is an artist. The eldest Daniel doesn't allow Whitt to engage in his passions with the exception of dominance. Whitt and Niel have bonded closely as they try to survive their family's machinations, both being told what to do at the expense of being their true selves. Unable to see Whitt's pretty face, I can feel the joy radiate off of him as he tattoos my wife's finger.

For Whitt, tattooing is like inflicting pain is for me– a gift.

Strong and determined, Monica wipes away the perspiration beading above her upper lip with shaky fingertips. She doesn't even whimper as the needle repeatedly grinds into her flesh. Whitt's steady hand slowly scrolls letters around Monica's finger– *DEXTER*.

Monica is branded as mine, my ownership screaming from her ring finger. My chest puffs up as it fills with pride. Inside my psyche, my inner caveman pounds his fists against his ribcage in victory.

It felt like it was only seconds in time, then it's my turn. In reality, it was nearly an hour. My eyes dart to the masters while I'm tattooed. I look to see if they have any discomfort for standing as long as they have. They remain motionless with their heads slightly bowed hidden beneath their hoods. Beyond them, the rest of the membership has turned around, facing the outside walls, their naked backs and rears on display.

MONICA is artistically scrolled around my ring finger. The letters are in the same calligraphy style as our *M* tattoo– the tattoo hidden in the webbing of our thumb and forefinger signifying our Master of Restraint status. In actuality, the M stands for Maître du Jeu, with our masters believing it's for Master or Marcus. If I were a curious sort, I'd go around grabbing everyone's hands to see if they have the answers I seek.

I wonder how Greta will cover up the fact that she already has a tattoo if she follows through with the training program long enough to reach master-status?

Relieved, I release a shuddering breath when the tattoo is complete and I'm unstrapped from the table. The pain is no issue– I don't enjoy being restrained, even if I trust those who are binding me.

I want to verbally thank Whitt, but it isn't allowed while we wear the cowls. Instead, I reach over to pat his back in thanks. I can feel the tension flee his body as I show my appreciation. I knew that he would worry about whether or not our tattoos pleased me. The young man is more like his father than he realizes.

The table is rolled away by an unknown person. I try to read their movements, but I can't. The person is smaller in both frame and stature. I notice the bright pink toenails peeking from the black fabric. I smile when I realize this must be Spyder or the daughter-in-law, Bianca. I elbow Marcus, trying to gain his attention, and he nudges me back in kind, followed by two taps to my wrist.

Marc's *no* is clear enough, said in the language we adopted when we were forced to suffer through charity functions as children. When silence isn't an issue, we'd just speak Hebrew– a neat trick despised by Hillbrook Academy's nuns.

Olivia regains her position at the head of the circle, next to an extremely tall person on her right– Devlin. The girl with the pink toenails stands next to Devlin, perfectly at ease. Marcus had listed off several submissives, but they wouldn't be allowed to wear cowls, probably relegated to the mass of naked spectators. I would hope Marcus would recognize his own daughter, so this must be Olivia's daughter-in-law, Bianca. So who the hell is the son?

All thought flees my mind as Monica comes to stand nose-to-nose with me. She's so close, only she can see my face from the depths of my cowl. I'm overcome with the need to take my wife to the floor and fuck her like a wild animal. I want to show everyone how Monica is mine and I can take her anywhere and anyway I please.

Monica's saucy smirk informs me how I'm being obvious with my hedonistic thoughts. I'm glad the cowl hides my raging erection and is obscuring the very private thoughts scrolling across my facial expression.

"*I want you,*" I mouth at Monica. Blushing, delighted, she laughs into the back of her hand. I tug her leash– hard –wrapping the thin leather around my fist until it's only a few inches in length.

"I don't think the groom can wait much longer." Sarcastic and a bit evil, Olivia laughs, finding me amusing for some unknown reason. "Master Dexter, please kiss your bride." She gestures to me, but I move toward Monica so fast I almost miss it.

Gripping the leash in my hand, I yank until Monica's mouth reaches mine. I bite her bottom lip viciously, enough so that she squeals as my teeth sink into her flesh. I devour her mouth, and take her along for the ride. Controlling the kiss, I lead my wife, and she follows, as we dance our mouths, lips, and tongues– teeth –in a searing kiss that completes the bond of our union.

My hand smooths down Monica's bare back until I grip her tight ass in my palm. Dipping inside, she's such a tiny thing that my fingers reach all the way to her slit. I part both sets of her lips– one set with my tongue and the other with my fingertips, both equally wet. Monica moans loudly into my mouth as I eat the song of her pleasure. Her chest and mine presses and retreats as our labored breathing and rapid heartbeats compete with one another.

Reaching down, I grab the backs of Monica's thighs and lift until she wraps her legs around my hips. I need her with a single-mindedness that borders on insanity.

"Hold on, wife," I raggedly breathe to her. Wrenching the cowl out from between us, I say a little prayer in thanks that I wore my favorite leathers. The pull-away snaps open with a subtle grip of my fingertips, releasing my cock.

Pulling lightly in a downward motion, the leash is clasped to the back of Monica's collar, making it the perfect position to arch her spine with a small tug. The arching of her back affords me access to her drenched pussy. With deft, practiced movements, I slip my cock between the folds of Monica's sex, and then thrust violently. Not deep enough, I yank the leash harder, lifting her hips, impaling me to the root inside my wife.

"Husband!" screams out Monica's mouth, just as I taught her weeks ago. Every pleasure and pain I afford her is released with my name– husband.

Never being an exhibitionist before, I take Monica for the first time as my wife while surrounded by members of Maître du Jeu. The instinctive urge to mark my territory overrode my need for privacy.

Standing on the dais, gripping Monica's hips, forcing her to ride my cock, my release builds to astronomical proportions. I murmur for only her ears to hear, "You always make me feel like a twelve-year-old boy during his first wank."

Laughing with me, the sound coming out as a labored pant, "Is that a bad thing?"

"Hell, no. It's a great thing." I tug the leash downward, arching Monica's back, forcing her to take me deeper. Running my lips along the column of her neck, I place whispered kisses. "I will feel forever young with you, even when we're old and gray." Vowing, "I will make love to you until my very last breath."

We embrace tightly, with Monica locked to the front of my body– her legs wrapped around my hips, heels digging into my ass, and her arms around my neck, fingers biting into my shoulders. We kiss slowly with our eyes locked open. I don't thrust, and she barely wiggles on me. The excitement of the watching crowd has Monica riding the edge of orgasm. The force of her pussy spasming around my cock is enough to draw my release. Our moans of pleasure mingle as we slowly build toward coming together.

"I love you, wife," I whisper as the first waves of orgasm flow through me. It's not a powerful release– it's sustainable and endless, flowing in waves radiating throughout my body, weaving the thread that binds us.

"I love you, husband." Monica whimpers as she falls off the precipice of pleasure. I catch her at the bottom before she lands, luxuriating in the way her pussy milks my cock. Locked together, we ride the wave for a long moment. We don't breathe or blink. We connect through the softest and longest release of our lives.

Sound whooshes back to me in a torrent. My ears suddenly sensitive, I can hear the labored breathing of all the guests. No one speaks or moves with the exception of rapidly moving chests as they struggle for breath.

I smile proudly at my loving wife and I can't wait to start our journey together.

"Ladies and Gentlemen, may I present, Mr. and Mrs. Dexter Hayes." Awed yet sarcastic, Olivia calls out amongst a myriad of shouts and whoops of congratulations. "This is most certainly the most unique wedding I've ever attended. You both made the BDSM Lifestyle Authority proud with your enthusiasm."

"Yeah, Dex!" Kris called out, issuing a shrill wolf-whistle. "You're a lucky bastard for nabbing Monica."

"They tried to make me the ring bearer," Tobias grumbles in a pouty voice, and my eyes widen when I take in how natural he seems to behave walking around completely nude. Extremely young and firm, I'm sure he's drawing more attention than he realizes. "You don't want to know where they wanted to tie the little pillow holding the rings."

"I would have paid to see that," murmurs softly from Olivia's daughter-in-law. Laughing, Devlin pokes the girl in the shoulder. "Joking, Dev. Jeesh, there were no rings."

"It's better than being the flower girl– think of where these deviants would put the flowers." Leaning into me, Marc whispers loud enough for me to hear, but quiet enough no one else can. "I did not need to know how you sound during an orgasm. I'll consider this payback for you walking in on me with Cort."

"The price wasn't high enough. Monica is hot. Cort is–"

"Bullshitter." Marc snorts. "Straight guys go bi-curious around him."

"Congrats!" Kat chirps, tugging Monica from my arms so she can have a hug. "I broke the vow of silence while wearing the cowl," she mutters defiantly to Olivia. "Go ahead and punish the matron of honor." Then she steals a sloppy kiss from the bride, with tongue and a tit grab.

Enjoying the view but confused, "What the–"

Releasing the bride, Kat draws me into a hug next. "I'm not deaf, even with how quiet Marc whispers," Kat reminds me, squeezing me tightly. "I heard what you said about Cort."

"Oh," I mutter lamely, the need to neuter Cort simmering in my blood. When Kat begins to draw away from me, "Doesn't the groom get a sloppy kiss?"

Kat looks over her shoulder at Monica, something important passing between them. Then she leans forward, snaring my lips in a brief kiss with her grabbing my pec to be a smart-ass. Our eyes never close, because the three of us are seeking out Ezra and Cortez, but the cowls obscure their reactions… and that is how our unholy alliance is born.

"Mmm… you suspiciously taste like my wife," I taunt, licking my lips. "You really shouldn't steal kisses from the bride."

"I gave Monica to you, remember?" Kat arches a red eyebrow in my direction.

"Best gift a trainee has ever given me." I tug Monica to my side, and she instantly sinks into me, arm wrapping around my waist. "You changed the course of our lives, and for that we will forever be thankful and indebted to you."

Chapter Twenty-Seven

"Children should not live in a museum," Monica whispers out the side of her mouth as we mount the front limestone steps to Shadow Haven for our family-only wedding dinner. "I grew up in a two bedroom house, and I turned out okay."

"Just wait until you see the Monet hanging in the foyer," I murmur, trying to keep my grin at bay.

Eyes flicking in my direction, Monica looks as if she thinks I'm joking. With the twist of my wrist, I enter Shadow Haven like I own the place– I've lived here a time or two in my lifetime between college and building my home. Not waiting to announce ourselves, I guide Monica to the Monet hanging on the wall.

"Seriously?" Monica gazes around the marble-on-marble foyer with a double staircase leading to the upper floor, completely flabbergasted– pissed, actually. "Kat lives here? Good God, she must hate it. It's about as comfortable as living in an institution."

Tugging Monica to my side, I nuzzle the top of her head. "Remind me to have us pay a little visit to the Whittenhowers. They dubbed their house Misery Castle, and it's a good four times the size of Shadow Haven."

Pulling away from me with an expression of horror written across her face, "You're joking, right?"

Smiling, I just shake my head left and right. Monica is gearing up to channel her anti-affluent father, but the sound of tiny feet smacking against the tile catches our notice. An angelic waif of a girl skips toward me with a huge grin etched across her face. Her long white hair flows behind her like wings.

"Dexter," the fourteen-year-old willowy girl chirps as she pulls me into a hug– and pull me she does. Ava's pushing six feet tall, dwarfing me and Monica. I hold the child back, unable to see her for the young woman she has become. I'll always see Ava as the eleven-year-old monster whose first love was sugar.

Ava pulls away from me to immediately engulf Monica in a hug. "I hear congratulations are in order. I wanted to go to the wedding, but Mom said no." Arms wrapped around my new wife, Ava pouts better than Cort can, displaying their genetic connection.

"It was the right decision," Monica murmurs. "If I'd known Niel was in attendance…" she trails off, mortified. But I shrugged the revelation off. The boy is a few months shy from eighteen– he saw nothing he hadn't been watching on the internet for years.

A shrill screech weaves through the foyer, echoing off the twenty-foot ceilings, followed by a baying. The mutant twins toddle after their big sister, shoes tapping wildly on the flooring.

"I'd be terrified they'd get lost in the house," Monica mumbles for only me to hear.

But Ava has bat-like hearing. "They have homing beacons. It's creepy, but they just know where I am in the house and find me. I get no privacy, no matter how many rooms I hide in."

"Hide and seek champions," I murmur with pleasure, longing to crouch down with my arms open in invitation but fearing the children don't know me well enough.

The tiny mistress of the pair is in charge. If her fiery red hair didn't inform you of her demon status, the name definitely would– Azrael, named after the fallen angel. She gets what she wants, when she wants, or all hell will break loose– just like Cortez. Marcus Zane was a calm and pleasant baby who cried only to get his sister what she wanted. His wispy pale hair, light gray eyes, and patient personality are just like his namesake.

The two toddlers tug on my pant legs and try to grab onto my fingers. "De-ex-ter," spills out Marcus Zane's lips. He has been learning names for the past few weeks, and he likes to test them out. He's a smart little guy. I think that he sees me as a large child to play with. I pick Marcus Zane up and give him a light squeeze, enjoying the weight of a child in my arms. I pass him to Monica, and he immediately burrows into her arms and closes his eyes, trusting my wife after seeing her at work with his mommy day in and day out.

"You're always so cuddly," Monica coos, but it suspiciously sounds like, "*I want a baby.*" I had to pass the kid off before I made a fool out of myself and actually said it out loud. A man doesn't go around making dreamy eyes at toddlers– I'd look creepy, not like a dad-wannabe

Ava tries to pick Azrael up before she's greeted me properly and is met with a tiny fist to the chest. The look that crosses Ava's face makes me flinch. Something tells me the girl will be joining the family's hobby sooner rather than later. Ava releases the wiggling child, and then steps away.

"Dexter," the small voice says eloquently. I pick Azrael up and give her a kiss on the cheek when she presents it to me.

"Hello, little one, how are you today?" I whisper into her ear.

"Pink." Azrael giggles and claps. *Pink?* Well, must be she's learning her colors. I laugh with the toddler, receiving an eye roll from Ava.

"What was this about food, I hear?" I speak to Ava, using baby-talk for the twins. "Marcus demanded our presence."

"Ah– Pop's favorite hobby, being demanding," Ava drawls with obvious annoyance. "I was commanded to bring you to the dining room upon your arrival."

"Still pissed at your grandfather for…" I trail off, not wanting to utter, *"Lecturing you on the perils of teenage sex."*

"I'm mad at Pop for messing around with Cortez when he thinks we don't see." Ava levels me with her gunmetal stare. "He's a hypocrite for telling me to leave my boyfriend alone, when he's sneaking behind closed doors with my parents' husband."

"You shouldn't know this," I warn, my eyes seeking out my wife. Monica looks horrified, an instant from stealing Kat and the kids and removing them from Shadow Haven. I don't want Monica to have any disillusions– most of the homes in our gated community operate like this one. Marc's and my parents were even worse. My cousin comes by this bullshit naturally. While Marc embraced it, I rejected it.

"I shouldn't, but that doesn't mean I don't know it." Ava walks off, leaving me and Monica holding the twins. With a shrug, we follow after her, but mostly because the kids are chanting their sister's name and waving *bye-bye*.

Surrounded by my family, we're sitting around the dining room table. I've decided to choose to be amused versus disgusted on our wedding night. Eating, holding polite conversation, they try to pretend they aren't furious with each other. They're trying their little hearts out for us, and I truly appreciate it. Ezra's doing his crazy-eye business, where he's fighting to remain in control of his inner Master Ez. How Katya can remain impassive as Cort and Marcus trade clever insults across the table is beyond me. The underlying resentment is hidden deep beneath their snide smirks.

"That fantasy life you live in every day must come in handy while writing a best-seller," Marcus tosses across the table with a pleasant smile and a flutter of his long lashes. He's simultaneously baiting and flirting with Cort.

Ava huffs a laugh while drinking a sip of wine and snorts it out her nostrils. She sputters and coughs, but continues to laugh. "That's a good one, Pop." Clearly Ava is a traitor, considering in the foyer she was pissed at Marc. Now she's pissed at Cort. Poor Ez and Kat, dealing with an irrational, hormonal teenager and these two big idiots who have no excuse for their horrific behavior.

"It's almost as impressive as when you put innocent people behind bars," Cort retorts angrily. "Or when the bad guys go free because you messed up their case with some loophole."

Marcus doesn't return an insult. He sits smugly, knowing he finally got underneath Cort's skin. Reaching over, Marc slowly rubs soothing circles on Ava's back until her face is no longer bright red from coughing.

"I'm so happy for you guys." Trying to change the subject while bringing the attention back to Monica and me— the reason we're supposedly celebrating —Ezra blatantly ignores how his adoptive father and husband are exchanging verbal foreplay. "That was one hell of a ceremony."

"Why was it different?" Ava feigns curiosity, the naughty gleam in her eye says she already knows the answer.

"Don't be coy, Ava. I know you talked to the little shit after he left Restraint." Ezra smiles at his daughter with pride. Unbelievable, but he seems to encourage her mischievousness and bad behavior.

"I just wanted to see how Dexter would explain it and watch Monica's expression as he did." Ava snickers evilly, sounding exactly like her father.

"How do you all not kill each other on a daily basis?" Monica demands, flabbergasted, looking a heartbeat away from pounding some sense into them. "Really, I want to know. This is no way to live— toxic."

"We all have different things we use as an outlet," Ezra mutters flippantly, his words tinged with bitterness. "It's a necessity if you live here at Shadow Haven. We don't go to bed angry, or we at least pretend we aren't. It's all a lie… frankly, I'm waiting for one of us to snap." With eyes gone cold with fury, Ezra glares between Cort and Marcus.

"They think I'm blind, especially Cortez, which is insulting." Kat's voice is short and to the point. "No matter what we do or say to each other, I know there is underlying love."

Ava rolls her eyes and looks at her mother like Katya's lost her mind. But the words spoken were that of a wife and mother trying to keep her family together– a desperate woman.

My wife and I share a shrug, knowing there is nothing we can do to fix this because it broke long before Katya entered our lives– it was broken when Cort and Ezra were merely children, and Marcus was dropped into their midst.

I'm thankful I've only fallen in love with one person in my entire life. It's so much simpler this way. There are too many people with conflicting emotions in this house. What makes this so much worse is the fact that these people are the only family I have on earth, and I have to sit here while watching them self-destruct.

It's time Monica and I start our own family. This version of the Zeitler family is so fucked up that I'm glad I only use my father's surname, not the hyphenated version on my birth certificate. I wouldn't want to be a Zeitler in this day and age. It was an hour-long ordeal just to get past the paparazzi camped outside of Restraint, and then again to gain access to Shadow Haven. We have two or three people milling around our lawn still, not the satellite-topped news vans anyone with the last name Zeitler attracts. I wouldn't want to live this way, and then add to that the bitter resentment boiling beneath the surface. I shudder to think of what is on the horizon for my cousin's adopted family.

We all go different directions after dinner. But the call of the little ones is too strong to resist. I follow everyone up to the nursery to say goodnight to the twins. Marcus Zane is cuddled up in his big boy bed, fast asleep. His fair skin and hair make him look like an angel. Azrael is sitting on the edge of her mattress, chatting with everyone like a tiny lady. Her mass of auburn curls and bright green eyes are striking against the golden skin tone she inherited from her father. Her small voice is so succinct and clear I can't help but smile.

"I want another story," Azrael demands.

"We don't want to wake your brother." Katya schools her youngest daughter. "We already read you two books."

"I want another story, Velveteen Rabbit." Azrael ups her demand, somehow picking that horrific trait up from Ezra. If you deny Ez something small, he will demand payment on something far larger, until you learn to never deny him again.

Instead of maintaining boundaries like a seasoned dominant, Katya gives in to the toddler, who will now grow up to be just like Ezra. Katya walks to the small bookcase built into the wall of the art themed room. Every wall has murals of different types of art: pointillism, mosaics, impressionism, and abstracts. Her fingers pull the requested book from the shelf without looking– I'm guessing it must be Azrael's favorite.

Everyone settles on the floor cross-legged, waiting to be entertained by Katya.

"No! I want Ava!" the demanding child orders. With a heavy sigh, Katya hands the book to Ava, looking demoralized and exhausted.

Maybe I don't want children just yet... but then again, I'd maintain those hard-fought boundaries to ensure my kid wouldn't grow up to be just like Ezra and Cortez. But that's an unwinnable war for Katya, as those very traits are what Cortez and Ezra love in each other. Whatever Katya tries to achieve would be undermined by the fathers of her children. My pot-smoking friend becomes very chatty once she's relaxed, and her pain is highlighted by how her *Ezes* disregard her opinions.

Ava rolls her eyes, but starts reading the story aloud with different accents and tones for the scenes. I immediately see why Azrael requested her sister for the reading. Ava has a natural dramatic talent.

I gaze around the room, watching everyone from where I'm perched, leaning against the wall near the door. Monica sits on the carpet, riveted by the tiny child who speaks like an adult. Content, Katya is seated between Ezra's legs, leaning against his chest with his arms wrapped around her– it's obvious they love one another, but it's too bad they also love Cort when he's having a conflict of conscience. It's different this time from all the times that came before. Cort isn't trying to get Ezra's attention because he already has it. It's something internal this time, but fuck if I know what it is.

Ava reads from the book, sitting in the glider rocker, thoroughly engrossed in her performance. I notice two are absent from the reading, only because it's pleasant for the first time this evening. My worry makes me curious, even though I know curiosity always kills the cat. With silent movements, I break away from the wall and I'm out in the hallway in the blink of an eye. A compulsion demands I seek out the missing Cortez and Marcus.

To Monica, Shadow Haven looked formidable. But to me, it's just a house slightly larger than the one I grew up in. It's only a matter of knowing where to look. Normal men have '*man caves*' but rich men have studies.

"I'm so fucking sick of your bullshit, Cortez. You're just begging for me to break you," Marcus hisses as he stalks Cort around the study.

Awed yet not entirely shocked, I freeze before the cracked door. The compulsion for knowledge grows, demanding I watch them when they are unguarded in their natural habitat. Melding to the wall, I watch as Marcus prowls toward Cortez through the gap between the frame and the door. My eyes widen at the grace they possess as they stalk each other like large felines.

"You're the one who always starts it." Cort whines, stepping to the side, using the desk as a barrier between him and Marc. "Dig. Dig. Dig. Bait. Bait. Bait. You force me to continually defend myself, humiliating me in public and private. If you act like a bastard, I'll give you an asshole in return." Whipping around, Cortez stands toe-to-toe with Marcus, jutting his chin in defiance.

"No, I think you want me to touch you, and you're too much of a coward to ask for it." Smirking smugly, Marc skates a fingertip down Cort's cheek. I lean forward, needing a better view, finding Cort to be visibly shaking. "You're begging for me to take you forcibly, disrespecting me, hoping I'll snap. I'm not Ezra– *I won't snap*."

With a snarl, Cort jerks backward, causing Marc's fingertip to fall from his cheek.

"Hmm…" Marcus purrs, eyes narrowed with rejection. "I think I'll turn the tables on you, and see how you like it. I won't give you the control by playing your games, and I sure as fuck won't touch you, even if you beg me."

"I don't know what you're getting at, fucktard." Palms slapping out, Cort pushes at Marc's chest, just begging to be hit or fucked. I'm not sure which he's angling for at this point, and that's the root of all of this. Cort is in a marriage with a man and a woman, raising three kids, and he doesn't know what he wants out of life.

"You remind me of the twins at naptime when they throw a tantrum," Marc taunts, words thick with bitterness. "They're exhausted, but refuse to sleep. You're horny, but refuse to fuck. The thing is, just as the twins have warm, cozy beds to rest in, you have a husband and a wife who want you very badly. But just like the twins wanting to stay awake so they won't miss a single second, you refuse to give in and be loved by Ezra and Kat."

"You make no sense," Cort grumbles, resolve crumbling.

"I make complete sense," Marcus replies, no longer sounding smug but pained. "If you feel you need to scratch this itch so you can finally be happy with Kat and Ez, realize once Pandora's Box has been opened you might not be able to close it. That's what is plaguing you. You're trying to wear me down so I'll snap and fuck you, taking the decision out of your hands because you're too cowardly to just admit it. Ez and Kat know this, but turn a blind-eye."

Leaning against the desk, Marcus intertwines his fingers with Cort's, pulling the man to him. "You're using me, just as you always have. But I'm an idiot who allows you to use me because I want to see you happy, knowing that's the only thing in the world that will make Ezra content."

For long moments, Marcus studies Cort's face, recognizing the pure, unadulterated lust written across his features. "I can't put into words how I feel right now," Cort grits out, voice thick with tears of frustration. "But I know I don't feel *right*. Something is wrong, and I can't put a finger on it."

"I know what it is, but if I told you what it was, you'd knee me in the nuts." Cocking his head to the side, Marc studies Cort. "In fact, you've done so to many, many people, especially Faith."

Blowing up in an instant, "I'm not gay, fuckhead!"

Voice wry, flat with taunting, "Hmm… If you say so, it must be true." Marc reaches up to run a fingertip along Cort's bottom lip. Like a switch being flipped, Cort pulls Marcus into his arms and kisses him brutally.

Unhinged, Cort attacks Marc like he's a starving man. "I'm not gay, I just fucking want you, is that what you want to hear, asshole?" Cort groans against the other man's lips.

"If you say so," Marc sounds unaffected, but his body is pitching forward to get closer to Cortez. "But you won't acknowledge that you said even this little bit after the fact. Just like every time you pull Katya or Ezra into an embrace, you spout how much you love them and want them and can't live without them, and then later you deny it. It's cruel. You've always been cruel to Ezra." Angry, Marc fists Cortez's hair, wrenching his head backward, controlling the man. "Now you're being beyond cruel to your wife, the mother of your children."

"I'm not gay," Cort slurs, but it doesn't hold as much weight as before. "I love women– I've been with enough of them."

"I don't care what label you put on yourself." Marc's grip loosens on Cort's hair. "I stopped using a label. I don't want men… but then again, I don't want women, either. I just want you and our family to be happy. Why aren't we good enough for you, Cort?"

"That's not–"

Marcus taps into Rebekah Zeitler's guilt. "It hurts so much. I know you love Ezra with every fiber of your being, and you're hurting him the worst." I can hear the deep well of sadness echoing in his voice, causing my chest to ache for them.

"I'm sorry. I'm so confused and scared," Cort sobs, pressing his face against Marc's cheek, looking for comfort and reassurance like a submissive being.

Pressing their lips together, Marcus offers a gentle and tender kiss– highly intimate, and not anything that should be shared between them. Marc's hands roam around Cort's back in a soothing manner, fingers tightening and loosening in a massage.

Suddenly Cort's sobs turn to moans. I blink my eyes several times over when his hand caresses over the bulge in Marc's pants. Then I blink some more, completely taken aback as he grinds his palm in a circular motion until Marc starts to hiss between his clenched teeth.

"I love you, Marcus," Cort murmurs as he melds their bodies together until their legs are tangled. He starts to rock back and forth against Marcus, using the edge of the desk as leverage. Palms skimming down Cort's back, Marc's hands immediately clench Cort's ass, fingers biting in, controlling the movement of their pelvises.

Even though I know this is private, even though I know I shouldn't be watching, I can't help but feel I understand Cortez better while simultaneously realizing I don't know my cousin at all. He keeps everything hidden from me. The scene before me is eerily familiar to the one I witnessed weeks back, except now they are clothed and standing up while leaning against a desk instead of tainting the Zeitler mattress in their private room at Restraint.

"You're a cunning and manipulative bastard," Marcus murmurs in awe. "Even if you'll refuse to admit you just told me you love me when I remind you tomorrow while you're shouting how much you loathe me."

I feel beyond guilty for watching such a raw and powerful moment that I have to leave the doorway. The study is directly off the family room, so I take the nearest seat on the sofa, trying to ignore the fact that I can still hear their mingled moans of pleasure. It feels less intrusive to not be physically watching. Plus, this way, I can direct anyone who enters the room away from the sounds flowing from the crack in the door.

If they wanted their affair to remain a secret, they should have closed and locked the door, which is why curious kiddies in the house see what they shouldn't.

Closing my eyes tightly, I count backward in my head, trying to block out the noise as it increases in volume and pitch. Shit, it's my wedding night. I should be fucking Monica's daylights out, not listening to my cousin getting dry-humped by his son-in-law. I pull a throw pillow into my lap to cover the increasing bulge in my pants.

Yes, big guy, I know you love the sound of satisfied lovers. All dominants do. But that's your blood in there getting it on with another dude. You don't even like dudes. Be a good boy and let me flow some more blood to my brain. I promise you a warm, tight Monica. Alright, so there is no reasoning with my cock. He recognizes a job well done and swells with pride.

I ignore the words of devotion Cortez is so fond of using in the throes of passion. I've heard similar ones spewed from his lips as he ravaged Katya in my private room at Restraint. I bite my lip and fist the pillow in my lap as they both find their mutual release.

Damn, bastards!

Five minutes later, the pair ambles out the door looking lax and replete. Cort falls onto the sofa next to me at the same time Marcus drops across from us on the adjoining sofa. Cort's eyes are at half-mast and his lips are raw and swollen. He groans as he gets comfortable on the couch, projecting his satisfaction. He blinks at me several times before his eyes finally stay open, while grinning with a sated expression.

"Feel better?" I mutter sarcastically, trying to dampen how angry their dynamic makes me feel for Katya and Ez.

"Much, thank you." Cort tries and fails to hide his satisfaction. He forced Marcus to touch him, now his eyes are glazed with the high from the power that brought. I guarantee, later on, Cortez won't own his actions. I heard what he moaned to Marc. There is no denying how much he was begging for it.

Marcus looks at me and nods. He can read me like no other, knowing exactly what I'm thinking. "It was worth all the annoyance. He knows I'll do it again and again and again to bring sanity to this household. It's a vicious cycle I don't know how to stop." Marcus wants to be angry, but he's too satisfied with himself.

"Who wants cake?" Katya calls from the doorway. We don't answer, because who doesn't love cake? She rolls in a small wedding cake that is intricately decorated in hues of purple with crimson accents. It looks similar to my Victorian era décor. Hmmm… I love my wife.

Kat wheels the cake near the sofas and narrows her eyes at the men who are now being agreeable, albeit looking higher than hell.

"Did you–" she trails off in a whisper, voice quivering, terrified of the answer.

"No," Marc utters a single word that speaks volumes.

"Sorry, Kitten." Cortez sounds completely unrepentant, proud even. "We didn't do anything beyond the norm. I promise I won't be cranky anymore."

Amber eyes holding mine, "*Like a child,*" Marcus mouths to me.

"You not bitching and complaining would be a welcome experience," Katya verbally jabs her husband, underlying resentment leaking through. But Cort doesn't complain, instead he shares a laugh with Marcus. Which only rubs Katya wrong as she looks between the pair with a bemused expression.

"In honor of the newlyweds, I think I'll fuck you tonight," Cort directs in Kat's direction.

"Did you drug him?" Kat mutters to Marc in mystification. "Because he hasn't touched me sexually in almost two years if Ezra wasn't involved." Voice warping with betrayal and dripping with sarcasm, "I feel so flattered right now."

"Drugs? Why didn't we think of that sooner," Marc teases. "It's only been five minutes since Cort got off. Give him a half hour and the asshole will return. I'm seriously thinking about tying him down and having him serviced every half hour for our mental wellbeing."

"You could just have Ezra prescribe some anti-anxiety medication," I offer with heavy sarcasm. "I think that would make more sense. Perhaps therapy for Cortez to figure out what he really wants out of life."

"Ha-ha, fucktard. You're lucky I'm so relaxed. There is absolutely nothing wrong with me." Cort mutters in denial.

"You're fucked in the head– admit it. After watching this bullshit tonight, it has reaffirmed my life choices," I announce to anyone who will listen. "Where's my wife? We have a cake to cut, and then I want to go home and be thankful for what I have."

Chapter Twenty-Eight

I'm not looking forward to getting back to the daily grind. Monica and I enjoyed two weeks of solitude locked up in a cabin in the middle of nowhere— no phones, no computers, no outside interference with the stress of work, insane family members tearing their own lives apart, the BDSM Lifestyle Authority, Generation Next, or Adelaide Whittenhower's mole hiding out at Restraint.

We made love, enjoyed my gift, and refueled with food and sleep. We did absolutely nothing else and it was relaxing bond-forging. I wish we never had to leave, except for the fact both Monica and I missed Tobias and Minion, and our home.

Monica is shining with self-satisfaction and I couldn't love her more. On our wedding night, I tossed her birth control into the garbage. She looked at me as if I'd lost my mind. I told her that if that clusterfuck of Zeitlers can raise three kids and want more, then the pair of us are more than qualified for the job. Plus, I'm steadily approaching forty. I'm in no rush. We'll let nature take its course.

I was thrilled to find out how Tobias made his own decisions while I was gone. I was even more surprised to see that he turned into quite the flirt on the few times he visited Restraint with Alex. Tobias makes me so proud. His need to please me makes him the most competent personal assistant on the planet. It's a cycle: his need to please me, my pride at his job well done, and the resulting confidence he has in himself. As the cycle strengthens, so does Tobias into an independent young man.

Two editions of Generation Next were waiting on my desk this morning. One edition was dedicated to Monica and me. It chronicled our lives together starting with our first meeting, to when I took her as my submissive, her betrayal with Dalton, our struggles with her insecurities and self-sabotaging issues, and then the wedding and reception in highly graphic detail.

If I ever had any doubt that the creator of Generation Next is in my family, I have no doubt now. Only the members were present at the wedding, but it was a small, family-only wedding dinner at Shadow Haven. The biggest clue and annoyance was the fact that the location of our honeymoon was printed as well. Generation Next stated that whoever bothered us at the cabin would be slandered in the publication.

I wish I knew who the hell its creator was. I've come to look forward to the gossip-style writing. Generation Next is most certainly a guilty pleasure read.

Restraint is still closed to the public after three weeks. We have a meeting with Gunner and Wil scheduled. I have no idea what their current professions entail, but it's hard not to trust a Marine. Roarke has taken to both of the guys, forming a security team meant to protect us at not only Restraint but to act as bodyguards to keep the paparazzi at bay. To create our security team, Gunner is rounding up retired service men and Roarke is contacting ex-police officers he trusts. Restraint will be open for business as soon as all the details are ironed out. It's a huge relief, but at the same time, I don't miss the hassle of a packed club.

What's bothering me the most, and is the most detrimental to Restraint, is the mole syphoning information to Adelaide Whittenhower, who is writing the Mistress & Masters of Restraint: The Collapse. I want to find the mole and string them up and beat them to death with my bare hands.

One of the bad things about being away for any amount of time is the stack of shit waiting when you return. Even with Tobias taking care of all he can, I still have personal correspondence and phone calls to return. There are over four hundred emails in my inbox that still need to be sorted by importance.

Leaning back in my chair, I stretch to wake myself up. The corner of an expensive envelope catches my eye from the center of the mail pile. Fingers snatching it up, the envelope feels heavy for its size. The gray paper is thick and coarse under my fingertips with my name in vibrant red written in bold calligraphy script. It must have been hand-delivered this morning. Curiosity getting the better of me, I open it knowing I might regret it later.

Reward

Tonight: 7p.m.

I should be excited, but I'm filled with trepidation. I almost hope that I missed the night. There is no date, just the word tonight. Marcus knew when I was coming home. He also knows how anal I am about getting right back to work. The bastard probably slid the invitation in the stack himself. I'm not sure I'm comfortable with Monica watching me fuck another woman the day we get back from our honeymoon.

"Monica!" I yell from my study, hoping the sound travels down the hallway to her home office.

My cock is trying to burrow up inside me. He doesn't want to do it, either. My inner caveman rolls a boulder in front of his cave and waves goodbye at me before he closes himself in. He doesn't want anything to do with it, either. We're finally having amazing sex on a regular basis. We're kind of raw right now from all the friction. My cock and my inner caveman are scared shitless. I'm a sadist who is frightened of having sex with my wife's and my best friend while her husbands watch.

My mind rolls through all my concerns and highlights on Monica. She's who we're worried about. Even though I've watched her punish herself with Dalton, watched her suck Ez off, and then have sex with Tobias, I'm not Monica. My self-esteem understands the difference between sex and intimacy, which is why I call Marc and Cort adulterers. I'm not about to sabotage the best thing that has ever happened to me.

Hearing Monica padding softly down the hallway, my cock fills with blood in anticipation. The boulder slides to the side and the caveman peers his face out in mild curiosity.

"Dexter?" Monica smiles at me from the hallway.

"Come here, wife," I growl. I draw Monica into my lap, forcing her to straddle my hips, and begin by running my hands up and under her t-shirt. It's the t-shirt Kat bought Monica. *I entered Restraint's Dungeon & stole their sadist.* I moan in pleasure when I notice the only thing she's wearing is the shirt. I hastily pull my sore cock from the confines of my pajama bottoms and enter her in one thrust. My cock can find Monica's sopping wet pussy in the dark at a hundred paces. He has a homing beacon placed inside her– his seed.

"Husband," she moans. Now, every time I hear the word husband, I nearly climax, even when it's said on the TV and not from Monica's mouth. I've conditioned myself that the word means instant pleasure.

I hand Monica the invitation as I slowly rock her hips above me. She's still so tight that all I have to do is sheath my dick and I could cum just resting inside her as she clenches around me. Me, my cock, and my inner caveman are worried that Monica will leave us if we go through with the reward. We show her the invitation while we make love to her, hoping and praying it's not our last time.

Not even looking at the note, Monica somehow anticipates what it says. "You're worried about me, aren't you?" Wearing a sex flush, Monica giggles at me, and she never giggles.

"Yes," I mutter shyly, heart beating a wicked tattoo inside my chest.

"I love you," is Monica's odd reply.

"You don't care?" Insulted, I almost wrench my wife out of my lap. "I'm your husband; I expect a slight amount of possessiveness when it comes to me. It's human nature."

Eyes heating with potent jealousy and lust, "Oh…" Monica purrs, fingernails biting into my shoulders. She begins to ride my cock in earnest. Her thrusts so forceful the top of my thighs are getting bruised by her ass slapping at my flesh. Growling, we explode with force.

"I'm the luckiest man on earth." Cum spurting into my wife, I grunt as my stomach muscles clench. "I won't accept the reward."

"You will," Monica breathlessly pants into my ear. "I wrote the invitation. Kat's going to fuck you and I'm going to assist. The Ezes will rue the day they thought they could toy with our girl's emotions."

"Christ." My head jackknives backward to hit my headrest. "Luckiest husband ever."

"And I'm the luckiest wife."

Chapter Twenty-Nine

Monica and I walk into Restraint hand-in-hand. It's early on a Sunday night and Restraint is closed. It's a different experience when you see the club without the music, lights, flowing alcohol, the smell of pheromones, and the suffocation of packed bodies filling every inch of space. It brings the nagging worry of the mole and the possibility of Restraint's chapter being dissolved from the Authority. I shudder at the thought of all we've accomplished in the past decade breaking apart because of one jealous bitch. I agree with Generation Next, may Adelaide Whittenhower rot in hell along with her mole and whoever's pulling their strings.

I squeeze Monica's hand in fear. My biggest fear isn't the pain Kat will cause me or the humiliation. Well, it is a type of humiliation– flaccidness. My cock is hiding out near my body, trying not to get involved.

I shudder again.

"It's going to be all right, Dexter." Monica trails an evil giggle, one that twitches my cock with interest. "It's not your execution. Kat is a gorgeous woman, and I can't wait until she gets her hands on you."

"I never want to lose you," I breathe the truth.

"You never will." Monica tugs me to a stop, stepping on her tippy toes to press a reassuring kiss to my lips. "I've had sex with Kat before– obviously. I know the difference between physical lust and friendship versus that twisted shit Marcus is pulling with Cort. *That* is why we are doing this, with the pleasure as an added bonus."

"Remind me of what we're trying to accomplish?" I look down at my wife, a smirk playing along my lips. In this, I know Monica and I want Katya with equal fervor, and she's making up excuses to do something about it.

"They need to learn Kat isn't a piece of furniture or a broodmare," Monica snarls, impassioned. "Cort hasn't touched Kat in years, not even a kiss goodbye in the morning. Yet he's playing with Ezra one-on-one without her, then fucking around with Marc. Plus, no one ever really knows what that fucking lunatic Ezra is up to– he could be fucking a swath of people for all we know. Kat shouldn't live her life without knowing she has friends who will teach the Ezes the lesson that if they don't want Kat, there are many who do."

"I get it– I don't want to contemplate their fucked-up relationship because it makes me want to punch something. I know Ezra loves Kat, but sometimes Ezra's love hurts."

"Exactly." Monica's eyes clear from stormy anger to that of unadulterated lust. "I'm going to assist our girl as she tops you. I won't play with you and you won't play with me. I'll watch and mind what Katya tells me."

"And you're okay with that?" I mutter incredulously. "Women are known to hate sharing."

"Truth?" I nod yes to her question. "Kat needs to gain her power back, and you're going to give it to her, so in the future she is strong enough to survive the Ezes' fallout."

Smirking, "Truth?" I ask Monica, waiting for her to nod yes this time. "I believe you just want to watch me fuck Katya."

"Oh, that too!" Monica tugs me forward, beyond eager to get this show on the road. My wife is so bizarre that it makes her extra sexy in my eyes.

We enter the main dungeon in the pitch-dark, with silence surrounding us. A hand grabs me roughly and I squeak like a girl.

"I warned you before, cousin." Voice menacing, "If you yell like a girl, some man may mistake your pretty ass for one."

"Asshole," I mutter underneath my breath. "You have no idea how much creepy incest innuendo that would spawn if someone else heard you say that. It's bad enough they saw you watch me take my wife at the altar."

Marc's evil chuckle is the only response he gives on that subject as he bags my head in a hood.

Voice stiff with annoyance, "Why are we using the initiation hoods? I hate those goddamn things."

"Ambiance." Marcus laughs again. "It's more fun for us this way."

"Joy," I deadpan.

"Monica, Ezra is a few feet to your left," Marc offers kindly. "He will escort you into our room."

"Thanks," Monica replies, chipper as all hell. Lifting the hood, she pecks a quick kiss to my cheek, and then shouts, "Marco!"

"Polo," comes a smoky voice filled with wry amusement.

"Ha! I found you," Monica says with excitement. "I'll see you in a minute, husband."

As with every time I hear the word *husband*, my cock is struck with lightning and my brain goes dizzy from blood loss. I don't have to fear erectile dysfunction with my wife around. I hope my enemies never find out that the word husband is my Viagra.

Nimble fingers take advantage of my distraction and zip-strip my wrists behind my back. "Hey!" I issue in complaint, struggling with zest. I hate this blacker than death cryptic bullshit Marc gets off on. I always sympathize with the initiate when the hoods are pulled out.

"Why?" I ask when I finally give up my fruitless struggles. Marcus only chuckles in answer. He allowed me to tire myself out as I fought for freedom. I'm sure I am amusing the hell out of him right now.

"Well, we all know Katya isn't strong enough to take you down, and you won't willingly allow someone to top you. So I decided to offer up some assistance by catching you by surprise." Each word flows quieter and quieter, until I can barely hear him, and then he bellows, "Surprise!" in the silent dungeon, causing me to jump out of my skin

"Asshole," I say louder this time.

Marc's immediate response to my insult is to laugh harder. I growl and start heading in the direction of the hallway. The dungeon is big, but the center is empty because of the stage. I can navigate it in total darkness. Plus, I can make out the faint light through the fabric of the hood– the light is at the end of the hallway glowing from the security keypad.

I've only been topped once in my life– my initiation. Marcus beat me with a whip. He said that I had to learn the feel of pain before I could accurately deliver it. I breathed through the pain and entered subspace for the first and only time in my life.

Orgasming from the pain gave me a new understanding and appreciation over how a masochist feels. I've adopted the same technique in all things– never utilize what you've never experienced.

The tool of my trade, the only whip I've ever held, was used on me first. As a reward, Marcus gave me the whip when he was finished.

With cocky strides, I release a smug snicker for finding my way through the dungeon, down the hallway, and to the door without help. I wish I could see enough to type in the damn code.

Back facing the door, with reaching fingers, I try to locate the keypad– my hands get slapped away. "Don't even try it. You'll miss, and then I'll have to reboot the entire system." Marcus chastises me, figuring out how I was going to try to type the numbers.

I not-so patiently wait as I hear the beeps of four numbers and the beep signifying the door unlatched. I tap my toe as the air moves around me when the door is flung open. Marcus pushes me with a hand on my back until my feet move forward. I head slightly to the right, knowing the layout of the mini-dungeon. The apartment-like side is to the left, and we won't be using the bed Cort and Marc were fucking on. I'm glad the hood covers my grimace.

Marc's hands grip around my ribcage, just underneath my armpits, and lifts until my feet are no longer on the floor. I stifle my need to struggle, knowing it will only delay the inevitable. Centering myself, I slow my breathing– in through the nose and out through the mouth. But it's not working.

I'm set on my feet and a heavy hand holds me in place. "Are you going to fight?" The fingers tighten, waiting for my response.

"No, Marcus, there is no sense." I mutter truthfully. I feel the fingers loosen as he gauges my honesty. "I've accepted my fate."

"We top, dumbass. So don't act as if those we top are being slaughtered." I can hear the eye roll in my cousin's voice, but then he commands, "Don't move."

I get the concept of dominance and submission– obviously. It's entirely in my nature to dread being controlled, even if it's by one of the hottest women I've ever met. When it's all said and done, my spank-bank will be overflowing.

I stand still as Marcus begins to remove my clothing. My cock runs and hides and my balls shrivel up into raisins. A dude touching me is one thing– it's gross when it's Marcus.

"You have absolutely no boundaries you're not willing to cross," I snap, feeling uncomfortable. "I can do it. I won't run. Just please let me do it myself." I'm not too proud to beg. "Or have someone else strip me. The creepy-factor is too high."

The air moves as Marcus steps away. A sharp snick, and then my hands are freed from the cable tie. With hurried movements, I remove my *Smack my bitch up* t-shirt. I toe my leather dress shoes off, and then kick them to the side, hearing the thump as they connect with an object.

I'm wearing my second favorite pair of leathers. Monica and I gave my favorite pair a thorough workout during our honeymoon. I have several pairs on backorder for replacements. These pants are supple black leather tightly fitted to my body. Riding low on my hips, the waist is created from large metal rings hooked into the leather that show a glimpse of flesh as I move. A ring is directly over the top of my bulge. With a practiced roll of my hips, I can pull my cock out through the ring.

These pants are going unused this evening since I have to be unclothed. I wore them for the exact opposite reason. I wanted to stay dressed with just my cock in contact with Katya. Que Sera, Sera…

When I'm completely naked and giving an unimpressive showing, Marc's hands are back, maneuvering me into place. The cold touch of metal is pressed against my feet and forehead. Warm fingers attach my feet to a metal bar, then my hands are lifted and strapped to the top bar. A leather strap is cinched around my back, and then another around my stomach. There is nothing supporting my body except for the straps on my ankles and wrists. I recognize the device just by how I'm attached to it. My entire body is on display and able to be turned in all directions, even upside down.

With an abrupt flourish, the hood is jerked over my head. Light blinding me, I blink several times through the sting until my vision begins to clear. I'm facing the gray back wall. The rack of toys hangs to my left and beneath it is the apothecary-style drawers holding all the tiny torture devices. The exit is to my right. I can hear quiet murmuring at my back in the location of the sofas.

I'm strapped to an inversion table minus the leather and foam body support– it's just the frame. My feet rest on the diamond plate and my forehead rests securely against the headrest. My hands are bound to the top support. The waist restraint is cinched tight around my back, the frame, over my stomach, and then buckled at the other side of the frame. I'm completely immobile and scared shitless.

A small hand yanks the hair at the back of my head, wrenching my neck in a long line. I feel the cool and smooth texture of latex as the woman who is going to dominate me this evening leans her chest against my back.

"Dexter," Kat purrs in my ear. In rare form, no doubt from the need to hurt those watching, Kat the seductress is in action. "I've waited a very long time for my reward– too long." Then she whispers softly into my ear, and I know no one else can hear. "Thank you for this. I haven't played in far too long. Ezra refuses to be topped and Cort ignores me on good days, but neither would allow me to play with anyone else. My only recourse was trading in our reward."

"You should have told me sooner," I murmur back so quietly no one else can hear. "I would have sent you to my basement with Tobias, not had you smoke weed. Jesus, Kat. How long?"

"Years," is breathed into my ear.

"Fucking assholes," I snarl loud enough for everyone to hear. "You had me train your wife as a dominant, but then you didn't allow her to dominate anyone?" I shout in the quiet as all conversation ceases. "What? Were you too busy to notice while you were fucking everyone else but your wife?"

"I was easy to ignore once they got what they wanted from me," Kat whispers in my ear. "Just let it go, and enjoy tonight. I promise not to be too rough with you– I'll use the utmost care."

"I trust you," I state loudly. There is no need for me to face the sofa, I can feel the frustration, shame, and possessive jealousy weaving its way through the room. Their relationship is more fucked than Monica or I realized.

My gift is sadism, particularly with the whip, but Kat's version is more defined. The first bite is a sting to the meat of my shoulder. I hiss out a breath as it hurts, but it gets my blood pumping. My cock immediately stiffens to attention.

I experience the indent of Kat's fangs sinking on the next bite. It's much harder, the fierce burn, and I try not to jerk in my restraints. As a point of pride, I don't make a sound. She bites down the column of muscle along my spine– each bite progressively harder until I'm biting my own lip to contain the bubble of pain building in my throat. My eyes roll back as my body flushes with goosebumps. She leaves a trail of stinging, aching bites down my back.

I breathe in a deep gulp of air when Kat reaches my tailbone. Then the air moves, fluttering against my oversensitive flesh, signaling that she stepped back to appreciate her work. Biting is Katya's art– her gift.

A silent scream escapes past my lips as the tender flesh of my ass cheek is laid open by one of her fangs. I order my pain receptors to feel pleasure instead of torture. I can already feel endorphins rushing throughout my system to aid me during this ordeal. My traitorous cock perceives it as bliss. Precum beads at the tip, then gravity takes over, slowly sliding it down the shaft, leaving a cold, wet sensation in its wake. I'm so hard that I'm pressed tight against my stomach instead of jutting out straight ahead.

Katya moans, enjoying her work. I no longer feel each individual bite as the sensations start to bleed together. I bite my lip hard to contain the yelp that almost escapes as she latches onto my thigh.

Sack constricting, I almost come when Katya suckles one of my balls into her scalding hot mouth. Breathing deeply, I wait through the panic as I anticipate her next bite to the most sensitive flesh on my entire body. Slowly, I begin to relax as she sucks and rolls her tongue around my tender ball. My cock throbs erratically, releasing precum in steady rivulets, the slickness streams down my shaft, reaching Katya's eager mouth lapping at my balls.

An agonizing scream is torn from my throat as tiny teeth nip into the delicate flesh of my sack. Bucking in my restraints, my body involuntarily writhes from the intense wash of pain. My scream ends with a tortured moan from deep within my chest.

My body no longer distinguishes pain from pleasure. Lightheaded, my eyes seem to float in water inside their sockets. Every inch of my skin throbs like a full-body toothache, only now I don't know if it's agonizing or amazing– exquisite torture. Chest expanding and contracting, I force air into my lungs, drying my lips out from the amount of air passing between them.

The frame flips before I find my equilibrium. I'm upside down facing the rest of the dungeon while my back is to the wall I was looking at moments ago. My eyes widen as I take in Mistress Kat for the first time in almost three years. The Zeitlers have played in private since Kat's initiation, but apparently not playing at all.

Katya is wearing the same latex catsuit she wore to her initiation with the exception that she is built differently than before. Her breasts are heavier and fuller since the birth of the twins. Her hips are wider as they stretch the latex. All the weed munchies did Kat's body good. My cock pulses as I take in the expanse of Katya's body. So much flesh to strike and watch its reverberations.

Good God, the fun Monica and I would have with Katya all alone in our basement. What is wrong with Cortez? Why is he jerking Ezra around, harming Kat in the process? Fucking moron.

"Motherhood was kind to you, Katya. You're better looking now. I couldn't see the differences without the latex smoothing you. Jesus," I hiss out in awe. My mind still isn't processing properly from the pain, or I wouldn't have said such a thing in front of my wife or her husbands.

My eyes rove the room until I spy our audience. Cort and Ezra are cuddled up on the sofa, watching with glazed-over eyes. It doesn't escape my notice how their mouths are swollen and raw– it makes me wonder if Marc ever feels jealous as he looks on. My eyes dart to the loveseat to find Marcus rubbing Monica's back in soothing circles. Their eyes are filled with lust, but not for each other. I think the audience enjoys Katya's work as much as she does.

Kat leans down in slow motion so I can anticipate her next move. Upside down, my face is near her shins with my feet slightly above her head. She bends at the waist until I see nothing but her large green eyes captivating me. Her tongue swishes out to lick my stomach, allowing me to blink out of the spell she cast me under. Panting rapidly, I shiver as Kat licks a path down my thigh from my knee to my hip.

"Mmm… you're tasty," Kat murmurs, licking her lips provocatively. Flashing me a fanged smile, I shiver in fear as my cock pumps precum in anticipation. It doesn't care if she bites us, just as long as she touches us with that scorching hot mouth.

The blood pooling in my skull from being upside down leaves me feeling lightheaded. The sensation adds to the endorphins pumping through my veins.

"I think it's time for you to taste me." In rapid succession, expressions flash over Katya's face: insecurity, fear, and lust. "Would you like that, Dexter?"

Without hesitation, "Yes," rumbles passed my lips.

Startling me, Kat's bare foot flies up to rest on the support beam near my hip. I watch in avid fascination as she parts the latex at the juncture of her thighs. My body flushes when I see the pale and hairless flesh of her labia. I start to pant as her fingers move to spread her slit, giving me an up-close and personal view of how pink and wet she is.

Kat's hand moves, and I hope she's going to have me suckle the taste of her off her fingertips. But from one breath to the next, she's squatting to lower her sweet cunt near my face.

"Lick me clean like a good puppy." Kat's command ends on a breathy moan. "Lap up all the cream."

Momentarily stunned with her pussy an inch from my mouth, I can't believe this is the Kat who sits in my parlor smoking weed with me a few times a week. The woman I watched bad science fiction television shows with the day before my wedding, her pussy is *right in my face*.

Awed, Kat's aroma tickles at my nostrils, causing my mouth to water and my cock to pound. My tongue flashes out to lick a long line from her cleft to her ass. We moan at the same time, me from the taste and her from the sensation.

"Good, puppy. You'll get a treat for good behavior." Kat rasps, teasing me. But I turn the tables by startling a gasp from her throat by drawing one of her pussy lips into my mouth and sucking. I nip her fiercely for all the bites she gave me. Her strangled moan informs me how she not only likes to bite, but loves being bitten as well.

A shout is torn from my lips when Kat's mouth closes over my cock in retaliation. A war for dominance, with me strapped upside down on an inversion table, Katya sucks me deep into her throat while I wrap my lips around her clit and suck it like a cock. Images of Katya on her knees during her initiation, servicing Marcus, flash through my mind.

I want to be completely deep-throated just once in my lifetime. Women say they want a huge cock, but it's just a novelty. They don't know what to do with it once they get it, but I know Kat does.

Lost in the past, fantasizing about being taken to the root, Katya's teeth press into my flesh when I stop tonguing her cunt. Not one to ever miss a tasty meal, I eat her with my lips, teeth, and tongue until she vibrates her pleasure around my shaft.

Finally deep-throating me, I sigh in bliss, but then Kat bites me hard at the base of my cock, fangs sinking into my flesh. The pain is excruciating, but I no longer process it as a bad thing. My mind believes having my cock nearly bitten off is the greatest pleasure known to man. Entering the foggy bliss known as subspace, my eyes roll back in my head and my body starts to writhe. Precum pours from my dick as she drinks me down, but I don't orgasm. The sensation is fantastic, but not enough to topple me over the edge.

Drawing Kat's engorged clit into my mouth, I suckle. Hard. My teeth close over the nub of nerves where it connects to her body and I bite just enough for her to go insane above me. Kat's keen is loud and long as she presses into me, riding my face, juices dripping off my chin.

The suction on my cock increases to the point of bruising. Kat's leg falls off the support beam and her pussy almost suffocates me. Before I can protest, she moves away and my cock is released from her mouth with a loud pop. Hot saliva glides down my dick and sack, cooling when the air hits it, causing a full-body shiver.

"No coming yet, Dexter– for either of us. I have plans for you." She grips the front of my curls and pulls my face up to her sight.

I don't need a mirror to know what I look like. My eyes are glazed and my pupils are blown. I feel high, drunk, fucked, and asleep all at the same time. Hell, I've passed the point of no return where only trust keeps you alive– trust that the person topping you won't abuse you while you're in your most vulnerable state.

My body thrums as every single nerve-ending begs for touch. A weak moan rumbles up my throat. "Earth to Dexter, are you still in this orbit?" Kat chuckles at the expression on my face. "Dexter's in subspace. Is it okay to move on?" She asks someone else, because hell if I could answer.

"Dexter?" Marcus calmly commands. He tugs the invisible leash which connects those he trained and all of our people who are weaker than him.

An epiphany strikes me. I'd thought it odd that my cousin would want to witness his daughter-in-law topping me. I kept thinking Cort and Ez wore off on him with their incest-fest. But, no. After so much time without dominating anyone, Katya needed someone to keep her in line. Someone I respect enough to accept their dominance in her stead if she were to fuck up.

I lick my lips a few times to moisten them. "Yes, Marcus?"

"Dexter's good. Whatever you do will feel incredible for him. Beware, you will no longer be able to take cues from his body language. He's floating too deep."

"You have no idea how hot you both look right now," my wife murmurs, voice raspy and filled with lust. "Jesus."

"You ready to be my bitch?" Kat asks, and I almost answer her.

"Yes, Mistress," Monica purrs, her feet coming into focus near me.

I'm flung from vertically facedown to vertically face-up until I'm upright in the position I started with– facing the back wall with my feet at the ground. I breathe a sigh of relief as my blood redistributes throughout my body. Maybe now I can get some blood and oxygen to my brain so I can think straight, but I doubt Katya will allow me clarity of mind.

The bite of the cane says, '*No– no thinking straight for you, Dexter*." The cane my own wife handed Katya.

No sound erupts from me during the hit. Logically I know it should feel like a searing hot strike, burning yet freezing. But all I experience is a tingling of pure pleasure that seeps into my mind. Every hit snaps loudly and my body moves from the force. I don't even grunt from the impact. The louder the hit, the harder the force, means the more pleasure I feel.

The hits come closer in intervals along my back, shoulders, ass, and thighs. I can no longer pinpoint the location of the hit. My body burns fiercely with a need I cannot fathom. My moans and groans go from separate entities to one long continuous sound.

Completely out of it, I try to get my eyes to focus by blinking repeatedly. But my lids are fused shut because I don't have the energy to hold them open, yet I can still see. I feel separate from my body as if my spirit removed itself of its earthly flesh.

My back and thighs are on fire, yet feel coolly numb. I manage to pry my eyes open enough to watch as my cock ejects cum all over the front of my body, jerking spurt after spurt. I gaze to the floor where a large puddle is forming by my feet.

Jesus, how long have I been coming?

My cock is still firm to my stomach, refusing to give up the fight until it has milked every ounce of pleasure and pain from the experience. This is our reward at long last– Katya and I will enjoy every second of it.

Mind not functioning properly, the only way I know the beating has stopped is because my body no longer moves from the force of the impact. But it doesn't end there. I cannot contain the weak sounds slipping past my lips or the semen spilling to the floor.

Abruptly, my body is jerked backward until I'm lying horizontally. I watch in rapt fascination as Katya latches a bolt near my hip and Monica the other. The ladies test out the resiliency of the device, making sure it's stable in its flat position.

Pupils blown, my eyes bulge from their sockets at the sight of my wife peeling the latex catsuit from Katya's body, with it getting stuck on Kat's hips and then her ass. My mouth waters at the sight of Kat's luscious tits jiggling with her movements. Of a like mind, Monica steals a hearty grope of each breast. Instead of punishing my wife for the liberties taken, Katya returns the favor.

"Are you still with me, Dexter?" Peering down at me, Kat is on my right and Monica is on my left as I lay flat on my back with nothing but a metal frame and leather straps keeping me from tumbling to the floor.

I lick my lips again, trying to force words from my mouth. I rasp, "More please," but I'm not sure if it comes out with sound or not.

"I'm going to ride your long, thick cock until I scream," Kat purrs in a sultry voice, driving my wife to distraction. Monica leans forward, groaning as if the words are caressing her lady bits. "You're nothing but my living, breathing sex toy. When we're done, you can be my friend again. Deal?"

"Deal," I try to say, but I think I just mouthed the word. Monica echoes my thoughts in a voice gone deep with lust.

"You're flying so high right now, Dex." Leaning over me, Kat's green eyes widen impossibly large. "I've never seen anyone so far into subspace. I'm amazed someone so dominant can go so deep."

I don't process what Kat's talking about. I feel just fine, thank you very much.

Katya's hands move so fast I barely catch the movements. It takes me a minute to realize she's moving at normal speed, but my brain is taking longer than usual to process it.

Katya and Monica wipe my thighs and chest free of semen with a damp washcloth smelling faintly of disinfectant. My cock jerks upright when my wife washes him too. Amazed, confused, feeling closer to Monica than ever, my cock starts to pound with my heartbeat as she rolls a condom over it, preparing me for her best friend.

Once I'm covered, Katya hops onto the inversion table. My eyes bug-out of my head when she straddles my hips, palms resting over my pecs. My wife grips my dick at the base, holding me upright for Katya to slowly lower herself onto my cock.

"Fuck, you're huge. How the hell did Ezra take you?" Kat laughs as she lowers down over me by another inch. "Jesus, girl," she cries out to Monica. "I know your pussy is dinky– you really are a masochist."

Hand finding mine, I worry Monica is having second thoughts, regretting this decision that was ultimately hers. Proving I need to trust her judgement, "It hurts every single time, but I've come to need it. I doubt I could get off any other way."

I try to stay as still as possible, refusing to follow the biological urge to thrust upward, which would be nearly impossible because of the restraints. I don't want to hurt Katya, and I can tell by her body that her Ezes aren't meeting her needs. Kat's almost as tight as Monica, and I bet she usually isn't if she is getting steady penetration from both Ezra and Cort.

"Your men are fucking crazy for ignoring you." I croak out, squeezing Monica's hand.

"Tell me about it. This would go easier if I was getting any." Kat laughs nervously, her cheeks pinking from embarrassment. Monica and I watch the transformation as the seductress Mistress Kat is shed, leaving behind our friend, Kat.

Mistress Kat wanted to torture and toy with me, but Kat only wanted to have sex with me. I smile at the ladies, feeling as if I'm floating on a wave of pure pleasure.

"You're as thick as Marcus and as long as Cort." Pained, awed, she hisses, "Fuck!"

"Hey, now… no comparing cock sizes," Ezra chastises Kat, but I can hear the humor in his voice.

"I didn't say anything about yours, Ezra. None of you have anything to complain about. But I will start tying you guys to this table and fucking some sense into you if I don't get some from Cort soon."

Kat sliding down my cock until I'm fully sheathed eclipses their collective chuckle. Whatever ground I had made up flees as I'm flung back into subspace. Mind altered, I stare down at us from the ceiling. Katya arches her back as she rides me in a wave-like motion, rolling her hips, grinding her clit on my pelvis. Her head is thrown back with her mouth wide open in a silent moan. The bend of her back thrusts her breasts forward. I watch in rapture as they bounce up and down when she bobs on me, and swirl when she rolls her hips on mine. Someday I want to put tassels on her nipples and have her ride me.

Monica can use the fact that she's a submissive for her lack of control– not that I need an excuse since the inversion table leaves me completely immobile. My wife and I are utterly fascinated with the movement of Katya's tits, and only one of us has the balls to steal a taste.

Groaning, I watch my wife's mouth latch on to suck an engorged nipple while her hands manipulate Kat's plump tits. Mentally and physically, sensations flow in a stream as I'm flung from the ceiling back into my body– my release starts to build to epic proportions.

"I hope they let us do this again, Dex." Kat moans deeply, rocking her hips faster as she nears her peak. "This is beyond imaginable."

"Mon–" unable to move, let alone be able to form complete words, I allow my wife to act and speak for me. With a palm wrapped around Katya's throat, Monica backbends her, gaining access to the apex where we're joined. Leaning over the table, Monica presses her face between us.

"Oh, my God!" Kat grunts sharply, pussy starting to clench around my dick, when my wife's tongue licks where we're joined. My eyelids are slowly lowering, but the last sight I see is Kat's fingers wrapping in Monica's hair, controlling how her pussy gets eaten as she rides my dick.

I choke in a breath and wheeze out the sounds of my climax, since I long ago lost the ability to scream. Kat rocks faster on me as her hot cunt clenches like an angry fist, pumping me dry with her spasms, coaxing my cock to spill into the sleeve of latex. My body begins to shake and tremble involuntarily. My mouth releases a strange sound as my body seizes. My eyes roll back into my head and my body shakes as my nerves explode.

"Is Dex okay? I think he may be seizing!" Kat shouts in a distressed voice as her body leaves mine. "Did I hurt him? Is he okay?"

"Shh… it's okay," Monica murmurs, suddenly sounding far away, but she's talking our friend down from panicking. "Dexter's crashing. It happened to me the first time I entered subspace. It was terrifying."

Fingers stroke my forehead. "Dexter?" Marc's voice penetrates my mind as my body spazzes out on me. "You'll be okay. Your body just went through too many sensations too quickly."

"Dexter's literally in shock," Ezra murmurs as fingers are pressed to the inside of my wrist while others unstrap me from the table.

I try to blink, but my eyelids won't cooperate, just as my body refuses. The darkness grips me as several pairs of hands lift me.

"Damn, Kat. I never thought it was possible to fuck a person to death." Ezra's concern floods into my numb body. "I guess we're not doing our husbandly duties enough if you drained poor Dex."

"Dexter is proof Kitten's a succubus," Cort's snarky tone fades into my subconscious.

I wake lying on a cloud. I blink several times before my eyes obey by staying open for more than a split-second. I'm on a big bed, lying on my stomach, with everyone surrounding me.

"Here, Dex. Drink this down." Cort wiggles a straw between my lips. It takes a few tries before I can force the liquid up the straw, then I regret it when I have to fight the need to gag at the horrific taste. I want to spit it back out, but I don't have the energy.

"It's a protein shake. Suck it all up and I'll give you some water. Drink it slowly so you don't choke," Cort nurses.

After finishing the vile drink, I win my prize. I sip the ice-cold water and sigh in bliss. I feel more like myself, vaguely able to think again. I've only journeyed to subspace one other occasion and it felt nothing like this. I was beaten briefly by Marcus, and then it was over.

This time it was euphoric, and I can understand how a submissive could grow to crave the trip. Dominants have their version as well, but it pales in comparison to this. I dread the drop that I fear is coming.

"Good… can you eat this now?" Cort pushes something gritty against my bottom lip. I open and immediately regret it. Fussing, I try to push it back out with my tongue as more is forced into my mouth.

"Hey, eat it. It's an energy bar, idiot." I want to hate Cortez for treating Katya and Ezra like shit, but then he does something like this for me– even if he is talking like an asshole, but that's usual for him. "C'mon. It won't kill you. Do this and you won't feel as hungover later. Be a good boy and I will give you some pain reliever next."

I eat the nasty bar piece-by-piece until it's gone. Then I'm rewarded with more water and three ibuprofen.

I'm still blissed out as I experience a tug and pull on my back. I hear a snip followed by another tug and pull. I feel pressure and no pain. "What's going on back there? Why can't I feel anything?"

"You seized and passed out," Cort answers. "While you were out, Ezra numbed you up. Now he's stitching a few marks on your back. He's making tiny sutures so you won't scar."

"What's he sewing up back there?" I want to freak out, but I can't find the strength.

"Nothing major. We would have just bandaged you up, but Kat would have felt guilty for the rest of her life if it left a scar. Three bite marks tore– Ez put a stitch in each. Then two strikes with the cane split you open– one with three stitches and one with two."

Ezra's voice comes from above me. "The perils of bottoming in BDSM to a dominant who doesn't top often enough. I'd ask why you didn't say something, but I doubt you could. I'm sorry I didn't pay closer attention. This isn't an excuse, but the lighting wasn't bright enough. I feel like shit because it's definitely my fault."

"Ever the martyr," I murmur into the mattress beneath me. "I remember feeling wetness on my back."

"Ezra already shot you up with some antibiotics. He'll get you a prescription. We don't want you to scar or get sick." Cort wipes my mouth with a washcloth. "You'll be as good as new."

"Thanks, Dr. Zeitler, but I think your partner's true calling should have been a nurse," I slur, and get flicked in the head for teasing Cort.

"That was the last one. I did a great job." Ez marvels from his perch on my ass.

"Get off my ass, Ez." I groan as pain starts to bleed through the fog.

Ezra hops off me, and a moment later he spreads a cool gel over my back. I sigh in relief. "One bite might leave a mark. It's always the small ones that leave a lasting impression." He squeezes my shoulder, working out a kink that formed.

"Where is my wife? Where are Kat and Marc?"

"Marcus took the ladies home," Cort is the question answerer. "We didn't want to freak Monica out as you seized. Your back was bloody, and we didn't want her seeing it. Plus, Kat was scared that you'd kill her when you woke. She was extremely upset that she may have hurt you. She lost control."

"Kat has played with me a handful of times, but nothing more than bedroom games– a little light bondage and getting her ass paddled with my palm." Ezra's roaming hands move on to the top of my thighs, massaging and taking the pain away. "We've never allowed Kat to stretch her sadist wings. No biting except for a love bite, and no impact play."

"That's irresponsible and selfish." I use all the strength I possess to roll my eyes toward Ezra and Cort, trying to get them to look at me. "I didn't train Kat for no reason. She's like me, living with whatever bullshit you've got going on, which isn't her fault, and you deny her the only release she could use?"

"We'll have to find her someone to work with, or allow her to work on me. I'm so sorry, Dex. I-" Ezra's eyes are glossy and his face pales, upset and going full-out martyr mode.

"We couldn't see what she was doing since the light was so dim. Plus, I was slightly distracted." Guilty, Ezra's eyes cut toward Cort, showing what distracted him. "I didn't think she would lose control. It's our fault. Please don't blame her."

"You're right. It is your fault, and I would never blame Katya." Voice stiff with anger and pain, the events of the past few hours culminate into me finally speaking my mind. "You're always distracted by Cort, who does it on purpose to be the center of attention. Tonight was about Katya– completely. Instead of paying attention to Kat for the past few years, let alone giving her an hour of your undivided attention, you were sucking face with Cort because he was giving you the time of day. You both need to grow up before you lose her– this is coming from the man who is your wife's shoulder to cry on."

"I'm sorry... so sorry for everything. I'll do better." Ezra's contrition flavors the air as he begins to massage my shoulders and arms again. I close my eyes in relief, hurting from being restrained for too long.

"Do better?" I grumble into the mattress, words slurring to sound like nonsense. "I'll believe it when I see it."

"I promise." Ezra proves he has impeccable hearing, or he's answering his own unspoken thoughts.

Chapter Thirty

"Students, I know you're all worked up right now. Since everyone was so attentive this evening, you're excused to go play in the dungeon. Don't do anything I wouldn't do, boys and girls," I say with a wink.

I twist back to the chalkboard and inwardly wince. It's been almost two weeks and I'm still hurting. Today I decided that whether or not I was sitting at home or training my students, I was going to hurt either way.

In my absence, Marcus took over all the training, making me feel like a big baby for a few stitches. But it wasn't that the sadist couldn't take the pain– I was burnt out. Burnt out on the whole lot of them, just wanting to be in my home with my wife and Toby and our cat, while shutting out the outside world.

Monica says it's a phantom pain, because I am all healed up, not even a single scar, and my muscles aren't cramping. I trust my wife's judgement. Psychologically, I have too much on my plate and need some help. So after class tonight, I've decided to sit down with Marcus and Devlin to demand I be told everything they know.

No more sticking my head in the sand, refusing to ask questions when I fear the answers.

My ignorance is not bliss. At the least, it's created a divide between Marcus and myself. At the worst, it could cause irrevocable harm to someone because I might have been able to head something off at the pass if I was paying attention.

I was shocked when I entered my room to find twenty desks filled with students. Katya's overzealous scene scared the piss out of Marcus, forcing him to finally get with the program. I thought my naughty students would take issue with Marcus lecturing them, but they sat absorbed while Marcus and I tag-teamed the lesson.

With Restraint closed, we've concentrated on the important things, not the club patrons' experiences. Our membership is on the rise, to the point that we're considering expansion of the club. Currently, the upper floors house apartments and storage rooms, and Ezra wants to convert a few into more private dungeons and themed rooms. Restraint was always small with a select clientele that hunted in the public section of the club.

Ezra and Cortez are the redesigning team while Marcus and I are teaching. We hope the training is infectious and contaminates the membership. The Masters of Restraint got cranky when they lost their playtime, but it's for the benefit of Restraint.

The club is still closed until further notice. We have the security ready to go, but Marcus wants to make sure we're at our best before we open the front doors. The riots and the paparazzi have taken a toll on all of us, and now we're scared to have Restraint up and running. The arrival of Master Fontaine has our tails between our legs. Olivia now walks around Restraint like she owns the place, and we're all on our best behavior, finally breathing only when she leaves us be. Weirder yet is that Devlin never once said he was the new head of the BDSM Lifestyle Authority. If the Master of all Masters is scared for us, surely we have a problem— and that problem is leaking like a sieve.

I lean against the dry-erase board and stifle a laugh as all the students pair up for the dungeon. It's like biology class with everyone running around, looking for a lab partner. Instead of dissection, they are learning the biology of reproduction— hopefully conception-free.

The enigma that is known as Dalton looks frightened as Kristal chooses him as her prey. I don't know what she sees in the drab douchebag, but every chance she gets she tries to entice him into a scene. He stares at the floor anxiously while she flirts with him. Whitt, being the knight in shining armor type, comes to the rescue and Dalton visibly relaxes. The three of them have an odd dynamic, recently hooking up every single time we have dungeon playtime.

My tight and itchy skin demands that I find a cozy spot to vegetate, and maybe manipulate someone into scratching my back and giving me a bit of a rub-down while they're back there. I follow the herd out to the dungeon, and release a sigh in bliss as I drop onto one of the new couches. The best thing Marcus ever did for the dungeon was placing the seating area so it faces the stage. If those attention whores want to be watched, we might as well watch them from a cushy seat.

My wife crawls over the back of the sofa to slide behind me with her legs on either side of my hips. Monica tugs at my t-shirt in silent demand. Eagerly complying, I grip the back of the collar with a couple of fingertips and pull it off. I groan loudly when her sharp nails scratch around all the itchy wounds.

"I swear I could come from this." A grunt of pure pleasure escapes my throat when Monica hits a particularly itchy spot. If I could purr, I would.

Monica's tongue licks close to an untouched spot and my hips jackknife off the sofa cushion from the ecstasy of it. For the first time ever, my favorite leathers pop open on their own— unleashing my wife-seeking cock.

"You're going to kill me, Monica." I half laugh, half cry.

The sound of knees dropping to the slate floor distracts me. I look down to see Katya abasing herself at my feet. I haven't seen her since our scene, but not because I didn't want to. I thought it best to give her some space, hoping Ezra would make due on his promise to give Katya the undivided attention she needs and force Cortez to join him.

Our scene was entirely for Katya. She needed an outlet while we showed her husbands that she is a woman with needs, and if they didn't provide, someone worthy would.

"Dexter, I'm sorry for my untrustworthy behavior. Please accept my sincerest apology." Katya has tears swimming in her eyes and shame written across her features. My hand rests on her cheek and my thumb wipes a tear away before the thought even crossed my mind.

"Hey, now. None of that," I chastise gently. Monica's fingernails cease their scratching to pat her friend on the shoulder, trying to console her. "Everything is always Ezra's fault, even if it's Cort's fault, simply because he ignored the issues. Okay?"

"I did it— not Ezra. I haven't been punished," Kat croaks out, swallowing audibly. "And I should be."

"Punishment is for when you willfully do something wrong. In this case, your needs were being ignored. Your only fault in this is not demanding they be met. If you continue to be passive in your marriage, when you're one of the most dominant people I know, I'm going to kick your ass. But not to punish you, simply because you're family."

"You can't force someone to love you, to *see* you," Kat stresses. "Because the tighter you grip them, the quicker you lose them."

Leaning over my back, Monica whispers fiercely. "You're right. You can't control how they feel, so don't worry about losing them. You need to make them see what they will lose when you're gone. Once you do, you demand what you need. If they won't give it to you, you leave. You don't live in misery– no relationship can survive two martyrs and a narcissist. You'll be sucked dry, not realizing you were losing yourself in the quest to not lose someone who was already gone."

"Jesus," I mutter, shocked at Monica's advice. "Now I see why Kat said I sucked at the best friend gig."

"I love you, Kat– you're the only true friend I've ever had. I want you to be happy, not always walking on eggshells around those crazies. I love them, too– but I love you more. You do you, and forget about those assholes who can't seem to remember you."

I reach a hand out for Kat to take, knowing Monica is right but understanding how it's a hard pill to swallow. Kat reluctantly places her hand in mine, trying to be strong by not allowing her tears to show. With a tug, I draw Kat up onto the sofa next to me.

Monica slides out from behind me to sit next to Kat. "Girlfriend, you're intelligent, beautiful enough to have any man who looks your way, stronger than hell, and not crazy. Someday Cort will accept the fact that he's gay, and things will change. But no matter what happens, you'll survive."

Smiling at the girls, "Now that is some priceless advice." I lean forward, kissing Kat on the cheek, then Monica on the lips. "No matter what, we'll be here for you. If you want me to kick Ezra's ass for allowing Cort to lead him around by his dick, I will."

Either having sonic hearing or some type of preternatural empathy, Ezra appears in front of us. "Would you sit with me?" Ez asks his wife, unsure of what answer he'll receive.

The love Ezra holds for Katya is evident by the adoration written across his face, but it's hidden beneath layer upon layer of guilt and shame. The real question isn't whether or not Ezra loves Katya, but does he love her enough to put her first– above Cortez's childish games.

Tentative, Katya stands, looking over her shoulder at Monica for some moral support. Then she crosses to the chaise lounge Marcus bought for Kat and the Ezes. Ezra sits first, tugging Kat into his arms, and then he buries his face against her neck. They don't attack each other like Cort and Ezra would. It doesn't turn sexual. Pure intimacy and connection is the only thread that is missing between Cort and Ezra, simply because it terrifies Cortez.

Ezra and Cortez have sexual passion, but that terrifies Cortez too.

Ezra and Katya have intimacy and connection that translates to explosive sex.

I'm terrified for the day Ezra connects to one but not the other on all levels.

Crawling behind me again, Monica returns to the task at hand—scratching the ever-loving fuck out of my back. "I'm so happy we found each other." I lean backward to restrain Monica between the sofa and my back. "I'm never letting you go."

"I never thought I'd ever say this…" Monica pauses, reading my body language better than a seasoned dominant. She hits a particularly itchy spot and I grunt in pleasure. "But we're the most normal people here, and that's just fucking bizarre."

"You're right— this place is filled with head-cases. As a sadist, I never thought I'd see the day when I was considered normal."

A guttural cry draws our attention to the center of the dungeon, where Whitt and Dalton are double-penetrating Kristal. "Holy fuck," I mumble in awe. "That's something you don't see every day."

Standing while being pounded hard, Kris is sandwiched with Dalton at her back and Whitt at her front. The look of undeniable ecstasy on Kristal's face is one worn by a sex addict getting their cravings fed. Kris screams bloody murder as she climaxes, both men gripping her hips to keep her in place.

The cry that sounded seconds earlier is repeated, and I shake my head in shock. I know the sound Whitt makes when he comes— a deep moan from his chest —after witnessing the kid getting blowjob after blowjob in this dungeon. What shocks me senseless is the fact that the cry is spewing out of Dalton's mouth. It's mournful and so filled with longing that my chest aches from its tone.

We now have tangible proof that Dalton had been faking orgasms for the past four years, because this is the real deal. It saddens me that he had to lie in the first place, and then I realize he's gone years without actually coming, which explains why he's baying like a dying animal.

Whitt's moans join the symphony echoing around the dungeon. Riding out his orgasm, Whitt's fingers latch onto Dalton's hips, and even from this distance I can see it's going to bruise. He stares intently into Dalton's eyes, drawing another reluctant cry from the man's chest.

Everyone else is silent as we voyeurs look around at each other in utter shock. In juxtaposition, Devlin stands abruptly and begins to clap. "That's my boy!" he joyfully yells at– Whitt? Dalton? I don't know, but he looks fucking proud for some reason.

Monica presses her lips to my ear and breathes, "Dalton wasn't all the way hard with me. I'd take offence, but Kris told me it was the same with her. You know she loves a challenge. Do you think this means what I think it means?"

"Oh!" I huff in shock. "Oh… yeah, that makes so much more sense, doesn't it?"

Embarrassed, Dalton turns his back to the dungeon and quickly tucks himself into his pants and zips up. "Not to bring up a sore subject, but if Dalton actually got hard inside Kris this time, I pity her ass."

"Yeah," I mutter begrudgingly. "The bastard looked hung even when he was flaccid."

Slipping into dominant-mode, when Dalton tries to leave, Whitt stops Dalton in his tracks by gripping his arm. "Kristal, clean Dalton up. We don't want his cum to stain his pants."

"No… no… that's okay," Dalton mutters frantically while trying to pry Whitt's hand off his arm. Whitt flashes him a potent look, and the struggle immediately ceases.

"Clean me, Kristal," Whitt demands in a raspy voice. "Don't leave a drop behind." We all watch in sick fascination as Kristal takes Whitt into her mouth and starts sucking, cheeks hollowing from the force. She continues for a few minutes, causing Monica and me to look at each other in confusion.

"Jesus," Ezra gasps from the chaise. "Can you really call it a recovery rate if his cock never flagged? Pretty Boy's gearing up for another one."

"*Is your gaydar online?*" I mouth to Ezra.

"Jesus Christ," Ezra hisses, sounding awed. "That explains so much."

A deep groan from the center of the dungeon brings my eyes back to Whitt. He's coming yet again– his cock is like a goddamn fountain. Fuck young men and their ability to recuperate almost instantly. Feeling inadequate, I curse Whitt for finding his second release with no downtime in between.

"Kiss Dalton in thanks," Whitt commands Kristal as soon as she sucks his cock dry.

Everyone in the dungeon takes a collective breath, all of us leaning forward to get a closer view. Dalton tries to flee for the hallway again, but all it takes is one potent look from Whitt and his feet freeze into place.

Doing as she was ordered, Kristal leans into the reluctant man and kisses him lightly. A second later, Dalton latches onto Kristal's mouth and violently devours her– drinking Whitt's taste down his throat.

Dalton abruptly releases Kris and turns his back to us, almost shoving her to the floor from the force. Whitt catches her, but his interest is with Dalton, whose back is rippling with the effort to still his movements and stifle his cry.

Whitt looks beyond smug as Dalton tries to come without making a sound.

"Well, that answers that, doesn't it?" Monica whispers, with several members muttering their agreement.

The humiliated man shoves his palms into Whitt's chest and glares. Astonishingly, the force shoves Whitt several feet. "Did I pass your test? Are you fucking happy now?" Dalton hisses between his clenched teeth, and then he bolts from the dungeon.

The look on Whitt's face says, *"Yes! You most certainly passed my test."* I shrug in confusion at Whitt's behavior. I've never known him to be malicious or to enjoy another's humiliation. But since it was humiliating Dalton, I try not to care.

"Bizarre," Kat mutters. "Bi-fucking-zarre. There are days where I experience this feeling like I'm not where I'm supposed to be, and this is one of those days. What the hell is wrong with our Pretty Boy?"

Ezra's maniacal laughter echoes around the dungeon for a long moment. "Things aren't always what they seem. Whitt?" he calls out to gain the young man's attention. "Good job, buddy! Good fucking job!"

Blushing all the way to the tips of his ears, Whitt mutters something underneath his breath, takes a deep bow for the members, and then flips us off before stalking down the hallway to his private room.

A few minutes later, we disband because no one can top whatever the hell that was. "I'll be right back. I need to grab my cellphone from my classroom," I say to my wife, and then I give her a soft kiss on the lips.

After grabbing my cellphone, I hurry down the hallway, hoping no one collars me to do something for them, particularly Marcus because there are always uncomfortable strings attached. Striding down the hallway, a frantic whispered conversation stops me in my tracks.

Dalton's door is ajar. "I'm trying my best, Master," he pleads. "Please don't be disappointed in me. I'll get you the information."

All the events from the past few months converge, dissolving my ability to control my baser instincts. My blood runs cold, and then turns fiery as Dalton outs himself as our mole.

"You should have shut your fucking door if you didn't want to be caught." I charge into the room, and then kick the door closed with the intent to commit violence. I don't need to have a mirror to know my eyes hold Dalton's death.

"Dexter, it's not what it sounds like." His voice is pleading as he holds out an arm in front of him in a stay motion. "It's not what you think. Please don't!"

With a predatory rolling gait, I move forward, cornering my prey. "Oh, it's exactly what I think," I mutter low and deadly.

There is no containing my inner caveman any longer. He unleashes his fury on the fucker who manipulated our wife and abused her before our very eyes. We kick Dalton in the chest with all our might. Flying backward several feet, Dalton falls to the ground. We hear a telltale snap and instinctively know a bone broke. We smile in satisfaction as Dalton's eyes tear and his face contorts from the agony.

"It's not what you think, Dexter." Even as he lies broken and in pain on the floor, Dalton tries to reason with me when there is no negotiating with me when my instincts rule.

As a sadist, I don't believe Dalton is in enough pain, and he will never be broken enough to cleanse his soul for betraying me and mine. With a menacing warning, I unleash my sadistic nature. "I'd fight back if I were you."

"Master, help me!" Dalton releases a bloodcurdling scream into his cellphone as my fists connect with his flesh.

Dalton
Mistress & Master of Restraint #4

The long-standing Mistress & Master of Restraint series is dark and mysterious, with a warped sense of morality. Erotic romance fans, would you prefer something just as twisted, but not as dark? Try the Blended Series, beginning with Good Girl. For a mix of both styles, try the Rusty Knob series.

To purchase any of Erica Chilson's titles, please visit her website (ericachilson.com) for details.

-Acknowledgements -

A lot of work goes into writing a novel, and it isn't just by the writer herself. **My parents:** for their unconditional support. **My readers**: thank you for reading my twisted words and spreading my books to the masses. For without you, no one would have ever heard of my stories. My readers are my lifeblood. A shout out to the members of the **M&M of Restraint Group on Facebook**: thanks for the endless entertainment and inspiration. Thank you to my street team: **Erica Chilson's Deviants!** You guys ROCK! **Wicked Reads**: (in all its incarnations) **Angela G.**, thank you for taking over and making Wicked Reads better than I could have done by myself. & thank you for helping promote my work and the work of other authors. Angela? Have I told you lately how much I appreciate you? A huge thank you to the **Wicked Writer's Betas** for keeping me grounded and encouraging me to keep trudging along when I get frustrated. Your thoughts and observations are invaluable. ((Hugs)) Beta readers: **Kris | Suz | Darcy | Sandy | Di | Angela | Diane | Jacki | Linsey | Alexis | Alicia | Billie Jo | Shelby | Tassie | Liz | April | Caroline | Judith | Jodi Lynn | Jodi | Lakecia |** Someday, I'd love to meet you all in real life– it would be the experience of a lifetime.

About the Author

Erica Chilson does not write in the 3rd person, wanting her readers to *be* her characters. Therefore, writing a bio about herself, is uncomfortable in the extreme.

Born, raised, and here to stay, the Wicked Writer is a stump-jumper, a ridge-runner. Hailing from North Central Pennsylvania, directly on the New York State border; she loves the changes in seasons, the humid air, all the mountainous forest, and the gloomy atmosphere.

Introverted, but not socially awkward, Erica prides herself on thinking first and filtering her speech. There are days she doesn't speak at all. If it wasn't for the fact that she lives with her parents, giving her a sense of reality, she would be a hermit, where the delivery man finds her months after expiration.

Reading was an escape, a way to leave a not-so pleasant reality behind. Reading lent Erica the courage she gathered from the characters between the pages to long for a different life. Writing was an instrument of change, evolving Erica into the woman she is today– a better, more mature, more at peace thinker.

Erica has a wicked mind, one she pours out into her creations. Her filter doesn't allow all of it to erupt, much to her relief. Sarcastic, with a very dark, perverse sense of humor, Erica puts a bit of herself into every character she writes.

I love hearing from readers. If you would like more information on release dates, works in progress, teaser chapters, and random bits of madness, please visit my Facebook Fan Page: https://www.facebook.com/thewickedwriter my website: ericachilson.com or please contact me via email: wickedwriter.ericachilson@gmail.com

DEVIANTS ONLY, if you'd like to join Erica Chilson's closed Facebook group, M&M of Restraint: https://www.facebook.com/groups/MistressandMaster/